"Romance, violence, technology are superbly blended by a master storyteller. Du Brul creates a fast-moving odyssey that is second to none."
—Clive Cussler on *Charon's Landing*

"Cliffhangers more ~~suspenseful~~ ~~your eyes~~ than you'll find in Clive ~~Cussler~~ ~~Alistair MacLean~~."
—*Kirkus Reviews*

"An intricate tale filled with action and intrigue where the stakes are high. Mercer is an action character with a brain, a penchant for beautiful women, and the ability to think fast and inspire respect and trust.

"Although his work is influenced by Clancy, Fleming, Cussler, and other masters of the genre, Du Brul's is a fresh voice.

"*Vulcan's Forge* is a fast-paced story well told by an upcoming new talent in the spy thriller genre."

—*The Cape Coral Daily Breeze*

"A study in triple-crosses . . . Finely tuned, buoyed by strong, fresh writing."

—*Kirkus Reviews*

"Mercer [is] a combination of Dirk Pitt and James Bond. A fun thriller."

—*Oklahoman*

"Du Brul has created a high-tempo action place. The reader is constantly intrigued. *Vulcan's Forge* is an action-packed and intriguing thriller."

—*The Mystery Review*

VULCAN'S
FORGE

JACK B. DU BRUL

A TOM DOHERTY ASSOCIATES BOOK
NEW YORK

This novel is thankfully
dedicated to those poor souls
who suffered through
the first drafts.

NOTE: If you purchased this book without a cover you should be aware that this book is stolen property. It was reported as "unsold and destroyed" to the publisher, and neither the author nor the publisher has received any payment for this "stripped book."

This is a work of fiction. All the characters and events portrayed in this book are either products of the author's imagination or are used fictitiously.

VULCAN'S FORGE

Copyright © 1998 by Jack B. Du Brul

All rights reserved, including the right to reproduce this book, or portions thereof, in any form.

A Forge Book
Published by Tom Doherty Associates, Inc.
175 Fifth Avenue
New York, NY 10010

Forge® is a registered trademark of Tom Doherty Associates, Inc.

ISBN: 0-812-56461-8
Library of Congress Card Catalog Number: 97-34382

First edition: March 1998
First mass market edition: January 1999

Printed in the United States of America

0 9 8 7 6 5 4 3 2 1

ACKNOWLEDGMENTS

Because this is my first novel, it is safe to say that I owe thanks to everyone who has ever influenced me, for a little of all of them is within these pages, from family and friends to casual acquaintances who may have imparted some piece of wisdom. A few notables are Elizabeth Ash for her scientific acumen and Dick Flynn for his firsthand account of a heart attack. I wish now I'd taken the time over the years to list all the others.

Actually writing this book was pretty much a one-person affair; however I've learned that publishing is very definitely a group activity. For that I must thank Todd Murphy and the other Jack Du Brul for proving it's not what you know but who you know, and Bob Diforio, my agent, for being that "who." At Forge I especially want to thank Melissa Ann Singer, my editor. If ever there was someone who knows how to hand-hold, it is she. I also want to thank you, the reader, for giving me a chance.

Author's note: For security reasons, the government forbids vehicle traffic on Pennsylvania Avenue in front of the White House. For reasons of continuity, I've left it open.

MAY 23, 1954

The moon was a millimetric sliver hanging in the night sky like an ironic smile. A gentle easterly breeze smeared the acrid feather of smoke that coiled from the single funnel of the ore carrier *Grandam Phoenix*. The Pacific swells rolled the ponderous ship as easily as a lazy hammock on a summer afternoon as she cruised two hundred miles north of the Hawaiian Islands. The tranquility of the night was about to be shattered.

The *Grandam Phoenix* was on her maiden voyage, having slipped down the ways in Kobe, Japan, just two months earlier. Her final fitting and sea trials had been rushed so that she could begin paying off the massive debts incurred by the company during her construction. Built with the latest technological advances in safety and speed, she was an example of the new breed of specialized cargo ship. The Second World War had taught that the efficiency of a specialized vessel far outweighed the cost in its design and construction. The owners maintained that their newest ship would prove that these principles worked as well for civilian craft as they did for the military. The 442-foot-long ore carrier was to become the flagship of the line as the shipping business greedily expanded into the booming Pacific markets.

Soon after taking command of the *Grandam Phoenix*, Captain Ralph Linc learned that the owners had a very different fate in store for their newest ship from the one proposed to her underwriters.

Not long after the development of maritime insurance, unscrupulous owners and crews intentionally began scuttling their vessels in order to collect often substantial claims. The underwriters had no recourse but to pay out unless someone, usually a crew member feeling twinges of guilt, came forward with the truth. For sinking the ore carrier, the crew of the *Grandam Phoenix* would receive bonuses large enough to ensure their silence. If the swindle worked, and there seemed no reason it wouldn't, the owners were looking at a settlement not only for the twenty-million-dollar value of the vessel, but also that of her cargo, listed as bauxite ore from Malaysia, but in reality worthless yellow gravel.

Captain Linc held true to his genre, a tough man with a whiskey- and cigarette-tortured voice and far-gazing eyes. Standing squarely as his ship rolled with the seas, he ground out his Lucky Strike. And lit another.

Linc had served in the U.S. Merchant Marine all through World War II. With losses rivaled only by the Marine Corps, the Merchant Marine seemed to be the service for maniacs or suicides. Yet Linc had managed not only to survive but flourish. By 1943 he had his own command, running troops and material to the hellfires of the Pacific theater. Unlike most of his contemporaries, he never once lost a vessel to the enemy.

At war's end, he, like many others, found that there were too many men and too few ships. During the late forties and early fifties, Linc became just another Yankee prowling the Far East, taking nearly any command offered to him. He ran questionable cargoes for shadowy companies and learned to keep his mouth shut.

When first approached by the *Phoenix*'s owners, Linc had thought he was being offered the opportunity of a lifetime. No longer would he have to scrounge for a ship, prostituting his integrity to remain at sea. They were giving him a chance once again to be the proud captain, the master of their flagship. It wasn't until after the contracts had been signed that the company told Linc about the predestined fate of his vessel. It took two days and a sizable bonus for his bitterness to give way to acceptance.

Now stationed on the bridge, a cup of cooling coffee in a weathered hand, Linc stared at the dark sea and cursed. He hated the corporate people who could arbitrarily decide to scuttle such a great ship. They didn't understand the bond between captain and vessel. For the sake of profit, they were about to destroy a beautiful living thing. The idea sickened Linc to the bone. He hated himself for accepting, for allowing himself to be part of such a loathsome act.

"Position," Ralph Linc barked.

Before the position could be given, a crewman stooped over the radar repeater and said in a remote voice, "Contact, twelve miles dead ahead."

Linc glanced at the chronometer on the bulkhead to his left. The contact would be the rendezvous vessel that would pick up the crew after the *Phoenix* was gone. They were right on time and in position. "Good work, men."

He had been given very specific and somewhat strange orders concerning the location, course, and time that he was to sink his ship. He assumed the North Pacific had been chosen because of her unpredictable weather patterns. The weather here could turn deadly without a moment's notice, building waves that could swamp a battleship and whipping up winds that literally tore the surface from the ocean. When the time came for the insurance inquiry, the rendezvous vessel would corroborate any story they manufactured.

"You know the drill, gentlemen," Linc growled, lighting a cigarette from the glowing tip of his last. "Engines All Stop, helm bring us to ninety-seven-point-five degrees magnetic."

This precise but inexplicable positioning of the vessel complied exactly with Linc's final orders from the head office. They had given no reason for this action and Linc knew enough not to pry. The engine speed was reduced, the rhythmic throb diminished until it was almost imperceptible. The ship's wheel blurred as the young seaman cranked it around.

"Helm?"

"We're coming up on ninety-seven degrees, sir, as ordered."

"Range?"

"Eleven miles."

Linc picked up the radio hand mike and dialed in the shipboard channel. "Now hear this: we've reached position; all crew not on duty report to the lifeboats. Engineering, emergency shut-down of the boilers and open the sea cocks on my mark. Prepare to abandon ship."

He looked around the bridge slowly, his eyes burning every detail of her into his brain. "I'm sorry, sweetheart," he mumbled.

"Ten miles," The radar man called.

"Open the seacocks, abandon ship." Linc replaced the mike and pressed a button on the radio. A klaxon began to wail.

The cry of a dying woman, Linc thought.

Linc waited on the bridge while the crew filed out to the boat deck. He had to spend a little time alone with the ship before he left her. He grasped the rung of the oaken wheel. The wood was so new that he felt slivers pricking at his skin. Never would this wheel achieve the smooth patina of use; instead it would become so much rot on the bottom of the ocean.

"Goddamn it," Linc said aloud, then strode from the bridge.

Gone were the days of men scampering down cargo netting into boats bobbing on the surface of the sea. Ocean Freight and Cargo had spared no expense in outfitting their flagship with every modern safety device. One lifeboat was already full of men and up on the davits. The winchman waited for a curt nod from Linc before lowering the boat to the sea below.

The warm night breeze blew smoke from Linc's cigarette into his eyes as he climbed into the second lifeboat. The other men in the boat with him were subdued, ashen. They didn't talk or look each other in the eye as Linc nodded to the winchman.

The winchman threw a toggle switch and the pulleys that lowered the lifeboat began to whine. The boat hit the calm surface with a white-frothed splash. Instantly two men stood up to detach the cables that secured them to the sinking ore carrier.

Captain Linc took charge of the lifeboat, grasping the tiller in his right hand while applying power to the idling engine. The boat motored away from the *Grandam Phoenix*, the crew craning their necks to watch their sinking ship. The klaxon echoed emptily across the waves.

It took fifteen minutes for the ship's list to become noticeable, but after that, she went quickly. The stern lifted from the water; her two ferro-bronze propellers gleaming in the low light. The watching men heard her boilers let go of their mounts and slam through the engine room bulkheads. The screeching hiss that followed was the sound of thousands of tons of gravel pouring across the vessel's gunwales into the ocean.

Linc refused to watch his ship die. He kept his eyes trained ahead, steering toward the dim lights of the distant rendezvous ship. Yet every time he heard a new sound from the *Grandam Phoenix*'s death throes, he cringed.

The rendezvous ship was not large, a ninety-foot general cargo freighter, the type referred to as a "stick ship" by seamen because her decks were studded with a forest of cranes and derricks. Her boxy superstructure stood amidships, her straight funnel atop it. As the two lifeboats approached, Linc could make out about a dozen men on her port rail. He guided his boat toward them.

"Captain Linc, I presume?" a voice called down cheerily.

"I'm Linc."

The reply was the rapid fire of ten Soviet-made PPSH submachine guns. The snail drums of the weapons could hold fifty rounds and the gunmen emptied them all into the lifeboats. The cacophony of shouts and screams, shots and ricochets, was deafening. Blood pooled on the floorboards of the boats, its sweet smell mingling with the cloud of cordite smoke.

Linc looked up at the ship, bloodied and dazed, astounded that he was still alive. Anger, fear, and pain boiled in his mind but the emotions and sensations were being driven back by darkness.

The gunmen lowered their weapons one by one as the bolts slammed into empty chambers. The lifeboat was a charnel scene of blood and mutilation, the water pouring in through the holed floor sloshed in a pink froth. In moments, both lifeboats capsized, spilling corpses into the ocean. Packs of sharks circled eagerly.

The lone unarmed man on deck had watched the massacre with flat appraising eyes. Though not yet thirty, he carried an air of authority held by only a few even twice his age. When the lifeboats capsized, he nodded to the commander of the gunmen and went into the freighter's superstructure.

Minutes later, he ducked into the ship's hold. The lights of the computing and sonar equipment packed into the cramped hold gave his skin an alien pallor.

"Depth of the target ship?" he snapped at one of the technicians bent over a sonar scope.

The target ship was of course the *Grandam Phoenix* as she plunged to the distant bottom.

The sonarman didn't look up from his equipment. "Six thousand feet, sinking at a thousand feet every seven minutes."

The man glanced at his watch and jotted down some numbers on a pad. After a brief pause he looked at his watch again. "Two minutes from my mark."

The hold was noisy. The sound of the ship's diesel generators filtered in through the steel walls and the air conditioners necessary to cool the computers sounded like aircraft propellers. Yet the seven men in the room could have sworn that during those two minutes there was not a sound in the world. They were too focused on their jobs to notice any distractions.

"Mark," the young man said with a casualness that was not forced.

Another crewman flipped several switches. Nothing happened.

The civilian counted down under his breath. "Four . . . three . . . two . . . one."

The shock wave started nearly seven thousand feet below the surface and had to travel a further ten miles to reach the ship, yet it struck only five seconds after detonation. Billions of gallons of water had been vaporized in a fireball with temperatures reaching 100,000 degrees. The main wave rushed to the surface at 150 miles per hour and threw up a dome of water half a mile across. The dome hung in the air for a full ten seconds, gravity fighting inertia, then collapsed, thunderously filling the six-thousand-foot deep hole in the Pacific Ocean.

Caught in a man-made Charybdis, the freighter tossed and pitched as if she were in a hurricane, her hull nearly out of the water one moment and almost swamped the next. The young man, the architect of such destruction, feared for a moment that he had cut the margin too thin, placed his ship too close to the epicenter. Before his concern could crack the glacial facade of his face, the sea began to calm. The huge waves leveled out and the gale wind created when the ocean fell back on itself, dissipated.

It took the young man a few minutes to reach the deck of the freighter, for she still rolled dangerously. On the horizon, a blanket of steam clung to the sea and glowed luminously in the weak moonlight.

''I have laid the foundation of Vulcan's Forge.''

WASHINGTON DC
PRESENT DAY

The only thing that the President really enjoyed about his new job was his chair in the Oval Office. It had a high back and a soft seat and was made of the most supple leather he had ever felt. Often he would sit in that chair after all of the staff had gone home and remember his simpler youth. He had achieved the most powerful office on the planet, fulfilling his life-long ambition but sometimes he thought the price had been too high. The college sweetheart he had married had been turned into an emotionless automaton by the pressures of her husband's career. The vast network of friends he had built during the years had become syco-phants groveling for favors and his once perfect health had deteriorated so he felt ten years older than his sixty-two.

He would sit some nights with all the lights off so the network watchdogs across the street wouldn't think the President was burning the midnight oil, and he would think about his younger days growing up outside of Cin-

cinnati. He missed guzzling beer with his hot-rodding friends, shooting trick pool to impress overly made-up, plump girls, and saying whatever came to mind when someone pissed him off.

A perfect example of why he longed for that puerile freedom was seated opposite him in full African splendor, robes and headband and sandals. He was the ambassador to one of the new central African nations. A tall man with sarcastic eyes and a complacent attitude about nearly everything that they had discussed.

The ambassador was saying, with a dismissive wave of his hand, that the intelligence gathered by the Red Cross, the United Nations and the CIA was all false; that his government was not involved in any type of tribal genocide through starvation or the intentional spread of disease. He insisted that his government was committed to all tribes under their care and all the people suffered, not just the smaller, less politically influential tribes.

Bullshit, the President wanted to shout and slap the smug smile off the ambassador's face. But convention stopped him.

Instead he would have to spout some platitude such as, "We haven't seen your situation in just that fashion, but it bears further investigation."

A glow under the lip of his desk caught the President's eye—the situation light, a signal from his chief of staff. In the six months of his term, this was the only time other than routine weekly tests that the light had been switched on. The last time the light had been used officially was during the Soviet coup in August of 1991.

The President stood up quickly, his professional smile masking his consternation. He extended his right hand and the ambassador knew that he was being dismissed.

"We haven't seen your situation in just that fashion, but it bears further investigation. Thank you, Mr. Ambassador."

"Thank you, Mr. President, for being so generous

with your time," the ambassador replied sourly. He'd been promised another half hour.

They shook hands briefly. The ambassador turned in a whirl of robes and left the Oval Office.

The President sat back down and had time to rub his temples for a second before the other door to the Oval Office opened. Expecting the angular figure of his chief of staff, Catherine Smith, the president was surprised to see Richard Henna.

Dick Henna was the new director of the FBI, one of the only important presidential appointees that Congress had so far approved. As always, self-serving political squabbling in the House was holding up the work of the federal government and costing the taxpayers tens of millions of dollars.

Henna was a career snoop who had managed never to step on the wrong toes. He had plodded his way through thirty years in the bureau, never grabbing headlines but always garnering respect. He had an exemplary family life, a modest slice of suburbia to call home, and absolutely no skeletons in any closet. Knowing of his reputation, the opposition party in Congress had not bothered with any serious investigation into his past.

The President, who liked Henna for his unshakable integrity, smiled when he saw the director enter his office. The smile faded when he realized that Henna, never a neat man, looked terrible. His eyes were puffy and bloodshot. The jowled lines of his face were blurred behind thick stubble. His suit was rumpled, his shirt looked as if it had been slept in, and his tie was cocked off and stained.

"You look like you could use some coffee, Dick." The President tried to put cheer into his voice, to penetrate the air of gloom that had permeated his office. His effort was as effective as a candle in a dark forest.

"I could use something a bit stronger, sir."

The President nodded toward the Regency table which

acted as a bar, and Henna helped himself to a triple Scotch.

Henna slumped into the seat opposite the President, the one formerly occupied by the African ambassador. Settling his attaché case on his lap, Henna opened it and withdrew a thin, violet file. The file was stamped PEO. President's Eyes Only.

"What's going on, Dick?" The President had never seen Henna so morose.

"Sir," Henna started shakily, "this morning, just after midnight, the National Oceanographic and Atmospheric Administration ship *Ocean Seeker* was reported missing about two hundred miles north of Hawaii. Search planes have been dispatched and found only debris in the water. A nearby freighter is assisting in the search, but so far it doesn't look promising."

The President had gone slightly pale; his fingers clenched. He had not obtained this office by being overly emotional and his mind was clear and sharp. "That's a terrible tragedy, Dick, but I don't see how it concerns you or the FBI."

Henna would have been surprised had the President not asked that question. He handed the file across the desk and took a sip of Scotch. "Please read the top sheet."

The President opened the file and began to read. Seconds later, the blood drained from his patrician's face and the tension lines around his eyes tightened so that he squinted at the paper.

Before he finished reading, Henna spoke. "That was brought to my attention two days ago, after it was proven to be Ohnishi's handwriting and not written under duress. When I received it, I checked with the coast guard and the navy. They didn't have any scheduled traffic to or from the islands, so I figured we had a little breathing room." Henna's voice broke. "I didn't check with NOAA, I forgot all about them. I had been warned that any government ship steaming outward from Hawaii would be destroyed. I had a goddamn warning. Those people didn't have to die.''

The President looked up. Pain and guilt and failure were etched into Henna's face. ''Take it easy, Dick. How many people know about this?''

''Three besides the two of us—a mailroom clerk; my deputy director, Marge Doyle; and a handwriting analyst.''

The President glanced at his watch. ''I've got lunch with the speaker of the house and if I cancel it . . . I don't want to think about the consequences. The rest of my day is booked solid. We'll keep things normal here in Washington, but I'll have all naval traffic to and from Hawaii suspended, just like this letter demands. I'm not about to give in to Ohnishi, but we need the time. I'm also going to put the military at Pearl Harbor on full alert. They've been on standby ever since the rioting started two weeks ago, but I think it prudent to up their readiness status. Let's meet tonight at nine in the Situation Room to discuss the situation and our possible responses. Use the tunnel from the Treasury Building so you don't arouse suspicion.''

''Yes, sir. Is there anything you want me to do in the meantime?'' Henna was regaining his composure.

''I assume you've already started a full background check on Takahiro Ohnishi.'' Henna nodded. ''Find out what he's all about. We're all well aware of his racial views, but this is an outrage. Also, I want to know where he got the capability to destroy one of our ships. Someone is supplying him with arms and I want it stopped.''

''Yes, sir,'' Henna replied, and left the office.

The President touched the intercom button on his desk. Joy Craig, his personal secretary, answered instantly.

''Joy, set up a meeting in the Situation Room for nine o'clock tonight. Call in the chairman of the joint chiefs; the directors of the CIA, NSA, and NOAA; the secretary of state and the secretary of defense.''

Most of those men were only acting heads, until their confirmation, but this crisis warranted trusting them as if they were already sworn into their respected offices.

The President sank back into his chair, his face blank, and stared at the gold braid–trimmed American flag near the office door. In his lap, his hands trembled.

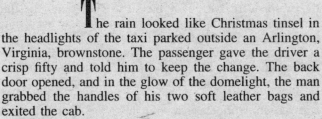

The rain looked like Christmas tinsel in the headlights of the taxi parked outside an Arlington, Virginia, brownstone. The passenger gave the driver a crisp fifty and told him to keep the change. The back door opened, and in the glow of the domelight, the man grabbed the handles of his two soft leather bags and exited the cab.

Philip Mercer had always believed that international airports were a type of stateless limbo, sovereign nations allied only to each other with no allegiance to their host countries. His flight had touched down at Dulles an hour and a half earlier, yet he only now felt that he'd returned to the United States. Although the cool rain soothed his dried sinuses, Mercer still groaned as he inevitably tried the wrong key on the Baldwin lock of the front door. He no longer wondered why he always tried the wrong key when his arms were full, yet choose the right one when they were empty.

Home at last, Mercer thought, as he stepped into the

foyer of his house, then chuckled. In the five years he had lived here, this was the first time that he had ever thought of the brownstone as home.

"Must be settling down," he chided himself mildly.

From the outside, the brownstone was as innocuous as the fifteen others on his side of the block. Yet once through the door, any similarity to the other 1940s-constructed row houses ended. Mercer had gutted the three-story building and completely redesigned the interior. From a thirty-foot-high entry that took up the front third of the seventy-five-foot-deep building, Mercer could see up to the second-floor library, and further up to his master bedroom. An ornate curved staircase salvaged from a nineteenth-century rectory connected the three levels.

All of the furniture was in place, yet the house still lacked many of the personal items that would make it a home. Tables and shelves were empty of mementos and the walls were barren of pictures. The design of the house showed much of the character of its sole occupant, but many of his subtleties lay hidden in cardboard boxes.

Mercer dropped his bags near the front door and walked across the little used formal living room toward the back of the house. Passing an oak-paneled billiard room and the kitchen, he went into his home office and slid his slim briefcase across the wide leather-topped desk.

He used the back stairs to climb to the second floor and on the landing he swore under his breath. The television in the rec room was on, the volume barely a mutter. The lights around the mahogany bar had been muted to an amber glow. Snores rose from a blanketed lump on the couch. Mercer walked behind the bar and placed a Clapton disc into the player. With a wicked smile, he pressed play and turned the stereo to maximum volume.

The Carver speakers rattled the bottles and glasses behind the bar. Harry White woke with a sudden jerk.

Mercer turned off the stereo and laughed.

"I said you could use my house when I was away, you bastard, not move in."

Harry looked at Mercer with owl eyes, his withered face still scrunched up with sleep. He peered around at the overflowing ashtray on the coffee table, the plates of congealed food, and the two empty Jack Daniel's bottles.

"Welcome back, Mercer. I didn't expect you till tomorrow." Harry's voice sounded like a rock crusher with a thrown gear.

"Obviously not." Mercer smirked. "Nice party?"

Harry ran his fingers through his gray crew cut. "I don't really remember."

Mercer laughed again, an infectious laugh that, despite what must have been a powerful hangover, made Harry smile.

Mercer pulled two Heinekens from the circa-1950 lock-levered refrigerator next to the stereo rack and opened them with the brass puller tucked under the ornately carved backbar. He drained one in four long gulps and started to sip the second.

"How was the trip?" Harry asked, lighting a cigarette.

"Good, but exhausting. I did seven lectures in six days all over South Africa, plus met with a couple of top engineers from one of the Rand mining firms." Rain rattled the darkened windows.

Philip Mercer was a mine engineer and consultant. According to those in the industry, he was the best in the world. His ideas and advice were sought by nearly every corporation in the business. The fees he charged were astronomical, but the companies never balked at the bills because their return on his input always paid off.

Over the years, dozens of firms had tried to hire Mercer exclusively, but he respectfully declined, always replying the same way: "My answer is also my reason, no thank you." He liked the freedom to say "no" whenever he wished. His abilities and independent status gave him the latitude to live his life by his own eccentric standards and to tell the occasional executive to shove it when the need arose.

Of course that freedom had been hard won. He had started out working for the United States Geological Survey just after receiving his Ph.D. For two years, he did mostly routine inspections of mining facilities which were cooperating with the USGS as seismic centers. The work was dull, repetitive and pointless. Mercer began to feel that his sharp intellect was being blunted by the ponderous weight of the federal bureaucracy. Fearing some kind of brain atrophy, he quit.

Recognizing that the independent streak which more or less dominated his personality would never allow him to work for any one organization for an extended period, Mercer decided to go into business for himself. He saw himself as a hired gun to help out in difficult situations but many others in the industry saw him as an unwanted interloper. It took seven months and countless phone calls to former instructors at Penn State and the Colorado School of Mines before he landed his first consulting job, confirming assay reports on a sizable Alaskan gold strike for a Swiss investment consortium. The three-month job paid twice what his annual government salary had been, and he never looked back from that point. The next job had been in Namibia and the mine had been for uranium. Within a few years he had built up the reputation he now enjoyed and commanded the fees to which he had grown accustomed.

Ironically, he had just accepted a temporary position at the USGS as a private sector consultant to liaise with major American mining concerns for the smooth implementation of the President's new environmental bill and discuss this plan for possible adoption by some foreign companies. His career was coming full circle in a way, but this time through the government's grist mill, he'd be walking away in two months with no strings attached.

"You look like shit," Harry observed.

Mercer glanced down at his wrinkled Hugo Boss suit and clammy-feeling shirt. Two days of dark beard shadowed the decisive line of his jaw. "You spend twenty hours on an airliner and see how you look."

Harry swung his leg off the couch and grabbed a flesh-colored piece of plastic from the floor. With three deft movements that his nearly eighty-year-old hands didn't seem capable of, he strapped the prosthetic leg on just below his knee and flexed the articulating ankle.

"Much better." He tugged down the cuff of his pants, stood and walked casually over to the bar without the slightest trace of a limp.

Mercer poured him a whiskey. "I've seen you do that a hundred times and it still gives me the creeps."

"You have no respect for the 'physically challenged'—I think that is the new politically correct term."

"You're a decrepit old man who probably had his leg shot off by a jealous husband as you leapt from his wife's boudoir."

The two men had met the night Mercer moved into the area. Harry was a fixture at the neighborhood bar, Tiny's, a place Mercer discovered to be a sublime distraction from unpacking ten years of eclectic junk collected from all over the world. The unlikely pair became best friends that night. In the five subsequent years, Harry, no matter how drunk, had never told Mercer how he'd lost the leg and Mercer had enough respect to never pry.

"You're just jealous that your body doesn't make a good conversation piece in bed."

"Harry, I don't pick up women at the exit to circus freak tents," Mercer retorted.

Harry conceded the point and asked for another drink.

If anyone had been listening, the next hour's conversation would have seemed as if it were between bitter enemies. The sarcastic remarks and biting jokes sometimes got downright vicious, but both men enjoyed this verbal jousting, which was often the main source of entertainment at Tiny's.

A little after midnight, age and whiskey forced Harry to a tactful retreat to the couch, where he promptly fell asleep. Mercer, despite the jet lag and beer, still felt refreshed and knew any attempt to sleep would be futile. He decided to get some office work done.

His home office was all rich leather and oiled woods, forest green carpet and polished brass. Other than the bar it was the only truly finished room in the brownstone. He knew that the decor was somewhat cliché, but he liked it just the same. The numerous prints on the walls were of heavy mining equipment: walking draglines, huge dump trucks, and skeletal drilling derricks that towered eight stories. Each print was signed with a thanks from the president or owner of some company that Mercer had helped. On the credenza, discreetly lighted from below, was a large chunk of opaque blue stone. Mercer's hand caressed it as he walked to his desk.

He had phoned his secretary at the USGS from Jan Smuts Airport in Johannesburg and had asked her to fax all of his memos and messages to his house, knowing that insomnia always followed an international flight. There were at least fifty sheets of paper in the tray of the fax machine.

The majority could be ignored for at least a few days; only a couple had any urgency at all. Working through the pile quickly, he almost missed the significance of one sheet, from the deputy director of operations at the National Oceanographic and Atmospheric Administration. It was an invitation, dated six days earlier, to work aboard the NOAA research vessel *Ocean Seeker* in an investigation of an unknown geologic phenomenon off the coast of Hawaii. The deputy director had requested Mercer's presence because of the paper he had written two years earlier on the use of geothermic vents as possible energy sources and rich mining areas.

Mercer had heard of the tragic loss of the ship with all hands. It had made the newspapers even in South Africa.

The invitation itself was not the cause of his racing heart or shallow breathing. At the bottom of the invitation was a list of the specialists already assigned to the survey. The first name was Dr. Tish Talbot, marine biologist.

Mercer had never met Tish, but her father was a good friend, a man to whom Mercer owed his life following a plane crash in the Alaska Range. Mercer had been returning from his first private consulting job when his plane had suddenly lost power. The pilot had been killed landing in a rock-strewn field and Mercer had broken a leg, a wrist, and a bunch of ribs. Jack Talbot, a grizzled tool pusher on the North Slope fields at Prudhoe Bay, had been camping near the crash site on a one-week leave. Talbot had reached Mercer within ten minutes of the crash and tended him overnight until he could signal a rescue copter with a flare salvaged from the wrecked plane.

The two men had seen each other infrequently in the years since then, but their friendship lasted. And now, Jack's only daughter was dead, a victim of a terrible accident. Mercer empathized with his friend, feeling hollow inside when he imagined the pain that Jack must now be facing. Mercer had known such pain, losing his parents when he was only a boy, but no parent ever thinks that they will outlast their child. Many say that that is the worst kind of agony.

Mercer turned off his desk lamp. He left Harry on the couch in the rec room, not wanting to kick his friend out at two in the morning. Mercer's huge bed didn't really look inviting, but he made the effort anyway. His sleep was fitful.

```
══════
══════
══════
══════
══════
══════
```

HAWAII

Jill Tzu eased on the brake of her Honda Prelude and slipped the transmission into neutral. Her car slowed to a stop about twenty yards away from the main gates of Takahiro Ohnishi's estate. She tilted the rearview mirror downward until her mouth was in sight and deftly applied another slick layer of lipstick. She pursed her lips, flashed a professional smile to herself then opened her mouth wide. Satisfied that the makeup was perfect, she canted the mirror back.

As a female reporter, she knew the necessity of a glamorous appearance on camera. Despite her abhorrence of such sexism, she was pragmatic enough to know that she alone wasn't about to change the custom.

Yet it wasn't her stunning beauty or her dancer's legs that got her this interview today, it was her heritage.

Takahiro Ohnishi was easily the wealthiest man in Hawaii. In fact, he was the twelfth richest man in the world, with interests as diverse as real estate, medical research, shipping, and mining. He had offices on six continents, seven palatial homes, and nearly thirty thousand employees. Despite the global aspects of his holdings, he remained rooted in one tradition, that of Japan.

He had built his empire on an ethnic pyramid with himself, a native born Japanese on top and his key managers at least pure Japanese regardless of their country of birth. The next level down had to be three-quarters' Japanese or more, and so on until only the lowliest of workers had no Japanese blood at all. Ohnishi employed two entire law firms to battle the hundreds of cases of discrimination filed against his companies. To date they had not lost a single case.

His obsession with his Japanese heritage consumed his personal life as well. Ohnishi had never mårried, but the numerous mistresses who had come and gone during his seventy years were all Japanese. If he found even the slightest trace of any other heritage the affair would end on the spot. All the servants in all his homes were Japanese, and even his rare press interviews had to be conducted by reporters who were at least half Japanese.

And that brings us to me, thought Jill Tzu, the daughter of a Hong Kong Chinese banker and a Japanese interpreter.

She eased her car into gear and approached the wrought iron gates of Ohnishi's principal American residence. The house, twenty miles northwest of Honolulu, was isolated by acres of sugarcane fields and pineapple plantations.

Once, asked why he remained so secluded, Ohnishi responded honestly, "Everyone I need is brought to me; why should I scurry around?"

A lean guard approached her car. Jill lowered the window, getting a delightful mixture of cool auto airconditioning and hot lush air.

The first thing she noticed was the automatic pistol slung from the guard's hip and the quality and cut of his uniform. This was no simple rent-a-cop.

"Yes?" he said courteously.

"Jill Tzu from KHNA; I'm here to interview Mr. Ohnishi."

"Of course," the guard replied. He pressed a button on one of the pillars supporting the gates and they slid open silently.

Jill accelerated, surprised that she hadn't been asked for identification.

The crushed limestone drive leading to the house was a pristine white trail through a vast emerald lawn. The drive curved around stands of trees and shrubs, artfully placed so the house was hidden until she rounded the last bend. When she saw the building, she was stunned.

Jill had expected traditional Japanese architecture on a grand scale, yet what was before her was unlike anything she had ever seen before. Takahiro Ohnishi lived in a glass house, modeled somewhat like the entrance to the Louvre designed by I. M. Pei, but much, much larger. Tubular steel struts supported small panels of glass in a framework that could only be described as obtuse. Spheres, cones, and slab-sided rectangles melded together in a multisided building that was not displeasing to view. Jill could see completely through the home to the shallow valley which stretched beyond.

Still not over her initial shock, Jill drove up to the porte-cochere and slid out. Her heels clicked against the white inlaid marble as she walked toward the glass front doors. Just as she reached them, they were opened by a servant.

"Miss Tzu, Mr. Ohnishi is waiting for you in the breakfast garden. Would you please follow me?" The butler was Japanese, of course, wearing a somber black livery reminiscent of the early part of the century.

"Thank you," she replied, slinging her purse over her shoulder.

The interior spaces of the house were broken by stark geometrical walls. The structures were not bound by any normal parameters of construction. Some hung ten feet or more in the air, and others were mere ripples across the floor. The foyer was a massive open space, domed by a delicate lattice of steel and glass that cast a spider-web shadow on the white marble floor. Stairs, landings, and balconies cantilevered into the foyer as if defying gravity. Having no basis of comparison, Jill simply assumed that the decidedly Oriental watercolors and paintings on the walls were priceless.

The butler led her through several rooms, some traditional Japanese and some Western in style. At the open doors of an elevator, the butler indicated that Jill was to proceed alone.

"Mr. Ohnishi is waiting to the right as you exit the elevator."

There was a discreet chime and the doors slid closed.

Feeling like an ant in the bottom of a kitchen sink, Jill smoothed her cream skirt against her legs as the brushed stainless steel elevator sedately ascended. When it stopped, Jill stepped onto a breezy loggia, forty feet above the ground. She turned to her right and saw a table set for two people, the silver glinting in the early Pacific light.

"I am delighted to be able to share my breakfast with you, Miss Tzu," Takahiro Ohnishi said as he stood.

"I am delighted that you invited me," Jill replied, walking toward the table.

She extended her hand, which Ohnishi ignored. Pissed at herself, Jill remembered whom she was dealing with and bowed deeply. Ohnishi replied with the barest nod of his head. "Won't you sit down?"

Ohnishi did not look like an industrialist. He was thin and frail, with a voice made tenuous by the years. His snowy hair was sparse, revealing red blotches of scalp. His face was cadaverous, sallow and drawn. His hands were darkly liver-spotted and bony, like the claws of a small bird.

"Miss Tzu, I did not invite you, I merely caved in to your persistence. One hundred and fourteen calls and seventy-eight letters are enough to make any man capitulate.'' Jill believed the comment was meant to be charming, but his flat delivery made her uncomfortable. In fact, Ohnishi made her uncomfortable. He looked like a corpse that refused to stop moving.

She smiled her best reporter's smile. "I'm glad you did. Any longer and the station was going to make me pay for the stamps I was using.''

A servant appeared and poured coffee into her cup, adding one spoonful of sugar. Jill looked at him queerly, wondered how he knew she took her coffee this way.

"I know much more than that, Miss Tzu, otherwise I would have never let you on the grounds,'' Ohnishi said, reading her expression, possibly her mind, for all she knew.

"Is that why no one asked to see my ID or search me when I came here?'' She meant the question to be friendly, but it sounded almost defensive.

"I had you followed from your home at 1123 Blossom Tree Court in the Muani Condominium development. In fact, I've had you followed every day since granting this interview,'' Ohnishi said so casually that Jill could not respond for a moment.

"Did you learn anything interesting?'' she said sarcastically, her anger now beginning to rise.

"Yes, a lovely successful woman like you needs to get out more.''

Jill's anger evaporated at his reply. "That's the same thing my mother tells me.''

Much later, Jill realized his use of her mother's exact words was no coincidence.

"I am sorry if my actions make you uncomfortable, but a man in my position must be cautious.''

"I understand. I don't particularly like it, but I understand.''

The servant reappeared and placed a bowl of fruit in front of Jill. Again he gave nothing to Ohnishi.

"As my aide Kenji told you on the phone, I do not

allow cameras on my property nor is this conversation to be recorded.''

''It won't be, I assure you,'' Jill said, setting her coffee cup into its saucer, fearful of spilling anything on the crisp linen cloth or cracking the translucent porcelain. She did not realize that she had been x-rayed twice since entering Ohnishi's home, once at the front door and again in the elevator. Her verbal assurances were superfluous.

''I must say this is an amazing home,'' Jill remarked to break the silence.

''Believe it or not, this structure was designed in 1867 by an obscure Tokyo architect, long before the technology was available for its construction. He took his own life only a few months after completing the drawings, knowing that his genius would never be appreciated in his time. It is supposition on my part, but I believe he thought his suicide would give his work the immortality it would never receive through construction.''

''I did not know that you were such a student of history.''

''Everything we know, Miss Tzu, is history. Just because it is not taught in schools from dusty texts does not lessen any information's importance.''

''I don't think I understand.''

''Allow me to explain. The latest piece of information, no matter how current, is already history. I can look at a stock ticker as the trading goes on and already the information I'm seeing is history. Maybe it's only a second old, but the events have already happened and nothing in my power can change them. If I decide to buy or sell based on that information, I would be basing that choice on history. All knowledge is like that and all decisions are made that way.''

''What if I decide to do something on a whim?''

''Such as?''

''I don't know, say, quit my job.''

''In that case, you would have a history of job dissatisfaction, a knowledge based on past performance that you could find another job, and confidence that you have put sufficient money in a bank to ensure security until you begin working again. All of these factors make your decision not whimsical at all, but rather calculating in fact.''

"I never thought about it in that way," Jill said, intrigued.

"That is why you are not worth eight billion dollars and I am," Ohnishi remarked, not boastful, just stating the truth.

"I asked your assistant if there were any taboo subjects for this interview and he assured me that you would be candid about anything I asked."

"That is true." The servant cleared Jill's fruit plate and brought a silver salver of raw fish and thinly sliced beef. He placed some on her plate along with rice and several varieties of seaweed.

"Aren't you eating, Mr. Ohnishi?" Jill asked after the servant vanished, again leaving his plate empty.

"My stomach and some of my small intestine were removed several years ago after I was diagnosed with cancer, Miss Tzu. I'm afraid I must eat intravenously. I may sample some of these dishes later, but I can't swallow them. It is an unpleasant sight I assure you."

Jill was thankful he did not get more graphic.

"I know your basic biography, Mr. Ohnishi," Jill began the formal interview, a Waterman pen poised over her notebook. "You were born in Osaka, but your parents immigrated to the United States with your two older sisters when you were an infant. Your father was a chemical engineer working for UC at San Diego."

"Correct," Ohnishi interrupted. "My family all died during World War II when Roosevelt imprisoned all Japanese nationals. My sisters died of typhus; they were barely into their teens. My mother died soon afterward of the same disease. The day he took his own life, my father told me to never forget them. I was seventeen years old."

"You had an uncle who became your legal ward?"

"Yes, his name was Chuichi Genda."

"If I read this correctly," Jill said looking through her notes, "he was released from an internment camp in January 1943, arrested one week later, released again at the end of the war and spent the remainder of his life in and out of prisons on various charges."

"Yes, my uncle had very strong beliefs about America and her treatment of our people both during the war and after. He often led violent campaigns against various policies. He was charged with inciting riots three times and convicted twice. He was, without a doubt, the most influential person in my life."

"In what way?"

"His ideas on race, principally."

"And what are those?" Jill asked, uncrossing her long legs. She knew that this was the most important part of her interview.

"You are a journalist—surely you are aware of my views."

"I know you've been called a racist by nearly every social group in the United States and that your hiring policies resemble Nazi purity laws."

Ohnishi laughed, a high thin note that startled Jill. "For lack of a better word, Miss Tzu, you are very naïve. There is no such thing as racism." Before Jill could voice a protest, Ohnishi continued. "According to anthropologists, there are only four races on this planet: Asian, negro, caucasian, and aboriginal. Yet there is tension and fighting between hundreds of different groups. Correct?"

He did not wait for a reply. "If race is the motivating factor as you in the press imply, why is there so much fighting in the nations of Africa, why do the English and Irish bomb each other on a regular basis, why did the

Nazis gas six million Jews? The answer is not racism, it's tribalism.

"There may be only four races, but there are hundreds of different tribes, maybe thousands. Many groups still maintain a tribal name, such as the Apache or Zulu. But numerous groups no longer have distinct names, the white Anglo-Saxon here in America, the Northern Irish Protestants, or the upper class of Brazil.

"Each group is fighting to maintain the integrity of their tribe. The French and Germans are two separate tribes of people, culturally and religiously different, yet each falling into the caucasian race. There is only one way to account for the four wars they have fought since the middle of the last century: tribalism. The need to protect and ensure the security in perpetuity of one's immediate group.

"Just because interracial strife makes good press does not make it the most common form. I will deny until my death that I am a racist. I care nothing for race. I am a tribalist. And my tribe, the Japanese, is all that I care for.

"Tribes are basically extended families, so when I give a top position to a fellow Japanese, I am merely helping one of my kin. That is no different than a man turning over his business to his son, a common practice all over the world. I have fought nearly three hundred court cases defending my right to hire and promote who I wish, and to date no one has been able to deny me."

"If you have such a pro-Japanese view of the world, why is it you recently took up residence in the United States?" Jill asked, trying to remain calm and professional despite her revulsion.

"I had this home built six years ago," Ohnishi pointed out.

"Yet you only moved here three months ago," Jill retorted.

"I feel that I am most needed here. As you know, the Japanese are now the largest ethnic group in Hawaii, and if you'll pardon my arrogance, I believe that they need my help."

"Your help?"

"I wish to see Japanese prosper wherever their work takes them. While the media focuses on material trade imbalances, they completely ignore the amount of brain power that Japan exports each year. We send only our brightest people to work in foreign countries, strengthening our position overseas year by year. Let America send wide-eyed college students to build huts in Africa. We send CEOs to build corporations. I just want to do my part and ensure the success of this program."

"And do you see your help extending to Hawaii's native population?"

"They have suffered under the yoke of a white government far longer than we, so of course I wish to see them gain more power here on the islands. After all, tribally speaking, they are closer to us Japanese than to their current white overlords."

"Surely you exaggerate when you use a term such as overlord to describe the state government," Jill said a little nervously.

"On the contrary. How else would you describe a governing body that does not speak your language, does not understand your culture or religion, and has done nothing to bridge the socioeconomic gap? If the true Hawaiians are so satisfied with the current system, why do you think the island of Niihau, with its strict language and culture laws, is attracting so many natives to their traditional way of life? But primarily, my assistance is to those who are of Japanese descent, Miss Tzu."

"Does your help include aiding Mayor Takamora? Some consider his acts treasonous."

"I have not hidden my support of Mayor Takamora. I believe in his programs for ensuring the prosperity of Hawaii. It is time that the true owners of this state come forth and claim what is theirs without paying undue taxes to Washington."

Ohnishi was referring to the Takamora-sponsored referendum now being discussed in the State House that would make foreign owners of Honolulu real estate exempt from paying most taxes if they agreed to place the money in social programs solely beneficial to Japanese and Japanese-American residents. If passed, the law would put tens of millions of tax dollars into the hands of the Japanese residents of the island. Some political analysts called it vote-buying, while others saw something deeper, state-buying.

The campaigning for Referendum 324 was at a crucial stage, with the vote only a week away. As with any controversial law, emotions across the state ran high and already had turned violent. The number of attacks against tourists and white residents had skyrocketed in the past few weeks. Roving gangs of Japanese youths prowled the city streets at night like modern-day ninjas, striking fear by their very presence.

"What about the increase in violence?"

"Miss Tzu, of course I don't condone those people who use violence to achieve their aims, but I do understand their commitment. Hawaii has special needs and considerations that only we understand and it is paramount that we gain more control over our lives."

"Some people see this as an attempt at secession," Jill said, referring to the vice president's speech of the night before.

"Some people would." Ohnishi smiled, but his dark eyes remained impassive. "The interview is over, Miss Tzu. You must leave."

Jill was startled at her abrupt dismissal, but she knew better than to protest. She tossed her pen and pad into her bag and stood.

"Thank you for your time, Mr. Ohnishi," Jill said formally.

"I wonder, Miss Tzu," Ohnishi remarked absently, "which part of your racial heritage makes you the most uncomfortable with yourself, your Chinese half, or your

Japanese which allows the Chinese to have any influence?''

Later, Jill was amazed how easily her reply had rolled off her tongue. "The Chinese, it's given me the patience to put up with all the freaks I meet on the job."

Her only memory of leaving the house was the echo of her heels against the marble foyer as she strode to the front door.

"Apart from her physical charms, what do you think of Miss Tzu?" Ohnishi asked after the elevator doors had closed behind her.

A dark shape split from the shadows of the loggia as if by mitosis. It padded across the terrace silently and eased into the recently vacated chair with the ease of a predatory cat.

"I believe that she is dangerous," the shadow replied.

"Kenji, you are a worrier. She is nothing more than a voice in the wind. She will report what every other journalist writes, some diatribe full of half-truths and hyperbole that will be lost among the juicy murder stories and baseball scores."

"Yet."

"Yet nothing. The people, I mean the real people of this state, the ones who matter, won't care what she says. The mayor and I have been whipping them into such a frenzy that her little report won't make a bit of difference."

"You and David Takamora may be creating a situation that you cannot control and one I am sure has no bearing on our true objective."

"You sound like Ivan Kerikov's lackey," Ohnishi accused.

Kenji's black eyes went flat. "That is not what I meant. But we have a responsibility to him that you may be jeopardizing by financing the youth gangs and talking to reporters like Jill Tzu."

"You have been in my employ since you were a boy, Kenji. You have only known the simplicity of one master. I, on the other hand, have known many, my conscience first and foremost and now that pig Kerikov. I know how to serve both. Kerikov will get his precious concession, but only at the price I dictate.''

"This uprising is proceding too quickly. That is not part of your bargain with him.''

"But it is part of *my* plan, Kenji, and that is all you need to know and believe.'' Ohnishi's tone of finality subdued his aide. "I am wondering about your loyalty, Kenji. You no longer act like my Hachiko.''

Ohnishi was referring to a much-beloved Japanese dog from the 1920s who waited each afternoon at a train station for his master to return from work. One day, the master did not return, for he had died at his desk at Tokyo University. The faithful dog returned every day to the very train platform for ten years, waiting for a master who would never come. The name Hachiko is still synonymous with loyalty in Japan.

"Two days ago you disappeared for the night without telling me,'' Ohnishi continued, "and now you are questioning my orders. Forget about Jill Tzu and concentrate on your other duties. Tonight we shall begin the bombings. Nothing serious, just a small show of force directed at those who oppose the referendum.''

Kenji stood, his body flowing from the chair as if made of quicksilver, yet tensed as only a martial arts expert can be. "I will see to it personally.''

He glided off the terrace, his tabi-shod feet merely brushing the tile. Once out of sight of Ohnishi, any trace of subserviance evaporated and his handsome face took on an even keener edge. He mumbled, "You feebleminded old fool; you have no idea who or what you're dealing with.''

He went back to his private office to ensure that Jill Tzu never filed her interview with Takahiro Ohnishi.

J ill raked her fingers through her thick hair in utter frustration. She pursed her full lips, forming a seductive kiss, then blew a loud raspberry. Her feet were up on the control console of the studio's editing room, her long legs stretched almost to the bank of monitors. She swung them down, ignoring the fact that her culotte shorts had just given her technician a view he'd brag about for a week.

"This isn't working, Ken," she muttered darkly.

"Give me a break will ya, Jill? We've been at this for six hours. It's not like you're going to get a Pulitzer for this," the scraggly-bearded techie said in his defense.

"Yea, but just maybe it'll be my ticket to the network. Just think about it, Ken, if I leave, you won't have anyone bitching at you at all hours of the day or night."

"Keep wearing those shorts and you can piss and moan all you want," Ken teased.

"Watch it, I know a good sexual harassment lawyer."

Jill smiled for the first time in an hour. "All right, let's go through this one more time."

This day in the editing room was the culmination of three months' work on Takahiro Ohnishi. Jill had begun hunting down her story shortly after the reclusive billionaire had moved to Hawaii and Referendum 324 had first been proposed. At thirty-two, she was already too cynical to believe in coincidences and she'd begun looking for a connection between Ohnishi and Honolulu's controversial mayor, David Takamora and his even more polemic actions.

She'd found, just through her own television station's financial and scheduling records, that Takamora had purchased more advertising space during his campaign than his public files showed he'd had the money for. At just her station, there was a discrepancy of nearly one hundred thousand dollars, and she knew he'd campaigned just as heavily on the other channels. Where had the secret funds come from?

Jill lacked any concrete evidence that Ohnishi had privately funded the majority of Takamora's campaign, but she was damned sure that was what had happened. Ohnishi, with his billions, had bought himself a city.

A journalism professor had once told her that only prosecutors in courtrooms needed proof. A reporter never needed to prove anything, all she had to do was implicate and wait for the self- incriminating defense. A few years later an aging editor said at his drunken retirement party that news never happened, it was created.

Jill's piece on Ohnishi was nearly ready. In fact this morning's interview had really been unnecessary; she'd just wanted to meet the man, to get a better sense of what made him tick.

She and Ken watched in silence as the first half of the piece ran. Stock footage of Ohnishi, David Takamora, and the violent street gangs currently preying on white tourists in the city were interspersed with close-up shots of Jill doing commentary in front of city hall. As the scenes began focusing more on the gangs, especially one violent image of four Asian youths beating an elderly white woman, Jill reached for the goose-necked microphone and began laying in a new voice-over, one not from the contrived script she had written, but one from her heart.

"Hawaii is the Aloha State. The word means love as well as good-bye in the native tongue, and in these times it means both simultaneously. Good-bye to love. Good-bye to everything that our island paradise has stood for since Captain Cook first came here two hundred years ago, and good-bye to the traditions that reigned on the islands since the first inhabitants 1,500 years before that.

"Where once we melded and blended into one people, neither all caucasian nor all Polynesian nor all Asian, today we stand divided from our neighbors and friends. Now all it takes is having eyes a little too round or skin a little too light and anyone on the street can become a target. Racial hatred has grown here like some cancer, some dread disease without cause whose cure seems equally elusive. Fostered by men like Takahiro Ohnishi, with his well-publicized views of racial purity, and vanguarded by youth gangs bent on violent expression, the state has been galvanized into two intractable camps: those who want Referendum 324 and those who fear it as many have feared tyranny before.

"Last night, the vice president called Referendum 324 the beginning of a secessionist movement, and perhaps he's right. The last time America faced a crisis like this, the Southern states withdrew from the Union because they believed in their way of life, one built on the conviction that people of other races are inferior. Today a segment of Hawaii's population believes they have a mandate to control everyone's lives because there is a little more Japanese blood flowing in their veins. They say that their Samurai ways are superior, that they can calm the streets once again if we agree to live under a system that stifles freedom of expression and the belief that every one is created equal. In this reporter's opinion, that sounds an awful lot like extortion.

"As the *ronin* scour the streets for white faces to victimize, their emperor sits inside his glass and steel home, safe behind a wall of hatred and bigotry. Since his arrival a darkness has descended, a black veil that no one seems able or willing to lift. Today, the hotels along the beaches, the condos near Diamond Head, and the cruise liners are all empty. People are afraid to come to Hawaii. I spoke with one hotel manager yesterday who told me that tourists are already canceling reservations for next year.

"A self-generating downward spiral has been created by the actions of those who now seem to control our streets. As more tourists are frightened away, more people will lose their jobs and seek the security and fraternity represented by the gangs, thus increasing their ability to terrorize. Only this morning the President placed the troops stationed at Pearl Harbor on full alert in order to protect the federal government's interest on the islands.

"Who is going to protect our interests?

"Mayor Takamora's police force does not act to control the gangs. Will he ever ask for the National Guard to step in and take control of a situation he can no longer handle? For surely we face a crisis as dire as any these islands have faced since the first time a Japanese force descended in 1941."

Jill angrily pushed the microphone aside as she watched a monitor displaying David Takamora's announcement four weeks earlier that he wanted to run in the gubernatorial elections in the fall.

Ken was too stunned to speak for an instant, and when he caught his voice, he stammered. "Jesus, Jill, you can't run that."

"Of course I can't. It's the truth, and right now we're not allowed to report the truth," she said bitterly.

The in-house phone rang. The unit was built into the

console next to where Jill's feet were propped back up against the complicated machine. She snatched it up, tucking her hair behind her right ear as she swung the receiver to her head.

"I know, I know, forty-five minutes to air." Only her producer would disturb her in the editing room.

"You've got five."

"What in the hell are you talking about, Hank? We don't air for an hour."

"You know the rules, Jill, every piece that chronicles the violence must be cleared by Hiroshi." Hiroshi Kyato was the station's news director.

"That's bullshit and you know it. You can shove your five-minute deadline. I'm not some second-class citizen."

"Wait, I didn't mean anything by it, I mean I don't mean any disrespect for who you are. It's just, well, you know . . ." His voice trailed off.

The producer backpedaled so fast that it truly stunned Jill. Race was polarizing the station, too. Jill was half-Japanese, and Hank was a caucasian from New Jersey, and he was now deadly afraid that he'd offended her.

"Hold on, Hank," Jill said quickly. "What I mean to say is that I'm not a cub reporter on her first assignment. I know what the boundaries are. I don't need Hiro and his thought police telling me what to say on the air."

"I'm sorry, Jill," Hank said tiredly. "I've been on edge ever since Hiro agreed to help Mayor Takamora reduce tensions in the city by running tamer pieces on the situation. So far you are about the only reporter who hasn't called me a graduate of the Josef Goebbels School of Broadcast Journalism."

"Haven't you talked to Hiro about this?"

"Sure did. He told me to hand over every segment about the violence or hand in my resignation."

"All right, listen, my piece isn't done yet, or, well, it is, but I'm not going to let that son of a bitch cut it up. I'm going to take it home tonight, tone it some. If anyone is going to censor my work, it'll be me. I won't be the person to cost you your job.''

''Jill, you can't do that, your story belongs to the station, it's not your private property.''

''Try and stop me, Hank.''

Jill set the phone back in the cradle and popped the tape from the editing machine, slipping it in her handbag slung across the back of her chair. She stood.

''What are you going to do?'' Ken asked from behind his thick glasses.

''I don't know yet.'' She left the darkened room.

THE subtle chirping of cicadas was a rhythmic accompaniment to the moon-drenched night. The air was warm, but charged with the humidity of a recently passed thunderstorm. Jill sat on the lanai of her condo, her bare feet propped against a patio table and a glass of zinfandel idly twirling between her long fingers.

She'd been home for a couple of hours, but the long bath and half bottle of wine had done little to calm her frayed nerves. Three months she'd been working on the Ohnishi piece, three fucking months, and it would be chopped up into tiny pieces on the cutting room floor and run as a human interest story, no doubt. If she'd ever questioned the connection between Ohnishi and Takamora, she had her proof now—and the links ran even deeper, to her own news director. Was no one immune to this racial factionalism other than her?

She was really wondering if it was all worth it. All the sacrifices she'd made in her life, all the thought she'd put into her career, and here she was, about to have her accomplishments hacked apart because they cut too close to the truth.

''Son of a bitch.'' Despite herself, she was almost in tears.

Everything in her life had been built around journalism. She'd let almost everything else go in order to reach the upper echelons of her profession. Few boyfriends lasted more than a month or so of her eighty-hour work weeks. She'd spent her last vacation working as a temporary secretary at a sewage treatment plant, tracking down allegations of groundwater contamination.

Her infrequent talks with her mother invariably turned to Jill's lack of a husband and children. Every time Jill bragged about a breaking story, her mother would ask where her grandbabies were. Jill would always end the conversation angrily defending her career, but would always be racked with guilt, knowing that her mother was partly right.

Jill did want a husband and children, but she also wanted to be a journalist. There was a balance between the two that she just couldn't seem to find. How much of her career should she give up for a family? How much family should she forego for a career?

And now her career might be about over. She could refuse to hand in her story and face probable dismissal, or she could cut the piece herself, destroying every shred of her integrity.

She wondered if she should send the story directly to New York. She had a few friends in the network— maybe she could get someone to watch it, see if it was worth running on the national feed. Lord knew nothing like it had been sent from Hawaii in a long time.

Her phone rang. Jill got up from the lanai to answer it, but as soon as she put the receiver to her ear, the line went dead. Crank call or wrong number, she didn't care.

She finished the last bit of wine in a heavy swallow and put the empty glass in the dishwasher, leaning against the tiled counter. She'd exhausted two of the three traditional female relaxation techniques, the bath and the wine, and there weren't any stores open this late, so she couldn't go shopping. She decided on a masculine diversion—she'd go out. Sitting at home and brooding wasn't her style anyway. She could do the voice-over in the morning, but tonight she wanted a diversion, something to get her mind off her job, off her parents, off everything.

There would be a vast assortment of eligible bachelors at the tourist hotels near the beach. Before heading into her bedroom, she put an Aerosmith CD into the player and cranked the volume to seven. The heavy bass and pounding tempo immediately made her feel better. Defiantly bad-girl music for a bad-girl-type night.

She spent over an hour choosing her outfit and makeup. Finally she was dressed to kill, from black tap panties to a hip-hugging Nina Ricci dress. Six hours a week in a gym ensured that she had a body that would turn even a blind man's head.

Just as she was resetting her breasts in the strapless dress, there was a crash of breaking glass. She whirled toward the sliding glass bedroom doors as a darkly dressed figure burst through the gauzy curtains. The first man was quickly followed by two more, their booted feet crushing the shards against the teal carpet.

Jill screamed shrilly. For an instant her panic overcame the natural urge to flee, and that hesitation cost her.

Two of the men raced toward her, guns clamped in their gloved fists. Jill began backing away, but a pistol whipped out and caught her on the jaw, snapping her head around and knocking her to the floor. She was unconscious before her diamond pendant necklace settled in her cleavage.

The man who had struck her peeled off his black ski mask. It was Takahiro Ohnishi's assistant, Kenji.

"Tie her," he ordered.

He searched the house until he found the room Jill used as an office. Two walls were lined with expensive video equipment, the type used for high-quality editing work. More than likely her piece on Ohnishi was here. Kenji rifled the filing cabinet and desk with professional adroitness, but turned up nothing.

In disgust he went back out to the living room. On a

small geometric lucite table near the front door rested a thick manila envelope. He tore it open and a videocassette slid into his hand. He returned to the office and slid the tape into a VCR.

Jill Tzu's story ran for the first and only time. As Kenji had suspected, it documented his employer's known violations of civil employment laws and Ohnishi's support of Honolulu Mayor David Takamora's gubernatorial election bid for the fall. Jill had also managed to slip in several references to the escalating violence surrounding the campaign and the possibility that Ohnishi was financing that as well. Popping the tape from the VCR, Kenji slid it into the inside pocket of his dark windbreaker.

He returned to the bedroom where Jill was laid across the bed, hands cuffed behind her and a gag stuffed into her lipsticked mouth. She was still unconscious.

Nevertheless, Kenji whispered into her ear, "An excellent piece of reporting, Miss Tzu. You are correct on all charges. Mr. Ohnishi is financing the violence in Honolulu. Though not for much longer, I assure you." He turned to his henchmen. "Let's go."

They bundled Jill into the bedspread and carried her from her home as if she were a rolled-up carpet. The cicadas paused as the party ducked through the bushes toward their hidden vehicle.

TWENTY miles away, thunderous applause swept across the Honolulu Convention Center as Mayor David Takamora took the stage, sending a palpable compression wave echoing through the cavernous hall. Twelve thousand people filled the room, many waving placards in support of Honolulu's controversial mayor. The air was charged with the energy of the massed throng as their hero raised his arms over his head in recognition of the crowd's adoration.

Under the glare of the television crew's kleig lights, Takamora appeared much more handsome than he did in person. The lights and makeup hid the pocks of adolescent acne on his face and darkened the thin strands of silver that wove through his thick hair. He held his body erect and confident, showing off a lean stomach that was nothing more than a girdle and a continual holding of his breath. The effort would inevitably cause severe back pain after the speech.

Such small hoaxes can be forgiven in most men in their fifties if they did not go deeper than the surface. In Takamora's case, it would take more than a little makeup to hide the flaws in his personality and morals.

Pathologically ambitious, Takamora had turned to the darker side of politics to gain his current office. From the very beginning of his career as a board member of the city's building commission, he had made it clear to any developer who cared to listen that he would almost joyfully take bribes to help a project gain quick approval.

He amassed several hundred thousand dollars in just a few years and used that money as a war chest to battle for the mayor's office. Some said that he cut so many deals to get on the ballot that he kept a knife on his desk rather than a pen. He waged one of the ugliest campaigns for mayor of any American city in history. His main opponent, a councilwoman of excellent standing, withdrew from the race when her daughter was brutally raped after leaving a Honolulu nightclub. Takamora didn't know if the rape was coincidence or the act of an overzealous assistant.

Now he stood poised to go far beyond his own ambition. He was the last of the speakers at this pro-Referendum 324 rally, and the crowd was already roused to a fever pitch.

"Ladies and gentlemen," Takamora said, quieting the crowd with hand gestures. He spoke in Japanese. "Ladies and gentlemen, a little over a year ago you gave me a mandate when you elected me to help this city prosper, to create new jobs and security for our way of life. Since then I have done everything in my power to make this happen. But I've found myself limited by the very office with which you entrusted me.

"While we've been able to attract Japanese companies to our city, state and federal regulators have stalled our efforts. When Ohnishi Heavy Industries wanted to build a computer assembly plant in Honolulu, the government in Washington refused to allow import permits for the machinery needed to set up the plant. When I wanted to privatize our police force, with the blessing of you, the voters, the Supreme Court called that an unconstitutional act because it might be construed as a private militia.

"Now I want to see our tax dollars stay here on Hawaii rather than disappear into the federal cesspit, and I'm being called a secessionist. Referendum 324 does not equal secession, it means parity. Our state is now wholly self-sufficient. We trade more with Japan than we do with California, so why shouldn't we be entitled to keep the tax revenue from our own labor? I no longer see any benefits from Washington, just inept meddling. I see us helping to prop up a system that has simply gotten away from itself, and I say: Don't take us with you.

"While the mainland sinks into a bottomless pit of crime and drug abuse, where drive-by shootings no longer make the news, where teenage pregnancy accounts for thirty percent of the children born, where welfare assistance has turned into a crutch for those too lazy to work, we have prospered.

"Do you think it fair we should pay for their corruption?"

The frenzied crowd shouted a defiant, "No!"

"Is it right that we must pay for their excesses?"

Again, with one hate-filled voice the crowd screamed, "No!"

"Last night, the vice president of the United States branded me a secessionist." The crowd was transmuting into a mindless mob, barely kept in check by Takamora's voice. "I say, *Don't tempt me*."

Takamora's last words were spoken in a low hiss, then he ducked from the stage, wearing the adulation of the crowd like a cloak. An aide handed him a bottle of beer and a towel. He took a quick swig and wiped the greasy makeup from his face.

"Listen to them," he said to the assembled aides, "they're fucking ready for anything."

As Takamora leaned into the sound of the crowd beyond the maroon curtain, an aide slid a ringing cellular phone from his pocket, listened for an instant, then handed it to Takamora.

"Yes."

"Congratulations, David, a rousing speech."

"Thank you, Mr. Ohnishi, I'm pleased you were able to hear it." The microphones in the convention center had been wired into a transceiver and the signals sent to Ohnishi's house. "Can you still hear the crowd, sir?"

"Yes, you are certainly the man of the hour."

"Only with your help, Mr. Ohnishi," Takamora replied honestly, acknowledging the massive support given to him by the aging industrialist.

"I think now is the time to step up our campaign, don't you?" Ohnishi's comment was not really a question, it was a command.

"I agree, sir," Takamora replied, keeping the pretense of a free will. "What do you have in mind?"

"A few bombings, better arms for the youth gangs, and a little more selectivity to their targets. Our day is rapidly approaching, so we must be more organized. Kenji will contact you in the morning with all the particulars."

"But the vote for Referendum 324 is still a week away—aren't we jumping the gun slightly?"

"Some unforeseen contingencies have arisen that may force me to abandon the subterfuge of Referendum 324. Who cares if the people won't be allowed their vote?

We will give them what they want anyway. What I want to know is if your National Guard troops will maintain their loyalty throughout our campaign.''

"You can count on them, sir, at least those units that I've personally built up since taking office. As you know, the crack units here in Honolulu are made up of Japanese-Americans, young men and women who feel the same as we do. It is only a matter of time until the governor calls them out, unwittingly putting more of our people on the streets. I guarantee that they will not interfere with your gangs.''

"And if the President calls out federal troops?''

Takamora hesitated for an instant. "The guardsmen will be willing to take them on. Remember, the military presence on the island represents the greatest source of antagonism among our people. It is the same here as it was on Okinawa following the rape of that little girl in 1996.''

"Good, and David, never question me again.'' Ohnishi's tone was saccharine, but hard edged.

Takamora shut off the phone with a snap, angered that his euphoria of a few moments ago had been chilled by Ohnishi. He tried to look composed as he handed the phone back to his assistant, but failed miserably.

ARLINGTON, VIRGINIA

The faint chime of the Tiffany alarm clock woke Mercer instantly. His hand snaked out from under the tangle of sheets and blankets and silenced the antique piece. He pushed aside the bed coverings and swung his legs to the floor. His deep gray eyes were already bright and clear. Mercer's eyes reacted to light much quicker than the average person's. He barely squinted at bright lights and adjusted to darkness with the speed of a cat. It was an ability he fully exploited in the subterranean world of hard-rock mining.

He shaved and took a quick shower before heading down the circular stairs to the rec room, passing through the library on the way. The built-in dark oak shelves were full of plain beige boxes containing his vast collection of reference books. For the thousandth time, Mercer promised himself he'd unpack the books and place them properly on the shelves. He also wanted to hang the dozens of pictures and paintings he had collected over the years, which currently lay crated in one of the brownstone's two spare bedrooms.

Cup of coffee in hand, he went to the front door and grabbed the morning *Washington Post*. He was just turning to the stories beneath the fold as he made his way to the bar in the rec room.

A story on the left corner riveted him to the stool.

SURVIVOR FOUND FROM NOAA SHIP

Hawaii

Dr. Tish Talbot, a specialist on the ill-fated NOAA research vessel *Ocean Seeker*, was rescued by a Finnish freighter at 12:30 local time this morning. She is so far the only survivor of the ship which sank three days ago. The *Ocean Seeker* was investigating the mysterious deaths of twelve gray whales found beached last month on Hawaii's north coast. Dr. Talbot is said to be in stable condition, suffering from dehydration and exposure. She is being flown to George Washington University Hospital this morning for observation. The rescue ship, SS *September Laurel*, had been assisting the coast guard and navy search for survivors since the mysterious sinking.

The article went on, but Mercer really didn't see the rest of the words; he was stunned. The sense of loss that he felt the night before slipped away, replaced by joy and relief.

"Harry, wake up." Mercer had to share the news.

Harry came awake slowly, groans and yawns followed by scratches and stretches. "What time is it?"

"Quarter of six," Mercer replied, glancing at his Tag Heuer watch.

"Christ, my mouth feels as if I just French-kissed an Angora sweater."

Mercer poured him a cup of coffee. Harry moved from the couch to the bar and slouched onto one of the stools, a cigarette already smoldering between his lips.

"Remember me telling you about Jack Talbot, the guy who saved my life in Alaska?" Mercer didn't wait for Harry to answer. "Last night I found out that his daughter was on board that NOAA ship that sank in the Pacific."

"Christ, Mercer, sorry to hear it," Harry said seriously. "I was meaning to ask you last night if you had heard about that."

Mercer held up the front page of the paper and Harry read it through still-bleary eyes. "Well, I'll be goddamned. How about that for luck."

"No shit."

"I wonder if your friend knows yet?"

"He probably didn't even know about the accident— last I knew he was working aboard an oil rig off the coast of Indonesia."

Harry looked at Mercer for a second, then stood up. "I better get home." Harry was through the door before Mercer could say another word. Mercer puzzled about his friend's abrupt exit for a moment, then went back to reading his paper.

At 8:30, Mercer strode into his office at the U.S. Geological Survey. His secretary, Jennifer Woodridge, tried to smile and say hi with a mouth full of cherry danish. Mercer marveled at her ability to eat. Her desk was nearly always covered with half-eaten junk food, mangled bags of chips, and at least three empty soft drink cans. Yet she weighed around one hundred pounds and had a figure that made him wish half the rumors in the office were true.

"Morning, Jen. I see nothing's changed in my absence."

She swallowed hard and took a sip of coffee. "Welcome back. I was so relieved that you were in South

Africa and not aboard that NOAA ship, you have no idea.''

"Trust me, you're not half as relieved as I am.''

Jen Woodridge had not always cared so much for her temporary boss. Two months earlier, when Mercer had started consulting at the USGS, Jen had prepared an extensive list of the things she would and wouldn't do in the course of her job. She read through the list at a staccato pace about two seconds after their introduction. Mercer had listened to her calmly, without comment. When she had finished all Mercer said was, "Okay.''

"What do you want me to do now?'' she asked, thinking she had the upper hand with him.

"Go back and sit at your desk.''

"And?''

"And nothing. Just sit at your desk. Don't answer the phone, don't fill out any papers, don't do anything.''

It took only forty fidgety minutes before Jen caved in and returned to Mercer's office, her blue eyes glazed with boredom. "Point taken and I'm sorry. Usually the consultants around here treat the staff like slaves.''

"Since you are the first secretary, excuse me, assistant, I've ever had, I really don't know how to treat you.'' Mercer's honesty had begun a great working relationship. Now he asked, "Did you read about that woman rescued last night?''

"Yes, isn't that fantastic?''

"Strange thing is, I know her, or rather, I know her father,'' Mercer said, heading for his office. "Come on and fill me in on what's been happening while I've been gone.''

Mercer struggled out of his jacket and threw it carelessly over the leather sofa. He laid his briefcase on the desk and settled into his chair. Jen hung up his jacket with a maternal scowl and sat in the chair in front of the desk to help him pore through the mountain of papers.

Around noon, Jennifer went to lunch; Mercer stayed in his office, catching up on the paperwork treadmill. A security guard knocked quietly at his office door a few minutes after Jen left. "Are you Dr. Philip Mercer?" the guard asked, confirming the name from the slip of paper in his hand.

Mercer winced inwardly—he hated to be called doctor. He grinned at the security officer. "So you boys finally caught me stealing toilet paper from the men's room."

The guard looked at him, puzzled, then realized that Mercer wasn't serious.

So much for a sense of humor, thought Mercer.

"Sir, Western Union delivered this telegram to the front office; it's addressed to you." The guard handed Mercer the envelope and left without another word.

The telegram had been sent from Jakarta. Mercer knew instinctively that it was from Jack Talbot. For some reason he felt a sense of foreboding as he unfolded the paper.

"Tish in mortal danger. Help her. *Ocean Seeker* intentionally destroyed. Will try to get to D.C. soonest."

It was signed *Jack*.

Mercer spent no more than ten seconds making up his mind. The Jack Talbot he knew was not prone to fantasy or hysteria. If Jack said that his daughter was in danger and that the NOAA ship had been purposely destroyed, Mercer believed him unequivocally.

Mercer stood quickly, his gray eyes hard and set, his lean body already slightly tensed for the unknown. He grabbed his jacket and strode to the elevators. Within six minutes of reading the telegram his black Jaguar XJS convertible was bulling its way through downtown traffic toward the GWU hospital.

The nurse at the hospital's front desk informed him that Tish was in room 404, but that no visitors were allowed. The nurse also told Mercer that the room was being guarded by the FBI.

The fact that the sole survivor of a shipwreck was under guard gave some credence to Jack's warning that his daughter was in danger and that the sinking of the *Ocean Seeker* had ominous overtones.

"Well, that takes care of that," Mercer said, and gave the nurse a smile that made her blush. "Where can I find a cup of coffee?"

"To the right and up the stairs, sir," she responded, patting her mousy hair. "The cafeteria is on the second floor."

Mercer thanked her, but once in the stairwell he climbed quickly to the fourth floor. The fluorescent lights, yellow-painted walls, and hospital smell were enough to cause nausea in the most healthy person. After a few minutes he found the wing which contained room 404. The two beefy no-necked men sitting at an impromptu security desk eyed him like sharks looking at a wounded mullet.

"Dr. Mercer to see Tish Talbot," Mercer said casually, flashing an ID card.

One guard looked him up and down, noting the stethoscope protruding from his coat pocket. Mercer had picked it up at an empty nurse's station. The other guard saw the GWU logo on the card and noted that the photo of Dr. Mercer matched the man in front of him.

"What's your business, Dr. Mercer?" The man's voice was flat and lifeless.

"I'm a urologist," Mercer replied, and stifled a small yawn. "I need to check for renal damage due to extended dehydration."

The guard waved him through without a second thought. The ID that Mercer flashed had in fact been issued by GWU hospital, but it merely signified that he was a recipient of the hospital's health coverage. Anything more than a cursory examination would have gotten him a quick trip to the J. Edgar Hoover Building.

So much for the vigilance of the FBI.

Mercer looked over his shoulder and saw one of the guards bury his face in a near-empty bag of corn chips and pour the remainder in his mouth. Since Tish was in possible trouble, there was no way that he would let these two idiots look out for her.

Tish was sitting up in bed, a magazine resting on her bent knees. Though she looked fatigued from her ordeal she was a beautiful woman on the easy side of thirty with short-cropped dark hair, arresting red lips, and high cheekbones. Her skin was burned dark by the sun but did not appear permanently damaged. She looked up at him with her father's eyes, impossibly clear blue and impish.

"Miss Talbot, I'm Philip Mercer. I'm a friend of your father's. In fact I owe him my life—maybe he told you the story?"

Her smile was warm and open. "I've heard that story about a million times, Dr. Mercer, and I must say it's good to have a friend here."

"Better than you know," Mercer said under his breath. "How do you feel?"

"Tired and sore but okay. I really don't know why I'm being kept here." There was annoyance in her voice.

"Believe it or not, you're a pretty hot item right now. Do you know that you're under guard?"

"I wasn't aware of that. What the hell for?" She was plain speaking, just like her father.

"I was hoping you could tell me. I received a telegram about an hour ago from your father in Jakarta. He asked me to look after you."

Tish stared at him.

"He felt that the *Ocean Seeker* was intentionally destroyed, and if that's true, I don't think that you're safe here. I was in South Africa when all of this happened, so I don't know any details, but for now I'll trust your father and assume that your life may be in danger."

Tish continued to regard him blankly.

"Does any of this make sense to you? Do you remember something or did you see something that could cause this stir?"

"In the first place, Dr. Mercer . . ." Before she could

continue a man opened the door. A lab coat covered his suit.

"Good afternoon, I'm Dr. Alfred Rosenburg, your urologist." His smile was crooked and his teeth stained tobacco yellow.

Mercer took one look at the man's shoes and reacted instantly. The punch was powered with a full twist of his body. The instant before his fist smashed into the man's face, Mercer bent his arm, and his elbow connected solidly with Rosenburg's cheek. Tish muffled a scream in her hands as the doctor's head whipped around and he slammed into the wall.

Mercer turned to her. "Get dressed now, I'm getting you out of here."

Rosenburg was already regaining his feet, a six-inch stiletto in his hand. Mercer bent at the knees and torqued his body around, extending one leg in a sweep. The man fell back, his body shaking the wall when he hit. Mercer planted a foot squarely in his stomach, then kicked up into his face as he doubled over. Rosenburg's head snapped back and crashed into the wall. He slumped over, unconscious.

Mercer looked at Tish, who was still in bed. "He won't be alone, now get dressed."

She flew from the bed and was dressed in jeans and a T-shirt within moments, though not before Mercer stole a glimpse of exquisitely long legs and a white silk-pantied backside.

Mercer opened the door slowly and looked toward the guard station. The pool of blood under the desk told him that both FBI agents were dead.

"Oh, Jesus," Tish moaned as Mercer led her past the desk. Pausing for an instant, he found an automatic pistol and a spare clip inside one of the dead men's jackets. He held the weapon discreetly under his own coat and slipped the clip into a pocket.

Mercer took Tish's hand as they went down the stairs to the lobby. A quick scan of the faces there confirmed that the killer upstairs was indeed not alone. Three men stood just outside the automatic door while another trio peered at a glass-covered bulletin board, their eyes watching the room in its reflection.

The fugitives turned away from the lobby. Mercer led Tish through a set of doors marked NO ADMITTANCE and out onto a loading dock. The man standing on the dock looked at Tish just a bit too critically, so Mercer smashed his knee into the man's groin. If he was an innocent bystander, where better to get treated for his injuries, and if he was an assistant to the assassin upstairs, fuck him. Mercer and Tish ran to his car.

The Jaguar V12 burst into life instantly. Mercer had hoped to get away without being seen, but two men were already running toward them from the loading dock. Mercer jammed the gearbox into drive and smoked the Pirelli tires pulling out onto the street. A few cars pounded their horns in anger and a pair of nurses jumped back to the sidewalk for safety. Three identical BMWs were already in pursuit as Mercer turned onto 23rd Street heading toward Washington Circle.

Mercer took the car around the circle twice, trying to snarl his pursuers in traffic before tearing off down K Street. The maneuver gained him only a second or two.

Mercer put the borrowed pistol, a Heckler and Koch VP-70, on his lap as he jinked around a Metrobus. The deadly 9mm German-made gun had eighteen rounds inside its wide grip.

He clicked off the safety, then pressed the button that lowered his window. The sounds of the city whipped into the car. Mercer wished that he had taken the top down to give him better visibility, but there was nothing that he could do about that now.

The first chase car was pulling up on Mercer's left. The driver was intent on the road ahead, but the passenger had his eyes glued on Mercer. He threw a sardonic wave and pulled a Beretta model 12 into view. The little Italian submachine gun could fire a blanket of 9mm bullets at a rate of 550 a minute. Just as the man brought his weapon to bear, Mercer lifted his pistol over the windowsill and let loose.

He fired as fast as he could. The first five rounds tore up the body of the gunman; his torso and head jumped at every impact. As he slumped over, the next five rounds pulverized the head of the driver. The BMW slowed and began to veer off the road. It careened off one of the huge trees that lined K Street and shot back into traffic. In the rearview mirror, Mercer saw the BMW fly into the other lane and slam into the front of a parked garbage truck. The windshield exploded outward as the two bodies smashed through it.

Tish had turned almost white and kept biting her lower lip. Mercer took one hand off the wheel to grasp her reassuringly on the shoulder. He wished he could do more, but there were still two cars chasing them.

Mercer ignored a red light as K Street turned onto Pennsylvania Avenue and so did the pursuers. They had just passed the World Bank Building when the first bullets smashed into the Jaguar. Tish slid to the floor and Mercer began weaving the car, but the bullets continued to find their mark.

Traffic was getting thicker. Once Mercer was forced to stop completely but luckily the two BMWs were stuck several cars back. As they approached the busy intersection at 17th Street, with the Jag doing about forty mph, the light turned yellow. Mercer jammed the transmission into second ignoring the tachometer needle as it arced across the gauge, and mashed the gas pedal to the black-carpeted floor boards. The engine revs peaked with an earsplitting whine before Mercer eased the car back into drive. They passed the point of no return as the light changed to red and the mass of cars started down 17th Street like a steel avalanche.

Mercer cut the car wide to the right, the tires squealing on the asphalt. Pedestrians dove out of the way as he took the car up onto the sidewalk for a few yards before veering back onto the road nearly in front of the White House. One BMW had tried to follow him, but had smashed into the thick concrete antitank barricades that protected the presidential residence. The other was stuck in traffic.

Mercer stopped the Jag at the corner of Penn and 16th. "Take my wallet," he said, handing it to Tish. "My address is on the license and there's enough money for a cab." He yanked the house key from the ring dangling in the ignition and handed it to her. "There's a security panel to the right of the door. 36-22-34 will deactivate it. I'll be there as soon as I can."

"Will you be okay?" Tish's eyes were huge with fear.

"Don't worry, just go." She nodded, then leapt out of the car and immediately blended with the flow of people on their lunch breaks.

The moment the door slammed shut, Mercer took off down 16th Street, past the Hotel Washington. He cut back onto Pennsylvania in front of the Department of Commerce Building. He glimpsed the BMW in the rearview mirror. They were still following him, so he figured Tish was safe for now.

The Willard Hotel and the Post Office Pavilion blurred past as Mercer used the power and control of the Jaguar to snake throughout the thick traffic. Suddenly he heard the unmistakable sound of automatic fire again. The first fusillade mangled the coachwork of the Jag and punctured the rear windscreen about a dozen times. The next burst blew out the left rear tire.

The car flew out of control, the steering wheel like a slippery, living creature in Mercer's hands. He knew the Jaguar was doomed. The car's mad lurching had cleared the road quickly, and Mercer exploited this by driving into the oncoming lane, bouncing off stationary cars like a billiard ball. He finally came to a stop at the entrance of the Archive Metro station. In the relative silence following the crash, he could hear the fast approach of police sirens racing from all across downtown.

Mercer jammed a fresh clip into the pistol and leapt from the car. He flew down the escalator, shouldering people aside as he raced toward the city's modern subway system. Commuters gasped or complained as he pushed through the crowd and jumped the turnstile. The Metro guard in the glass booth was the last of his worries. As he reached the platform, Mercer was dismayed to see that the two sets of parallel tracks were empty and that there was not enough of a crowd to conceal him. He whirled around to see three men running toward him, weapons barely concealed under their jackets.

The floor lights lining the near track began to flash, indicating that a train was about to arrive. The station began to rumble as the train approached, pushing a wall of air ahead of it. The far track was still clear. Mercer knew that if he boarded the train he would be cut down instantly—these men obviously had no compunctions about a public murder.

The noise in the station reached a tactile level as the train burst from the tunnel in a whoosh of air and a squeal of brakes. Mercer's pursuers were only twenty yards away and already one was reaching into his jacket for his weapon. Mercer had only one chance for escape and he took it without thought. He ran for the edge of the track and leapt, barely two yards in front of the oncoming train.

The engineer blasted his horn and jammed on the brakes, but Mercer didn't even notice. He was too intent on the ten-foot jump. If he overshot, he could fly into the next track, land on the current rail, electrocute himself and save his attackers the trouble.

He landed safely on the low platform between the two tracks. As his body rocked forward from the momentum, he was stunned to see another train rushing toward him from the opposite direction. He windmilled his arms, trying to regain his balance, and almost succeeded.

The oncoming train glanced into his shoulder, sending him flying back so that he bounced off the first train, which had ground to a halt. Mercer lay between the now-stationary trains for a moment or two, recovering his senses. Finally he stood and, ignoring the shocked faces of passengers on both trains, levered his back against one of the trains and his legs against the other to shinny up to the roof of the far carriage. Over the shouts and police whistles that echoed through the station, he heard the quiet double ping that indicated the train doors were closing.

A shot rang out and the roof next to Mercer's head exploded. He flipped onto his back, extending the H&K toward the assassin who stood on the pedestrian bridge which spanned the tracks. Mercer fired just as the train lurched forward; his shot shattered concrete far to the left of his target. The assassin lined up another careful shot. Mercer rolled across the roof until he nearly slipped off, dodging the bullet.

An instant later, the Metro car slid under the bridge and Mercer rolled back across the roof, holding the pistol by his head, arms tucked close to his body. There was a four-foot gap between the bridge and the entrance to the subway tunnel. As Mercer passed through the gap, he spotted the assassin. Mercer pulled the trigger and saw the gunman fall back just before the Metro plunged into the darkened tunnel.

The ride through the tunnel was a nightmare. Though the train's speed was nearly forty miles per hour, in the dark it felt like four hundred. The rattling car threatened to shake Mercer off the roof and he had the constant fear of being smeared against the low ceiling. The noise and vibration were maddening, but he grimly held on, jaw clenched tightly to keep his teeth from jarring loose.

After a couple of minutes that seemed like an eternity, the train thundered into L'Enfant Plaza, the next station on the yellow line. Mercer moved forward until he was under the pedestrian bridge. No doubt that there would be a backup team in this station by now and probably in all the stations on the line. They had him boxed in. Whoever "they" were.

The wait in the station dragged on as passengers left and entered the train in the confused ballet called commuting. Mercer feared that the train would be held because of the body he had left in the Archive station. But a moment later the bell chimed and the pneumatic doors hissed closed. The train began to inch along and in a second, Mercer was exposed to another gunman standing on the bridge.

Mercer raised the VP-70 to take aim just as the other man swung the barrel of a Beretta toward him. Neither man had time to fire before Mercer disappeared into the blackness of the tunnel. Mercer's raised hand, the one grasping the pistol, smashed into the concrete wall. Instantly numbed fingers sprang open and the weapon slid from his grasp. It bounced against the roof, once, twice, then slipped over the edge, lost forever.

Mercer flipped back onto his stomach, cursing the pain and his own stupidity. He was now unarmed and facing an unimaginable number of enemies.

As the Metro climbed above ground just south of the Jefferson Memorial, Mercer realized that he had a chance to escape while the train was crossing the Potomac River. He swore at himself for even thinking it, but knew he had no other option. As soon as the train reached daylight, he sat up and kicked off his shoes. The train sped onto the truss bridge that spanned the sluggish river, rattling and clanging like an old steam locomotive. Mercer stood, the wind whipping his jacket around his body. He shed it quickly and peered at the river below. It was a sapphire blur.

Mercer jumped.

The jarring vibration of the Metro vanished as he arrowed toward the water, and for a moment all was quiet except for the wind in his ears. The impact as he hit the choppy water nearly knocked him unconscious, but the cold brought him back quickly. He was deep under the river's surface. With lungs emptied by the blow, the swim upward was agonizing.

He finally broke the surface and coughed the water from his lungs. He looked up at the bridge, but the train had already vanished from sight.

Twenty excruciating minutes later, he dragged himself onto the shore.

"Welcome to Virginia," he gasped.

THE PACIFIC

By its very nature a modern nuclear submarine makes an optimal platform for sensitive intelligence gathering. With its ability to remain submerged for extended periods and its absolute silence, a sub can maintain station near an unfriendly coast for weeks or even months with relative impunity.

The sub now lying in wait two hundred miles northwest of Hawaii had been there for seven months and apart from one minor incident had not once come close to detection. There was only about another week or two left of this patrol, so morale, which had been dismal, was finally picking up.

The crew, mostly northerners, no longer snickered at the captain's thick Georgian accent. The bickering, which had become an almost daily occurrence even among this highly disciplined crew, had ceased. The men knew that very soon they would feel the warm sun, breathe unrecirculated air, and have the company of their families once again.

The captain, an unlaughing, hawk-faced man in his midfifties, scanned the control room slowly. The red lights of battle stations, which had glowed continuously since the beginning of the mission, stained the faces of his men and hid every corner of the room in shadow. He too was looking forward to going home. Though he had lost his wife years before, he did have a daughter. A daughter who would have given birth to his first grandchild in his absence.

A boy or a girl? he mused. And if it was a boy will she name him after me or that idiot husband of hers?

"Captain, contact bearing two-oh-five degrees range fifteen miles," the sonar operator barked.

The bridge was galvanized with anticipation, each pair of eyes riveted on the captain. He checked his watch and decided that this might be the ship they were expecting.

"Sonar, scrub the target's signature please," the Old Man said calmly.

"Range too far, sir, we have to wait. Range thirteen miles. Single screw turning thirteen knots."

The captain picked up a hand mike. "Fire control, plot a solution to target and give me a lock. Torpedo room, flood tubes one and two but do not open outer doors."

Even on the bridge, thirty yards from the torpedo room, the captain could hear the water flooding into the tubes. He just hoped that there was no one else out there to hear as well.

"Sonar, can you scrub the signature yet?"

"Affirmative, sir, working now."

The boat's multimillion-dollar acoustical computer was analyzing the sounds coming from the approaching ship, digitally washing out the grinding rotation of her screw, the liquid friction of her hull cutting through the waves, and the omnipresent background noise of the living sea, until . . .

"We have our target, her signal is coming in strong. Repeat, she is our ship." Amid the ambient noise of the vessel, an ultrasonic generator pulsed a signal through the water to be picked up by only those listening for it. It was this signal for which the computer searched and the captain waited.

The captain picked up the microphone again. "Torpedo room, stand down."

"Shit!" the sonarman screamed and ripped off his headphones.

"What is it?" the captain demanded.

There was a thin trickle of blood from the man's ears. He spoke unnaturally loudly. "Another underwater explosion, sir. Much more powerful than any other."

"You are relieved," the captain said.

The sensitive sonar gear was designed with a fail-safe acoustical buffer to shield the hearing of the men who listened in, yet his four top operators now suffered permanent hearing damage due to the buffer's inability to screen out the nearby subsurface explosions. The equipment simply wasn't designed for this kind of abuse. And neither were the men.

ARLINGTON, VIRGINIA

Mercer tapped the cabdriver on his shoulder and handed the young African immigrant a twenty. "Keep the change and I'm sorry about the seat."

The cloth-backed seat of the yellow Ford Taurus was soaking wet, just like Mercer's suit. He walked toward his house in stocking feet, his socks making an obscene sound against the concrete with every step.

The front door of the house was unlocked. Mercer breathed a heavy sigh once the door was closed behind him. It had taken him nearly an hour and a half to get home after he'd pulled himself from the river near the Pentagon. His first act, after wringing the water from his clothes behind a derelict bus, was to phone a friend with the metro police.

The friend promised that Mercer's shot-up Jaguar would be towed to an auxiliary lot in Anacostia, not to the city's main impound. He also assured Mercer that the paperwork on the car would be "lost" for at least a couple of days. It would take some time to trace him through his destroyed car.

He now had a little breathing space to figure out what in the hell had just happened and why.

Mercer heard the sound of the television and knew that Tish Talbot had made it here safely. He walked through the house, not caring about the water he was getting on the tile or the antique stairs. Tish was asleep in the bar, stretched out on the couch under a steamer rug that Mercer had bought in an auction of ocean liner memorabilia. The name SS *Normandie* was embroidered in gold silk on the thick dark wool.

Tish woke slowly, extending her hands over her head in a decidedly feline gesture.

"How do you feel?" Mercer asked. Making a quick decision between keeping his floor dry and his need for a drink, he gingerly stepped behind the bar.

"I'm not sure," Tish responded, then noticed his appearance. "My God, are you okay?"

"Let's just say, I'm not ready to do that again." Mercer pulled two beers from the antique fridge and popped the lids.

"No, thanks," Tish said. "I took the liberty of opening a bottle of wine." She indicated the half-filled glass on the coffee table.

"I wasn't offering," Mercer replied as he tilted the first bottle to his lips. The beer vanished in seven heavy swallows. "I need a shower and a change. I'll be back in a few minutes." He left the empty on the bar.

Ten minutes later, Mercer returned wearing jeans and a Pittsburgh Penguins jersey. Tish had folded the blanket and was sitting at the bar. "Your home is beautiful. I made the mistake of going for cute rather than practical when I bought my condo in San Diego. My whole unit is smaller than this room."

"One of these days I'll finally admit that I live here and decorate some of it."

"I did notice a definite lack of decorating skills." Tish smiled warmly. "Oh, my God, your hand!"

Mercer looked down at the back of his right hand, where the skin had been scraped off by the rough subway tunnel. In the bathroom, he'd awkwardly wound a bandage around it, but the self-minstrations had come apart and the angry cuts had opened again. They were painful and still bled freely, but weren't serious. He grabbed for a clean bar towel, but Tish snatched it from him.

"Let me do that," she said, and began wiping the blood from his skin.

As soon as her hand touched his, she gasped as if she'd touched something hot. She turned Mercer's hand over slowly, inspecting it like the scientist she was.

His hands were exactingly sculpted by labor and pain. His palms were horny callused pads and the backs were criss-crossed with the raised white ridges of old scar tissue. The nails, though neatly tended, were scored and pitted and one nail, on his pinkie, was cracked all the way to the cuticle. Despite the damage, they were beautiful hands, rugged like a new mountain chain yet with a tapered masculine elegance.

Tish released his hand and looked into his eyes searchingly.

"I work for a living," he grinned, "and these are my tools."

"Then I guess this scrape doesn't bother you much?"

"Hell, yes, I just won't admit it."

Tish looked away and when she spoke, her voice had a serious timbre. "I want to thank you for saving my life today." She chuckled. "Christ, does that sound like a cliché."

Mercer smiled at her. "It's the least I can do since your father once saved my life. How is Jack?"

"My father died about a year ago. You didn't know?" Mercer's face went ashen. "I tried to tell you back at the hospital, but that man came in."

Mercer managed to croak, "How?"

"He was killed on an oil platform near Indonesia. It capsized in a freak typhoon."

A numbness started at the base of his skull and raced through his body in seconds. He almost had to hold onto the bar for support. Without a word, Mercer ran up to his bedroom and returned a moment latter holding a soggy scrap of paper, the telegram sent by Jack Talbot. He held it out to Tish, but she seemed reluctant for a moment, fearful of even touching the page. Finally, she took it and read it quickly.

Bewildered, she looked up at him. "I don't understand."

"Neither do I," Mercer said slowly, "neither do I. But someone wants me involved in this, whatever 'this' is. And they were right about you being in danger." He finished the beer and pulled another from the fridge. "You said at the hospital that you had no idea why you were under guard or why your father or whoever sent this telegram might think you're in danger?"

"That's right. Listen, I'm just a marine biologist. Who would want to kill me? And by the way, how did you know that man in my hospital room wasn't a real doctor?"

"For one thing, he said he was a urologist, which was the same line I used to get past the FBI guards. One of them would have come to recheck my credentials. Also, no doctor making rounds would wear shoes as uncomfortable-looking as his." Mercer shrugged. "As to why someone is trying to kill you, that is what we have to find out. It's obvious that it has to do with the last voyage of the *Ocean Seeker*. Why don't you tell me about it?"

Tish was almost at the point of tears and had to slow her breathing before she could speak. "Do you think all those people were killed because of me?" She sobbed once.

Mercer came around the bar and took her into his

arms. She sagged into him gratefully. Her hair smelled like hospital soap, and was smooth and slippery against his skin. He let thirty seconds go by before straightening up. Looking deeply into her eyes, he spoke softly. "I don't think anyone was supposed to survive that trip. Now tell me about the last voyage."

Tish took a moment to compose herself.

"A few weeks ago, seven gray whales were found beached just west of Hana on Maui. They were all dead. A biologist from the University of Hawaii performed a necropsy."

"A what?" Mercer interrupted.

"Necropsy—an animal autopsy," Tish replied as if everyone should know the word. "He found that their digestive tracts were clogged with minerals. About fifty-five percent silica, with some magnesium, calcium, and iron, plus traces of gold."

"You're describing lava."

"That's what the biologist thought as well. His theory was the whales had been attracted to the huge schools of plankton that would surround a new undersea volcano for its warmth. The whales, while feeding, would also ingest the particles of lava suspended in the water. Eventually, their digestive tracts would fill with the minerals and they could no longer feed."

"So what happened then?"

"Well, NOAA was called in to investigate. An aerial search of the waters north of Maui showed nothing. No new island, no clouds of ash or even steam. Then some sonar buoys were dropped, and within twelve hours we had found our new volcano, about two hundred miles from the Hawaiian islands.

"The *Ocean Seeker* was sent out late last Thursday night." Tish stopped speaking for several seconds. "Twenty-four hours later, the ship exploded. When I was first rescued, I just assumed that it had been some sort of accident, but now I don't know what to think."

Mercer poured her another glass of wine and opened

another beer for himself. The adrenaline rush from a few hours ago was wearing off, leaving him thirsty.

"Why are all those pins in that map?" Tish said, changing the subject and referring to the map of the world hung behind the bar. It was studded with numerous pushpins in several different colors.

Mercer felt that the distraction would let Tish calm down enough to answer the dozens of questions he still had for her. "It's a map of places I've been. The different colors indicate why I was there. Green is for pleasure, like most of the Caribbean islands. Red is for work overseas for the U.S. Geological Survey, mostly meetings in Europe and Africa. And blue is for private consulting work that I've done for various mining companies."

Tish noted that this last category included some pretty exotic places—Thailand, Namibia, South Africa, Alaska, New Guinea and at least fifteen others. "Why is there a clear pin in central Africa? I can't tell which country."

Mercer looked pained as he replied, "The pin's in Rwanda. I was there for six months in 1994 when the world looked on as 800,000 Tutsi tribesmen were slaughtered by the Hutu majority. I was on a consulting job when the violence erupted, and rather than run away, I joined a band of soldiers trying to defend fleeing villagers."

"My God, why would you do something like that? I heard that the fighting was absolutely savage."

"I was born in that part of the world. My parents and I lived in Rwanda during the early days of independence. I was too young to remember the massacre of 1964, but I've never lost my sense of loyalty to the Tutsi friends I had growing up."

Tish knew he was keeping something from her, but she didn't press. "And what about the clear pin in Iraq?"

Mercer smiled. "I was never there—and even if I was, I can't talk about it."

She threw him a cheeky grin. "Real James Bond, hush hush."

"Sort of." Mercer still carried scars from that mission. The information he had brought back had been the trigger for Operation Desert Storm. "Now tell me about your rescue."

Tish spoke quietly. "The ship exploded late Friday night. I was on the fantail, rigging some acoustical gear. I didn't hear or even see the explosion. One second, I was standing there, and the next I was in the water. There were a lot of flames. I remember that I couldn't hear anything. I think I had gone deaf for a moment."

"The concussion stunned your ears—it's common. Go on."

"There was an inflatable raft near me and I swam to it."

Mercer interrupted again, "It was already inflated?"

"Yes, it was. Come to think of it, that's awfully strange. They're usually stowed in big plastic cylinders. Maybe the explosion released the CO_2 used to inflate it." That sounded a little far-fetched to Mercer, and he made a mental note to come back to it later. "I was in the raft all of the next day until the *September Laurel* rescued me."

"That's the freighter?"

"Yes. A couple hours later, a helicopter from the navy came to pick me up. The doctor on board gave me a shot, and when I came to, I was in D.C."

"Can you describe the freighter?"

"I don't know, it was just a ship. I don't know the length or anything like that. It had a bunch of cranes and booms. There was a black circle with a yellow dot on the funnel which was near the back of the ship."

"What else can you tell me?"

Tish paused, her smooth forehead furrowed. There was something she wanted to say, Mercer could tell, but he didn't think she was sure of the facts herself.

"I heard Russian," she blurted out.

"Russian? Are you sure?"

"Well, no, not really."

"When did you hear it?"

"When I was being pulled aboard the freighter. The crew were shouting orders to each other in Russian."

"How can you be sure it was Russian? Some of the Scandinavian languages sound similar."

"A year ago I was part of a research team in Mozambique, investigating the ruin that the government there has made of the prawn beds just off the coast. It was a joint venture between NOAA, Woods Hole, the Mozambique government, and a team of Soviets. I, well, I became involved with one of the Soviets. When we were alone together, he would always speak to me in Russian. I don't think I'll ever forget the sound of that language."

She looked at Mercer, as if defying him to judge her.

"Okay, so you heard Russian, could be they had some expatriate Russian crewman or something like that. What happened when you were in the life raft?"

"Nothing. I was unconscious until just before I was rescued."

"You don't remember anything?"

"I had just been blown off a ship, what the hell am I supposed to remember?" Fatigue was taking its toll on her.

"I'm sorry, you must still be exhausted." Mercer glanced at his watch. It was four-thirty in the afternoon. "Why don't you get some sleep? I'll wake you at seven. I'm sure you're dying for a non-hospital meal."

"Yes, that would be wonderful."

Mercer led her to one of the two guest rooms. He showed her the bath and gave her several towels. He heard the water running even before he returned to the rec room.

Mercer pulled two more beers from the fridge and went to his home office. He switched on the desk lamp and grabbed the phone.

A moment later a female voice chirped, "Berkowitz, Saulman, and Little."

"David Saulman please, tell him it's Philip Mercer."

Of the dozens of lawyers that Mercer had dealt with in his life, David Saulman was the only one he liked. Saulman had been a ship's officer during the late 1950s and early sixties, but an engine room accident had scalded his left hand so badly that it had to be amputated. Forced out of the Merchant Marine, he put himself through law school and within just a few years he was the man to talk to about maritime law.

Thirty years later, his office in Miami had over one hundred associate attorneys and his counsel rated five hundred dollars an hour. At seventy-five, Saulman was still sharp and his knowledge of ships and shipping was voluminous.

"Mercer, how are you? I haven't heard your sorry voice in months. Tell me you're in Miami and ready to get into trouble."

"Sorry, Dave, I'm in D.C. and I'm already in trouble."

"Don't tell me the cops finally picked you up for flashing the tourists in front of the White House?"

"Hell, no one even notices when I do it. Dave, what do you know about a ship called the *September Laurel*?"

"An official call, is it?"

"Yeah, charge it to NOAA."

"NOAA, huh? Do they know?"

"Not yet, but if I'm right, they won't mind."

"The *September Laurel* was the ship that rescued that woman from the NOAA research vessel last night, right?"

"That's the one."

"The *Laurel*'s owned by Ocean Freight and Cargo, head office in New York, but all of their ships are registered in Panama and have Italian crews. She's just a tramp freighter, usually runs the north Pacific. Let me think, about four hundred feet, thirty thousand gross tons. Only notable thing about her is this rescue."

"Dave, I want you to check her out—normal cargoes, big contracts—also I want the lowdown on her parent company. Dig deep. Also, could you get me any information on all the ships that have sunk in the same waters as the *Ocean Seeker*?"

"What's going on in that paranoid mind of yours?"

"I'm not sure yet, and I can't really talk about what I suspect. Do you happen to know the design on her stack?"

"Yeah, a bunch of laurels."

"You sure?"

"Yes, its OF&C's trademark. Their ship *August Rose* has a bunch of roses on the stack and the *December Iris* has irises on hers."

"So there's no way that her stack could be painted with a black circle surrounding a yellow dot?"

"Not unless the company has changed a forty-year tradition."

"Thanks Dave, I owe you. Just fax the info to my home and I'll take it from there."

"Are you up for a trivia challenge?" Saulman asked. This had been a tradition since they'd first met in 1983, at a reception honoring the few remaining Titanic survivors.

"Fire away."

"Who was the last person to own the *Queen Elizabeth* and what did he change her name to?"

"C. Y. Tung, and he called her *Seawise University*."

Mercer just barely heard Saulman call him a bastard before he hung up.

Mercer flipped through his Rolodex for a second, searching for a number at Woods Hole Oceanographic institute.

"Time to call in another favor," he muttered as the phone began ringing.

"Yo," answered a familiar deep baritone.

Mercer instantly recognized the easy negligence of the

greeting. The voice was pure Harlem. "Spook, whatever happened to hello?"

"Only one man dare call me that. Is that you, Mercer?"

"No, this is the Massachusetts chapter of the KKK soliciting donations."

"So it is the Rock Jock, how the hell are you?"

Three years earlier, Mercer had been contacted by a Pennsylvania mining firm about a piece of property they had just purchased in upstate New York. The company was hoping to reopen a hard-rock anthracite mine first excavated in the 1890s. While doing the first exploratory trips into the half-submerged mine, Mercer and a small team from the mining company had come across a school of swift but blind fish. Not recognizing them as a normal subterranean species, Mercer had called in Woods Hole to investigate the mutated specimens. They sent over two marine biologists and several assistants. The mine was never reopened, but the research had given a young grad student named Charles Washington his Ph.D. thesis and a guaranteed tenure at Woods Hole. Mercer had given Washington the nickname Spook, not because of his black skin and inner-city manner, but because of his love of Stephen King novels and the frightening stories he'd tell to keep the crew entertained while working in the dark mine tunnels.

"Another day older and deeper in debt."

"Shit, man, you ain't seen debt until you see the payments on my new BMW."

"Whatever happened to scientists with leather-elbowed jackets, untrimmed beards, and beat-up Saabs?"

"That's for old white farts, not us lean and mean black brothers. 'Sides which, last I knew you was drivin' a Jag."

"Just to prove I'm not an old white fart, that's all."

"Bullshit, but I love ya anyway. This ain't no social call, what up?"

"A year ago, Woods Hole sent a team to Mozambique to look at shrimp beds. You know anything about it?"

"No, but hold on, I know someone who does."

Mercer could hear him shout to someone else in the room. A few moments later a frail female voice came on the line. "Hello, this is Dr. Baker."

"Good afternoon, Doctor, my name is Philip Mercer, I'm a geologist with the USGS." Mercer thought it best to sound formal. "I'm trying to get some information about an expedition to Mozambique that Woods Hole was involved with last year."

"That's what Charley said. I was on that expedition as lab director."

"Do you happen to remember any of the Russian scientists? A youngish man in particular. I'm sorry, I don't have his name."

"Probably you're referring to Valery Borodin. Supposedly he was a biologist, but he knew more about geology than anything else. He spent most of his time with one of the women from NOAA, lucky girl."

"Why's that?"

"I may be sixty-six years old, Mr. Mercer, and have four delightful grandchildren, but these old eyes can still appreciate a handsome man. And Valery Borodin was a very handsome man."

"So you say he knew more about geology than anything else, huh?"

"That's right. If you want to know more about him, I suggest you contact the woman from NOAA. I can't think of her name right off the top of my head, but if you give me a second I can get it."

"That's okay, Dr. Baker, you've been more than kind. Thank you, and please thank Dr. Washington." Mercer hung up and leaned far back into his seat.

He reviewed the information he'd gathered. A bunch of dead whales. An explosion on a research vessel. An assassination attempt on the only survivor. A telegram from a dead friend. One freighter with two different designs on its stack. An Italian crew that speaks Russian. A Russian biologist that doesn't know biology and probably has nothing to do with what's going on, and, Mercer looked ruefully at the empty beer bottles on his desk, the beginning of a good buzz.

"In other words, I've got nothing," he said aloud, and switched off the desk lamp.

BANGKOK, THAILAND

While many of the Pacific islands are described as sparkling jewels by those who visit them, anyone seeing the Spratly Islands would agree that they are nothing more than a handful of gravel tossed haphazardly into the center of the South China Sea. The Spratlys are spread across an area the size of New England, yet comprise a total land area of less than two square miles. The more than one hundred islets, coral outcroppings, and atolls are completely unremarkable—except that they are claimed as sovereign territory by no less than six nations.

These countries, in a bid to legitimize their claims, have gone so far as to set up gun emplacements on some of the larger islands and garrisons on the smaller ones, islands so small that high tide obliterates them and leaves the troops standing thigh high in the sea. Vietnam has occupied twenty-five of the islands while China claims seven, the Philippines eight, Malaysia three, and Taiwan one. The sultan of Brunei wants to claim one island in particular, but that tiny speck is underwater for more than six months of the year.

At first, many Western observers scoffed at the conflicting claims, calling them a poor man's imperialism. A naval engagement between China and Vietnam in March 1988, which claimed the lives of seventy-seven Vietnamese and an undisclosed number of Chinese, changed their attitudes.

These two vehemently Communist countries did not come to blows for merely territorial reasons nor national pride. The motivation for the battle was the basest of interests: greed. Since oil was discovered off the coast of southern Vietnam in the mid-1980s, the nations ringing the South China Sea have shown a keen interest in what other natural resources might lie beneath the warm waters. Hydrocarbons, huge fishing banks, and the Spratlys' location, in the middle of the shipping lanes between the Pacific and Indian Oceans, have made them one of the most contested spots on the globe.

To open a dialogue between the disputing parties, the government of Indonesia invited them all to Bandung, about sixty miles east of Jakarta, in 1992. For several weeks, ministers met to discuss their aims. China promised to consider joint economic development of the Spratlys, provided that all other claimants relinquished their territorial interests. In response, Malaysia purchased two guided missile corvettes from Great Britain.

The meeting broke up with nothing resolved.

Since then, the situation had continued to deteriorate. Vietnam began shelling vessels that strayed too close to the island of Amboyna Cay and Malaysia further solidified her position by building an airfield on Terumba Layang-Layang. Taiwan grabbed two more islands, setting up manned outposts. The Taiwanese also faced down a threat from a Chinese gunboat, an act that almost brought the two nations to war.

Taiwan's new aggressiveness, coupled with a massive infusion of money from American and European oil companies prompted the government of Thailand to make a new attempt to bring about a peaceful settlement. Thus, ministers from the six rival nations, plus binding representatives from the United States and Russia, were meeting in Bangkok at the invitation of the Thai foreign minister.

The meetings were held at the Shangri-la Hotel just off Sathon Road along the banks of the Chao Phraya River, the river which runs through the sprawling city of Bangkok the way the aorta runs through the human body. Behind closed teak doors in the hotel's new convention center, the eight representatives, plus their coterie of aides and translators, had been hard at work for six straight weeks, meeting ten hours a day, and it was beginning to look like the conference would be a success.

The Chinese representative, Minister Lujian, was willing to forgo total sovereignty of the islands if his nation was granted a continuation of Most Favored Nation status from the United States. In return, the United States representative, Undersecretary of Commerce Kenneth Donnelly, received guarantees that several American oil companies would be allowed exploratory rights to a couple of areas in the Spratlys.

All of the assembled delegates agreed to this, yet the Taiwanese and Russian representatives continued to bring up fine points of law that served only as delaying tactics. The Bangkok Accords, as they were to be known, were ready, yet Minister Tren and Ambassador Gennady Perchenko continued to delay the final signing.

Ambassador Perchenko had been mostly silent during the preceding weeks of negotiations, yet a week earlier he had taken his customary place at the round table in the richly tapestried room with a new set to his shoulders. He had begun to speak, and had rarely stopped since. At first, Minister Lujian thought Perchenko and Tren were buying time for a Taiwanese military buildup, but satellite images and hard data from spies around the naval bases at Kao-hsiung and Chi-lung showed no increase in activity. Kenneth Donnelly finally assumed that these tactics were a way for the Russians to gain some sort of economic interest in the Spratlys in exchange for a timely settlement.

Drawing on his twenty-five years of adroit statecraft experience, Perchenko had changed his role from observer to dominator, ready to dictate terms.

With a discreet click, a member of the king's personal bodyguard closed the heavy doors to the conference room and took up station just to their left, a gleaming M-16 hanging from his thin shoulder. The Thai foreign minister, Prem Vivarya, paused for a few moments to let the men in the room settle down before opening the morning session. Set before the Asian delegates were cups of delicate porcelain decorated with ermine lotus blossoms, filled with steaming tea. The Americans and the Russians drank thick coffee from institutional white cups, the type found in hotels all over the world.

Through the partially shaded plate-glass window, Minister Prem could see the gleaming concrete tower of the hotel. Beyond it, the green torpid river was choked with power boats, barges, water taxis, and long-tailed skiffs caught in the midst of the city's rush hour. He hoped that this day would not become as deadlocked as the river traffic.

"Gentlemen, at yesterday's meeting," Prem intoned, and the assembled translators began whispering to their charges, "the representative from the Russian Federation, Ambassador Perchenko, was beginning to outline several concerns that his government had for the treaty that we are all considering."

Even through the cumbersome translations, Prem's annoyance at the Russian was plain. Perchenko, a heavy rumpled man in his late fifties, smiled tightly.

As an aide, Perchenko had attended the landmark 1982 United Nations Convention on the Law of the Sea in Caracas. With more than 150 nations represented it was the largest gathering of its type in history, a truly

global event. It took nine grueling months to write the
final document. It pertained to every aspect of the
oceans, from environmental protection to the harvesting
of their bounty, from the free passage of vessels to undersea mining. In the end, every representative signed it,
yet the convention was killed soon after its birth because
the United States Congress refused to enact it into law.

Though UNCLOS had miscarried, it had given Gennady Perchenko one of the finest educations possible on
maritime law. Now he was using that knowledge for the
Bangkok Accords. Or, more precisely, to stall the Bangkok Accords.

After Minister Prem's opening remarks, Perchenko
launched into a ten-hour-long monologue, interrupted
only by a one-hour pause for lunch. This speech, though
informed, was entirely irrelevant. Perchenko chronicled
sovereignty issues dating back more than a century and,
although the conflict over the Spratlys was based on such
historical clashes, they had been reviewed ad nauseam
during earlier meetings. There was no logical reason for
the wily Russian to bring them up again. As soon as the
other delegates realized that Perchenko was stalling once
again, they quickly tuned out the voices of their translators and blankly watched the shadows progress around
the room as the hours passed.

This was the third straight day of Perchenko's mon-
ologues, and this one was as pointless as the preceeding
two.

At six in the evening, Minister Prem politely interrupted Perchenko. ''Ambassador Perchenko, the hour
once again grows late. The hotel's chef informed me
earlier that his dishes cannot be held long, so it is in our
best interest if we pause here and resume again in the
morning.''

''Of course, Minister.'' Perchenko smiled mirthlessly.
His voice was still controlled and level after hours of
speaking, and unlike the other men in the room he
showed not the slightest trace of discomfort or boredom.

The delegates stood quickly and shuffled from the room. Perchenko remained seated and made a show of lighting a thin Dutch cigar. Undersecretary of Commerce Donnelly clapped Perchenko on the shoulder in a friendly gesture, but the big Texan's hand dug deeply into the Russian's soft muscles. "See ya' at dinner, pardner."

Perchenko waited until the room was empty before wincing at the pain in his shoulder and attempting to massage it away.

"Fucking cowboy," he muttered.

Perchenko left the hotel quickly, forgoing the dinner, as he had most evenings. Exiting the gleaming concrete tower on the river side, he called over one of the hotel's river taxis. Perchenko told the bellman his destination and he, in turn, informed the liveried boat driver. The Russian stepped lightly onto the taxi, a Riva twenty-four footer, and settled himself into the wide backseat just forward of the craft's idling engine.

The driver eased the boat into the teaming river traffic, heading north and passing the classic Victorian elegance that was the Oriental Hotel. Like its brethren, Shepherds in Cairo, or the Mount Nelson in Cape Town, the Oriental stood as a reminder of the once mighty and far-flung British Empire.

The Riva drove north, cutting a quick stroke through the river, dodging other boats with the agility of a thoroughbred. Bangkok tumbled down to the edge of the river in urban sprawl. Barges sat tied to the banks four and five deep, forming cluttered neighborhoods of their own. The numerous canals that once sliced off into the city and earned Bangkok the title "Venice of the East" were all but gone, turned into automobile choked streets, but all of Bangkok's diversity could still be seen from the river; the wealth stacked up in glittering high-rises and the abject poverty living in stick and sheet metal shacks crammed between warehouses.

On the river, the sharp water smell almost masked the

reeking cloud of pollution which shrouds the city, ejected from sweatshops and cars in a pall that rivals Los Angeles or Mexico City.

The boat sped along, under the Memorial Bridge, where cars and the three-wheeled jitneys called tuk-tuks were strung like beads. They shot past the Arun Wat, the Temple of Dawn, a squashed cone that typified Thai religious architecture. The dying rays of the sun shone hard against its gilded facade.

The taxi passed the royal palace, the Temple of the Emerald Buddha, and Wat Po. As they pounded north-ward, the city became older, the buildings more tumbled, the Western influence not nearly as strong. The houses and tenements were so jammed together that they leaned against one another. It seemed as though if one were torn down, whole neighborhoods would tumble like dominos.

Finally they came to the Royal River Hotel, the only major hotel on the western bank of the river. A new hotel, it was immensely popular with European and Aus-tralian tour groups. Tourists clustered around white ta-bles on the hotel's landing, their shorts and open-necked shirts garish splashes of color that clashed sharply with their sunburnt skin.

Gennady Perchenko stood and shuffled to the Riva's gunwale. Ignoring the proffered hand of a bellman, he stumbled to the dock and told the driver to wait, in both English and mangled Thai. He approached the waterside bar's host, a tuxedoed man with a deeply pocked face and slicked back hair. As the maître d' led Perchenko to the only unoccupied table, he spoke quietly from the side of his mouth, his thin lips barely moving.

"There is no word yet, you should wait."

Perchenko bristled at the order from this man who was no more than a cutout in the spy trade, a disposable piece of garbage whose worth was so small it was uncounta-ble, yet he knew the man was right. He must wait.

As a slim waitress set a Rum Collins on his table, Perchenko thought, as he had every night since coming to Bangkok, about how he had gotten into his current situation.

He had been a successful diplomat under the old Soviet regime, a functionary of some standing who might have one day reached a cabinet position. The coup, the collapse of the Soviet government, and the subsequent formation of the Russian Federation had all but crushed his career. In the sweeping changes that washed across his homeland like a tsunami wave, Perchenko had found himself tumbling in the swirling back eddies. Former allies in the Politburo vanished, others switched loyalties so fast that even they had no idea in what they believed. Gennady watched assignment after assignment pass him by. The old cronyism had been replaced by a tougher but more subtle system of political patronage that left him idle while other men flourished.

It was at that time that a hand reached out and dragged him back onto the crest of the wave. Later he realized that that hand belonged to the very devil himself: Colonel Ivan Kerikov, Director of Department 7, KGB Scientific Operations. Kerikov was a shadowy figure in the stygian world of espionage, a man no one claimed to know yet the list of those who feared him was lengthy.

A full month before the Bangkok Accords were announced, Kerikov had invited Perchenko to his offices in a nondescript building near the Moskva Hotel, far from KGB headquarters. He was told about the upcoming meetings and given a choice—attend as Kerikov's agent or never receive another posting in the foreign service.

Perchenko did not question how Kerikov knew of the impending meetings, nor did he question the meaning of the word ''agent,'' he simply accepted and began making preparations.

Five weeks later, Gennady was told by his superior in the Foreign Office that he would represent the federation in Thailand. Gennady innocently asked if Kerikov had any final orders. His superior shot him a scathing look, then sharply denied that he'd ever heard of Kerikov.

The full extent of Kerikov's power became apparent in Bangkok when the Taiwanese ambassador took Gennady aside and explained that he too was working for Kerikov and would follow Perchenko's orders. At that moment, Perchenko began to fear for his life. Engineering his posting to the conference was one thing, but Kerikov seemed to control people outside of the Russian Federation. Perchenko couldn't, nor did he wish to, understand that level of dominion.

At first, Perchenko simply had to attend the rounds of meetings and pay attention, but a week ago, the situation changed. Kerikov contacted Gennady through the maître d' at the Royal River and instructed him to delay the final signing of the Accords. No explanation was given and the fear that Gennady had built of Kerikov had prevented him from ever asking for one. If Ivan Kerikov wanted the Bangkok Accords stalled, that was exactly what Gennady would do.

So Gennady stalled—and waited for some sort of inquiry from his superiors in the Foreign Office. Their silence, he assumed, was another sign of Kerikov's influence. Perchenko could easily handle the pressure put on him by the other delegates, and the assistance given by the Taiwanese ambassador made the situation even easier. Still, he wanted some sense of Kerikov's final plan. How long would he have to delay the meetings and what was the ultimate goal?

As Perchenko watched the maître d' wend his way through the crowded tables to seat a group of Dutch tourists, he knew the answers wouldn't be found here.

"Yes," he muttered, "I must wait."

MOSCOW

Colonel Ivan Kerikov dragged his hard, flat gaze from the face of the man across his desk and lined up the glowing tip of a nearly spent cigarette to the fresh one pressed between his thin lips. As soon as the smoke filled his lungs, he ground the old cigarette into an overflowing ashtray and stared again at his guest. The man seemed to shrink under Kerikov's scrutiny.

Through the cloud of acrid smoke Kerikov continued his assessment of his guest. Though he had never met the man before, he was cut from the same mold as so many other bureaucrat accountants that Kerikov seemed to know the man intimately. The accountant wore the uniform of a KGB major, but the tailoring was poor so it hung loosely across his thin shoulders and sunken chest. The few decorations seemed to be more apology than a statement of valor. His skin was pasty white and, had Soviet doctors not perfected cheap ocular surgery, Kerikov was sure that this man would sport thick-lensed glasses. Kerikov remembered with distaste that the auditor's handshake was limp, like squeezing a plastic bag of entrails.

Kerikov had not been surprised when this man had presented himself to his secretary an hour earlier. In fact, he had been expecting a general audit from the KGB's Central Bureau, of which this man was the vanguard, here merely to pave the way for the dozen or so other little ferrets who would tear through Kerikov's budgetary reports with the anticipation of hounds tracking a fresh scent.

This audit was a long time coming. After the collapse of the old Soviet Union, every sector of the government had been reevaluated. The budgets, once lavish under Brezhnev and Andropov, had dwindled under Gorbachev and Yeltsin, and accountability had risen. Every ruble and kopek now had to be tracked and disbursed. Financial discrepancy was unacceptable. It was an indication of the power of the KGB that they were the last of the major organizations to fall victim to the auditors' slashing pens.

Kerikov had known a full six months earlier that the auditing teams were interested in the affairs of his particular division of the KGB, Department 7, Scientific Operations. It was only a cruel quirk of fate that this interest coincided with a massive amount of new spending, which he was now forced to justify to the thin major sitting on the other side of his oak desk.

As the auditor busied himself in his imitation leather expandable briefcase, Kerikov reflected on the easier times Scientific Operations had once enjoyed.

Born in the tumult of the Great Patriotic War against the Nazis, Department 7 had been established by Stalin himself to help assimilate captured enemy technology into the Soviet army. As the Russian forces advanced into Germany and liberated various factories and laboratories, members of the newly formed Scientific Operations were there to see that secret works were preserved and brought back to a huge facility near the Black Sea port of Odessa.

If a site was deemed important to the members of Department 7, they gave the order and whole buildings were dismantled, packed up and shipped back to Russia, oftentimes with the original staffs kept as virtual slave labor. In this fashion, a deuterium plant was taken from outside Berlin and reestablished, giving Russia her first source of heavy water, a critical component in the building of fission bombs. A factory outside of Warsaw that produced Zyklon-B, the nerve agent used in the death camps, was shipped to a remote site in the Ural Mountains and began stockpiling gas weapons by the summer of 1945. Officers of Department 7 seized a Heinkle workshop just as the staff were destroying their accumulated research. The papers and models captured from that raid led to the development of the MIG-15, the Soviet's first jet fighter.

Since the strategic rocket site at Penemunde was liberated by the Western Allies, Department 7 lost out on that windfall of missile technology, yet still managed to secure many top scientists and designs for their homeland. By far, their greatest boon came during the occupation of Berlin.

While the Western Allies busied themselves searching the city for war criminals, the Soviets searched for secrets. A safe in the home of a Messerschmitt engineer yielded the formula for a synthetic oil necessary for turbine engines. The diary of a Krupp manager held the key to the metallurgy of the exhaust nozzle of the V–2 rocket.

In this fashion, Department 7 brought secrets home to Russia and gave Soviet scientists the facilities they needed to adapt them to the Red Army.

By the summer of 1952, all of the captured German technology had been evaluated, much incorporated, and some abandoned. With its primary mission complete, the head of Department 7, Boris Ulinev, decided to change the objective of his section.

Scientific Operations had been a passive agency; it had no agents in the popular sense, nor did it create anything original. Ulinev set out to change all that. Because Scientific Operations had always dealt with technology that was ahead of its time, Ulinev began setting up operations that would only come to fruition far into the future. Spending millions of rubles supplied by the Soviet government, Ulinev directed the eight hundred scientists on his staff to concentrate their efforts leapfrogging current technology and developing devices far more advanced than anything on any drawing board in the world.

Like Kelly Johnson's "Skunk Works" at Lockheed, which developed the SR-71 spy plane long before the materials were available to build it, Scientific Operations began designing and testing rudimentary multiwarhead ballistic missiles even before Sputnik was conceived. A Department 7 theoretician came just a couple of molecules away from discovering carbon fiber. And a team of experts began working on circuit boards for computers while the rest of the world still marveled at the power of the vacuum tube.

One project in particular became the pet of Boris Ulinev and subsequently the potential triumph of Ivan Kerikov. Presented to Ulinev by an intense young geologist named Pytor Borodin, the project was as audacious as anything yet attempted by Department 7. In fact, it might rival the greatest feats of mankind.

The undertaking, code-named "Vulcan's Forge," had its genesis on Bikini Atoll on July 25, 1946, when the United States conducted the first underwater nuclear test as part of Operation Crossroads. It took four years, until 1950, for the data from that test to reach Department 7, stolen by a female agent who seduced a lab technician at the White Sands Testing Grounds in New Mexico, where the volumes of information and tons of samples were warehoused. Pytor Borodin became involved due to a happenstance comment from a colleague, who mentioned that a hitherto unknown alloy had been created by the Bikini explosion. Borodin quickly became obsessed, going so far as to request a clandestine submarine reconnaissance to Bikini in late 1951 in order to collect additional samples of sand, water, and debris from the seventy-four ships the U.S. intentionally sank as part of the test.

For eighteen additional months, Borodin labored at his task until he was able to present a far-reaching plan to Boris Ulinev. It seemed tailor-made for the new direction Scientific Operations was to take.

The opening phase of Vulcan's Forge called for the detonation of a nuclear weapon deep under the Pacific Ocean. Because all atomic materials were under the direct control of the army, Ulinev had his team secretly build one. This alone took more than a year. Department 7 also established a large dummy corporation and secreted money in various accounts in Europe and Asia. All in all, Vulcan's Forge wasn't ready to commence until the spring of 1954.

Once the opening gambit had been played, the only thing left to do was wait for nature to take her course. For forty years the waiting dragged by, through the height of the Cold War, through the opening of Eastern Europe, and through the collapse of the Soviet Union herself. During this time, Boris Ulinev died and was replaced, and his replacement was himself replaced, and so on, until Ivan Kerikov reigned as the head of a much diminished department. Of all the plots and projects launched by Ulinev in the 1950s, only Vulcan's Forge remained viable.

Unfortunately, its raison d'être had vanished. The mighty struggle between communism and capitalism was all but over. The massive arms race during the 1980s had brought the Soviet Union to her economic knees. Though gamely trying to keep pace in conventional and nuclear forces, Reagan's gamble on Star Wars technology had chimed the death knell for Russia. The Soviet Union had no response to SDI but capitulation. America paid for the arms buildup with a four-year recession, but Russia paid with her very existence.

Bit by bit, Russia began withdrawing into herself. Aid to Cuba was slowed to a trickle, then shut off completely. Troops were pulled from the fifty-year occupation of Berlin. Aeroflot suspended most international flights. Within Russia, programs and departments began to vanish. The state-run diamond mines at Aikhal in central Siberia were surreptitiously sold to a London consortium linked to the Consolidated Selling System. The Blackjack bomber, the MIG–29 Fulcrum, and Russia's aircraft carrier program were all shelved. Officers began committing suicide because they were worth more to their families dead than alive. The staff of the KGB was cut by more than fifty percent.

Bold projects like Vulcan's Forge had no place in the New World Order. During his first four years as head of Scientific Operations, before the collapse of the Soviet Union, Kerikov had guarded and nurtured Vulcan's Forge for pure patriotism and duty. But now, the very fabric of what he believed had torn through, and Kerikov started to protect the project from the auditors for simple greed. He planned to steal Vulcan's Forge for himself in a coup as brilliant as the original plan laid down by Pytor Borodin forty years before.

Time, once so abundant, had run incredibly short for Kerikov. The Bangkok Accords had seemed a providential gift when first proposed, but now it had become necessary to delay them at a substantial cost in bribe money paid to the ambassador of Taiwan and to Gennady Perchenko and Perchenko's superior in the Foreign Office.

Department 7 could ill afford the huge payoffs. Kerikov had been able to dodge the auditors for months, but now they were here, in his office, asking questions that he was unwilling to answer.

"Ah, here we are," the ferret said, pulling a sheaf of notes from his briefcase. "It seems that your department paid for the refitting of a refrigeration ship called the *August Rose* four years ago at a cost of twenty-seven million dollars. An affidavit from a shipyard foreman in Vladivostok states that the sonar system installed on the ship is far superior to anything he'd seen on our strategic submarines. Would you care to comment on that?"

Kerikov felt a pressure building behind his eyes, a force that threatened to blow apart his entire head. Security concerning the refit of the *August Rose* had been airtight, yet here was the entire story being laid out before him. The constraint of time he'd felt a moment ago had just tightened with the relentlessness of a garrote.

Kerikov opened the top right-hand drawer of his desk. "I happen to have something here that is very pertinent to that."

The accountant leaned forward in his chair, eyes bright with anticipation.

There was only one round in the Makarov semi-automatic pistol, the one round Kerikov had planned to use on himself if the need ever arose. It blew a perfectly round hole through the accountant's forehead, then splattered the contents of his skull onto the wall and door behind his slumping body.

Kerikov rummaged through his desk until he found a flimsy cardboard box of ammunition. He loaded one round into the pistol and slipped it back into the drawer. He pressed the intercom button on his black telephone.

"Yes, Mr. Kerikov," his secretary answered.

"There has been a slight change in my plans, Anna." Kerikov lit another cigarette. "Inform Evad Lurbud that I want him in Cairo as soon as possible; I believe he is still at my dacha. Also, I want you to get me the earliest flight to Bangkok. I'll travel on the Johann Kreiger passport."

"What about the KGB accountant?" Anna asked.

Kerikov assumed from her tone that she had heard the shot.

"He'll be resting here for a while. As soon as you've reached Lurbud and booked my flight, leave the building. When you're questioned, tell them that you took an early lunch and know nothing. Good luck, Anna. And good-bye."

"I understand." If she was disappointed that their four-year affair was ending, she gave no indication.

Kerikov took some time going through the secure files in his wall safe, pulling out a select few that might one day prove useful or profitable. He knew after he boarded the flight to Bangkok, he'd never again return to Russia.

THE PACIFIC

Valery Borodin bolted upright in his bed, a muffled gasp clutched in the base of his throat. His lean body was slick with nervous sweat, his dark hair plastered to his neat head. His chest heaved and his heart pounded as he fought to regain control of himself.

It took nearly two minutes to realize he was no longer the frightened six-year-old boy of his dream, being told by faceless uniformed men that his father had died in a laboratory accident. He was a man now, a respected scientist in his own right. Yet the haunting sobs of his mother still lingered in the quiet of his cabin aboard the motor ship *August Rose*.

That dream had tortured him since the day those events actually occurred. It woke him most nights, but he had always remained silent, because his mother was grieving in the room next to his in the small Kiev apartment that the Department of Scientific Operations had allowed them to retain as recompense after the accident.

To Valery, that had been the worst, stifling the scream

that always rushed through him, suppressing it, crushing it so he would not disturb his mother. To Russians, grief was something to be worn openly, passionately, yet he could not express it. He did not believe that his pain was worth encroaching on his mother's. Years later, retelling this story always evoked sympathy from the listener, but never understanding. Somehow he got the feeling that people thought there was something wrong with him, some flaw.

It wasn't until last year, in Mozambique, that Valery found someone who finally understood, an American girl who was herself a victim of losing a parent young.

He swung his legs off the narrow bunk of his private cabin. Had the Soviet government not developed a keen interest in his mind, Valery surely would have found a career in the ballet. There was not an ounce of extra flesh on his frame; muscled plane blended with supple joint in the perfect symmetry that comes not from hours spent in gyms, but the blessing of genetic inheritance.

He raked his fingers through his hair, pulling it back from his forehead, and at once a thick cowlick sprang up and hung over his right eye.

The dream which had haunted his childhood had returned just last year in the office of Ivan Kerikov, a man whom Valery had never heard of, but who seemed to know everything about him. Valery learned that this man was the current head of the department that had employed his late father. Kerikov calmly explained that Scientific Operations had watched Valery with interest over the years and in fact helped him along at times. As Valery incredulously tried to digest this piece of information, Kerikov dropped another bombshell.

He pressed a signal buzzer on his desk and a man walked into the room. Valery barely heard Kerikov introduce Dr. Pytor Borodin. Thirty years had aged his father, filling out his body and silvering his wild hair and beard, but he was still the man who stared from the photograph hanging over the dinner table in his mother's apartment.

That night Valery had the dream for the first time since his early teens.

It wasn't until their next meeting that Valery had recovered enough to actually listen to the things his father and Kerikov were discussing.

The elder Borodin had faked his own death so many years ago as a security precaution. His work at the time had been so secret that only such drastic measures would ensure protection. After most of Borodin's coworkers were summarily executed in the summer of 1963, Borodin had worked alone monitoring his secret project, nurturing it along to its now fast approaching conclusion.

Kerikov explained that they needed a new staff of scientists to see the project concluded. Would Valery be interested in joining as second-in-command?

At the time Valery was working for the State Energy Bureau, investigating the potential of Russia's tremendous methane hydrate reserves, which were locked in the permafrost of western and central Siberia. His background in geology was as strong as any of the new breed of Russian scientists, men and women whose worth was valued by results rather than the ability to regurgitate party dogma.

Valery only agreed to join after being assured that his consideration was based on his merits, not on the family connection. Pytor Borodin's casual dismissal of such a notion was terribly painful, as if Borodin wasn't even acknowledging his own son.

Two weeks after those early meetings, Valery was given a holiday in Mozambique under the cover of a marine biology mission, a chance to defrost his body after so many months in Siberia and prepare himself for the work ahead.

Since then, the work had been nothing short of incredible. Kerikov had managed to assemble some of the sharpest minds in the Russian Federation and place at their disposal the latest cutting edge technology.

Valery pulled on a pair of American denim jeans and a military green T-shirt. It was just past midnight, but he knew trying to go back to sleep would be futile.

The ship's galley, one deck below his cabin, was deserted, but a large urn of coffee was kept warm on a side table. Valery filled a white mug and took a cautious sip of the strong, bitter brew. He nodded to the kitchen hand noisily cleaning pans in the scullery before leaving for the nerve center of the *August Rose*.

Built as a bulk carrier designated UT–20 by Hitachi-Zosen in 1979, she had been converted to a refrigeration ship in 1983 when she had been bought by Ocean Freight and Cargo. The 1.13 million cubic feet of bulk storage area had been reduced by nearly thirty percent to make room for massive Carrier refrigeration units and the special cargo-handling equipment needed to transport frozen goods.

That refitting was well documented by the Japanese shipyard that carried out the work, by Continental Insurance, and by the Finnish bank which floated most of the loans held by Ocean Freight and Cargo. The *August Rose*'s next refit was kept much more secret.

She spent seven weeks in a secure drydock in Vladivostok in the spring of 1990. Cosmetically she still resembled the vessel she had always been: 20,000 deadweight tons and 497 feet long, with a sharply raked bow and an aft-positioned superstructure that resembled a four-story steel box. But within her steel-plated hull she was transformed into the most unique scientific vessel ever built.

The cavernous main hold was turned into a geophysics laboratory augmented by smaller labs, offices, and data storage rooms. The refrigeration units were left in place, but now they worked to keep the sophisticated computer system at a constant temperature.

The computers themselves were huge, taking up nearly two thousand square feet of space for the mainframes and half again as much for the peripherals. There was more computing power aboard the *August Rose* than at Baikanor, Russia's equivalent of Cape Kennedy. Enough cargo space remained for the *August Rose* to operate under the cover of a refrigerator ship, though she could no longer haul enough frozen goods to ever turn a profit, yet the ruse allowed her to sail the Pacific un-impeded.

Valery reached the main laboratory through a tortur-ous maze of bulkhead doors and narrow companion-ways. The final door was secured by a magnetic keycard lock. A guard noted his time of entry on a log sheet and took custody of his card, which would have been erased by the magnetic fields created by the equipment in the lab.

It was past midnight, but nearly a dozen scientists, technicians, and assistants were at work, monitoring the numerous sensors that hung from two towed arrays beneath the vessel's keel. A large metal plotting table dominated the center of the room. Above it, on an artic-ulating arm, a holographic laser projector hung down like some monstrous dentist's drill. Bundles of fiber-optic cables ran from the projector to the mainframe computer and to the table itself.

Pytor Borodin was seated at the console nearest the projection table, his slim body hidden under a volumi-nous white lab coat. Valery took a deep breath of the filtered, sterilized air and strode across the rubber-tiled floor.

"Working late again, Father?"

He might have been the oldest member of the scien-tific team by twenty years, but Pytor Borodin kept a pace that far surpassed that of all of his staff, including his second-in-command. He usually spent thirty-six hours in the computer room before taking a grudging six-hour break for sleep. His crumpled appearance alarmed his son.

"Father, have you been taking your medication?"

"No," the elder scientist fired back irritably. "That Coumadin is nothing more than rat poison and Vasotec, the beta blocker, affects my breathing because of the air-conditioning. Now don't bother me again about my heart. Have a look at this; we've gotten the cameras back on line."

Valery glanced at the monitor and saw a close approximation of hell on earth. Dangling from a Kevlar cable and encased in carbon fiber with a thick artificial sapphire lens cover, the camera hung directly above the central vent of the fastest growing volcano in the world. Molten rock, forced upward by the tremendous heat engine of the earth's core, poured through the narrow rent in the crust in a never-ending stream, amid billowing clouds of noxious gas and dissolved minerals. There was no microphone attached to the camera, but Valery could almost hear the protesting moans as the earth vomited up her guts.

"The rate has increased again," Valery remarked.

"And?"

"The flow is forming more westerly now."

"Right, it's caught in the North Equatorial Gyre, just as I'd predicted."

"But that current only moves maybe three miles per day. Surely that can't cause a shift in the formation of the cone."

"It wouldn't normally, no, but the rate of ejection from the volcano is so great that the two forces create a skew in the lava flow. It's a simple matter of vectors. I'm glad you're here, Valery, the computer is about finished with the past day's data and is ready for a growth projection."

Because of the massive amount of raw data gathered by the sensors and the inherently chaotic movement of anything within nature's realm, the *August Rose* needed huge computers in order to create a reasonable prediction of the volcano's future growth. Even with the gigabytes of power, the computers needed a full twenty-four hours to remap, down to the millimeter, the thrusting cone below the ship and then to predict where the cone would broach the surface of the Pacific Ocean.

The countdown clock on one computer screen indicated that the holographic projection would be complete in one minute and twenty seconds. Valery and his father waited in silence, both preferring to stare at the camera images than fake inane conversation. Pytor Borodin didn't seem to notice the tension between them, but Valery was well aware.

Finally the counter ran down to zero, and Pytor Borodin activated the holographic imager. The model projected against the plotting table began as just a hazy conical outline, but quickly sharpened. Crags, radiating dikes, and smaller vents were easily distinguished. The projection looked as solid as a plaster cast but was composed entirely of laser beams.

"Activating the extrapolation logarithms."

The computer had already done the tens of billions of calculations necessary to predict the growth of the volcano, so the image began to change immediately. A shimmering blue plane representing the ocean's surface appeared and the volcano quickly rose through it, tiny simulated waves pounding against the bleak basalt shores.

Borodin pressed several more buttons on his console and longitude and latitude lines were added to the projection, accurate to the second of a degree.

With a note of satisfaction, Pytor Borodin remarked, "This is the third straight test where the summit has broached more than a thousand meters outside of Hawaii's two-hundred-mile exclusionary limit. I think it is now time to inform Kerikov." He turned to a female assistant. "Tell the captain that I wish us to remain on the site for an additional twenty-four hours."

She nearly bowed as she left the lab. Borodin strode back to his console and called to the room at large, "Reset the sensors and the computers. I want to run another simulation immediately.''

Just as Valery turned to go, his father grabbed him lightly by the arm. ''You have yet to see the latest from the gas spectrometry lab.''

The two left the lab together, Borodin's hand still on his son's arm, as if he expected him to bolt at any moment.

The spectrometry lab was crammed with gleaming stainless steel equipment and several computer monitors slaved to the mainframe. The gas spectrometer itself was as large as an automobile, but infinitely more complex. It used the spectrum of light given off by vaporized material to decode its chemical composition. The system was also paired with a seismic wave echo sounder as a back up.

''Vassily, show our second-in-command what you showed me earlier this evening.'' Borodin never called Valery his son.

The sheets of paper the scientist thrust into Valery's hands were covered in bands of rainbow hues broken up by black lines of varying thicknesses. The lines corresponded to the wavelengths of light absorbed by the vaporized materials.

As easily as a geographer deciphering the myriad lines on a topographical map, Valery leafed through pages, noting no deviations from the normal composition of asthenospheric magma, until he came to the last set of spectrographic images.

He recognized the lines denoting basalt, silica, and ferro-magnesium, but there was also a series of conspicuous lines indicating the presence of vanadium, and next to that, a jumble of alternating thick and thin lines that he had never seen before.

''The earliest writings on alchemy date from the mid-fifth century and have been found in Arab and Chinese codices as well as European,'' Pytor Borodin said softly, looking over his son's shoulder at the printout. ''For the following twelve centuries, alchemists represented the best scientific minds of their time and gave rise to modern chemistry and pharmacology, yet they all failed at their self-appointed task. Not one was ever able to transmute lead into gold.

"Now, in the age of supercomputers, satellites, and atom smashers, we have returned to the very roots of science. We have done what thousands of people have wasted generations trying to accomplish. At the time of the great alchemists, gold represented the true power of the world. Today, power in the literal sense is what drives the planet. We have done something that mankind had given up as hopeless—we have turned base earth into the most precious substance in the universe. Not some gaudy metal with only limited use, but a power source that can recreate itself even as we use it up. With that kind of strength, Valery, no one will ever have the strength to challenge us."

Uncomfortable with his father's words, Valery silently let the papers slide to the desk and walked out of the lab. He was reminded of a quote from Hindu mythology, in which Shiva announced, "I am become death, the destroyer of worlds." They were the same words used by Robert Oppenheimer after his creation vaporized a portion of the New Mexico desert.

ARLINGTON, VIRGINIA

Mercer woke just before six in the morning, the jet lag he'd expected burned away by the previous day's adrenaline overdose. He rose stiffly, gently fingering the livid bruises on both shoulders. He shaved and showered before descending to the rec room. With a cup of thick black coffee in hand, he tried unsuccessfully to concentrate on the morning papers. Throughout the night, his sleep had been interrupted with new questions about Tish's story, but there were no answers. He resigned himself to waiting for the information from David Saulman in Miami.

By quarter of seven, his coffee cold in the cup, Mercer impatiently folded the newspapers and slid them down the length of the bar. Behind the bar, between a bottle of Remy Martin and one of Glenfiddich, lay a one-foot section of railroad track. Half of it was rust-colored and pitted, the other burnished to an almost mirror finish.

Mercer retrieved the heavy rail and set it on a towel on the bar. Beside it he placed a shoe box containing a metal polishing kit, usually stored next to the antique fridge. He began polishing the rail with a remarkable amount of concentration, as if when the steel was beneath his fingers, nothing else in the world mattered. As the rust and grime slowly dissolved under the chemical and physical onslaught, he silently thanked Winston Churchill for giving him the idea for such a meditative device. When the British prime minister found himself under even greater stress than his legendary constitution could handle, he would build brick walls in the courtyard behind Number 10 Downing Street. The repetitive act of mortaring, setting, and pointing allowed his mind to disengage from the frantic pace of the Second World War and focus on one particular problem. When a solution was thrashed out in this fashion, an aide would tear down the wall, chip the mortar from the bricks, and stack them neatly for the next crisis.

Emulating this idea, but adapting it for apartment life, Mercer had begun polishing railroad track while attending the Colorado School of Mines. He would polish a section for an hour or so before a big exam, clearing his mind and focusing his energy on the upcoming challenge. He graduated eleventh in his class and swore that this ritual was the key.

Of course, he chuckled as he worked on the rail, a near photographic memory didn't hurt. Since school, Mercer estimated that he'd polished nearly sixty yards of track.

He was still polishing when Tish entered the rec room a little past nine.

"Good morning," she said.

Mercer laid his polish-soaked rag in the shoe box, feeling no need to explain his actions. "Good morning to you. I see they fit."

Tish pirouetted in front of him, the thin black skirt twirling around her beautiful calves. Her top was a simple white T-shirt from Armani. Mercer had bought the clothes for her at a local mall while she had slept through the previous afternoon.

"I assumed that you're not a transvestite and these were for me." Tish grinned, smoothing the skirt against her thighs.

"No, I gave up drag years ago. Are the sizes all right?"

"Right down to 34C cup, thank you for noticing." She threw him another saucy grin. "Is that coffee I smell?"

"Yes, but let me make a new pot, this is my own blend, brewed especially to wake the dead."

"Sounds fine to me." She took a tentative sip and winced. Mercer started a fresh pot. "Why didn't you wake me last night for dinner?"

"I figured you needed sleep more than you needed my cooking."

"I've found that most bachelors are excellent chefs."

"Not this one, I'm afraid. I travel so much that I never took the time to learn how to cook. I live by the principle that if it can't be nuked, it can't be edible."

Mercer saw Tish's eyes dart to the map behind the bar. "I've only been on a few field trips. Most of my time is spent in a lab in San Diego. It must be exciting, all that travel, I mean."

"At first it was, now it's cramped airline seats, cardboard food, and dull meetings."

Tish scoffed but didn't press. "Do you have any new clues as to what's going on?"

Before answering, Mercer glanced at his watch. It was well past his personal cutoff limit of 9:30. He strode around the bar and pulled a beer from the fridge. "I placed some calls yesterday, after you went to bed. We should be hearing something soon. Until then, I think it best that you stay here. Is there anyone you need to contact? Boyfriend, anything like that?"

"No."

"Good. I hope by this afternoon we'll know something that will lead us in a direction. But right now, all we can do is wait."

"Don't you have to go to work?"

Mercer laughed. "I'm consulting for the USGS, they expect me to be irresponsible."

They talked for the next hour or so, Mercer deftly turning the conversation away from himself so that Tish spoke most of the time. She had an infectious laugh and, Mercer noticed, several charming freckles high on her cheeks. She had never been married, just engaged once, when she was younger. She was a Democrat and a conservationist, but she didn't trust her party's candidates or the mainstream environmental groups. She never knew her mother, which Mercer already knew, and idolized her late father, which he'd guessed. She enjoyed her work for NOAA and wasn't ready to settle down into a teaching job just yet. Her last serious relationship had ended seven months before so right now the only thing she needed to worry about were several house plants that her neighbor promised to look after when she had gone away to Hawaii.

Around eleven, a phone rang in Mercer's office. He made no move to answer it. A few seconds later, the fax machine attached to that phone line began to whirr. When it finally stopped, Mercer excused himself and retrieved the dozen sheets from the tray.

He walked slowly back to the bar, eyes glued to the first page. As he finished each page, he handed it to Tish. They read for twenty minutes; occasionally Mercer would grunt at some piece of information, or Tish would gasp.

"I don't understand that question at the end of the report."

"It's a trivia challenge between Dave and me. Goes back years. I have to admit he has me stumped."

Tish read the question aloud. " 'Who was the captain of the *Amoco Cadizo*?' I've never even heard of that ship."

"She was a fully loaded supertanker that ran aground in the English Channel in March of '78. I'll be damned if I can remember her captain's name."

Tish regarded him strangely, but changed the subject. "What do you make of this information?"

"I'm not too sure yet." Mercer opened another beer. Ocean Freight and Cargo, the company whose ship rescued Tish, was headquartered in New York City but the corporate money came from a Finnish consortium headed by a company once suspected of being a KGB front. "Slicker than Air America," was David Saulman's assessment. Their ships sailed mostly in the Pacific, running fairly standard cargos to established ports of call. Saulman did find that OF&C had a "Weasel Clause"—his words—written into all of their contracts concerning the *August Rose*. The clause allowed the five-hundred-foot refrigerator ship to break contract with only twelve hours' notice, provided that cargo had not already been onloaded. In all of Saulman's years of maritime law, he had never seen such a stipulation and couldn't even guess its purpose. Since 1989, OF&C had evoked this clause several times, refusing to load cargo onto the *August Rose* in the States. The clause was odd, Saulman concluded, but certainly not nefarious.

Her present position was north of Hawaii, hove-to because of engine difficulties. Saulman's sources said that she would be underway within fifteen hours and that the company had not requested outside help for their idle ship. Her cargo of beef, scheduled to be picked up in Seattle, was currently being loaded onto a Lykes Brothers' vessel.

Mercer's request for information about vessels sunk in the same waters as the NOAA ship *Ocean Seeker* had opened quite a Pandora's box. No less than forty ships had sunk in that area in the past fifty years, although sinkings had been less frequent since the 1970s. Mercer assumed this was because of new weather-tracking technology. He noted that most of the vessels lost were charter fishing boats, pleasure craft, or day sailors. He checked off the notable exceptions with a black Waterman fountain pen.

Ocean Seeker, NOAA research vessel, June this year. One survivor.

Oshabi Maru, Japanese long-line trawler, December 1990. No survivors.

Philipe Santos, Chilean weather ship, April 1982. No survivors.

Western Passage, American freighter converted to cable layer, May 1977. No survivors.

Curie, French oceanography research ship, October 1975. No survivors.

Colombo Princess, Sri Lankan container ship, March 1972. Thirty-one survivors.

Baltimore, American tanker, February 1968. Twenty-four survivors.

Between the loss of the *Baltimore* in 1968 and the sinking of an ore carrier named *Grandam Phoenix* in 1954, no large ships had sunk north of Hawaii. Any large vessel lost before 1954 could be attributed to World War II.

"I don't know what to make of it either," Tish added.

"Well, if the ship that rescued you is somehow connected to the KGB, that would explain why you heard Russian as you were being rescued."

Mercer scanned the pages again, but kept returning to the list of sunken ships, noting that the *Grandam Phoenix* had been lost with all hands. There was something . . .

"Jesus."

"What?" Tish said.

He hadn't realized he'd spoken aloud. "I have to go to my office."

"What for?"

"I have a hunch." Mercer reached for the phone. A second after dialing, Harry White's bleary voice rasped, "Hello."

"Harry, Mercer. I need you over here to keep an eye on a friend of mine. . . . No, don't bring a guest and yes, I do still have some Jack Daniel's. . . . Right, see you in a few."

Mercer hung up and turned to Tish. "A friend of mine will be here in a few minutes. I want you to stay here with him; I can't trust you out on the streets just yet. Not until I know more."

There was a pleading look in Tish's eyes. Mercer couldn't tell if she wanted reassurance or more information. "I'll be back in a few hours. If what I suspect is true, we'll have this cleared up by tonight and you'll be on a plane home in the morning. Besides, Harry is better company than I am."

Ten minutes later the doorbell rang and Harry let himself in. When he entered the rec room, a few millimeters of unfiltered cigarette dangled from his lips.

"Christ, Mercer, no wonder you called me over. This girl is too pretty to be here of her own free will. You must have kidnapped her."

"Actually, I did. Tish Talbot, this pathetic creature is Harry White. Harry, Tish."

Harry ran a hand through his hair. "If I were twenty years younger, I'd still be old enough to be your father, but it's good to meet you anyway."

Mercer could see that Tish was immediately charmed. The old lecher still had it, he admitted. She would be in good hands while he was away.

"I'll be back in an hour or two."

"Take your time," Harry responded. "I'm free all day and I'm sure that the lovely lady is eager for some good company."

"Harry, you're a paragon. Tish, I won't be too long. Try not to encourage him, bad heart, you know."

"Leave us," Harry barked, and turned to stare into Tish's eyes.

Mercer heard Tish's rich laughter before the front door had closed behind him.

JENNIFER Woodridge looked up in shock as Mercer entered his outer office.

"And where have you been since yesterday?"

"I took a long lunch, Jen, and just lost track of the time."

"Right. Next time you do that, let me know first so I can cover for you. Richard has been frantic trying to reach you."

As if by mystic perception the phone rang. It was Richard Harris Howell, the corpulent, whiney deputy director of the USGS, Mercer's immediate boss.

"Dr. Mercer, I need to see you in my office right away. I have a list of travel vouchers in front of me that we need to discuss." Howell was more accountant now than scientist. "It seems that you abused government money on that South Africa trip."

Mercer held the receiver away from his ear while Howell continued in this vein for another minute. "You're right, Rich." Mercer knew that Howell hated that nickname. "Listen, I've got some stuff to clear up here. I'll be in your office in ten minutes."

Mercer hung up the phone, forestalling any complaint. "I'm sure he'll waddle right over. Tell him I went to the bathroom."

"Where are you really going?"

Mercer sat on the corner of her desk and affected a mock serious tone. "Jen, I can't implicate you in this. What if Howell resorts to torture?" She giggled. "As soon as the little toad leaves, take the rest of the day off. Ah, hell, take the week off, I don't think I'll be around much."

"Is there anything I can help you with?"

"Just keep Howell off my back."

He grabbed his briefcase from his inner office and descended to the basement of the USGS building, where the extensive data archives were stored.

Although Mercer had not met the USGS chief archivist, Chuck Lowry, he had heard about him. Most people who fought in the Vietnam War agreed that their tour had changed them in some profound way. The staff at the USGS believed that two tours in 'Nam had perhaps made Chuck Lowry a little more sane, but by no stretch of the imagination was Lowry a normal man. He wore eight-hundred-dollar sports coats and tattered jeans. His face was hidden behind a beautifully manicured beard, but his hair was a gnarled mess. The black eyeglass frames perched on his squat nose had no lenses, and he swore like a truck driver but possessed an amazing vocabulary.

When Mercer entered the computer room of the USGS archive, Lowry was seated behind his desk, a trashy romance novel in his hand. A brass plaque next to the telephone read, "Eschew Obfuscation."

"I purchased this yesterday," Lowry said, holding up the garishly covered book, "along with a packet of condoms and an economy-size jar of Vaseline. Fucking cashier didn't even bat an eye. The times are fecundating a truly preternatural disinterest between people. The book, though, is delightful. Except the authoress constantly describes the heroine's breasts as supple and the hero's torso as glistening under a sheen of manly sweat. If she does it once more, I will track her down and truncate her. Who are you?"

"Philip Mercer. I'm a temporary consultant."

"Oh, Jen Woodridge works with you."

"You know her?"

"Just as a potential stalking victim." Mercer hoped Lowry was joking, "You're the guy that's busting Howell's balls, right?"

"Let's just say he and I don't get along."

"That's been his problem since he first darkened our door. He doesn't play well with others. He's also a vexatious little dilettante with a permanent fecal ring environing his mouth from so much ass-kissing. What brings you to my Dante-esque nook?"

Mercer ignored the fact that he understood only about a quarter of Lowry's words. "I need to see the seismic records of Hawaii during May of 1954."

"Somewhat obtuse request, but I can oblige. Come back tomorrow, I'll have everything you need."

"Sorry, Chuck, this can't wait. I've got Howell breathing down my neck again, so I have to get out of here ASAP."

"In any way will this research piss off that cock-in-the-mouth?"

"Only to the effect that it has absolutely nothing to do with my contract with him."

"Good enough, walk this way." Lowry hopped off his chair and shuffled into a back room, doing a perfect impression of Lon Chaney's "Igor."

Lowry seated himself in front of a computer terminal that was hooked into the data retrieval mainframe and lifted a heavy data reference book from the drawer beneath the keyboard. He thumbed through it slowly, whistling the theme from *Gilligan's Island*. Several minutes passed before he put the book aside and began hammering at the keys.

"I always type fortissimo rather than pianissimo—lets the fucking machine know who is Maestro around here."

Mercer could not suppress a grin at Lowry's antics. After a few minutes at the keys, the computer chirping, whirring, and beeping, Lowry pushed himself away from the terminal. "There, seismic records of the Hawaiian Islands for May of 1954. Why the fuck you want it, I'll never fathom. Now I'll return to Bimbo St. Trollop and her hero, the redoubtable Major Tough Roughman."

Lowry left the room and Mercer took his seat at the computer. Because of the tremendous volcanic activity in and around Hawaii, the records, even for a single month, would take days to assimilate, but he had a specific date in mind.

Twenty minutes later, Mercer shut off the computer and thanked Lowry for his help.

Lowry's response was a quote from the romance novel. "Tough tore the bodice from her young flesh, exposing her supple breasts to the pirate crew." Lowry looked up. "This bitch writer is going to die."

Mercer chuckled and closed the door to the archive. He took the stairs directly to the street. Because the Jaguar, or what was left of it, was still impounded, he was forced to take a cab back to his house.

Tish and Harry were not home, but a note taped to the television screen in the rec room, stated they had gone to Tiny's bar. Mercer was furious for a moment, but realized that Tish would be just about as safe there as at the house. Before he could join them at Tiny's he had to place a call to New York City, to set up what he hoped was the beginning of a plan.

Ocean Freight and Cargo, the KGB, or whoever was behind all of this had gotten Mercer into the fight. Now it was time to return the favor.

THE WHITE HOUSE

Our man's name is Mercer. Dr. Philip Mercer,'' Dick Henna announced as he entered the Oval Office.

"About fucking time," Paul Barnes, the acting head of the CIA, said. There was no love lost between the two men.

Also in the office with the President was Admiral C. Thomas Morrison, the second African-American to be chairman of the joint chiefs in U.S. history and a man who didn't play coy about possible political aspirations.

"Who is he, Dick?" the President asked.

"He's a mining consultant, currently working for the USGS. The reason it took so long to ID Mercer was that a cop friend of his impounded his Jaguar at the Anacostia auxiliary lot. If I hadn't put extra men on the case, we never would have found him." Henna took a seat. "I can only assume the woman is with him."

"Why does that name sound familiar to me?" the

President said more to himself than the men seated around him.

"Sir," Barnes spoke up, "he was involved in a CIA operation just prior to the Gulf War. I'm sure his name was mentioned during a briefing by my predecessor."

"That's right. I was serving on the Senate Armed Service Committee then."

"Yes, sir. Dr. Mercer accompanied a small team of Delta Force soldiers into Iraq to investigate their capabilities of mining weapon's-grade uranium. The International Atomic Energy Agency confirmed that the Iraqis hadn't obtained any from foreign sources, but we needed to know if the uranium ore mined near Mosul was pure enough to be enriched into plutonium 239. The data Mercer's team brought back guaranteed that our troops would not face a nuclear threat. That was the last piece of intelligence President Bush needed before commencing Operation Desert Storm."

"As I recall, there were some losses during that mission," the President commented.

"Yes, there were. Four of the commandos were killed in an ambush at the mine site. In the debriefing afterward we learned that Dr. Mercer took charge of the remaining force and led them safely out of Iraq."

"He seems to be a capable man," the President remarked.

"That's true, but we're still left with the question, why did he kidnap Tish Talbot, killing a half-dozen men in the process, including two agents of the FBI sent to protect her."

"He did not kill my men." Henna snorted. "The man found dead in the hospital room had blood under his fingernails. It matched the blood of my men on guard down the hall."

"Then who the hell was the man in the hospital room?" Admiral Morrison asked.

"He's not in our files," Henna replied. "But INTER-

POL thinks they have a match. They also might be able to identify the bodies found on the street and in the metro. I should know in an hour or so.''

"We still don't have a why yet, gentlemen," Barnes said acidly, his scalp an angry red.

"We'll have Mercer in custody shortly," Henna snapped. "We just missed him at his office, but I have agents planted around his house in Arlington as of ten minutes ago. When we have him, we will get our why. Oh, there is one more thing. NOAA received a bill from a maritime law firm in Miami—for information that was faxed to Philip Mercer's house."

"What was the information?" asked the President.

"We don't know, sir. We got the runaround from the law office. A court order is being rushed through right now to search their files. We should know what Mercer wanted by late today."

"I must say that, so far, Dr. Mercer has been a lot smarter than any of us." The President spoke softly, a sure sign that he was keeping his temper in check. "And if Dr. Talbot is with him, she is probably in more capable hands than ours. So far he has saved her life at least once and managed to elude our best efforts to find him. Now he's launched an investigation of his own—which seems to have more direction than ours. Am I right?''

The President's accusation was met by silence.

"When Dr. Mercer is found, I want him brought to me. There will be no charges filed against him. Perhaps he can shed more light on what's happening in the Pacific. Does anyone have anything else to add?''

"Since our briefing yesterday," Admiral Morrison said, "I have put our Pacific Fleet on standby alert. Two carrier groups are steaming toward Hawaii from the Coral Sea. The *Kitty Hawk* is in position right now, along with the amphibious assault ship *Inchon*. Both vessels and their support ships are three hundred miles south of Hawaii.''

"I don't know if they'll be needed, but it's a good idea to have some firepower standing by." The President rubbed his hands against his temples. "Gentlemen, we are right now facing a puzzle with no clues. If Ohnishi is behind the sinking of the *Ocean Seeker*, Dr. Talbot may be the only person who can provide any evidence against him. We must find out what she knows. Until then, we're playing blindman's bluff with an enemy who has surfaced twice, but has yet to be seen. That is all."

The President asked Dick Henna to stay and dismissed Barnes and Morrison. "Dick, since this whole episode is taking place within our borders, you are the man in charge. I want to know, right now, what your opinion is."

Henna took a few moments to think, then said, truthfully, "I don't know."

He let the statement hang in the air for several seconds.

"That note we received a couple days ago wasn't any different from hundreds of crank letters sent to us every week. Until the *Ocean Seeker* went down, that is. Then we stood up and took notice. Two days later the only survivor was kidnapped by a man who I think is a patriot. He leaves a trail of bodies across the city, requests some type of maritime information from Miami, and requests the seismic records of Hawaii during May of 1954 from the USGS archives. Please don't ask me why, my top people can't even come close to figuring that one out. He's onto something, I have no doubt."

"Why, though? Why is he even involved?"

"His motivation may be revenge. He was asked to join the NOAA survey crew aboard the *Ocean Seeker*, but he was out of the country. I asked Paul Barnes for the background check the CIA did on him before the mission to Iraq. Maybe there's something there that'll help."

"And what about the letter from Takahiro Ohnishi?"

"Look at any newspaper today and it seems that every

small ethnic group in the world is declaring their independence, no matter how long they have coexisted with their neighbors. Africa, Europe, even Asia. Who's to say we're immune? The majority of the people of Hawaii are of Japanese ancestry, most of whom have never seen the continental states. Maybe we don't have the right to govern them with our Western ideas. I don't know.''

"Dick, do you know what you're saying?"

"I do, Mr. President. I don't like it, but I do know what I'm saying. You might be confronted with a situation only once before faced by a President.'' Henna stood to go. "But sir, that situation started a war that lasted five years and caused more deaths than all the wars in American history combined. Lincoln walked away a hero, but maybe only because he was martyred.''

HAWAII

Takahiro Ohnishi scraped a Frank Lloyd Wright–designed stainless fork across the Limoges plate, piling rich Bernaise sauce around a cut of Kobe beef. He brought the food to his mouth and chewed thoughtfully. Honolulu's mayor, David Takamora, watched the elderly industrialist with well-hidden distaste.

Ohnishi chewed for several more seconds, then leaned over and spit the thick mass of meat into a silver wine bucket, already a quarter filled with his chewed but indigestible meal. Ohnishi patted his lips delicately and waved a butler over to clear the plates.

"Tell the chef that the asparagus was a bit wilted and the next time it happens, he'll be fired." There was no malice in his withered voice, but a man of his position needed none to ensure that his orders were carried out. "I can't believe you didn't eat more, David. That beef was flown in this morning from my farm in Japan."

"My appetite isn't what it used to be." Takamora shrugged.

"I hope my condition doesn't upset you."

"Not at all," the mayor denied too quickly. "It's just the pressure I'm under right now. Planning a silent coup isn't all that simple, you know."

At home, Ohnishi usually used an electric wheelchair to get around easier. Now he wheeled away from the mahogany table. Takamora tossed his napkin onto the table and followed, silently cursing the revolting spectacle of Ohnishi's eating practices.

Though still in his fifties, Takamora's face was developing the languid cast common to many elderly Japanese men. His eyes had begun to retreat behind permanent bags. His body, once slender and toned from years of exercise, had paunched and bowed, so his trunk now appeared too large for his thin legs to support.

Warm light glinted off the frames of the paintings and brought out the beautiful burnish of the cherry wood paneling of Ohnishi's private study. Takamora took the leather winged-back chair as Ohnishi wheeled behind his broad ormolu-topped desk.

"Smoke if you wish," Ohnishi invited.

Takamora wasted no time lighting a Marlboro with a gaily colored disposable lighter.

"What have you to report?"

From behind a blue-gray cloud of smoke, Takamora spoke slowly to mask the tension he felt whenever he was in Ohnishi's presence. "We are nearly ready to send the ultimatum to the President. I have two full divisions of loyal National Guards ready to blockade Pearl Harbor and the airport. The governor will return from the mainland next week; we will detain him as soon as he lands. Our senators and representatives can be called back from Washington with only a moment's notice. If they resist our plans, they too will be detained—however, Senator Namura has already expressed an interest in joining us.

"I have full assurances from all the civic organizations involved that they are prepared to do their part with the strikes and marches. The press, too, is ready. There will be a full blackout for forty-eight hours after the start date. The news will be broadcast as usual, but will make no references to the coup.

"I have here," Takamora reached into his jacket pocket and removed a sheet of paper, "the names of the satellite technicians on the islands who could broadcast unauthorized stories. I will have them detained or their equipment destroyed, whichever is necessary."

"And the phone service?"

"The main microwave transmission towers and the mainland cable junction will be taken and controlled by our troops. It's inevitable that some news of the coup will escape before we're ready for our own broadcasts, but it will be largely unconfirmable."

"You have done well, David. All seems to be in order, but there is a slight problem."

"What is that?" Takamora asked, leaning forward in his chair.

The study door opened and the menacing form of Kenji, Ohnishi's assistant/bodyguard, moved to stand behind the mayor's chair, his steel-hard hands held at his sides.

"And what is that problem?" Takamora repeated, a bit more nervously, after a glance at the newcomer.

"The letter I had written as an ultimatum to the President has been removed from my office. I can only assume it has been sent to Washington."

Takamora couldn't hide his surprise. "We still need more time, why did you send it?"

"I did not say, David, that I sent the letter. I said that it had been removed from my office. The only person to know of this letter and to have spent time in my office alone is you. Therefore, I must ask if you sent the letter to the President without my authorization?"

"I have only seen that letter once, I swear." Takamora quickly realized the danger he was in. "I would never take it from you."

"I want to believe you, David. I really do, but I find

that I can't. I don't know what you wished to gain from your action, but I assure you that I know its results.''

"I swear I didn't take the letter." Sweat beaded against Takamora's waxen skin.

"You are the only person to have any access to this room and to know the location of my safe. I must congratulate you on your safecracking abilities. Most impressive." There was no admiration in Ohnishi's voice. "If you think your act will cripple my efforts in any way, you are very wrong.

"As we speak, arms are being readied for transit here. I have made arrangements for a highly motivated mercenary army. Of course, it would be easier to use your National Guard troops, but I will manage without them.

"David, you could have been the President of the newest and possibly most wealthy nation on the planet if you hadn't become greedy and crossed me."

"I didn't." Desperation edged Takamora's voice up an octave.

"I find it admirable that you retain your innocence even to the end," Ohnishi said sadly.

With those words, Kenji struck.

He whipped a thin nylon cord around David Takamora's neck in a lightning-quick maneuver. With amazing strength, he torqued the cord into the mayor's throat. Takamora clawed at the garrote as it bit deeper and deeper, his tongue thickening as it thrust between his tobacco-stained teeth. His chokes came as thin reedy gaps as the life was pulled from him.

Ohnishi sat neutrally as the grisly murder took place, his wrinkled fingers laced perfectly on the cool desktop.

Kenji pulled tighter as Takamora's struggles diminished. After a few more moments all movement ceased. Mayor David Takamora was dead.

Kenji slipped the cord from around the corpse's neck, revealing a razor-thin line of blood where the skin had parted under relentless pressure. He cleaned his garrote on Takamora's suit coat, coiled the weapon, and slipped it into the pocket of his baggy black pants.

"I'm relieved that his bowels didn't void," Ohnishi remarked, sniffing delicately. "Feed the body to the dogs and return to me."

Kenji returned from his gruesome task after nearly thirty minutes. Despite a change of clothing, Ohnishi noted that the stench of death still clung to his assistant, as always.

"It is done," Kenji said.

"What is it?" Ohnishi asked, knowing something was bothering this man whom he considered a son. "Don't let Takamora's ambition upset you."

"It is not his ambition that upset me. It is yours."

"Don't start that again, Kenji," Ohnishi warned, but his assistant continued.

"I have followed your orders concerning this operation, but I do not agree with them. What you planned with Takamora was only a sideshow for our true aims, yet you treat it with your full attention. Our priority lies elsewhere. Takamora's betrayal should be a sign to stop this foolish coup, which was meant as a contingency plan in the first place. It cannot succeed; you must realize that. And it puts into jeopardy what we are really working for."

"Has our Russian friend so intimidated you, Kenji, that you no longer trust in me?"

"No, Ohnishi-San," Kenji replied. "But we must first concentrate on our obligations to him."

"Let me tell you something about our Russian ally. He will cross us just as quickly as we do him. We are merely tools to him. Our first loyalty must be with the people of Hawaii, not some white taskmaster bent on our control."

"But we made promises . . ."

"They mean nothing now. Takamora's ambition has changed everything. When I first wrote that letter declaring our independence, I knew that it would be sent whether Kerikov ordered it or not. What we are doing must proceed. Takamora's betrayal has merely pushed up our deadline. I'm certain that the President is planning some sort of reprisal. That is why we must strike now. The coup can be successful without Takamora. We can control his people."

Kenji was silent for a moment, his dark eyes downcast. "And the arms you spoke of?"

"I dealt directly with an old friend for those, an Egyptian named Suleiman el-aziz Suleiman."

"And the mercenary army?"

"Suleiman is also arranging for them. Hard currency is a powerful tool in such matters. The mercenaries will augment Takamora's National Guard troops—or replace them if they refuse to follow me."

"I did not realize," Kenji said dejectedly.

"You are like my son, but even a father must do things without his son's awareness. It changes nothing between us, Kenji. Do not be hurt."

"I am not."

"Good," Ohnishi said with a thin smile. "I wish to celebrate tonight. Are you in the mood?"

"Yes, of course," Kenji answered the rhetorical question.

Ohnishi wheeled out from behind the desk and toward his bedroom on the top floor of the glass mansion. Once there, Kenji helped him undress and reclothe himself for bed. Kenji easily lifted his frail form into the wide four-poster, propping several pillows behind his back. Ohnishi laid a withered hand on Kenji's cheek and thanked him with a smile, his eyes shining as if in fever.

"You are like a son to me, you must know that."

"I do," Kenji replied, stroking the old hand gently. "Please allow me a few minutes to prepare."

As Kenji strode from the room, Ohnishi turned to a control panel near his bed and pressed several buttons in quick succession. The electrochromic panels in the glass ceiling of his bedroom darkened, blocking out the rich tropical moonlight. Throughout the house, the walls and roof also darkened, enclosing the mansion in a blackened cocoon.

On the far wall, past the foot of the bed, heavy velvet drapes parted, revealing a two-way glass wall and a small bedroom beyond. A nude woman lay supine on the bedspread, her small breasts peaked with long erect nipples.

Because of his age, Takahiro Ohnishi could no longer enjoy intercourse, but his sexual drive had diminished little over the years. Rather than give in to his body's inability to respond, he had devised a method of voyeurism that partly slaked his still healthy urges. He was incapable of erections let alone emission, but he could still enjoy the act in his own way.

He patiently waited for Kenji to make his entrance, enjoying the lithe body of the sleeping girl. When Kenji finally entered the room, his muscled body was bare and his arousal was plainly evident. He crossed to the sleeping woman—girl, really, since she was not yet fifteen— and woke her by rubbing his erection against her parted lips. She had been well schooled in her responses according to the script that Ohnishi had provided.

Pretending to be still asleep, she took Kenji into her mouth and began a gentle fellatio. Ohnishi pressed a button on the console and the sensitive microphones in the other room broadcast the subtle noises of the girl's lips and mouth. She moved a hand up from her side and began massaging one of her nipples softly, quickly picking up the rhythm as if coming awake.

Ohnishi leaned forward in his bed as the Japanese girl's eyes fluttered open and she began sucking in earnest. He could feel a slight tightening near his prostate muscles and smiled. Kenji reached down and toyed roughly, with her other breast, and the speakers in Ohnishi's bedroom sounded with her moans of building passion. Ohnishi resisted the temptation to touch himself, knowing he would be disappointed at his body's lack of response.

Kenji spread the girl's legs, revealing her still hairless mons. Slipping one thick finger into her body, he thrust through her virginity so that blood slicked his hand and her inner thighs. The girl winced but did not cry out. He crawled onto the bed and positioned her so Ohnishi would have the best possible view before he entered her.

He mounted her roughly, thrusting sharply into her still undeveloped pelvis. Despite the pain she must have felt, the girl writhed and moaned, clenching Kenji's torso with her coltish legs and lifting her firm buttocks from the bed, arching her back higher and higher. Ohnishi could not resist the temptation; his hand snaked under his blankets to find himself semierect. He grasped it and began pumping in time with Kenji.

His erection lasted only a few moments and there was no emission, but it was more than he'd had in years. As soon as he lost it, he lost all interest in the performance still being played out behind the glass. He pressed the button to close the curtains and lay back on his bed. The sounds of Kenji's lovemaking still filled the room. He made a mental note, as he settled into sleep, to use this girl again.

SHE had been in the room for only twenty-four hours, but already Jill felt as if she'd been imprisoned for a year. She had gone through the classic steps taken by nearly every person who is locked up against their will. First she had raged at her captors, screaming and pounding against the solid steel door that kept her from freedom. When she had exhausted herself, she spent the next several hours going over her cell in minute detail, exploring the cement block walls, the ceiling that was too far over her head to reach, the empty pegboard rack with the outlines of tools still painted on its brown glossy surface. The twenty-square-foot room smelled of fertilizer, old gasoline, and oil—Jill assumed it had once been a gardener's supply shed.

After she'd paced her cell for another hour, Jill had

finally settled on the concrete floor next to the dripping spigot. She'd watched dully as the tiny drops pooled, then snaked to the rusted drain in the middle of the room. Eventually she slept, her body overriding her mind's racing questions.

When she woke a tray of food rested next to the door. There were a couple of oranges, half a loaf of crusty french bread, and a quarter stick of butter, along with a waxed paper cup of cool coffee. Jill noticed immediately that nothing on the tray could provide her with a weapon, no glass or tin cans, no utensils that could be sharpened by scraping them against the floor.

The waste bucket in the far corner of the room had been removed during the night and replaced with a fresh one, much to her relief.

Now Jill sat quietly, stoically, like a twenty-year veteran of prison, taking the time as it came, with neither expectations nor hope. For a while she'd tried to understand why someone had kidnapped her, but she realized that knowing the truth wouldn't do her any good. She suspected that Takahiro Ohnishi was behind her abduction, but the knowledge was worthless to her in her present circumstances. Her only interests were in survival.

Since Ohnishi had gone through the trouble of snatching her from her home, he must not want to kill her. He wanted something from her, something that only she could give.

It had to be her credibility as a reporter. If she was correct about Ohnishi and Mayor Takamora's attempt to break Hawaii away from the rest of the Union, then they would need the legitimacy that only the media could give, the soothing voice and face on the television assuring the people that everything was all right and under control. It would be simple to coerce her into giving false reports and no one who'd placed their trust in her as a reporter would ever know that they were being deceived.

It was the same question of ethics and integrity that

she'd faced before storming out of the studio, but this time the stakes were much higher. Yesterday it had been a question about her job, her career. Today it was her life at risk. Jill had thought about all of this throughout the long morning, but by late afternoon and into the evening her mind dulled and lost focus. She had settled into a torpor. She was just thinking about falling back asleep, her back was already pressed against the wall, her head held only limply by her slender neck.

The door opened without warning. Jill jerked out of her lethargy, edging along the wall to gain distance between herself and the dark figure that entered her cell. She noted idly that night had fallen once again, though she didn't know the time since she'd been stripped of her watch and shoes when she'd been left in the cell.

"I did not mean to startle you, Miss Tzu, my apologies." The man's voice was flat and lifeless, echoing inside him like a distant whisper.

"I know you, don't I?" Jill had gotten to her feet.

"We have not formally met, but we have spoken on the phone several times. I am Kenji."

"I knew Ohnishi was behind this." There was little triumph in her voice.

Kenji slid further into the room, his feet gliding on the floor with the ease of quicksilver. There was a dangerous elegance about him. It was the charm of the serpent, slow, seductive, evil. He eased himself to the floor, hunching down in the very place where Jill had been a moment earlier.

"You are a very perceptive woman and an excellent reporter. I watched your latest piece, and I must say you made a bold and accurate assessment of my employer and his involvement with Mayor Takamora. You are correct in assuming that they both want Hawaii to be an independent nation, albeit one with strong ties to Japan. However, you are wrong in guessing that Ohnishi is behind your abduction."

"You?" Kenji nodded. "Why?"

"You are intelligent enough to know why you were kidnapped."

"You want me to report some sort of propaganda," Jill said accusingly.

"Correct. In fact, the propaganda, as you call it, will not be that far from the truth. You can even air that piece you just finished."

Jill was startled and confused. "Why would you want that? It fully exposes your little plot."

"Not my plot, Miss Tzu, Ohnishi's plot."

"I don't understand." Despite herself, Jill couldn't help slipping back into her comfortable role as a reporter, digging for facts.

Kenji gazed off into the middle distance for a moment as if he could see the words he was thinking, watch them ricochet around like billiard balls after a strong break. "I have worked for Takahiro Ohnishi almost my entire life. I owe him everything. He is my master and I am his slave. I have killed for him and I have raped little girls for him. In fact, I did both again tonight. There is nothing I would not do if he asked.

"But there is something about me that he does not know, something that I myself didn't acknowledge for many years." He paused for a moment, then chuckled quietly. "Given his concept of honor, I actually believe he would understand my betrayal.

"My parents met only twice in their lives. The first time was when my father raped my mother, when he was stationed in Korea during the Second World War. She was a comfort girl, an unwilling prostitute like so many other young women who had the misfortune of being poor and attractive during the Japanese occupation. Her own father had sold her into prostitution so the family could survive.

"The second time my parents met was six years later, when my father returned to Korea to buy me from her. An injury during the war had left him impotent so I was to be his legacy, his only chance at immortality. Until his death, he worked for Ohnishi-San. I inherited his position.

"For most of my life, I saw myself as pure Japanese. I hid my Korean side in shame. But something has happened in the last few months—something that has given me reason to feel proud of my Korean heritage. Surely you understand this. You are half Japanese and half Chinese."

"I am an American," Jill stated firmly.

Kenji turned to her, his face both handsome and cruel. "Let us hope that you can see beyond that, or our relationship and your life will end very quickly. Very soon it will become necessary for Ohnishi's coup attempt to fail. Mayor Takamora is dead and soon Ohnishi will follow him. When this happens, we will need you to use your influence to calm the people and put an end to the violence."

"I'm a reporter. I report the news, I don't make it." Even as Jill spoke she remembered the words of her former colleague.

Kenji said, "A journalist can sway more opinion and change more policies than every politician alive today. You have a power that most people don't even recognize they have given to you. When the time comes, a few days from now, a week at most, you will divulge everything you know about Ohnishi and Takamora. Since they will be dead, whatever you say will not be refuted. I will provide you with many more details. People must be focused on the coup attempt; it must remain the top story for several weeks." At Jill's questioning look, Kenji shook his head. "The reasons for this do not concern you. Once this is done, I promise that you will never be bothered again, and your complicity never revealed."

"And if I refuse?" Jill asked with more bravery than she felt.

"Refuse now and I will kill you immediately," Kenji

said matter of factly. "But I don't need an answer yet.
I want you to think about it."

As he left, he added, "I chose you because I believe
you will actually have a hard time making your decision.
Do not disappoint me."

ARLINGTON

Tiny's Bar was, of course, named after its owner. On his first visit to the pub four blocks from his house, Mercer had expected to see a huge man behind the bar. Yet Tiny, Paul Gordon, was tiny, no more than four foot eight, about ninety pounds with his pockets full of bricks.

The bar was small, only eight stools and six four-person booths. The linoleum floor looked as though it hadn't been swept in years. The walls were decorated with horse racing pictures and trophies from Saratoga, Belmont Park, and Yonkers Raceway, just a few of the tracks where Paul had raced as a professional jockey. He had never reached the status of Willy Shoemaker, but he was a consistent rider with proven ability. But he gambled, and went on a particularly long losing streak. To pay back the debt, his loan shark ordered him to throw a certain race.

Explaining it once to Mercer, Tiny had said that the horse was too much of a true winner to allow any other to beat her. He didn't have the heart to rein her back and come in second. That night he was treated to a sumptuous victory banquet by the horse's owner. The next morning the loan shark's enforcers broke both of Tiny's kneecaps with a steel wrecking bar. During the following months of painful rehabilitation, Tiny cursed the stupid nag for being so swift. He finally forgave Dandy Maid only after he opened a bar in his native Washington.

When Mercer entered the bar, Tiny waved one small arm and immediately poured a vodka gimlet, easy on the Rose's lime.

"Thanks, I need this." Mercer took his drink to the red leatherette booth occupied by Tish and Harry White. Apart from two workers from the industrial laundry around the block, the bar was empty.

"Sorry I had to take Tish out of your house, Mercer, but you ran out of Jack Daniel's."

"I have a fresh bottle under the back bar."

"Had, Mercer. You had a fresh bottle under the back bar. Besides, who the hell would look for her in this hole in the wall?

"I agree, no harm done." Mercer turned to Tish. "How are you doing?"

"I'm fine." She giggled, slightly drunk. "But I must say I'm not used to drinking in the afternoon."

"Stick with Harry and me, we'll show you the ropes." Mercer smiled warmly. Perhaps a little buzz would be good for her. Brace her for what he was going to ask her to do.

"What did you find in your office?"

"More clues, I think. There's one more thing I want to check tonight and then I'll turn us both over to the authorities."

"What do you mean 'turn us over'?"

"Tish, you were under the protection of the FBI when I nabbed you, and I'm sure they want you back. Also, I have to answer for the corpses I left in the gutters down-town.''

"Oh."

"Hey, Harry, I see two suits coming in," Tiny said, peering out the filthy front window.

Mercer turned to Harry, one eyebrow cocked in question.

"Tish told me the story about yesterday, so I took the precaution of having Tiny keep an eye out."

"Good thinking." Mercer held out his hand to Tish. "Come on."

He led her out of the barroom and into the small kitchen in the back. They paused in front of a pane of glass set into the tiled wall, and Tish realized that the mirror behind the bar was a two-way mirror. She looked over Tiny's shoulder as two beefy men strode through the front door and flashed badges. FBI, not local cops, was Mercer's guess.

"Philip Mercer?" Tiny responded to their question. "Yeah, I know him. I haven't seen him in a week or more. He travels a lot." Tiny's thin voice raised a notch. "If I had seen him, he wouldn't owe me eighty bucks in old bar tabs."

Tiny thrust a wad of chits under one agent's face. Mercer winced, hoping the agent didn't look too closely. Those tabs all belonged to Harry.

Harry stood up and staggered one step, steadying himself on the back of the booth. Mercer wondered if his friend was acting.

"I seen Mercer," Harry nearly shouted, spit spraying from his lips. Acting, for sure.

"Where?" one of the agents asked eagerly.

"It was 1943; he was a cook for my battalion. Couldn't cook worth a damn; gave us all food poisoning on Tarawa, or maybe it was Iwo Jima." Harry downed a heavy slug of bourbon. "If it was on Iwo, that must have been '45. Poor Frank Merker bought it on Oki-nawa."

"No, it's Philip Mercer were looking for."

"Don't recall any Philbert Mercy," Harry said slowly. His eyes glazed over and he slumped into his seat. "I once knew a stripper named Phyllis mmmm . . ." His head hit the table with the sound of a fallen coconut, snores following a moment later.

The two agents left after warning Tiny to call if Philip Mercer showed up. Tiny and Harry played their roles for a few minutes more, until they were satisfied that the FBI men had moved on. As Mercer led Tish out of the kitchen, he noted that he had not let go of her hand during the whole episode. The simple touch was comforting.

"Harry, you should get an Oscar for that."

Harry sat up and smiled brightly. "I did once know a stripper named Phyllis. Phyllis Withluv she called herself; hot little redhead I met in Baltimore."

"What are we going to do now?" Tish interrupted before Harry could begin some lurid story.

"We can't go back to my place, that's for damned sure," Mercer said, sipping a fresh gimlet.

"If you need to, you can stay with me," Harry volunteered.

"No, I'm allergic to roaches. Seriously, I have other plans. We're going to New York."

Tish looked at him sharply. "What?"

"Tiny, call us a cab, have him meet us at the Safeway." The giant grocery store was a couple of blocks away. "Harry, thanks for your acting job." Mercer pulled a hundred dollar bill out of his wallet and slapped it on the bar. "This should clear your tabs."

He led Tish through the deserted kitchen and out the back door.

"Why are we going to New York?" Tish asked as they walked up the street.

"When we read those faxes, you must have seen that David Saulman suspects that Ocean Freight and Cargo may be a Soviet front. If that's true—and I believe it is because you heard Russian—then checking out their offices is our next logical step.''

"You mean we just waltz in there and make accusations?"

"Not at all." Mercer laughed. "We're going to break in tonight."

Tish stopped to look at him; his gray eyes were hard as flint and just as sharp. "You're serious?"

His voice was soft when he responded, but his conviction stung the air. "Deadly."

YOU'SE guys sure you'se want to do dis?" the Hat asked.

"Yeah. Hat, we're sure," Mercer said evenly.

They were sitting in a late-model Plymouth, on lower Fifth Avenue, about ten blocks from the brownstone that was the OF&C headquarters.

"My scags could hit it no time, lift any swag you want and be out before nobody knew nottin'. Youse don't need ta go in a'tall."

"That's the whole point, Hat. We do need to go in, and I want them to know that they were hit."

For the first time Mercer had a vent for the anger that had begun the moment Tish entered his life. Until now, he had been simply reacting to the actions of his unknown enemy. Now he was about to act, to take the fight to them, as he had promised.

"Babes in da woods," Hat said with a wave of his hand. The ember of his cigarette was like a comet in the dark car.

Danny "The Hat" Spezhattori was a professional thief. His gang of burglars were responsible for making New York City's wealthiest denizens several million dollars poorer over the years. The Hat's fourteen-year-old son had once made the mistake of trying to pick Mercer's pocket in front of the United Nations Building. Rather than turn the boy over to the police, Mercer had forced him to tell him who his father was. Mercer and the Hat met an hour later.

In a world where more business is done through people owing each other favors, Mercer had decided that a favor owed to him by a man in the Hat's position might someday be worthwhile. He was right. Tonight, that three-year-old debt would be paid off.

"Hat, give us an hour to get in position and then send your boys in, all right?"

"Mercer, once we hit da doors and d'alarms trip, dey will station a guard in da building."

"I'm counting on that."

"Youse ain't gonna murder no one, are you? Cause if ya do, I'll have nottin ta do wit it."

"Hat, we had a deal." Mercer's voice was like ice. "No questions asked. Your boys do what they're told and they will be in their pajamas in no time. No risk to any of them."

"I just gots ta say dis, Mercer. What kinda swag can be worth it, man? Youse got money; we bote knows it. It's a fuckin' shippin office; even their payroll will be shit."

"It's none of your business, Hat. Just do your job and we're square." Adrenaline sang in Mercer's veins like the heroin injection of a career junkie. "I know what I'm after."

Mercer looked at Tish in the backseat. Her face was very white, framed by shimmering black hair. Her blue eyes were wide but trusting. Mercer looked into them, searching for a sign of weakness, but saw none. "Ready?"

"Yes." Her voice was a whisper, but her eyes were hard.

They left the car. The dome light had been broken so there was only the soft click of the door latches to give away their exit. In seconds, they had both blended into the shadows of the steamy New York night.

One hour later, a little before one in the morning, a

Camaro, its body work covered with more Bondo than paint, streaked down Eleventh Street, just off Fifth Avenue. A dog barked at the noise of the racing engine on the quiet street.

The driver was intent on the road. A slight drizzle had made it slick, but his passenger was enjoying and savoring the moment. The shotgun in his hand was cool and heavy. The wind blowing through the open window was hot and humid but fresh in his nostrils. The adrenaline in his body had heightened all of his senses.

Hat owed Mercer a great debt. The driving he could trust to a lieutenant in his organization, but he would do the shooting himself. Four doors away from the target, the driver pounded his hand against the horn and shouted like a Comanche.

Hat thrust the barrel of the Remington pump-action 12-gauge out the window. He had loaded the ammo himself and was pleased with the result when he fired. The first shot obliterated the window of one ground floor apartment, the explosion of the cartridge and the shattering glass one continuous sound.

The second shot blew in the door of another brownstone. The thick oak splintered under the charge of lead. Another shot and another window vaporized. The driver was still yelling and the horn continued to blare, but Hat heard none of it. His eyes were locked onto his next target.

He fired, pumped the gun, and pushed his body nearly out the window to fire again. The door of the Ocean Freight and Cargo Building was much stouter than others on the street, but it couldn't withstand the shock of the double blast. The door, as if mauled by a predatory animal, dangled from its top hinge; the hardened lead shot had shredded the wood completely.

Immediately an alarm began to shriek within the brownstone, piercing the night even above the din of the Camaro's horn. Hat shot out one more window before lowering his weapon. The driver released the horn and the car raced out of the area, anonymous after only a couple of blocks.

Two police cars reached the scene within six minutes. The officers made a cursory search of the area and began taking statements from panic-stricken residents. Already the cops had figured that the shooting was just a joy ride by a couple of kids. Random violence in a city that was renowned for it.

Greg Russo knew that nothing that happened to OF&C was random. He arrived as soon as possible after the alarm company had phoned him. According to company records, he was the vice president in charge of the head office in New York, but Ocean Freight and Cargo had no company president. The Swedish group named as the directors of the corporation was nothing more than a Stockholm post office box. The only person above Russo was Ivan Kerikov, the head of Department 7, Scientific Operations, KGB.

Russo spoke to the police officers for several minutes, getting the details of the incident but not really listening to their explanations. Twenty years in the KGB had taught him to take nothing at face value.

"Again, Mr. Russo," one of the cops was saying, "I don't think you have anything to worry about. This is like no break-in I've ever seen. It's just kids, out for a night of terror. I'll make sure that this area is heavily patrolled tonight. There won't be any more disturbances."

"Our company pays a great deal in city taxes, Sergeant. I expect that you will provide ample protection." Russo spoke in a flat, accentless English.

"I'm sorry, but I cannot place men here to guard your office. If you want the name of a private security firm, I can give it to you. They could have men here in ten minutes." The sergeant moonlighted for them on Saturdays when his wife visited her mother in Trenton.

"That is all right." Russo acted mollified. "I'm sure that it's just my imagination. Whoever hit this street didn't seem to be targeting our offices. You are probably right that it was just kids.''

"Just to make you feel better, Mr. Russo, I called in a helicopter. It should be here in about a half hour. They'll hit the back of your building with a spotlight and make sure nothing is goofy back there.''

"You did go back there yourselves, didn't you?''

"Yes, sir, we did. Nothing in that courtyard but a couple of winos and a heap of trash.''

"Well, having that helicopter coming is a relief.''

A few minutes later both cop cars left. The few people out on the street, the type attracted to all police activity, slowly made their way back to their apartments, the excitement over for the night. Russo, whose real name was Gregory Brezhnicov, waited until the street was deserted before giving a signal to the driver of the van that had arrived only moments after him.

Two men dressed in black leapt from the back of the van. They marched toward Brezhnicov, thick arms held stiffly by their sides, chests puffed as if on parade. Their eyes continuously scanned the street, never resting on one object for more than a fraction of a second, but seemingly missing nothing.

No matter how long they remain in the West, Brezhnicov thought, a KGB assassination team never loses the discipline drilled into them during years of training. They were some of the best trained men in the world, capable of killing with nearly every weapon conceived as well as with their bare hands.

They stopped in front of Brezhnicov, grim-faced men with lifeless eyes.

"Search the entire building, look for anything out of place, then take up guard duties. Also check the courtyard out back. There are two derelicts there, get them out. No one enters the building until after nine in the morning. I will be the first here.'' There was no reason for Brezhnicov to stay; these men were more than capable of handling any situation.

THERE was a slight squeak in Mercer's miniaturized earphone before a voice came through. "Mercer, two of the baddest dudes I've ever seen just entered the building. Seems the bossman is heading back home."

Mercer clicked the button on the transmitter, acknowledging the information from Hat's son, called Cap, standing on a roof across the street.

"Get ready," he whispered to Tish, who was lying next to him. "They should come back here first."

A minute later, the two assassins eased out the back door of the OF&C building, pistols held competently. Their eyes searched the dark courtyard, checking the back windows of the buildings opposite, penetrating the shadows created by the single street lamp before resting on the two winos lying next to an overflowing Dumpster.

One guard came across the courtyard, hugging the shadows. Mercer, watching, knew this man was a true professional. The other man stayed hidden near the doorway, his gun covering his partner. Mercer tensed.

The first man approached a wino and, without warning, jerked the derelict to his feet.

Mercer winced as if physically struck. He could only imagine the strength it took to pull a man from the ground and onto his feet and make the action look effortless.

Hat's decoy stood limply in the man's grasp, babbling incoherently. The other wino, also part of Hat's team, slowly started to waken, as if from a lifelong binge.

"Get out of here now," the guard hissed, shaking Hat's man in his grasp. He kicked at the other wino. "You, too. Get out of here, before I break your fucking necks."

Mercer noted from his vantage in the Dumpster that the man's English was thickened by a heavy accent.

"We ain't done nothing," the wino on the ground

said as he rubbed his mouth with a filth-stained hand. "We got rights."

"Out, now." The assassin dropped the first of Hat's crew and took his pistol from a holster behind his back. At the sight of the gun, the two winos retreated hastily from the courtyard, nearly falling over each other as they ran toward the alley that led to Sixth Avenue.

When Hat's men had gone, the guard kicked at the pile of rubbish next to the Dumpster until satisfied that there was nothing hidden within. He turned his attention to the Dumpster. Inside, Mercer crouched lower.

The guard lifted the plastic lid and recoiled in disgust. The Dumpster reeked of human feces, rotted food, and decay. He let the lid drop, gagging slightly.

Mercer groped through the filth until he felt Tish's hand, then gave it a reassuring squeeze. He couldn't feel her skin through the thin rubberized protection suit, but he knew that it had to be as sweaty as his. He adjusted the oxygen mask over his nose and mouth and took a deep breath. The oxygen from the small tank at his side was crisp and cool. The suits and oxygen tanks, the same type worn by sewer workers, had been provided by Hat, who asked Mercer if he could use them to take an art gallery that he knew backed against a Chinese restaurant. The restaurant produced some particularly pungent rubbish.

The two guards, fooled into believing that the two "winos" were the only humans in the courtyard, cut short their search and reentered the OF&C building.

Ten minutes later Mercer opened the lid of the Dumpster and climbed out. He helped Tish to the ground and both peeled off the protection suits. They threw the suits into the Dumpster and gratefully closed the lid.

"This is one side of New York I never thought I'd see on a first date." Tish grinned.

Mercer would have cautioned her about silence, but he knew that she needed to speak in order to relieve some of the tension.

"Only the finest for you. Next time we'll go for a moonlight dip in the East River near an industrial vent I know. Very romantic this time of year."

"You are a charmer."

Mercer pulled a duffel bag from beneath a pile of garbage and unzipped it. He retrieved a pair of night-vision goggles, purchased from the Hat, and scanned the back of the OF&C building.

It was a typical New York brownstone, five stories high with a flat roof speared by chimneys and TV antennas. Firewalls separated it from its neighbors. There were four windows on each floor except for the ground floor, which had no opening other than a thick steel door. Wrought-iron grilles covered the windows on the second and third floors, making it impregnable from the ground. The upper windows were unguarded, but Mercer knew that a sophisticated security system protected the whole building.

When Mercer had outlined his plan to Hat, the professional thief's opinion was, "You're fucked if da system's zoned." If the brownstone's security system lacked individual secure zones, then the destroyed front door would have crippled the entire system. But if individual zones could be compromised without effecting other areas of the building, then Mercer's attempt to breach the back of the offices would trip further alarms.

Mercer didn't see movement in any of the darkened windows, but knew that a watcher would not give himself away so easily. He had to take a chance. From under a urine-soaked tarpaulin that Hat had placed in the courtyard hours before, Mercer took four lengths of ten-foot pipe, each with rungs protruding at regular intervals. Joined, the sections became a crude forty-foot ladder.

Mercer carried the ladder to the base of the building and set it up with minimal effort, resting the top between the building and a rusted drain pipe. Then he drew his gun, a Browning Hi-Power, a souvenir from Iraq. The 9 mm pistol could not carry as many rounds as the H&K

he had lost in Washington, but its stopping power was fearsome. The gun and the spare clip were loaded with mercury-filled hollow point bullets that would break up on contact. If a man were hit, nearly anywhere on his body, the shock alone would kill him.

He cocked the pistol and thumbed off the safety, the silencer attached to the barrel made it slow for a quick draw, but he needed both hands for the next few minutes. He reholstered the weapon and climbed the ladder.

On the train ride to New York, Mercer had explained his plan to Tish. At first she had balked at his intentions, but as he spoke, he could see the trust growing in her eyes. He outlined the four weeks of CIA training he had received prior to his insertion into Iraq, and that seemed to alleviate most of her fears. Though his training had focused on weapon tactics, he had learned the basics of breaking and entering and felt confident in his abilities.

At the top of the ladder, just level with the fourth-floor window, Mercer paused and scanned the darkened room. He saw nothing. From a pocket in his black pants, he withdrew a three-quarter carat cubic zirconia engagement ring he'd bought that afternoon while shopping for clothing for Tish. The retailer at the jewelry store had scoffed at Mercer's poor choice, but he didn't know that the ring would never be used as a betrothal gift.

At 8.5 on the Mohs' hardness scale, the zirconia easily etched the glass. Mercer traced one of the panes of the window. The protesting squeal of the cutting glass was loud in his ears. Judging that three times around had weakened the glass sufficiently, Mercer paused for a deep breath. He was about to find out if the system was zoned. If the alarm sounded, neither he nor Tish would have enough time to escape the courtyard before the guards rushed out to investigate. He took another deep breath, his pulse pounding.

"Fuck it," he said as he gave the weakened pane a slight tap with the heel of his hand.

The tiny filament wires of the security system parted

and the glass fell softly to the carpeted floor of the building. An alarm screamed in Mercer's head, but the building itself remained silent.

He could hear his heart pounding a furious tattoo in the eerie gloom of the courtyard. Then he realized that the noise wasn't his heart. Searching the square of visible sky above his head, Mercer saw the lights of an approaching police helicopter. The chopper was no more than ten blocks away and already the powerful halogen spotlight mounted in the nose was piercing the dark streets.

He tried to open the window, but countless coats of paint applied to the frame had glued it solidly shut.

"Shit," Mercer cursed under his breath, and hammered at the underside of the open pane. The small amount of glass left in the windowframe sliced painfully into his hand.

After several hard blows, the window sprang up, slamming into its upper stop. Mercer didn't worry about noise being heard inside—the sound of the police helicopter would easily drown it out. He wriggled through the window as the downblast of the chopper's rotors whipped up a maelstrom in the small courtyard. Dust and debris choked the air. The sound was deafening.

"Tish, come on," Mercer called, trying to be heard above the din.

Tish scrambled up the ladder as the searchlight beam blasted into the courtyard, probing into the darkest corners, seeking its prey.

Mercer grabbed Tish by the wrists when she reached the top of the ladder. The searchlight was systematically spotlighting every window of the OF&C building, and it was only seconds before her form would be in the beam. He yanked her into the room. She yelped as her breasts scraped over the hard wooden sill. Mercer lunged up and slammed the window closed just as the searchlight probed into the office. He thought for a moment that the cops above had seen his face, but quickly the light passed on. He could see its beam forming bizarre shadows in the hallway beyond the room. From the helicopter, the ladder would look like any of the wiring conduits that clung to the building like ivy.

"Jesus, that hurt," Tish said, massaging her chest.

"I'd do that for you, but you'd probably slap me."

The grin she gave told him that she would be all right. Mercer pulled a flashlight from his jacket and switched it on. A red lens diffused the light, but he could see easily enough. Before beginning the search, Mercer pulled the Browning from its holster.

He didn't know how long they would be in the offices, so he had to eliminate the pair of guards. He couldn't chance being discovered unexpectedly. Mercer had no illusions about taking on two professional assassins in a fair fight, but he had no intention of being fair.

"Do you have any doubts about what we are going to do?" Mercer asked Tish, perhaps more for his own benefit.

"If these people have anything to do with the destruction of the *Ocean Seeker*, then they deserve to be punished." The steel in her voice was chilling.

"All right then, I want you to wait here until it's over. I'll come back to get you." Her eyes were fearful in the dim light, but there was a determined set to her jaw. When he took her hand for an instant, the trembling he felt was mild.

All the lights on the top floor were off, but dim light spilled up the stairway. Mercer handed Tish the flashlight and began his search, the night-vision goggles over his face giving the building an eerie green glow.

The rooms on the top floor, storerooms mostly, were all empty, dust coated, and neglected. Mercer padded silently down the stairs. On the third floor, a single wall sconce illuminated the narrow carpeted hallway. The doors which led off the hall were all locked and there was no one in sight. Mercer licked his fingers and unscrewed the bare bulb, plunging the hallway into darkness.

The old wooden stairs creaked as Mercer eased himself down one more flight. The entire second floor was one huge room, divided into small cubicles each containing a desk, chair, and computer. There were plenty of lights in the large work area, so Mercer removed the goggles and left them on a desk. He was thankful to have his peripheral vision restored.

He slid down to the floor and scanned the room. He saw only the legs of desks and chairs and not those of a guard. Like a snake, he slithered through the room, every sense tuned to perfection.

An instructor at the CIA facility had said: More often than not, you will find your enemy with your nose or ears before you will ever see him. When the wisp of tobacco smoke tickled Mercer's nostrils, he silently thanked that instructor. The room was so quiet he could even hear the sizzle of tobacco as the guard drew on the cigarette. The man was no more than ten feet away, on Mercer's right, shielded by a thin cubicle wall.

Mercer glanced at his watch. He had left Tish more than fifteen minutes ago, so he had to hurry. Panic would begin to overwhelm her soon.

He decided to be bold. He removed his black leather jacket, figuring that the black pants and shirt he wore were similar enough to the guard's to confuse him for a second. He stood and began to whistle cheerfully. Immediately, he heard the unseen guard spring from a chair and begin moving toward him.

The guard turned a corner directly in front of Mercer, a machine pistol held at the ready. In the millisecond it took him to realize that Mercer wasn't his partner, Mercer brought the Hi-Power to bear. The guard died an instant before his own trigger finger could squeeze. His body crumpled against a steel desk, his arm sweeping a pile of papers to the floor. The massive tissue damage caused by the Hi-Power sickened Mercer; a hole had been punched almost completely through the guard's body.

Reclaiming his jacket, Mercer retraced his steps to the stairway and cautiously made his way to the ground floor.

The lobby of the building also occupied an entire floor. The waiting area was furnished with several taste-ful couches, a large Turkish carpet, and an expansive reception desk. The walls were painted a calming salmon color and the prints which lined them were all of ships. A few dim lights kept the room more in shadow than light.

A figure leaned against the front doorframe, a holster cocked off one hip. For a moment, Mercer wondered if he could kill a man from behind, without warning.

As if alerted by some primal instinct, the guard whirled around, drawing his pistol and firing in one con-tinuous motion. The bullet grazed Mercer's pantleg as he dove out of the way. Mercer hit the floor rolling as bullets gouged the marble floor near his head and torso. He managed to duck behind the reception counter, and when he looked back to see where the guard had gone, another round slammed into the wood, driving splinters deep into his jaw and right cheek.

"Son of a bitch," he muttered, wiping blood from his face.

Suddenly, the lights went out in the lobby.

Mercer rolled silently from behind the counter, hug-ging one of the walls. His plan was to crawl to the light switch and flip it back on, hopefully using the surprise to target his opponent. Halfway to the switch, he bumped into the guard's leg.

· Neither man had anticipated the contact, so neither had an advantage. Mercer reared back, then sprang for-ward like an all-pro lineman playing in the Super Bowl, his shoulder connecting with the guard's knee. The joint failed and the guard fell forward, but he still had time to whip his pistol at Mercer's head, shearing skin from his already bleeding cheek. Mercer smashed a fist into the guard's thigh, paralyzing the leg momentarily and giving himself time to bring up the Hi-Power.

The guard kicked out with his good leg and sent Mercer's pistol skittering across the marbled floor. Mercer twisted away from the guard who was already trying to regain his feet. The room was too dark to see where the pistol wound up, so Mercer ignored it and concentrated on his opponent. He leapt to his feet and charged again, catching the guard low in the stomach and forcing the breath out of him in a loud whoosh. The guard back-pedaled as Mercer continued to push him but twisted aside just before they hit the sofas. Mercer flew over one of them and crashed to the floor, wrenching his shoulder painfully.

There was a brief spark of muzzle flash as the guard fired his silenced pistol at Mercer, but the shot was several feet off target. Mercer used the flash to locate the other man in the darkness and leapt at him, but missed. The guard had moved. Mercer hit the floor and rolled twice, coming up hard against another wall. It was cat and mouse again. Neither man could see the other in the gloom and neither could hear the other over his own labored breathing. Mercer edged forward, feeling along the floor, and found his pistol. The cool steel was a needed reassurance.

Just then the lights snapped back on in full brilliance. The nerves and muscles that controlled Mercer's pupils reacted just the barest fraction of a second faster than the assassin's. While the other man was squinting through nearly closed eyes, disoriented by the glare, Mercer's gaze was sweeping the room. Tish stood next to the bank of light switches, one hand still on the reostat, the other holding the bulky night-vision goggles. The guard was twenty feet away, peering off to Mercer's left. Mercer didn't take the time to properly aim. He fired from the hip, his first two shots going wide but his next six catching the guard squarely, pounding his torso into an unrecognizable mess.

Mercer moved over to Tish and took the goggles from her slack hand. "Tish." Her eyes swiveled to his. "I told you to wait upstairs. Please, from now on, never listen to me again, okay?"

He slid his arms around her and her body eased into his embrace. He calmly stroked her hair for a moment. "Now we're even. I saved your life and you just saved mine. Thank you."

"I waited until you had your gun and he was turned away from you," she replied after a moment.

They went back up to the third floor, dousing all the lights again and relying on Mercer's goggles to get them to the executive offices. Quickly scanning the names on the doors, they found the locked door of the highest ranking employee, a vice president. Mercer smirked at the man's name: Russo.

"Nice touch," he commented.

"If they are Russian," Tish replied.

"To have guards like those two, they're something."

It took Mercer five frustrating minutes to pick the lock. Although he remembered the technique from his CIA training, theory and practice were two entirely different things. One of Hat's men could have done it in ten seconds.

The office was paneled in rich oak, the carpet was soft under their feet. A window behind the broad desk looked out onto Eleventh Avenue. Mercer shut the thick drapes and turned on the desk lamp. Pictures of the OF&C fleet adorned the walls. David Saulman in Miami had been right. Each ship had a different bunch of flowers painted on the funnels: *April Lilac, September Laurel, December Iris*, and a score of others. There was a fish tank against one wall, and though it was large it only contained a single fish.

Mercer turned to the four squat filing cabinets and

opened a drawer at random. He started leafing through the folders within.

"Pick a drawer, any drawer," he said lightly.

"What are we looking for?"

"Anything that might jog your memory. There could be something here that you may remember from when you were rescued, a name, anything."

Tish pointed to a picture on the wall. "That's the ship that rescued me, I think."

Mercer looked at the picture and recognized the *September Laurel* as she calmly plied some distant sea.

"That may be the ship that reported finding you, but I don't think it's the ship that pulled you from the water. You remembered a black circle and a yellow dot on the funnel, not a bunch of flowers. Besides, Dave Saulman told me that her crew are mostly Italians, not Russians."

"I could have been wrong about hearing Russian."

"Even if you are, it's obvious that something is going on here. Let's just go through the files and see if anything turns up."

For the next half hour, Mercer and Tish pored through the files without turning up anything conclusive. The only odd thing was a loose file tab labeled "John Dory" lying on the bottom of the drawer containing the ownership papers of the OF&C ships. There was no file to go along with the tiny scrap of paper. Because all OF&C vessels were named after a month and a flower, Mercer guessed that John Dory was the name of a captain or ship's officer employed by OF&C.

"This has been a complete waste of time, hasn't it?" There was hopelessness in Tish's voice.

"I know I'm right. There has to be something here that we haven't seen," Mercer persisted. "But we have to get out of here."

"Did you kill those guards without a reason?"

Mercer looked up from the file. It was a question he did not want to address. Was there a chance he was wrong about OF&C's involvement?

"No, we didn't, and I'll tell you why. Look around this office. There's nothing personal anywhere, no photos, no diplomas, nothing. This may be a legitimate shipping line to some, but to the man who occupies this office, shipping is not his career." Mercer walked to the desk and scanned the address file. "There isn't one ship broker's number in here, not one chandler. Christ, he doesn't even have the private numbers of his captains."

"He could be just a figurehead."

"He is, don't you get it? Most shipping lines are built by individuals and based on personal contacts. I'm willing to bet this Greg Russo wouldn't know a hawsepipe from a hole in the wall. Whoever occupies this office has a job to do, but it has nothing to do with shipping."

"Hold it right there," a male voice commanded.

Mercer froze, his pulse pounding. Hat's son had said only two men had entered the building, and they had already been eliminated. Whose was the voice behind them?

"Step away from the desk and turn around slowly." The command was punctuated with the cocking of a revolver.

An overweight security guard stood in the doorway. He was a frightened rent-a-cop with a pale, jowled face and a trembling grip on his weapon.

"You got a lot to answer for. Keep your hands where I can see them. Move toward the fish tank."

Mercer backed away from the desk, Tish right beside him. She hadn't screamed when the guard entered and seemed in control. Mercer wished that he felt as calm as she appeared. The guard had scared the hell out of him. Greg Russo must have called in additional security after Cap had left his post across the street. Mercer had no way of knowing if more men were scouring the building. The guard crossed to the desk, his eyes and gun never straying from Mercer. With his free hand he fumbled for the telephone. Mercer's chance was coming.

The instant the guard glanced down at the phone, Mercer launched himself.

Time slowed to a crawl. Mercer's senses were heightened so that he could see the individual hairs on the guard's face, smell the nervous sweat of the man, and hear his labored breathing. Mercer flew across the room, focusing on the hand holding the revolver, the rings of fat around the man's wrist, the knuckles tightening around the trigger. The hammer began to drop and Mercer's fingers were still inches away from their mark.

The gun discharged just as Mercer grabbed the guard's wrist. The sound was like a burst of thunder in the small office. Cordite smoke burned Mercer's eyes, blinding him. Next to Tish, the large fish tank exploded, water, gravel, and the fish cascading to the carpet in a frothing wave.

The recoil lifted the gun high over the guard's head so that Mercer's shoulder barreled into the guard's unprotected flank. Mercer could feel the man's ribs snap as he smashed into them. The guard was thrown across the desk, the gun spinning from his hand. He fell against a wall, moaning.

Mercer recovered the revolver, aiming it at the fallen guard, but did not pull the trigger. "You're not with those others, you don't have to die." Mercer lowered the revolver and turned to Tish. "Are you all right?"

"Shaken, but not stirred."

"We've got to get out of here—someone must have heard this gun go off."

Mercer held out his hand and Tish came toward him and took it in hers. He stared at the dying fish for a moment as it flopped on the soaked carpet and the sight triggered a vague memory. "Benoit Charleteaux," he mumbled.

"What?" Tish asked as they started cautiously back to the fourth floor and the ladder outside.

"Another clue." Mercer's muted voice sounded triumphant.

Richard Henna was just getting back into bed after a late-night foray into the kitchen when the bedside phone rang. He grabbed the handset before the second ring. His wife, a twenty-five-year veteran of middle-of-the-night calls, didn't even stir.

"Henna."

"Dick, it's Marge." Margaret Doyle was a deputy director of the bureau and Dick Henna's oldest and best friend. She didn't bother apologizing for waking him. "Philip Mercer has left the Washington area."

"How?" Henna snapped.

"By train. The agents we had watching Union Station never saw him because he boarded the Metroliner at New Carolton. We just found out through his credit card. He purchased two one-way tickets for New York from the conductor on the train."

"Christ."

"What is it, dear?" Fay mumbled in her sleep.

He covered the mouthpiece with his hand. "Nothing,

hon," then spoke softly but clearly into the phone. "All right Marge, call the New York office, have them put a few men at Penn Station in case he tries to return by train. Fax them the picture of Mercer we got from the U.S. Geological Survey."

"I've already made the calls."

"If they pick him up, I want to be notified right away. Then I want him and Tish Talbot flown immediately to Andrews Air Force Base."

"Should we cancel the surveillance on his house?"

"No, I'm willing to bet he'll get by us again. Call me back if there are any new developments."

"Sorry about this fuck-up, Dick."

"Not your fault. I think we've all underestimated Mercer."

Henna hung up the phone and slipped into a bathrobe. He knew he would get no more sleep this night. He went downstairs, made a cup of coffee, and sipped it in the darkened kitchen for a few minutes before crossing through the large federal-style house to his study. He turned on his desk lamp, groaning as the light flashed into his eyes.

He dialed the combination of the Chubb safe behind his desk and removed a single file. The file, headed "Antebellum," recorded Henna's personal observations about events since the letter from Ohnishi came to his attention.

He read his own handwriting slowly, mostly because it was too sloppy to scan. The first page was a bare chronology. Henna now added Mercer and Talbot's trip to New York at the bottom of the list.

On a clean sheet of paper, he began drawing flow charts, tying events into each other. In minutes, he had created an indecipherable series of lines, circles, and swirls. The only thing he knew for certain was that Mercer had gone to New York in response to the information he had received from the law offices of David Saulman.

He reread the information that Mercer had requested

from Saulman, obtained by the FBI through a Dade County judge's court order. Saulman's office had grudgingly turned over a few lists of ship's names and some basic information on Ocean Freight and Cargo.

This time he saw it—the ship that rescued Tish Talbot was owned by OF&C, whose offices were in Manhattan. Henna spilled his coffee as he grabbed for the phone. Ignoring the mess, he dialed the New York FBI office.

"Federal Bureau of Investigations," a tired voice answered the phone.

Without preamble, Henna gave his personal recognition code to the night duty officer, establishing his identity without question. In situations like this, the code numbers saved valuable minutes needed when a person high up in the organization wanted to speak with someone out in the field. Henna had heard a similar system was used by many of the crime syndicates the FBI fought. Henna asked to speak with Special Agent Frank Little.

"I'm sorry, Agent Little is on the day shift, may I be of assistance? This is Agent Scofield."

"Who else is there now?" Henna needed to speak with someone he knew personally, someone who wouldn't want to use this phone call for some favor in the future

"I'm sure, sir, that I can be of some . . ."

Henna cut the man off, "Just tell me who else is there."

"Agent Morton is here and so is—" Pete Morton had been a rookie agent when Henna was station chief in New York six years earlier.

"Great, let me talk to him.

A moment later, "Morton."

"Pete, this is Dick Henna in Washington."

"Jesus." Henna could almost hear the man spring to his feet.

"Relax. I need a favor."

"Yes, sure, anything Mr. Henna."

"Get on the horn to one of your contacts in the NYPD. I want to know if there was any trouble near Eleventh Street tonight."

"I don't see how—"

"Pete, just do it, all right." Henna remembered that Morton used to ask a million questions about everything. "Call me at this number when you're done," Henna gave him his home number, "and then lose the number." He hung up.

He skipped through the file in front of him until he came to Philip Mercer's dossier, compiled by the CIA in 1990. Mercer had been born in the Belgian Congo. His father was an American mining engineer employed by Mines Belgique, a firm mining diamonds from the rich Katanga province. His mother was a Belgian fashion model. They had met during a photo shoot in Leopoldville, the capital of the Congo. Philip was their only child. Both parents had been killed during an insurrection in Rwanda in 1964; the details of their deaths were sketchy.

Mercer was raised by his paternal grandparents in Barre, Vermont. His grandfather worked in a granite quarry and his grandmother was a homemaker. He graduated top of his class in high school and cum laude from Penn State with a degree in geology. He then went to the Colorado School of Mines in Golden, again graduating near the top of his class. After four additional years of schooling at Penn State while doing contract work for various coal mines around western Pennsylvania, he received his Ph.D. in geology. His thesis on metamorphic rock dynamics as it pertains to quarry mining was still supplemental reading for graduate students at Penn State.

After completing his doctorate he went to work for the U.S. Geological Survey, but lasted there only two years. Interviews with coworkers from that time showed that Mercer was simply unchallenged by the work the USGS had given him.

Henna noted that Mercer's case was another example

of the government's inability to retain top minds in
whatever field. He couldn't count the number of agents
he had known who left to work for private security firms.
It wasn't just the pay or the benefits that caused people
to leave, government work simply drained people of
their spirit.

After the USGS, Mercer went into business for himself assaying mining properties for investment firms eager to know potential returns before committing huge
amounts of money. He built a reputation quickly within
the industry. After just a few years, two weeks of his
time cost up to fifty thousand dollars plus, in some cases,
bonuses in the form of stock if he believed the property
to be extremely valuable. The year that the CIA did the
background check, Mercer's income, as reported to the
IRS, was slightly over three quarters of a million dollars.
The CIA had also contacted the U.S. Customs Service,
who listed thirty overseas trips since his latest passport
was issued.

The next section of the report detailed his involvement
with the CIA and the mission to Iraq. When the plan to
infiltrate Iraq was first conceived, forty-eight candidates
were considered for the position of on-site expert on
mining practices and geology. Mercer was the eighth
candidate to be interviewed, and after his first series of
tests, all the other interviews were canceled. He scored
just above genius level on the IQ test and did perfectly
on all the memory tests. One of the testers noted that
Mercer was able to recall a forty-digit number twenty-
four hours after seeing it. After agreeing to join the team,
he was sent to a training facility in rural Virginia, where
he had excelled in marksmanship and the grueling obstacle course, but fared just average in communications
and what was termed ''basic trade craft.''

The attached psychological report documented an
acute fixation on self-reliance and a deeply rooted fear
of abandonment, probably due to his being orphaned. He
was a natural leader but had chosen not to develop those

skills. The staff psychiatrist summed up his report by stating that Mercer's motivation for joining the infiltration team was simply his need for continual challenge. The doctor feared that this would lead to reckless behavior, but recommended Mercer's approval.

In mid-January 1991, Mercer and eight Delta Force commandos parachuted into northern Iraq near the city of Mosul. The site was chosen by Mercer and a team of satellite analysts as the most likely spot for uranium mining.

Mercer had quickly confirmed that the mining facility there was not even close to production and the uranium ore was too poor a quality to make nuclear weapons. They were attacked by the mine's security detachment as they were sneaking out through the perimeter fence. Two commando officers were killed during the opening gun battle and another fell shortly afterward as they retreated through the mountainous desert.

The extraction helicopter they had depended on couldn't pick them up because of the heavy weapons fire from Iraqi scout cars. Mercer led the remaining troops through a scree field that the pursuing scout cars couldn't pass and managed to lead them to Mosul. There, they stole a produce truck and made a mad dash to the Turkish border. The Delta commandos all agreed that Mercer was the person most responsible for their success, and that without him, none of them would have survived.

Two days after their debriefing, President Bush ordered the beginning of Operation Desert Storm.

Henna stood and began pacing, his chin buried against his chest. He knew from the dossier that Mercer was acquainted with Tish Talbot's late father, which would explain why he had gone to the hospital. But his actions since then defied explanation. How had he known the other man in her room was not part of the hospital staff or another FBI agent? Why hadn't he contacted the FBI as soon as he had gotten Talbot safely away? Why had he pursued the matter on his own? And if he had gone to New York to investigate the shipping company, what had he found?

"Christ, there are too damn many questions and not enough answers," Henna said aloud.

The phone rang shrilly and Henna snatched at it.

"Henna."

"Mr. Henna, Pete Morton in New York, sir."

"Yeah, Pete, what've you got?"

"How did you know there was something up on Eleventh Street?"

"Skip the questions and tell me what happened." Henna's heart was racing and his palms were sweaty.

"At 12:53 this morning a gunman drove down Eleventh Street and fired a shotgun five times, blowing out several windows and doors. He then raced away. There are no suspects or clues."

"Was one of the buildings hit owned by a company called Ocean Freight and Cargo?"

"Yes, how did you—"

"Never mind that. Get some men down there right away, take into custody anyone they see. Call me back as soon as you're done."

"I'll take care of it myself, sir."

Henna set the phone down and slumped back into his chair.

"What the hell is Mercer playing at now?"

BANGKOK, THAILAND

The Scotch in Ivan Kerikov's glass was quickly diluting as the ice melted under the onslaught of the Asian heat. The tumbler was jeweled with condensation and the small napkin on the Royal River Hotel's table was sodden. Kerikov took another heavy swallow of the questionable Scotch, mindful of water dripping from the napkin that clung to the glass.

He had been in Bangkok now for two uneventful days, basking in the delights of his hotel, the venerable Oriental, where he had taken a suite in the original Author's Wing, and indulging in carnal vices on Pat Pong Road, Bangkok's famous red light district. He had also spent some of that time contemplating his hurried escape from Moscow, wondering if he had been too rash in executing the KGB auditor in his office. Hindsight said that he should have suffered through the little man's investigation and left afterward, but killing him had given Kerikov the sense of completion that he needed before he fled his homeland.

His leaving Russia was never in doubt, but the abruptness of his departure left a few loose ends that he now could never tie up. "So be it," he mused lightly, and ordered another Scotch from the attractive waitress. He had reason to be in a good spirit and regrets for the past would not be allowed to dampen it.

Last night he had been contacted by Dr. Borodin from aboard the *August Rose*. Borodin reported that he had a definite location for the volcano's summit and it was nearly a thousand meters beyond Hawaii's two-hundred-mile limit. The news was like a yoke removed from Kerikov's shoulders.

When Dr. Borodin had first proposed Vulcan's Forge forty years before, his selection for the most optimal geologic site did not take into account any political considerations. The area he chose had the right combination of natural volcanism, ocean depth, temperature, salinity, and currents as well as some native minerals that were necessary. Unfortunately this spot was forty miles from Oahu. Because this site was obviously unusable, Borodin had cut his margin as fine as possible, detonating his device as far from the Hawaiian Islands as he could without jeopardizing the results of his work.

At the time, Hawaii's entrance into the United States was a foregone conclusion, giving her the territorial rights afforded a sovereign nation rather than those of a colony or protectorate. Yet Borodin's calculations demanded that the explosion had to take place within that two-hundred-mile demarcation if Vulcan's Forge was to succeed. Boris Ulinev trusted Borodin's assertion that oceanic currents would skew the volcano enough so that it would surface outside the limit, yet the wily head of Scientific Operations hedged his bet by initiating an audacious contingency plan.

He selected a young Japanese-born American, an adolescent with a tortured background but an incredible mind. He surreptitiously groomed him, guiding him from afar through university and into business. Using the massive support of the KGB, Ulinev shepherded wealth and power to this young man for many years, all the while introducing him to people who shaped his personality and goals. This shaping was done subtly over many years and continued even after Ulinev had died and left Department 7 in the care of others.

The end result was the fanatical racist and megalomaniac, Takahiro Ohnishi. He had become a global industrialist with a far-flung empire and had unwittingly been programmed his entire life to attempt to break Hawaii away from the United States if Scientific Operations ever decided that was necessary for the success of Vulcan's Forge.

Kerikov, when he took over Department 7, had read about Ulinev's original contingency plan and inwardly cringed. He knew from experience that humans were easy to program, especially considering the extraordinary depth given in Ohnishi's case. Yet experience also showed that controlling those who had been so programmed was difficult at best. They often became active without authority, or not activate at all when called upon. The idea of a "Manchurian Candidate" worked well for fiction writers but not for true spy masters.

Kerikov was relieved now that this phase of Ulinev's original plan was no longer needed. Borodin's call confirmed that a revolution in Hawaii was no longer necessary to ensure they would be able to control the volcano. And although the KGB had spent millions of dollars creating Ohnishi, Kerikov really didn't care about the write-off. The volcano was outside American influence and within his personal grasp.

Eight months earlier, Borodin, on a regular pass-by of the burgeoning volcano aboard the *August Rose*, had reported that it would most likely crest outside the two-hundred-mile line yet he would not have conclusive proof for some time. Kerikov seized that moment to enact a contingency plan of his own.

With one million dollars in cash and a promissory

note of an additional five million dollars, Kerikov bought
someone high up in Ohnishi's personal staff to report on
all of the eccentric billionaire's activities. If the coup in
Hawaii was unnecessary, Kerikov wanted to ensure that
Ohnishi would not continue his end of the plan. The
mole was his insurance that Ohnishi could be controlled.
Permanently, if necessary.

At the same time, Kerikov set into motion a plot to
steal the wealth of the volcano for himself. Had the Soviet Union remained the world power that it had been
when Dr. Borodin launched Vulcan's Forge, Kerikov
would have been proud to turn over the marvelous
achievement to his superiors. But the decades since then
had seen Russia degenerate into a Third World country,
a nation whose very survival depended on loan guarantees from America and Western Europe.

After quietly capitulating the Cold War in 1989, Russia had suffered a cruel peace. She was turning into a
market for goods and a source of raw materials, much
the way Europe had once treated the backwaters of Asia
and Africa. In just a few years, the Soviet Union had
toppled from superpower to colony, and the decline was
far from over.

Watching dispassionately as his nation rotted, Kerikov
decided that if he could not save the *Rodina,* then perhaps the Motherland could save him. Since Russia no
longer possessed neither the political clout nor the financial resources to develop Vulcan's Forge, Kerikov
opened negotiations with a group of men who could.

The nine members of Hydra Consolidated, a Korean-
based holding company representing billions of dollars
of real estate, manufacturing, and electronics, recognized
the value of Vulcan's Forge when Kerikov approached
them. They did not balk at the one-hundred-million-
dollar price tag that he attached to the volcano and its
unusual riches, for the strategic element being produced
in the charnel guts of the volcano would make its pos-

sessor the most powerful force on earth, in both the literal and figurative sense.

Just a week after initiating talks with the Koreans, Kerikov learned of the proposed meetings in Thailand to discuss the Spratly Island situation. Sensing that the Bangkok Accords could aid his plan, Kerikov pulled in some favors and employed a little bribery and blackmail to get Gennady Perchenko assigned as the Russian delegate to the meeting. He also managed to get the Taiwanese ambassador to act on his behalf in return for some information that would ensure Minister Tren the prime minister's office whenever he wanted it.

Even before the accord meetings began, Kerikov knew how he would use his two agents-in-place to solidify possession of the volcano when it crested through the Pacific swells.

When his second Scotch arrived, he glanced at the Piaget watch on his wrist. Perchenko would arrive at any moment. Kerikov looked at the maître d'. It was his first night here at the Royal River, yet he seemed comfortable in his job.

The regular man hadn't arrived for work this afternoon. His body was secured to several cement blocks in a canal about ten miles from the city.

An hour after receiving the confirmation from Borodin, Kerikov had killed the maître d' as the ultimate insurance that he would never discuss his dealings with the Russian delegate to the Bangkok Accords. After dispatching the young Thai, Kerikov phoned his sociopathic assistant, Evad Lurbud, in Cairo and ordered him to commence his housekeeping. This would mean killing an Egyptian arms merchant and then flying to Hawaii to take care of Takahiro Ohnishi and Kerikov's mole.

Kerikov might have left behind some loose ends when he fled Russia, but he'd be damned if there would be any from the final gambit of Vulcan's Forge. In just a few days, he'd be spending the one hundred million dollars from the Koreans and there wouldn't be a soul left alive who would know how he got it.

Kerikov spotted Gennady Perchenko leaping from a Riva River taxi onto the quay of the Royal River. In a moment, the new maître d' would guide the diplomat to his final briefing.

WASHINGTON, D.C.

The big Greyhound over-the-road bus
hissed to a stop just outside the city's main terminal,
near the convention center. Mercer was stiff legged as
he trailed Tish down the three steps of the bus to the
already sizzling pavement. His whole body ached, not
only from his ordeal in New York but from the torturous
seats that all transportation manufacturers seem intent on
using. He tried, without success, to knuckle the kinks
from his lower back as he and Tish ambled into the bus
terminal. Announcements echoed off the tiled walls,
mixing with the din of the passengers arriving and de-
parting. The terminal stank of the homeless who spent
their nights on the steel benches.

"I still don't understand why we had to take the bus
back to Washington," Tish complained, swiveling her
head to stretch her tense neck muscles. They had cabbed
to Newark and caught the bus there.

Mercer grimaced as he stroked the new beard that
stubbled his face. "Because by now the FBI will have

the train stations staked out and I needed time to think before we turn ourselves in.'' He strode to a bank of telephones and dialed an international operator. ''After I make this call, we'll give up.''

Mercer waited a full five minutes for the connection to be made, then spoke in French. Tish, not understanding the language, walked over to a bench and sat down. Mercer joined her after a few minutes.

''All set,'' he announced.

''What was that all about?''

''I had to call an old fishing buddy in the Ruhr Valley.''

Tish had learned not to be surprised by any of Mercer's actions. ''Did he tell you what you needed?''

''He sure did.'' There was a sense of triumph in Mercer's voice that cut through the exhaustion etched around his eyes.

They grabbed a taxi in front of the terminal and Mercer gave the driver his home address.

''Why don't we go straight to the FBI?'' Tish said, and leaned her head against his shoulder as she had for much of the six-hour ride from New York.

''If we showed up at the Hoover Building, it would take them hours to verify who we are and direct us to the person who was in charge of your protection at the hospital. This way, the agents at my house will take us straight to him.''

''Clever.''

The cab ride took nearly forty-five minutes in the snarled downtown traffic. The driver refused to use the car's air-conditioning, so great blasts of hot air blew into the taxi, plastering Tish's hair around her face.

''Since you fell asleep as soon as we got on the bus this morning, I just want to thank you for the way you handled yourself in New York. You came through like a true professional.''

Tish smiled at him, her beautiful lips framing dazzling

teeth. "Jack Talbot didn't raise a daughter who couldn't take care of herself."

Mercer laughed. "No doubt about that."

"Mercer, what's going to happen to us once the FBI pick us up?"

"I don't know, Tish. I think the information we've gotten in the past couple of days points to the people responsible for the *Ocean Seeker* disaster. Once we deliver it to the FBI, we should be out of it."

"What if they don't believe us?" she persisted.

"We just have to make sure they do. The story I have to tell is too chilling to be ignored."

The cab stopped in front of Mercer's house. He paid the driver, unlocked the door of the house, and keyed off the security system. He almost had the door closed when a voice from behind interrupted him.

"Dr. Mercer, please step away from the door and place your hands over your head. This is the FBI."

Mercer backed away and turned to the FBI agent, his smile ironic. "The last person who told me that was left tied up in an office in New York and he already had his gun drawn."

The agent, not catching Mercer's graveyard humor, sensed a threat and pulled his service weapon. "I said, place your hands on your head. You too, Dr. Talbot."

The agent stepped forward. He was Mercer's age, but had a baby face under a mop of light blond hair. Mercer noted that his gun hand was very steady. Another agent joined the first.

"I've been instructed to take you downtown. You're not under arrest, so please go easily."

"I don't think so. You'd better make this official," Mercer replied with a slow smile. He turned around and lowered his hands behind his back. As if by programming, the second agent came forward and slapped on a pair of handcuffs. "Think of how good you'll look to your friends when they see you captured us in irons."

When they were in the agents' brown sedan heading

back into the city, Tish whispered, "Why in the hell did you do that?"

"I want to see the reaction of whoever has summoned us. It might tell me a lot."

The car ducked into the city via Route 66, and exited just North of the Lincoln Memorial, then streaked down Constitution Avenue, parallel to the Mall, where countless tourists sweated in the Washington heat while viewing the monuments. They turned left onto 15th Street as Mercer expected. He was certain they were headed for the J. Edgar Hoover Building, FBI headquarters, but just before reaching the Treasury Building, the car slowed and made another left onto East Executive Avenue. A moment later they entered the White House grounds through a back gate. Mercer and Tish glanced at each other, speechless.

The car pulled into an underground garage just behind the White House. The agents escorted Tish and Mercer to an already waiting elevator. Two more agents joined them there. Mercer noticed, just as the elevator doors closed, that the garage didn't smell of oil and was absolutely spotless. He suspected that the garage was washed every day to prevent a stray spark from lighting any spilled oil.

The elevator took them up to the ground floor and disgorged them into a blue-carpeted hallway. Young staffers rushed past, reports and faxes clutched in their fists as if their jobs meant the safety of the free world. Which, in reality, they did. Only a few stopped to notice the cuffs that secured Mercer's hands behind his back. He wondered if they thought he was a fellow staffer sacrificed to some as yet unknown scandal.

"I won't give any of you away," he called over the din of the countless ringing phones.

The agents pushed him roughly down the hall past numerous cramped offices until they reached a cluttered desk just outside a wide door. The presidential seal hung from the wall behind the desk.

"Miss Craig, this is Philip Mercer and Tish Talbot. Is everything set inside?"

"Yes, it is," the plump woman said. She looked up at Tish and smiled sweetly. "You poor dear, I've heard about what you've been through. Come with me. I'm sure you'd love to freshen up a bit."

Tish looked at Mercer, stricken.

"It's all right. I'm sure you'll be fine." Tish allowed the President's personal secretary to lead her away.

Mercer turned to the agents flanking him. "Well, gentlemen, let's get on with it."

They opened the door and Mercer stepped into the Oval Office.

Mercer's first impression was that the office was much smaller than he had imagined. He envisioned the president governing the country from a much larger room. He stepped over the seal embroidered into the pale blue carpet and studied the people in the room. He recognized most of them. Seated were Admiral C. Thomas Morrison, Richard Henna of the FBI, and Catherine Smith, the President's chief of staff. Mercer guessed that the bald man standing against the far wall was the director of the CIA. The President sat behind his desk, his large hands resting on the leather top. Ms. Smith wore a conservative suit, white blouse, and a muted bow at her throat, and the assembled men were all wearing the customary Washington uniform—conservative suit, white shirt, and muted tie. Only Admiral Morrison, in his summer whites, and Mercer still in the black clothing from the break-in, were dressed any differently.

"Mr. President, I wish to congratulate you." The President looked at Mercer quizzically. "I saw in the paper a couple days ago that your wife's dog just had puppies."

"We are not here to discuss dogs, Dr. Mercer," Paul Barnes, the head of the CIA, said sharply, clipping each word.

"We're not going to discuss anything until I know

why Tish Talbot was brought to Washington and why she was placed under FBI protection.''

"She is no longer a concern of yours," Barnes snapped.

"I'm beginning not to like you, friend." There was no malice in Mercer's voice, but his gray eyes hardened.

"Dr. Mercer, we will answer all of your questions in turn. Rest assured that Dr. Talbot's ordeal, as you put it, is at an end. She is upstairs right now with my wife and the puppies you just mentioned. She will be looked after." The President cut through the mounting tension.

"Christ," Henna exclaimed as he realized that Mercer was cuffed. "Get those damn things off him and leave us."

The two agents removed the handcuffs and skulked from the room. Mercer helped himself to a cup of coffee from the silver urn next to the fireplace and took the last available chair.

"So you wanted to see me," Mercer said innocently, taking a sip of coffee.

"Dr. Mercer, you have a lot of explaining to do," Henna replied. "But first we all want to express our gratitude to you for saving Dr. Talbot's life in the hospital. How did you know that the man in the room was an impostor?"

"Lucky guess," Mercer demurred. "We both used the same cover to get into her room. I figured your watchdogs might let in one urologist, but not two. I also noticed that his shoes were too uncomfortable looking for a doctor making his rounds. It was a calculated risk, but at worst I was risking an assault charge from an irate citizen. It turned out I was right. Who was he, anyway?"

"Josef Skadra, a Czech-born agent who used to free-lance for the KGB."

"Do you have any idea who he was working for when he went after Dr. Talbot?"

"We're not certain," Henna admitted. "Remember,

you didn't leave him or any of his team in the position to answer questions.''

''Dr. Mercer, you are here to answer questions, not ask them.'' Barnes spoke again.

''Paul, take it easy,'' the president cautioned. ''Dr. Mercer is a guest here, not a prisoner.''

''Before you start asking questions, why don't I fill you in on what I know,'' Mercer said, and the president nodded.

''On the night of May 23, 1954, an ore carrier named *Grandam Phoenix* sank about two hundred miles north of Hawaii in the middle of the Musicians Seamounts, a five-hundred-mile-long string of undersea volcanoes. Whether she was destroyed by the nuclear blast that occurred that night or she was already sinking, I don't know. The bomb was under about seven thousand feet of water when it went off.'' Mercer's audience was too dumbstruck to speak, so he continued, ''I pinpointed the epicenter by triangulating time delays and Richter scale differences from six different stations in Asia and the United States. The sharp spike recorded on the seismograph tapes that night is identical to ones measured after underground nuclear tests. There is no natural occurrence that even remotely resembles it.

''Since that time, seven large vessels have sunk in a fifty-mile radius of the explosion's epicenter, including, most recently, the NOAA research ship, *Ocean Seeker*.''

''What are you talking about?'' Henna finally found his voice.

''Let me finish and you'll see. That many ships sinking in such a relatively small area is strange enough, but there is a connection between them that defies random mishap. Of the seven ships that went down, only three had survivors—a tanker in 1968, a container ship in 1972, and the *Ocean Seeker*. The four other vessels, the ones where no one survived, all had something in common, very accurate bottom-scanning sonar. The trawlers lost since 1954 use them for finding shoals of fish, a cable layer sunk in 1977 would use it for locating a smooth path on the ocean floor, and a Chilean survey ship was mapping the Pacific basin in 1982 when it vanished without a trace.''

''Is that from the list of vessels you received from that law office in Miami?'' asked Henna.

''Yes. I stared at it for quite a while until I saw a connection between all the ships that sank with no survivors. Once I saw that they all had bottom-scanning technology, I pieced together what it was they may have seen. I believe they were all sunk so they wouldn't report a new volcano building its way to the surface.''

''Is this volcano connected to the nuclear detonation?'' the President asked.

''I'm certain that it is. I believe that the explosion was the trigger that started the volcano's eruption. The area around Hawaii, including the Musicians Seamounts, contains an intraplate hot spot. Put simply, a hot spot is a localized area of intense heat deep in the earth's mantle that punches holes through the crust as a tectonic plate slide across it, forming chains of volcanoes that are progressively older the further from the spot they are.

''By detonating a nuclear bomb over a hot spot, weakening the crust further, magma from the lithosphere was given a new, artificial outlet.''

''Why would somebody want to do that?''

''I have no idea, but it's proved to be worth killing for.''

''Let's get back to more recent history,'' Henna prompted.

''The *Ocean Seeker* was sent out on an unscheduled survey to find the cause of some whale deaths. The whales had been found beached on Hawaii about a month ago with their digestive tracts filled with lava particles. Tish Talbot was an invited guest on the expedition. Twenty-four hours after leaving port, the ship exploded and Tish was thrown into the sea. After her rescue, she was transferred to George Washington Uni-

versity Hospital for observation. I received a telegram
the day after she was admitted to the hospital saying she
was in grave danger.''

''Who sent the telegram?''

''It was signed by her father, but I later found out her
father has been dead for a year, so I don't know who
sent it. It's obvious that someone wanted me to get involved.''

''Why?''

''Mr. President, that is the million-dollar question.''

''This is a waste of time,'' Paul Barnes snorted. ''He's
got more questions than answers.''

''You're right, I do have a lot of questions. Why was
Tish Talbot purposely saved when the *Ocean Seeker* was
destroyed? The *Seeker* has the most sophisticated sonar
systems found outside the U.S. Navy, so Tish being
found alive breaks a well-established pattern. Why was
she held prisoner for a few days before her official 'rescue' by a freighter called the *September Laurel*? And
then why did someone try to have her killed?''

''Are these all things she told you?''

''No, I've figured it out myself. When the ship exploded she was thrown clear by the blast and suddenly
there was an inflatable raft right next to her.''

''The raft could have been dislodged by the explosion,'' Admiral Morrison pointed out.

''Impossible. The raft would have been shredded, not
inflated. She also told me she swam to it, but admitted
that she could barely hear anything. How could she have
swam in the turbulent water around a sinking vessel if
the blast had stunned her so badly? I'm certain there was
someone aboard who was forewarned about the ship's
destruction and whose job it was to save her life.''

The men in the room all exchanged glances. Mercer
felt that they knew something he didn't.

''To get back to your question about why Dr. Talbot
was brought to Washington and placed under the protection of the FBI, you must know that we received a

warning a couple of days before the *Ocean Seeker* disaster.'' The President spoke slowly. ''We felt putting her at George Washington University Hospital would raise less suspicion than bringing her to Walter Reed. You see, she is the only living witness to a terrorist act directed at the heart of America.'' He pulled out the letter sent from Takahiro Ohnishi and read it aloud.

'' 'To the President of the United States. After World War II, Europe, faced with economic necessity, released her long-held colonies and let them struggle through the arduous process of independence. Some made the transition smoothly, while others continue to struggle internally and with their former masters. It is a painful chapter of human history that is still being inked in blood.

'' 'It is time now that the United States, too, face economic realities. The colonies that America maintains must be released, and that is how we on Hawaii feel we've been treated by you. The four-trillion-dollar debt that you carry is a burden too heavy to maintain. The stopgap efforts that you and your predecessors have attempted have done little but stave off the complete collapse of your system.

'' 'While U.S. tax dollars flood the coffers of foreign nations and banks and bloat already engorged government contractors, the American people slide deeper into an unquestioning torpor spawned by inane rhetoric and slick presentations.

'' 'Mr. President, this cannot be allowed to continue for Hawaii. The people of Hawaii are by origin not white Europeans nor should they be governed by them. We are a separate people with different beliefs and a different set of values, and it is wrong that we too should be bankrupted by the dying system to which you cling.

'' 'You must realize by now that mankind does not thrive with cultural diversity. We are a tribalist species, one most comfortable within well-defined groups, and it is wrong to deny this. The idea of a 'melting pot' is as outdated as the 'white man's burden.'

" 'I fear that soon the United States will join that growing list of nations torn by factional fighting and I do not wish to see this come to pass for my people. Hawaii's transition to independence must be made peaceably, but it must be made. Already plans are being implemented to draw us away from the United States and establish ourselves as a sovereign nation. Do not attempt to resist this action. I can promise peace, but only if you do not interfere.

" 'As a demonstration of the seriousness of my concern and conviction, I have at my disposal the means to destroy any American government vessel within two hundred miles of these islands. If I detect any such vessel in the coming weeks of transition, I will not hesitate to sink it.

" 'Please do not test my resolve or the resolve of the people of these islands. We are united in purpose and our goal will ultimately benefit all.' It is signed, Takahiro Ohnishi."

The President placed the pages facedown on his desk and looked up at Mercer.

Mercer remained expressionless while his mind churned through what the President had just read. He knew the eccentric billionaire's views; in fact, he'd read one of Ohnishi's books about the need for racial integrity. But he'd never believed the industrialist capable of this. Race relations between Hawaii's Japanese majority and the island's white population were strained, but what the President had just read was tantamount to a declaration of independence. He said as much.

"As it turns out, there were no naval vessels scheduled to arrive or depart Pearl Harbor at the time that we received this letter, but NOAA did have the *Ocean Seeker* heading northward. Dick brought the letter to my attention only after she'd had been lost. Before that, he had assumed it was just a crank. Since then, I've suspended all activity within the two-hundred-mile limit Ohnishi outlined in this letter. Dr. Mercer, you are the first person outside this group to know the situation.

"We believed that this was a recent plot by Ohnishi, but the information you've brought us indicates that it goes back forty years."

"Mr. President, I'm not even finished yet. This goes even further than some crackpot billionaire with a decidedly Hitleresque mien," Mercer stated.

The men in the room turned to him intently.

"You see, the *Ocean Seeker* was sunk by a Soviet submarine called *John Dory*, not by Takahiro Ohnishi."

CAIRO, EGYPT

The sun was still a sizzling torture over the crowded city streets despite the onset of evening. The Arabs in their long white *galabias* seemed immune to the hundred plus heat, but the Westerners in the city suffered. Evad Lurbud bought a cup of warm date juice from a passing vendor who had a huge petwer urn strapped to his back. The juice tasted awful, but his body needed the fluids.

Lurbud stood on Shari al-Muizz Le-din Allah, the main road in the Khan el-Khalili, a huge sprawling bazaar located three miles and about a thousand years from modern Tahrir Square at the center of Cairo. A rabbit warren of twisting alleys choked with people, the Khan is the true shopping center for the locals. Harried, red-faced tourists make it an obligatory stop after the pyramids, the necropolis at Memphis, and the crowded Cairo Museum.

Founded by Sultan Barquq's Master of Horse, Garkas el-Khalili in 1382 as a way station for camel caravans, the Khan had grown enormously over time. By the Ottoman conquest of Egypt in 1517, items from as far away as England were being traded in the sprawling bazaar. The Ottoman sense of order established a guild system within the bazaar that is still evident today. Perfume sellers congregate just south of the Khan's main crossroads. Gold and silver are sold in specific areas, while carpet merchants are found in another. The heady aromas from spice merchants and food sellers compete throughout the Khan while tourist curio shops cling to the Khan's perimeter.

There were no cars in the Khan, but the din of the pedestrian traffic more than made up for the lack of engine noises. Hawkers touted their wares and the Arab tradition of haggling reached a great cacophony. The loudspeakers of the two mosques just outside the bazaar throbbed with cries of *"Allah Akbar"* with pious regularity.

Soon, Lurbud knew, the Muslims would close up their shops and head to the mosques for sundown prayer. He scoffed at the notion of a God, especially one that demanded prayer five times a day, yet he respected their fealty. As a veteran of the Afghani campaign, he knew full well the strength the rebels derived from their religion. The Mujahedeen called their resistance a "Holy War," and whipped the tribes into an amazing, cohesive force that possessed the power to resist the largest army ever maintained.

Lurbud had spent his first tour of the war as an intelligence operative for the KGB, spending weeks and sometimes months away from the relative security of Kabul on deep cover insertions. Because of his swarthy complexion and knack for languages, he could ingratiate himself with a rebel band and act as one of their own while gathering data on their strengths and weaknesses, assessing the future plans of other groups of resistance fighters. When his task was complete, he would call in the feared helicopter gunships. The craft would thunder

into an encampment where he was a trusted member and
kill every man, woman, and child in sight. Lurbud would
conveniently be on patrol during these massacres. During the two years he spent on this duty, Lurbud's Afghani compatriots never once suspected that he was the
cause of the devastation.

His amazing nerve caught the eye of the KGB hier-
archy, especially Ivan Kerikov. After one helicopter attack, when Lurbud couldn't extricate himself from a
rebel village yet managed to survive the scathing fire
from the Hind-D gunships, Kerikov pulled him from the
ranks of field operatives and seconded him to his personal staff in Kabul.

There, Lurbud's chief function was breaking captured
rebels in the dank prisons the Soviets had established.
Lurbud learned that the binding force that held the Mu-
jahedin together was also a major weapon in the interrogation rooms. The Muslim faith forbade the devout
from coming into contact with swine, and even the threat
of such contact was enough to break the hardest rebels
Lurbud faced. It amazed him how the most solid fighter
would panic when threatened to be placed inside the
decayed carcass of a pig.

What kind of God made men fear hogs, considering
so many of them lived just like them? Lurbud wondered
idly.

The voice of the Muezzin blared from speakers high
above the streets in the minarets, calling the faithful to
prayer. Lurbud crouched deeper in an alley, shrinking
into the shadows of stacked spice bags as the streets
began to empty. The smell of saffron was nauseating.
Glancing at his feet, he saw that he'd stepped into a pile
of dog shit. He muttered in disgust and smeared the filth
against one of the bags.

Looking up, Lurbud recognized his quarry as the man
left his shop across the Khan's main road. The sign
above the shop's door stated that Suleiman el-aziz Suleiman was a jeweler, and the size of his shop indicated

that he was prosperous. Evad Lurbud knew differently.

Suleiman was one of the richest arms merchants in the Middle East. Not having the notoriety and ostentation of other death merchants, Suleiman had been able to practice his trade unmolested by the United States or Western Europe. Although his arms were used to fight in Beirut, Italy, Ireland, Germany, the drug-choked cities of America, and countless other places, he had never once been questioned by the authorities.

The obese Arab waddled down the street to the Mosque of Sayyada al-Hussein, his body waggling with every step as huge sacks of extra flesh slid against each other. His face was round with an almost childlike openness.

Acording to his KGB dossier, Suleiman was far from the fool whose image he projected. He had distinguished himself in two of the wars against Israel and in the subsequent years had established a relationship with nearly every terrorist organization on the planet. The KGB figured that Suleiman's personal wealth was somewhere in the neighborhood of two hundred million dollars.

Too nice a neighborhood for a stinking Arab, thought Lurbud as he crossed the now empty street.

Lurbud paused by the door. The streets were now eerie. He had been watching Suleiman's shop since noon from various vantage points, and during that entire time the streets had been crowded and loud. There was no one about now; even the countless cats that skulked through the alleys had vanished. Since crime is nearly nonexistent in the Khan, there was no need for elaborate security systems. Lurbud expertly picked the frail lock to Suleiman's shop.

He knew from the dossier that the Arab always returned to his shop for a few minutes after prayer before leaving the Khan for his home on Shari El Haram, the road which leads to the Great Pyramids at Giza. Lurbud closed and locked the door after once again checking the empty street.

Inside the shop, Lurbud passed display cases that gleamed with gold in the dusty light that streamed in through the transomed windows. The setting sun cast long shadows across the room. Lurbud eased a Takarov pistol from its holster under his jacket and parted the beaded curtain that led to Suleiman's back office.

A battered wooden desk, covered with stacks of books and a gold measuring scale, occupied the center of the small office. A coffee urn, tarnished and pitted, sat on a low settee against one wall. The room smelled of dust mingled with the sweet odor of hashish. Lurbud sat behind the desk, the pistol in his lap. For twenty minutes, until Suleiman returned from prayer, the only movement in the room was the occasional blinking of Lurbud's dark eyes. He waited with the same patience as the Sphinx just outside the city.

Lurbud's entrance had disturbed the room, its air pattern, its volume, its feel. As he remained, motionless, the room had calmed, accepting his presence. This was a skill he had learned at a training camp on the shores of the Black Sea, where students were put into a completely dark maze. The one who walked out alive, graduated.

He remained motionless even when he heard the front door of the shop open and close. An instant later Suleiman's immense bulk parted the curtain separating his shop from his office.

Suleiman had grabbed a demitasse of coffee and was almost upon Lurbud before he noticed the intruder. The thimble-sized cup fell from his pudgy finger, shattering on the stone floor. Behind his beard, Suleiman's face drained of color and he staggered back several paces.

"I read in your dossier that you are never guarded here in the Khan." Lurbud spoke fluent, unaccented Arabic. "You believed that your standing in the bazaar would protect you, yes?"

"Who are you?" Suleiman demanded, recovering from his initial shock.

"My name means nothing to you, Suleiman el-aziz,"

Lurbud spoke without emotion. "You were hired to supply and ship nearly a thousand tons of arms, ammunition, and material to Hawaii. Is this not true?"

"I know not what you talk about."

"I believe that you do. The order was placed by Takahiro Ohnishi possibly several weeks or months ago."

"I am a simple jeweler. I don't understand."

Lurbud continued as if Suleiman had not spoken. "I represent a group that does not wish to see this order filled. We don't want those arms shipped to Hawaii. In fact, we don't want you to have any further involvement with Ohnishi at all."

"Who are you to tell me how to run my business?" Suleiman retorted with a sneer.

"Ah, so no longer are you a simple jeweler." Lurbud's smile was devoid of amusement.

"I know your type," Suleiman said, his tone scornful. "You're some soldier of fortune who happened on that piece of information. Do you think you can blackmail Suleiman el-aziz Suleiman?"

"I am not here to blackmail you. I'm here to tell you that the order is canceled."

"You are too late, mercenary. Those arms are on a freighter halfway to Hawaii." Sweat had beaded on Suleiman's creased forehead.

The Arab was lying. Suleiman hadn't even purchased the arms yet. He was currently using Ohnishi's deposit money to push up the bond prices of a hydroelectric project in Sri Lanka. Because of his contacts in the terrorist underworld, Suleiman knew that Tamil separatists were going to bomb the huge network of dams within two weeks. By pushing up the bond price and then selling at a slight discount just prior to the attack, Suleiman stood to quadruple the money. Only then would he put together Ohnishi's order for weapons.

"I believe that you're lying, Suleiman." Lurbud brought the Takarov into view for the first time. "But to be honest, I don't really care what the truth is."

For such a large man, Suleiman's reaction time was incredibly fast. He dove across the room, his body sailing through the air like a giant zeppelin.

Lurbud swung his pistol in an arc matching Suleiman's leap, but his first shot amazingly missed the huge target. Suleiman crashed against the wall near the settee, one arm sweeping the coffee urn to the floor. Coffee flooded across the floor in a thick black tide. Suleiman's hands, made dexterous through years of precision jewelery making, tore at a pistol which had been taped to the back of the old urn.

Evad caught a look of murderous rage in the Arab's eyes as Suleiman torqued his huge body to bring the gun to bear. Lurbud fired an instant before the muzzle of Suleiman's automatic caught a bead on him. The shot tore into the arms merchant's body, the fat rippling in shock waves around the impact.

Suleiman's arm was thrown up by the shot, the tiny Beretta spinning from his hand. Lurbud fired again, and again. The killing light in Suleiman's eyes began to fade. Lurbud came around the desk, his pistol aimed directly at the Arab's head.

With his free hand the Russian pulled a flask from inside his jacket. He unscrewed the lid from the pewter flask and knelt next to the dying Muslim.

"As a final thought, Suleiman el-aziz Suleiman," Lurbud began, pouring the viscous red liquid from the flask onto Suleiman, "you will meet Allah with your body covered in pig's blood."

Suleiman opened his mouth to scream at this ultimate desecration, and Lurbud fired one more round down the gaping throat. The blood of the dead Muslim mingled with that of the unclean pig on the hard floor of the office.

Lurbud reholstered his gun, noting for the first time the thick pall of cordite smoke that hung in the air. The room reeked of smoke, but beneath that odor he detected the smell of blood and Suleiman's voided bowels.

At the front door of the shop, he paused. There were a few people on the street, mostly old men heading back to the coffee houses and their hookahs. The thick stone walls of the shop had muffled any sound from the silenced Takarov. Lurbud eased out of the shop and mingled with the crowd as best he could. Ten minutes later he was out of the bazaar, searching for a cab. He had two hours to dispose of the pistol and get to the airport before his flight to Hawaii.

THE WHITE HOUSE

There was a stunned silence in the Oval Office after Mercer made his revelation. He watched as everyone's expressions turned from surprise to confusion and finally to doubt.

"What makes you think Russia has anything to do with this?" Paul Barnes broke the silence. "Just because the assassin who went after Dr. Talbot once worked for the KGB doesn't mean anything."

Mercer realized that he had just stepped on the toes of the director of the CIA.

"Tish Talbot told me that after her rescue from the *Ocean Seeker*, she heard some of her saviors speaking Russian."

"Christ," Barnes said, glancing around the room. "You said she was blown from the ship, stunned. Who knows what she heard—she was half dead at the time."

"I doubt that St. Peter speaks Russian during his interview at the Pearly Gates, Mr. Barnes," Mercer said evenly. "But that's not the fact I'm relying on.

"A friend of mine in Miami is an expert in maritime law. I had him research Ocean Freight and Cargo, the owners of the *September Laurel*. He found that the company is a front for the the KGB."

"I had a court order demanding Saulman turn over all the information that you requested," Henna said incredulously. "He withheld that from the FBI."

"If you knew Dave Saulman, you wouldn't be surprised. He's as crusty as a Paris bakery. But he is a walking encyclopedia concerning maritime commerce and his word is gospel truth."

"If we take his word about the KGB for the time being," Paul Barnes said suspiciously, "what about this submarine idea of yours?"

"The first piece of evidence is really just simple reasoning. According to the news reports there was a combined naval and Coast Guard search of the area, using, I'm sure, the most sophisticated hardware in the world. Yet they failed to find any survivors. The *Ocean Seeker*'s last known position was well documented by her Loran transmissions, yet the search turned up nothing except an oil slick and a few pieces of debris.

"Then, two days later, the *September Laurel* happens along, 'aiding' in the search, and miraculously they find Tish. That freighter, which was a hundred miles away from the *Ocean Seeker* when she blew up, managed to accomplish something the coast guard and navy couldn't do. I don't buy it. There were no weather problems during that time, no storms, no fog."

"You're wrong there, Dr. Mercer," Admiral Morrison interrupted. "There was a tremendous amount of surface fog, and because of the President's order not to send out surface ships, we were confined to an aerial search only."

"Admiral, tell me honestly, is there any logical reason why your planes would have missed her, even with the fog?"

The chairman of the Joint Chiefs ran a hand across

the tight whorls of hair on his large head before answering. "If she had been out there, my boys would have found her."

"Since there is no logical reason why she wasn't found by the coast guard or navy, I looked for an illogical one. The only one that fits, gentlemen, is a submarine."

Morrison turned to the President. "It makes sense, sir. There could have been a sub out there and we never would have known it. None of the search aircraft used sonar buoys or acoustical gear in the search for survivors. That sub could have sat just under the surface and listened to us flounder around."

The President nodded. "What other proof do you have, Dr. Mercer?"

"Since I couldn't learn anything more about Ocean Freight and Cargo from Dave Saulman, I knew I needed a firsthand investigation, so Tish and I broke into their offices in New York."

"What did you find?" asked Dick Henna.

"For one I found a fish tank in the vice president's office, a large tank that contained only a single fish."

"So?"

"Well, OF&C has a practice of naming their ships after months and flowers and painting those flowers on the stack of the vessels. Tish remembers seeing the design on the stack of the ship that rescued her. It was a yellow circle surrounding a black dot, yet the *September Laurel* is marked with a bunch of laurels. The distinctive pattern that Tish remembered matches that of a European game fish I once caught in France."

"What's the connection?"

"The name of the fish is John Dory and that tank at the OF&C office contained a prime specimen."

"That's the thinnest connection I've ever heard," Barnes remarked.

"I'd agree with you, if I hadn't found a base file tab in the drawer with the ownership papers for the company's vessels. The tab read 'John Dory.' At the time I thought the reference was simply a misfile, but it makes more sense that they own a ship by that name but don't keep any paperwork on her. When I got back to D.C., I called the friend I went fishing with and he confirmed the name of the fish. The design on the stack pins down the source of the name, and the only ships ever named after fish are submarines.''

''You've got to be joking.'' Barnes chuckled indolently.

Mercer stood up. ''Mr. President, you said I was a guest and not a prisoner. If that's true, I want to leave. If you don't want to listen to what I have to say, then I see no reason to stay here and try to explain. In the past few days I've been shot at a dozen times, and not because I have a bad standing in the community. I've stumbled on something, and if you gentlemen are not interested in what I have to say, I'm going.''

''Dr. Mercer, please wait,'' Henna said. ''Tell us what happened in New York.''

Mercer told them about the break-in, the armed soldiers guarding the building, and his impressions about the office.

''There is something nefarious behind Ocean Freight and Cargo, and so far all indications point to the Russians,'' Mercer concluded. ''I just don't know why.''

''Mr. President,'' Henna said, turning in his seat, ''I had some agents go to the OF&C offices soon after Dr. Mercer and Dr. Talbot had left. The scene had been sanitized—no corpses or blood. My men could tell that a gun had been discharged in the building. The air fresheners couldn't mask the smell of the cordite. I can't confirm what Dr. Mercer reported, but I certainly can't deny it either.''

''I just remembered something.'' Paul Barnes rejoined the conversation with a more accepting tone. ''I can't remember any details, but a report crossed my desk a few years ago from a metallurgist in Pennsylvania. It sounds similar to the conditions Dr. Mercer described about the explosion in 1954. He had obtained a sample of some element; I can't remember what it was called, but it had something to do with radiation and seawater.''

"Do you remember anything else?'' Admiral Morrison prompted after Barnes had lapsed into silence.

"Abraham Jacobs,'' Barnes finally replied. "The scientist's name was Abraham Jacobs. I'm sure he knew something about what we're discussing.''

"Can you find him?''

"Yes, sir.''

"I want him in my office by this afternoon.'' The force in the President's voice galvanized the room. "We now have a more grave situation in Hawaii than we first estimated. If Dr. Mercer is right and this does go beyond Ohnishi's personal coup and in some way involves the Russians, I don't even want to think of the consequences.''

"It seems too far-fetched to me that Takahiro Ohnishi and the Russians have been planning this since the 1950s. Too much has changed in the world to make a plot of this type viable.'' This from Henna.

"This could be an alliance of convenience,'' hazarded Mercer. "Something that was formed recently, as new situations developed.''

"That makes sense,'' the President agreed. "But we have to get in touch with this Dr. Jacobs. Hopefully he can tell us exactly what's at stake here.''

"You mean over and above the possible secession of Hawaii?'' Henna said caustically. The President shot him a scathing look.

"Mr. President, may I make a request?'' asked Mercer.

"Yes, Dr. Mercer, what is it?''

"I have a feeling that we're working under a time limit. Ohnishi or the Russians must know we're on to them in some respect. They are probably being forced to push up their deadlines because of my action in New

York. I have a feeling that the situation in Hawaii is going to get critical real soon."

"I know what you are going to ask and it's already been taken care of. The carrier *Kitty Hawk* and the amphibious assault ship *Inchon* are already on alert three hundred miles from Hawaii."

"A good idea, sir, but not what I wanted. I think to better understand what we're up against, a series of infrared photos should be taken of the area where the *Ocean Seeker* was sunk."

The President looked toward Barnes, who rummaged through a briefcase at his feet. "Let's see, there's a KH–11 flyby of the north Pacific in thirteen hours. That bird has the right cameras and it wouldn't take much to change her orbit to pass north of Hawaii."

"Thirteen hours, that's too late." Mercer said.

"What do you suggest?"

"Either an SR–71 Blackbird or one of the air force's superspy planes that no one is supposed to know about."

"Paul?"

"There's an SR-1 Wraith at Edwards, but I need your authorization to get her airborne."

"Do it. How long before we get some pictures back?"

"At mach six the Wraith will be there and back in about an hour and a half. Say a half hour for film processing and transmission here."

"Dr. Mercer, I needn't remind you that you have not heard any of this, correct?" the President cautioned.

"I'm sorry, sir." Mercer smiled. "I haven't been listening. Did you say something?"

"Very good, gentlemen, we all have jobs to do."

The group started for the door. "I want everyone to meet back here in two hours. Dr. Mercer, ask my secretary for a temporary pass if you plan to leave the grounds."

"I'll do that."

Mercer spoke with Miss Craig and learned that Tish was asleep in one of the White House guest rooms. He scribbled a quick note for her in case she woke up while he was gone and then hailed a cab near Pennsylvania Avenue. He was home twenty minutes later. After a quick shower and an even quicker beer, he went to his study, touched the large bluish stone that was his good luck piece, and sat behind his desk.

He dialed a number and two rings later the phone was answered. "Geology department, Carnegie-Mellon University."

"I'd like to speak to Dr. Jacobs, please."

"One moment." After about a dozen moments the same voice came back on the line. "I'm sorry, Dr. Jacobs is with a class."

"My name is Vince Andrews from the Hiller Foundation, the group that supports Dr. Jacobs's research," Mercer said putting as much bluff into his voice as he could. "Dr. Jacobs is in serious trouble and will probably lose his grant. It's imperative that I speak to him now."

"I understand, please hold the line."

A minute later a more mature voice spoke. "I don't know who this is since my grant comes from Cochran Steel, but you've piqued my interest."

"Hi, Abe, it's Philip Mercer."

"I should have known." Abraham Jacobs laughed. "Mercer, give me a second to get into my office. I don't want my assistant realizing the low caliber of some of my friends."

A few seconds later, Abe Jacobs was back and the assistant had hung up the antechamber extension. "So, to what do I owe the honor of this call, and by the way thank you for getting me away from that class. They're an even bigger group of idiots than you and your class when I taught at Penn State."

Abe Jacobs had been Mercer's academic advisor during his graduate work at Penn State, and Mercer had continued to seek his former professor's advice in the years since school. They rarely saw each other now, but the tight bond between master teacher and star student had not dimmed.

"Abe, I was just in a meeting where your name came up."

"Don't tell me you're on Carnegie-Mellon's ethics board?"

"Abe, we both know your wife's leash on you is just long enough for you to roam to your classes and your lab."

"Too true."

"Well, she might be in for a surprise tonight, because you won't be home for dinner. A couple of years ago you apparently sent a research paper to the CIA."

"Hold it right there, Mercer. How did you know that? That information was top secret."

"I was told by Paul Barnes, the head of the CIA."

"Ah."

"The CIA is tracking you down right now, but it'll probably take them a few hours to find you. They think you're a metallurgist, not a geologist. I thought I'd beat them to the punch and teach Paul Barnes a lesson in humility at the same time. They want you in Washington as soon as possible with any relevant material about your paper."

"What's this all about? It was basically a theoretical paper. Without twenty years of development, what I found would be unfeasible."

"Let's just say someone may have already put in the development effort. Get to the Pittsburgh airport general aviation counter. I'll have a charter plane ready to bring you down here."

"I don't understand. How could—"

Mercer interrupted. "Abe, I'll explain on the way to the White House this evening."

He cut the connection, then called general aviation at the airport. Securing a plane and pilot for Abe maxed out two of his credit cards, but Mercer shrugged off the expense. He was keeping a running tally of what the government owed him, and the price of the chartered Lear jet wasn't even close to the repair bill for his shot-up Jaguar.

BANGKOK, THAILAND

Minister Lujian, the Chinese representative, scratched his name into the heavy book slid to him by Minister Tren of Taiwan. Lujian finished his signature with a flourish and slid the book across the burnished mahogany table to the person at his left, Ambassador Marco Quirino, the representative from the Philippines.

With each successive signature, the oppressive air in the meeting room lightened. There were murmurs from the small gallery of spectators allowed to see the ambassadors pledge their nations' consent to the document. Those in the gallery had not been privy to the weeks of frustrating delays that had plagued the Bangkok summit, but still they sensed the great accomplishment these diplomats had achieved.

The official signature book was passed to the Russian ambassador, Gennady Perchenko. A close observer could easily detect a slight rise in tension among the delegates. The wily Russian had been the reason for the past weeks of utter frustration. Then, inexplicably, this morning he announced to the delegates that he had no further comments. Because the symbolic documents for the representative's signatures had been prepared at the start of the accords, Thailand's ambassador Prem motioned that the delegates commence with the signing and the others nearly fell over themselves seconding him.

U.S. undersecretary of commerce Kenneth Donnelly leaned over toward Perchenko and whispered out of the corner of his mouth, "I sure hope you know what you've been playing at, pardner."

"Mr. Secretary, I'm not playing at anything, I simply wanted to ensure all nations' rights were explored here."

Perchenko heard America's delegate mutter, "Bullshit," under his breath, but let the comment pass. No sooner had he signed the document than a wave of applause rippled through the room. Perchenko acknowledged the ovation with a smug smile and slid the book to Donnelly.

Donnelly signed with a tight smile focused on Perchenko and closed the book with a resounding snap.

A pounding rain lashed the night, the drone of the water interrupted only by the booming thunder that echoed across the city. The storm did little to cool the overpowering heat, and Perchenko found himself nearly panting as he raced from the courtyard of the Arun Wat toward the protection of the temple itself.

Kerikov's orders had been explicit; that he wait by the low stone wall that separated the Temple of Dawn from the Phraya River at eight PM, but the spy had said nothing about drowning in a torrential downpour.

Gennady dashed into the shadow of one of the four ceramic-tiled towers which surround the conical two-hundred-and-sixty-foot spire of the Wat. His suit was soaked through and his sparse hair hung limply against his pale face, a face once tight and healthy looking, but now worn by exhaustion so that bags drooped under his eyes and slabs of skin hung down his cheeks and throat.

He could hear the faint chanting of monks within the huge temple, but the storm drowned out all other sounds save his labored breathing.

"What the hell am I doing here?" he wheezed aloud.

"Not following instructions, Gennady Perchenco," Ivan Kerikov replied from the deep shadows to Perchenko's right.

Kerikov stepped into the light given off by the temple's numerous floods and spots. He seemed unaffected by the rain; his shoulders were squared against the deluge and his eyes remained open and alert. In contrast, Gennady hunched miserably, and he squinted at Kerikov as if he were a spectral apparition.

"I told you to wait by the wall." Kerikov gestured with his arm, then smiled warmly. "But under the circumstances, I understand."

Gennady relaxed a bit and smiled, but still regarded Kerikov with a wary, nervous eye.

"I assume that all went well?" Kerikov moved toward Gennady so that he stood in the protection of the temple's massive portal.

"Yes," Gennady muttered. His fear of Kerikov, oppressive yesterday in the open crowd of the Royal River Hotel's bar, was crippling now that the two were alone.

He had been terrified of Kerikov since learning of the KGB man's unlimited influence so when he had shown up the day before, Kerikov had dismissed Gennady's concerns over the missing maître d' and assured him that the time had come to wind up the Bangkok Accords. Gennady wanted to ask why the delay had been necessary in the first place, but fear froze the question in his throat. Even in the relaxed atmosphere of the open-air bar, Kerikov was the most malevolent man Gennady had ever seen.

"Relax, Gennady, it is done and you have triumphed." Kerikov slipped a sterling hip flask from his jacket pocket. "Vodka from home."

Gennady took a long pull from the flask. Even warm, the vodka went down his throat with the smoothness of silk. Kerikov motioned for Gennady to take another drink, and he did so gratefully.

"Tell me, were you able to insert my amendment into the accords?"

"Yes, that was done weeks ago. It was simple, really. I've had more difficulty in actually delaying the signing ceremony. I've made some promises to the Taiwanese ambassador that may be out of my bounds."

"Yes, yes," Kerikov said dismissively. "You had no trouble with my amendment, though?"

"The wording had to be changed some to accommodate the American, Donnelly, but they all agreed to it."

"Changed?" There was no panic in Kerikov's voice, but its pitch had raised slightly. "How?"

"I thought you'd ask, so I brought that section of the accords with me." Perchenko pulled a sheet of paper from within his jacket and read aloud:

> *No sovereign nation has the right to claim additional land created through volcanism or coral buildup or any other natural process, i.e. not created by man, not within a two-hundred-mile line radiating from that sovereign nation's territory. Any land created in this fashion is open to exploration and exploitation by any nation or other party which lays upon it first rights as laid down in Article 231 of this treaty. All contentions for said lands are to be settled by the World Court in The Hague.*

"Donnelly wanted that last bit about the World Court in Holland." Gennady took another swallow of vodka, waiting for a reaction from Kerikov.

Kerikov thought for a few seconds, letting Perchenko's words soak in, then decided that the diplomat had followed close enough to the original wording. Thanks to that single amendment, Kerikov could turn over the volcano to the Korean consortium without any fear of international recriminations. The United States and Russia had just signed away any title to the volcano and its unimaginable wealth.

Kerikov did not betray his emotions to Perchenko when he spoke. "This is acceptable. Come, I have a boat waiting in the river; we will celebrate your success."

Kerikov hurried Gennady away from the towering temple. They nearly sprinted through the driving rain toward the stone wall and the river beyond. Despite the water streaming into Gennady's eyes, he could see enough to realize that there was no boat waiting at the quay. He had just turned to question the KGB man when Kerikov struck.

Kerikov moved with the speed of a mamba, smashing a short truncheon over Gennady's head. Blood sprang from the wound over his left eye, mingled with the falling rain, and ran down Perchenko's face in a pink sheet.

The diplomat crumpled to the ground in an untidy heap. Kerikov easily dragged Gennady to the low stone wall; the river beyond was as black as an oil slick. Hidden in some shrubs near the wall was a large plastic ice chest. Beside it were two large cement blocks connected by a chain. The chain was wrapped in soft cloth and its two ends were joined not by a padlock, but rather by the thick chunk of ice that nestled in the cooler.

Kerikov rubbed the falling water from his eyes. On a night like this he didn't have to fear discovery by a casual stroller, but there was always a chance that a monk might come to the river to make an offering. He hoisted Gennady's still-unconscious body onto the low wall; the diplomat's breathing was shallow but even. Good.

After lifting the two cement blocks and the ice chest onto the wall, Kerikov slung the chain around Perchenko's neck. He had to hurry—the ice was melting faster than he'd anticipated. Kerikov heaved the loyal ambassador into the turgid water. The dark river swallowed Perchenko with a minimal splash, the cement blocks dragging him quickly toward the bottom.

Kerikov threw the cooler in also and watched as it was washed away by the river's subtle current, then started back to his hotel, shoulders hunched against the biting rain. He could imagine the police report when the body was finally discovered. Perchenko had been out celebrating the conclusion of his meetings; the alcohol in his system would show he wasn't drunk but certainly tipsy. He had slipped in the rain near the river, smashed his head against the stone wall, and fallen in.

There would be no indication of foul play because the padding around the chain would leave no marks around his throat and the chain that anchored him to the muddy bottom while he drowned would have vanished. The ice that held it together would melt in about ten minutes and then Perchenko's lifeless body would simply float free.

An hour later, Kerikov was seated in the living room of his hotel suite, showered and dressed in a conservative suit with a Scotch in his hand. He could hear the rain pelting the patio just outside the curtained French doors. The lighting in the elegant room was muted except for the lamp over the couch, which shone brightly on the papers spread across the coffee table. Kerikov had gone over them a dozen times in the past few days and felt he could recite them by heart. They were his ticket to a future outside Russia, a future that he had barely dreamed of.

The ice in the glass tinkled delicately as he took a sip. He placed the glass exactly onto its condensation ring on the glass-topped table and picked up a sheet of paper at random. It was the assay values of the mineral compiled by Dr. Borodin in his survey runs over the past few months. The figures were staggering. In one ton of mined volcanic material, eight pounds of usable ore were present. Processed, those eight pounds would produce about one pound of high-grade metal with all its extraordinary properties. By comparison, Borodin had explained that in open-pit diamond mining, 250 tons of overburden had to be removed per carat of diamond recovered, a ratio of one billion to one.

Kerikov selected another sheet of paper. This one was Borodin's plan for the actual mining of the mineral. A ship fitted with a huge cycloidal pump would be stationed near a less active vent of the volcano. A tungsten steel tube would be lowered into the vent and the pump turned on. Lava would be drawn directly from the volcano into the ship, where it would be cooled and systematically broken up into workable chunks, which would be off-loaded onto waiting ore carriers for refinement at a land-based smelter. The only real cost in the mining operation was the pump ship and since selling the idea to the Koreans, they had already had the ship built in Pusan.

There was a knock at the door. Kerikov stacked the papers neatly, took another sip of Scotch, and went to answer it. Two young Orientals stood there, each holding a bulky suitcase. He let them in without a word.

The Koreans opened the suitcases, revealing a daunting mass of electronics. They hurriedly set up the equipment: camera, monitor, and computerized transceiver. One man placed a small collapsible dish antenna on the teak railing of the patio. From the street seventy feet below, the steel mesh dish was invisible.

Once the equipment was set up, one of the young men began typing commands. The machines beeped and whirred and a test pattern appeared on the color monitor. The other man held a cardboard card in front of the camera. In Pusan, the image of that second test pattern filled the screen of a huge wall-mounted high-definition television. The two technicians nodded to each other and retreated from the room. An instant later the test pattern vanished from the monitor and was replaced by a view of a beautiful room.

Kerikov sat on the couch in front of the cyclops eye of the minicam. On the monitor, nine aged gentlemen were seated around a black lacquer table. None of them was under seventy years of age, yet their dark eyes were all alert and steady. Each man's face was deeply lined and there was not a single dark hair to be seen. Behind the men hung a red tapestry chronicling Genghis Khan's conquest of Asia, flanked by two huge terra-cotta vases.

Kerikov nodded slightly to show respect to the nine heads of Hydra Consolidated. In turn, the men merely dipped their eyes for a moment. That piece of Eastern nonsense complete, Kerikov spoke. "Good evening, gentlemen."

"Good evening to you, Mr. Kerikov." The satellite feed scrambled their voices and automatically translated from Korean into Russian and vice versa. The system worked well enough, as long as their sentences were not filled with enigmatic phrases. Way Hue Dong spoke for the syndicate, as he had during all their earlier negotiations. "I trust that this method of meeting is agreeable."

"I am ready now to commit to our agreed-upon proposal."

"We would like to know why the delay was necessary?" The electronics masked the annoyance in Way's voice, but the question made his emotions clear.

"It was needed, I assure you, gentlemen." Kerikov knew that a placating smile would be lost on these men, so he refrained. "When you see the location of the mineral deposit, you will understand that significant steps were needed to ensure its safety."

"I trust that our future activities will not be disturbed?"

"No, they will not," Kerikov responded hurriedly. With the Americans and Russians' hands tied by the Bangkok Accords, only Takahiro Ohnishi presented any obstacle, and by the time the Koreans reached the volcano, Ohnishi would be eliminated.

Dealing with the race-crazed billionaire was a necessary hazard during the final play of Vulcan's Forge. Ohnishi had been programmed to attempt his break away from the United States, and up until the last possible moment, Kerikov had needed him. But now the mineral wealth lay beyond America's control—and beyond Ohnishi's, if he ever succeeded in his bid for independence.

"Then all is in order?" Way asked, snapping Kerikov's attention back to the present.

"Yes, I am ready to transmit the final data to you now." Kerikov hid the tension that tightened his stomach.

"And we are ready to give you the account number." Kerikov could see Way's lips moving long before the computer's sterilized voice could be heard. "As a sign of good faith we will transmit first."

Way nodded to an off-camera assistant. An instant later the teletype attached to the transceiver began to pound away. Kerikov made it a point to keep his eyes glued to the camera. To look toward the teletype would be a major loss of face.

When it stopped, Kerikov fed several sheets of paper into a portable fax machine attached to the satellite up-link. These pages included the latest assay and elevation reports and gave the exact location of Dr. Borodin's island.

Kerikov saw that Way's eyes were locked on someone outside the camera's field of vision, so he took a moment to scan the teletype. One hundred million American dollars had just been transferred to the National Cayman Bank in the Caribbean. The transfer number and the account number were at the bottom of the page.

Way Hue Dong received an acknowledgment from some technician out of view and turned back to the camera. "The information seems legitimate, Mr. Kerikov. I believe now I know why there was a delay and I applaud your audacity.

"You must forgive me, sir," Way continued, "but there is a restraint order on the money. You cannot touch it until I send the bank another set of code numbers."

Way displayed no emotion as he revealed his double-cross. "Once my engineers are on-station and prove what you have told us, the money will be released into your care."

Kerikov listened and could barely contain his rage.

Way added, "I'm sure you understand that we must protect this large amount of money from fraud. Not that you are suspect. Once the value of this new mineral is established I will send the new code and the money will be yours. Good evening, Mr. Kerikov."

The monitor went blank. In Kerikov's hotel suite, the camera continued to record and transmit, so the nine Koreans saw Kerikov pound his foot through the monitor screen and then begin attacking the video transceiver. The image faded when Kerikov fired a roundhouse kick at the camera and sent it slamming into a wall.

"Those motherfucking bastards," Kerikov ranted once he could control himself enough to speak. "Those piss-drinking shit eaters."

Kerikov fumed for about ten minutes, dredging up curses he hadn't used since Afghanistan. When he finally calmed, he finished the diluted Scotch in his glass and then drank right from the bottle, the raw spirit singeing his stomach when it hit.

Somehow the Koreans had figured out that he was acting outside his own government's authority, that the hundred million dollars was destined for Kerikov himself and not the Russian State Treasury. Knowing that they wouldn't garner any government wrath, they could delay the transfer of money indefinitely while they reaped the benefits of Borodin's volcano. Without an armed force to back him, Kerikov would be powerless to stop them.

He laughed to himself amid the wreckage of the computer equipment. He admitted that he had been outsmarted. Once his laughter subsided, Kerikov's eyes gleamed with an unholy fire. There was no way that he would allow those Korean bastards to double-cross him when he still had an ace up his sleeve.

THE WHITE HOUSE

Paul Barnes, nearly cowered in his chair in front of the President, as if the supple leather would shield him from the chief executives's scathing censure. The President, usually a level-headed man, was furious. The CIA director had failed to find Dr. Jacobs.

"Sir, that report came across my desk years ago," Barnes said lamely.

"You are the head of the most powerful spy network in the world and you can't find a man who is no more than two hundred miles from Washington."

The President's intercom chimed. "Yes?" he responded.

"Sir, the others are back."

"Thanks, Joy. Send them in." The President turned back to Barnes. "We'll continue this conversation later."

Dick Henna and Admiral Morrison filed into the Oval Office. They were subdued, their faces drawn and ashen. Henna helped himself to a slug of Scotch.

"Where's Dr. Mercer?" the President asked.

"He'll probably be along in a few minutes," Henna said. "Should we wait for him?"

"No, we can't afford the time," the President replied slowly. "Dick, what's the latest from Hawaii?"

"I'm afraid I don't have much to report, sir. There's been no further communication from Ohnishi. I've got some agents keeping his estate under long-range surveillance, but they haven't reported anything suspicious. Our phone taps have turned up nothing, but I doubt that any sensitive conversations would go over unscrambled land lines."

"Have you found a tie-in between Ohnishi and Mayor Takamora?"

"Takamora went to Ohnishi's mansion last night, but has not left as of an hour ago. We assume that they are working together on this coup attempt. As near as we can figure, Takamora will be the front man, given his popularity in the islands, while Ohnishi plays the role of kingmaker."

"What have you got, Tom?"

Morrison cleared his throat. "Well, sir, I've been in contact with the base commander at Pearl. He reports that there's a fairly good-sized mob, maybe three hundred or so, on MacArthur Boulevard, just outside the base's main entrance. They don't appear to be armed, but he also reports that the National Guard, which was called out a few hours ago, seems to be part of the mob.

"I had some records pulled from the Pentagon files on Hawaiian National Guard enlistments. In the past couple of years a disproportionate number of applications have been rejected, nearly all white, black, and hispanic. In the past three years, eighty-six percent of the new members of the National Guard are of Japanese ancestry. Given the situation, I'd say Takamora has built himself a private army right under our noses."

"Have you been working on some options in case they do try to pull this off?" The President's cool blue eyes scanned the room, waiting for responses.

"Well," Admiral Morrison started after a pause, "we have the carrier *Kitty Hawk* and the amphibious assault ship *Inchon* on station, well within striking distance of Hawaii. Pearl Harbor is on full alert, although they're bottled up per your order. If Ohnishi tries to take the islands by force, we can just as easily take them back again. His mobs and guard troops can't stand up to what we can throw at them."

"Ordering our troops to fire on American citizens is not an option." Anguish etched the President's handsome features. "Goddamn it. I control the best trained and best equipped fighting machine ever built and it's fucking useless to me."

The men seated around the office watched the President's pain stoically, each man thankful that they did not sit behind that desk.

Admiral Morrison cleared his throat again. "A precise surgical air strike against Ohnishi's house would neutralize the problem. Cut off the head and the snake dies, so to speak."

"How do I explain that to the people of Hawaii? They revere him. Christ, he donates something like twenty million dollars a year to Hawaiian charities. If we killed him, we'd touch off a grassroots revolution."

"What about a commando raid of some sort?" Paul Barnes suggested. "And then tell the people about the Russian involvement. Make a clean breast of it and put Ohnishi on trial."

Henna gave the answer to that. "Our intelligence reports Ohnishi's house is heavily guarded. A raid would turn into a pitched battle. The furor over something like that would be ten times worse than the Waco fiasco back in 1993. I doubt the administration could survive, given the current polls. No offense, sir."

"None taken," the President said gloomily.

For the next hour, the men in the Oval Office batted around ideas, but each option they debated was rejected.

All of them ended with the same result, the end of the administration.

"Maybe that is the only way," the President mused.

The intercom buzzed and Joy Craig announced that Mercer had finally arrived, with a guest.

When Mercer introduced the stooped Dr. Abraham Jacobs, the President shot a brutal glare at Barnes, and Henna laughed delightedly.

"Dr. Mercer, when your contract's up at the USGS, the FBI would love to have you."

"I just can't see myself as one of your fair-haired boys, Mr. Henna. I don't take orders very well."

"Dr. Jacobs, have you been told anything?" the President interrupted.

Jacobs, still a little stunned by the men in the room, merely nodded.

Seeing his old teacher's discomfort, Mercer came to the rescue. "I told him that he was needed here because of the paper he presented to the CIA a few years ago."

"Yes, that is correct." Jacobs had found his voice, but sweat still gleamed on his wide bald head.

"Would you care to elaborate on that paper?" the President prompted.

After a preamble of coughs, throat clearing, and mumbles, Jacobs began. "Eight years ago, I was invited by the White Sands Testing Center to do some analysis on mineral samples from their 1946 Bikini tests. The samples had lain neglected in an old storage shed that was being demolished, so the White Sands people contacted a number of independent researchers across the country. They had something like eighteen thousand mineral samples in that shed, dating back to the early 1940s." Jacobs's voice was now sure and firm, confident of his subject.

"Of the groups of samples I agreed to assay for them, one was a collection of rocks, about twelve pounds worth, recovered from the seafloor around Bikini Atoll after the second test, the one where the bomb was detonated underwater. After some initial work, my interest was piqued and I requested all the data from the original tests conducted on soil, rock, and water samples collected from Bikini in 1946. For the next few months I researched twelve thousand pages of documents.

"After this, I realized only one small sample had any potential value, a two-pound chunk of rock taken directly from the epicenter of the explosion. It had been a ballast stone from the LSM–60, the ship under which the bomb was suspended. It was truly a miracle that the rock wasn't atomized by the blast. Or so I thought."

That phrase made the men in the room lean a little further forward in their seats.

"The ballast rock consisted mostly of vanadium ore, a surprising fact since vanadium is mainly found in North and South America and in parts of Africa. How it got to be ballast on a ship in the Pacific is one of those bizarre quirks of war, I suppose.

"Anyway, for those who don't know, vanadium is used to strengthen steel for use in precision machine tools and other high-stress jobs, so it is very tough. That might have explained why it hadn't vaporized, but it didn't seem likely. I crushed the sample and ran it through a spectrometer to see what other elements occurred in the rock.

"The standard stuff, like mica, I discounted, but I found something interesting. Bonded to the vanadium were traces of a metal alloy. At first, I thought the metal was pure vanadium, extracted from the ore because of the heat of the explosion. But when I tested my theory, I found I couldn't have been more wrong.

"The metal was something completely new. Something I couldn't explain. I crushed the rest of the samples given to me by White Sands and found even more of this new metal, about twenty grams in all. Not very much, but enough to continue my research.

"Have any of you gentlemen ever heard of invar?"

Mercer was the only person in the room not to reply

with a blank stare. "Yes, it's an alloy of thirty-six percent nickel, traces of manganese, silicon, and carbon, and the rest is iron."

"A-plus to my star student. It was developed by Nobel Prize–winner Charles Guillaume. Its principle characteristic is a mini-mal heat expansion, about seven ten-millionths of an inch per degree Fahrenheit of temperature increase. The incredible temperature of the blast, one hundred thousand degrees or more made me think of invar during my tests, and I wondered if the two metals had similar properties. I heated my samples. At seven thousand degrees the metal didn't expand at all, and at twelve thousand the change was measured in angstroms."

The technical language was beginning to lose Jacobs's audience, but he seemed not to notice.

"I continued applying heat, but I never could find the metal's melting point."

Mercer had a sly smile on his face; he thought he knew where the scientist's discussion was heading. Yet his expression changed to one of astonishment when Jacobs made his next revelation.

"My next test was with electricity. I ran one millijoule of electricity through the sample and created an unidirectional magnetic field of about six thousand gauss."

"Jesus," Mercer exclaimed.

"I don't understand." The President voiced the incomprehension on everyone's face.

"Mr. President, had I been wearing a steel watch, that magnetic field would have stripped it from my wrist at a distance of ten feet." Now everyone looked astonished.

"After that experiment, I reconfigured the sample so it would create a closed loop field and then I put the power to it, so to speak. I was able to sustain a field of eighty million kilogauss for seventeen seconds before an equipment short shut me down."

"The equipment failed, not the sample," said Mercer,

again the only one to grasp Jacobs' dissertation.

"Heat buildup melted the conductor wires despite the liquid oxygen cooling, but I hadn't reached the magnetic saturation or Curie points of the sample. The Curie point is where heat arrests magnetism. The Curie point of cobalt is around sixteen hundred degrees centigrade, the highest known until my work. My experiment failed when the wires melted, at about seven thousand degrees centigrade. At the time, the magnetic pressure within the field was in the neighborhood of forty thousand tons per square inch.

"You must remember that this really wasn't my area of expertise, so I didn't have the proper equipment to continue experimenting, but I'm sure that this new element could generate a strong enough field to create a magnetic well."

"A magnetic well?"

"It's something like a black hole, but using magnetism rather than gravity. The field within the well is strong enough to bend light, and time would slow as you neared its event horizon."

"Are you saying that this stuff can be used to make some sort of time machine?"

"Eventually, yes, Admiral Morrison, though it would take years to develop that. But bikinium has many applications in the here and now. When I discovered its strategic importance I immediately contacted the government. I'd done some consulting for the Pentagon, so I turned over my findings to the same people I'd dealt with before. A few months later I was told to drop the whole thing and have barely thought about it since then."

"Bikinium?"

"That is what I called the new metal. I considered naming it after myself, but calling it jacobinium just sounded too ridiculous." Jacobs smiled at his little joke.

"What are some of those uses?" the President prompted.

"Mr. President, the metal I have just described has

more uses in defense, aerospace, and power production than I could possibly name.''

''I don't understand.''

''The greatest challenges currently facing many leading high-tech corporations are the limitations placed upon them by the materials with which they work. They have the ideas and techniques to produce wondrous inventions. Unfortunately, they have nothing to build them with. Technological leaps must wait for materials to catch up.

''Think about the weight savings in automobiles when ceramic engines become a reality. These engines have already been designed, yet the ceramic itself cannot meet the strength requirements for internal combustion. Do you understand?''

''I think so.''

''I'll give you some of bikinium's more exotic applications to existing ideas: thermal and magnetic containment for fusion reactors, a way to channel nuclear blasts for propulsion of deep-space vehicles, desktop supercolliders, endless charge electric cars or supersonic maglev trains that don't need superconductivity. Anything that uses magnetic power or is limited by thermal friction could be made thousands of times more efficient.''

''I see your point.''

''I've saved the best for last, Mr. President.'' Jacobs's dark eyes shone with feverish excitement. ''The free lunch.''

''Excuse me.''

''It's a term used by physicists to describe a system that creates more energy than it requires. Einsteinian theory says that it's impossible due to conservation of mass and energy, but man has been searching for one anyway. Sort of a physicist's Holy Grail.''

''A modern power-producing plant burns coal or oil or splits atoms to release the energy stored within, correct?''

The men in the room nodded attentively.

"Bikinium, used in the dynamos of an electric generator, would create a much stronger electrical field than the amount of power put into it."

"I'm sorry, you've lost me again."

"An electric motor and an electric generator are basically the same machine. Add electricity to a motor and it spins around. Add spin to a generator and it creates electricity. Each machine transforms energy from mechanical to electrical or vice versa."

"Yes."

"Because of bikinium's abnormal magnetic properties, during that transformation more energy would be released than was first introduced."

"You're neglecting the energy put into the system by the initial nuclear blast," Mercer pointed out. "In fact, you would still remain within the laws of the conservation of mass and energy."

"Don't be a smart ass," Abe chided as if they were back in the classroom.

Dick Henna put into words what the rest of the men in the room were thinking.

"Dr. Jacobs, you're describing an unlimited power source."

"Yes, that's right." Jacobs looked smug.

"Dr. Jacobs," the President's tone was respectful, "how would you go about creating bikinium in useful amounts?"

"Well, to answer that, you have to know how bikinium was formed in the first place and even my findings are only theory. I researched all the mineral samples taken from nuclear detonations in New Mexico, going back to the original Los Alamos test, and found no trace of it, so the effect must have something to do with water, that much I am certain. I began to search for other dissimilarities between the land tests and the one conducted underwater.

"I found no traces of vanadium ore at any test site other than the 1946 Bikini test. I could conclude that the vanadium must act as a catalyst or possibly a host in the formation of this new metal. Furthermore, it is known that the neutrons released after a nuclear blast can be absorbed by any sodium in the area. It is my belief that all of the neutrons from the Bikini test were absorbed by the sodium in the surrounding seawater.

"Another dissimilarity between the two is the period of cooling. The seawater at Bikini cooled the test site much faster than those tests conducted on land. There is a strong possibility that rapid cooling also aids in the formation of bikinium. I also theorize that pressure may be a factor in its creation. Of course, there is no way to test any of my assumptions.

"But to create it again, I would detonate an atomic bomb in the seas near a vanadium deposit."

"Abe," Mercer turned to Jacobs, "is there anyone who might have stumbled onto this before you?"

"No one at all," Jacobs replied with confidence. "Though there were some ore samples missing from White Sands, I don't think anyone in the world could have come up with this."

"Are you sure?" Mercer persisted.

"Yes, quite. Only the Soviet Union and China have done the kind of test we conducted at Bikini. The Chinese don't have scientists of high enough caliber to find bikinium, and the only one in the Soviet Union that I've heard about testing exotic metals like this died years ago."

"When?" Mercer snapped.

"In the 1960s, I believe. He had published some brilliant articles about the changes in metals after nuclear tests, but his work centered mostly on the effects on the armor of tanks and ships. His name was Borodin, Pytor Borodin."

"Oh, Jesus," Mercer moaned. "Do we have those photos yet from the spy plane?"

Paul Barnes slid the 8 × 10s from a thin envelope and placed them on the President's desk. Their colors were phantasmagorical: fuchsia, teal, blinding white, indigo blue, vibrant yellow. They created a concentric pattern on the photos, each color ringing another so that the image looked like a distorted bull's-eye. At the bottom of each photograph was printed the time, location, and altitude of each shot. Mercer couldn't help but notice the shots were taken above one hundred and fifty thousand feet, miles above the earth's atmosphere. He was very impressed with the new SR-1 Wraith.

He wondered idly, as he waited his turn to closely study the photos, why all the men crowded around the desk to see them. Apart from Barnes, he doubted any of them had ever seen an infrared photo of this type. He passed it off as the same kind of curiosity that caused people to stare into construction pits.

Mercer looked at the near identical photos until his eyes found the one he wanted. Longitude and latitude lines had been etched onto the film by the computer that controlled the camera.

Mercer muttered something under his breath.

"What was that?"

"The Bangkok Accords," his voice barely a whisper in the quiet room. "I said, the Bangkok Accords."

"What is . . ."

"Meetings taking place right now that may just give away the greatest discovery of this or any century," Mercer said, anticipating the question. "Abe, did this Dr. Borodin have any children?"

"I can't see how that—"

"Answer me, goddamn it." The vehemence in Mercer's voice made Jacobs pale.

"Yes, one son."

"We've been had." Mercer leaned away from the photographs, his eyes betraying respect for the master of the plan.

"What do you mean?"

"Dr. Borodin is alive and well, gentlemen, and he beat us to the punch by forty years." Mercer spoke slowly as his brain began unraveling the four-decade-old mystery. "Bear with me for a few minutes.

"Let's assume that this Borodin somehow discovers the existence of bikinium back in the early fifties and wants to create his own. He persuades the Russians to give him an atomic bomb. Remember, those things were in short supply back then, so his project must have gotten a high priority.

"Then he fills an ore carrier with high-grade vanadium ore, sails her to a predetermined location near volcanic activity, and sinks her, along with the bomb. Once she settles on the ocean floor he touches off the nuke. Later, he fakes his own death, so there wouldn't ever be any connection to him."

"Is there any record of a lost ore carrier?" Abe asked.

"*Grandam Phoenix*, missing since May 23, 1954," Mercer replied sharply. "She was listed as running ballast from Kobe, Japan, to the States, but Christ only knew what she carried."

Mercer's voice trailed off, his eyes glazed for a second and then snapped back into focus. His voice was firm, commanding. "I need a phone, now."

In a moment that Mercer would remember for the rest of his life, the President of the United States obeyed and handed him the receiver to one of the telephones on his desk. Mercer gave the White House operator a number and waited patiently for the connection, oblivious of the stares.

"Berkowitz, Saulman . . ."

Mercer cut off the secretary. "Skip it, give me Dave Saulman right away; this is an emergency."

The secretary was used to emergencies in the uncontrollable world of ocean commerce and cut in on Saulman while he was on another line.

"Saulman here," the old lawyer answered quickly.

"Dave, it's Mercer."

"Oh, you finally have an answer for me?"

Mercer knew that Saulman was asking about the trivia

question at the bottom of the faxes he had received two days earlier. Without thinking, Mercer replied, "The captain of the *Amoco Cadiz* was Pasquale Bardari."

"You son of a bitch."

"Dave, I need to know who owned the *Grandam Phoenix*."

"Never heard of her."

"She was on the list you sent me of the vessels that disappeared north of Hawaii."

"Oh, right." Recognition lightened Saulman's voice. "Might take me a couple days to find. I'm swamped in work right now on a towing contract for an Exxon tanker that's drifting off Namibia. The fucking Dutch tugs are holding out for Lloyd's Open and the value of that tanker and cargo is somewhere around one hundred and thirty million dollars."

"Not to name drop," Mercer said with a fiendish smile, "but I'm sitting with the President, the chairman of the Joint Chiefs, and the heads of the FBI and CIA, and we're all waiting for your answer."

There was a moment's silence from the other end of the phone. Mercer marveled that there was no static on the President's phone line. Must be nice, he thought.

"You're not kidding, are you?"

"Want to talk to one of them?"

"No. It'll take a few minutes to get the info. Do you want me to call back?"

"I don't think AT&T cares how long the President is on the phone, I'll hold."

"What's this all about?" the President asked, not really caring that Mercer was now sitting on the corner of his desk.

"Conclusive evidence," replied Mercer enigmatically.

The President exchanged glances with the men around the room, but none of them spoke. They waited five long minutes, clearing throats, shuffling feet, and rattling papers, but their gaze never left Mercer.

"I've got it." Saulman was breathless. "The *Grandam Phoenix* was owned by Ocean Freight and Cargo." Saulman continued to speak, but Mercer was already hanging up the phone.

"The ore carrier that sank in 1954 and the ship that rescued Tish Talbot have the same owners, Ocean Freight and Cargo, the same company I broke into last night."

"The ones suspected of being a front for the KGB?"

"Right."

"You said something about the ore carrier being sunk over a volcanic area, why?" Henna asked.

"Correct me if I'm wrong, Abe, but the deeper the explosion and the more water pressure, the purer the bikinium."

Abe Jacobs nodded, then added, "That's just my theory, though."

"Well, in 1954, there was no way to mine any minerals from even a few hundred feet underwater and we're talking depths in the thousands. Even today, the Frasch process of using superheated water for mining can't work any deeper than two hundred feet.

"Dr. Borodin borrowed a line from the Koran and, like Muhammad, had the mountain come to him. By setting off the blast over a volcanic area, he would trigger an eruption, and the lava would transport the bikinium to the surface."

"Jesus, that would work," Jacobs said, respect lowering his voice. "I never would have even considered it."

"But volcanoes take millions of years to grow," the President pointed out.

"Normal geologic processes are that slow," Mercer agreed. "But volcanoes, like earthquakes, are very dynamic. A volcano in Paricutin, Mexico, grew out of a farmer's field beginning in the summer of 1943. After the first week, the field was a five-hundred-foot-tall mountain and growing by the second. Borodin's volcano has had more than enough time to reach the surface.''

"What do we do now?" The President locked eyes with each man in the room.

"The first step is to stop the Bangkok Accords," Mercer replied.

"What does that have—"

"Mr. Henna, if you look at this photo, you'll see that the center of Borodin's volcano lies directly atop Hawaii's two-hundred-mile limit. I'm willing to bet that Borodin's there now, studying the epicenter of the volcano. As soon as he knows it'll surface outside that limit, he'll contact the Russian ambassador at the meeting in Thailand and have him sign the treaty.''

"That would make the volcano anyone's property, right?" Admiral Morrison asked.

"The first one to spot it, gets it."

"What happens if the volcano is within that line?"

No one had an answer for Dr. Jacobs. Actually they all knew the answer, but no one was brave enough to put it into words. Mercer looked at the doctor and saw that his old teacher had asked the question because he really didn't know.

"Then we go to war, Abe."

As soon as the word was said everyone in the room started speaking at once, clamoring to be heard. The President snapped them to silence by slapping his palm against his desk, though when he spoke, his voice was calm.

"Dr. Mercer is right. We can't allow such a priceless commodity to belong to anyone but the United States. Now that we know the stakes, Takahiro Ohnishi's threats take on a much more ominous dimension. We now know why he's doing it. If the volcano does crest within Hawaii's two-hundred-mile limit, and his coup is successful, he can sell off possibly the most valuable commodity on earth. I just can't believe that the Soviets are still mixed up in this. Our relations with them have never been better.''

Mercer noted the President was now calling the old foe by their old name. No longer were they the Commonwealth of Independent States. Once again they were the Soviets.

"Paul, use everything at your disposal to find out about Pytor Borodin—who he used to work for before he disappeared, and what happened to his old bosses. Dick, keep digging at Ohnishi. I want to know why he turned traitor."

"I've got something on that already." Henna fumbled through his briefcase. "Ah, here it is. Both his parents were born in Japan and immigrated to the States in the 1930s. During the Second World War they were sent to one of the interment camps in California, and both died there, his mother on June 13, 1942, and his father just six months afterward. Ohnishi was raised by an aunt and uncle who also spent the war in the camps. His uncle was on file at the bureau for anti-American protests and petitions. He had two arrests: one for trying to break into Pearl Harbor and the other for assaulting a police officer at a pro-Japanese rally in Hawaii during the summer of 1958. Seems he didn't like the idea of statehood.

"I saw a copy of one of the pamphlets he printed. It's full of anti-American propaganda and urged Hawaii's Japanese residents, then and now the majority on the islands, to fight the statehood referendum and become an independent nation loyal to Japan.

"Ohnishi's uncle committed suicide right after Hawaii was admitted into the Union in March of 1959. There is no record that Ohnishi shared his uncle's radical politics, but there's no record that he didn't, either." Henna looked up from his notes.

"Thanks, Dick. I think that's our answer." Knowing the answer did not alleviate the problem. The President straightened his shoulders and when he spoke his voice was like steel. "I don't know what Ohnishi's next move will be, but I want a detailed battle plan drawn up, not only for Hawaii but also for this new volcano. I don't know what legal right, if any, we will have to this new island, but there's no way we're not going to win. If need be, I'll have the goddamn thing nuked. Now, if you gentlemen will excuse me, I have to call our diplomats in Bangkok and stop them from signing that treaty." The men got up to leave. "I want hourly reports from all of you. Dr. Mercer, please make yourself available in case you're needed again. Dr. Jacobs, thank you. We'll see that you have a safe trip home."

Mercer said farewell to Jacobs, gave his home number to Joy Craig, and collected Tish. On the cab ride home, she pumped him for information, but Mercer remained silent. He wondered, as the cityscape passed outside the cab's filthy windows, how the President would react if he knew that his wife had just spent the afternoon with a Russian spy.

HAWAII

JAL Flight 217, a 747 jumbo jet from Tokyo, was the last plane given permission to land at Honolulu's international airport. Employees loyal to Ohnishi and Takamora had followed their instructions and sabotaged the IFR equipment and the computers that controlled the other sophisticated systems. Only those planes without enough fuel to be rerouted were allowed to land. Hawaii was now completely isolated from the outside world.

Flight 217 touched down with an acrid puff of smoke and a bark of tires. Because of the danger in landing without electronic assistance from the tower, the pilot gave himself plenty of room to make sure the craft returned to earth safely. The Pratt and Whitney turbo fans shrieked as the pilot applied reverse thrust, the tremendous airframe shuddering with their awesome power.

The three hundred and sixty passengers had no idea of the danger they had just been through. Those controlling the airport had ordered the pilot to keep his charges ignorant of any problems during the landing, in direct violation of standard safety practices.

"Welcome to Honolulu, ladies and gentlemen," the flight attendant said in Japanese. "The temperature is seventy-eight degrees and the local time is one-thirty on a cloudless afternoon. Please remain seated until the aircraft has come to a complete stop and the pilot has turned off the seatbelt sign."

Evad Lurbud had absolutely no idea what the diminutive attendant said until she repeated her announcement in English.

He was the only Westerner on the jumbo jet; the rest were Japanese tourists or businessmen, lured to the islands by the increased trade promoted by Ohnishi and Takamora during the past months.

Though Lurbud had flown across eleven time zones since leaving Egypt and had endured hours'-long layovers, one in Hong Kong and the other in Tokyo, he felt relaxed and refreshed. This last flight had lasted nearly seven hours and he had slept through six and a half of them. Before each leg of his trip, he had taken a timed sleeping pill developed by the KGB. By calibrating the doses, he could sleep a specific number of hours. The only drawback to the medication was a slight nausea, which lasted about an hour after waking.

The 747, so graceful in the sky, lumbered to the terminal like a hippopotamus, her huge wings flexing with each bump in the tarmac. Lurbud remained seated and buckled as requested rather than draw attention to himself by standing as several hurried businessmen had done. The aircraft taxied to its hardstand, the huge engines spooling down to silence. The truck-mounted stairs eased to the exits and passengers began shuffling off the Boeing.

Deplaning, Lurbud was staggered by the amount of security within the airport's customs area. Armed National Guard troops, all Orientals he noted, patrolled the area, their M–16 assault rifles slung low, their eyes never lingering on one person too long.

At the customs counter, the bored agent gave Lurbud's forged German passport a cursory glance and didn't bother with his briefcase. Lurbud relaxed once he passed customs, but became wary when two suited Orientals strode toward him through the throng of passengers.

"Passport, please," one of the two men demanded, his hand thrust out waiting for the slim booklet.

"I'm already cleared by customs," Lurbud replied politely, staining his flawless English with a German accent.

The other Oriental flashed a silver badge in a cheap vinyl covering. "Airport security. Your passport."

Lurbud fished it from inside his suit coat and handed it over. "What's this all about?"

"Routine, Mr. Schmidt," one agent said, reading through the passport. "Would you come with us?"

Lurbud followed the two security men through a set of double doors and down a well-lit flight of stairs. They passed a couple of airport employes plodding upward as Lurbud and his two minders made their way down. At the base of the stairs they turned down a long hallway to the last doorway on the left.

As he stepped over the threshold, Lurbud's instincts told him that this was an interrogation room and his being here was far from routine. In the stark room, two chairs stood behind a unitarian trestle table, with a third chair set in the center of the neutral beige carpet. The room smelled of stale cigarettes and fear.

The moment the door closed, one of the men shoved Lurbud, propelling him across the room. He exaggerated his momentum and slammed himself against the far wall, sliding to the floor with a moan.

One of the security agents walked over to Lurbud, probably intending to throw him into the chair and begin the formal interrogation of this *Gai-Jin*, foreigner. The instant the man's hand touched Lurbud's shoulder, the Russian uncoiled himself from the floor, clutching an undetectable Teflon knife in his fist. He buried the knife between the Oriental's ribs, piercing his heart.

Lurbud pulled the knife from the dying man's chest, ignoring the fountain of blood that pumped from the obscene wound, and dove across the room.

The other agent was just going for his shoulder-holstered pistol when Lurbud reached him. The impetus of Lurbud's charge threw them both against the table, the Russian's body pinning the other man. Lurbud raised the knife over his head and stabbed down viciously, slicing into skin and cartilage, severing the carotid artery of the shocked security man.

The man died hard, gasping and choking and clutching at his punctured throat. His writhing body smeared blood across the table and onto the carpet and white walls.

After the man had stilled, Lurbud cleaned his knife against his victim's suit and stashed it back in its ankle sheath. He checked himself quickly. A few red splashes of blood were invisible against the dark tropical wool of his suit. He opened the door and, seeing that the hall was empty, made his escape. At the opposite end of the hall Lurbud reentered the public part of the airport just off the main concourse.

Outside, he passed banks of beautiful tropical flowers and ponds loaded with huge goldfish. He hailed a cab and gave the driver an address in downtown Honolulu, confident that he wouldn't be followed.

Ten minutes into the cab ride his hands began to quiver and his stomach knotted up. He wished he could pass it off as a reaction to the sleeping pill he'd taken during the flight, but knew in his heart that his close brush with the authorities had shaken him. He'd been living on adrenaline his entire adult life and, like any addict, his drug of choice was beginning to wear him away.

At the Cairo airport, Lurbud had been given a sealed
envelope by an embassy courier. It had contained a briefing from Ivan Kerikov. The top sheet had outlined the
current situation in Hawaii, so Lurbud knew that Honolulu was under martial law, with a strictly enforced
eight PM curfew. It had been a calculated risk bringing
the packet into the state, but there was too much information to memorize. He read through some of it in the
taxi to distract himself from the disturbing cityscape outside the Ford's windows. The envelope contained Lurbud's final orders, names of the critical targets,
opposition strength, and codes for contacting the *John
Dory*. Lurbud assumed that Kerikov had an agent in
place near Ohnishi because the orders contained a detailed map of Ohnishi's house, and also stated that
Mayor James Takamora was already dead. Yet the KGB
master made no provisions for sparing his agent's life.
Lurbud furtively wondered if he too would be considered a loose end after Ohnishi and the mole had been
eliminated.

Although it was just midafternoon, the city seemed
nearly deserted. Only groups of National Guard troops
and armed cadres of students wandered the streets. The
citizens were hidden in their homes, fearful or expectant,
depending on their loyalty. The scene outside the cab's
windows reminded Lurbud of the time he'd spent in war-
ravaged Beirut, where religion-intoxicated youths systematically ripped the Mediterranean's most beautiful
city into minute strips of terror.

Columns of smoke lifted from numerous fires to min-
gle in a murky haze over the city. The rocky outcrop of
Diamond Head was invisible in the gloom. Near the
commercial port, thick black smoke belched from two
burning oil storage tanks, their noxious fumes reaching
Lurbud's cab many miles away. Buildings had been rid-
dled with small-arms fire and the cab passed numerous
husks of burned-out cars and buses. The area over Pearl
Harbor resembled a bee's nest, angry helicopters buzzing

in frenzied flight as federal and National Guard choppers performed a dizzying *Danse Macabre*.

After the uneasy forty-minute drive, Lurbud paid off the driver and left the taxi in one of Honolulu's worst neighborhoods. His destination was a flat-fronted, three-story edifice with a liquor store on the ground floor and apartments on the other two. The building had been bought by Department 7 when they had brought Takahiro Ohnishi into Vulcan's Forge in case they ever needed a safehouse to monitor the local situation. This was the first time that members of the operation had ever used the building.

Lurbud surveyed the decayed neighborhood, the vacant, rubble strewn lots, the peeling paint, the empty looks in the eyes of few passersby, and knew that this location had never been compromised. In the humid air, his jacket was already beginning to stick to his body.

On the top floor, he knocked twice on the stout metal door at the head of the stairs, paused, then knocked once more.

"Yes?" a voice called from within.

"United Parcel Service, I have a package for Charles Haines," Lurbud replied, beginning a recognition code he'd learned from Kerikov's packet.

"Who's it from?" The voice behind the door responded suspiciously.

"Kyle Leblanc," Lurbud finished the code, and the bolts were thrown open.

The man who'd opened the door kept his automatic pistol in view as Lurbud entered the safehouse. Only after Sergeant Dimitri Demanov spoke from across the vast room did he reholster it. "So, what have you been doing since you can no longer rape boys with heated pokers?" Demanov was referring to one of Lurbud's more effective interrogation techniques from his time working for Kerikov in Afghanistan.

"Cutting off the testicles of disrespectful sergeants," Lurbud retorted. The two men crashed together in the center of the room like sea lions, pounding each other's backs in reunion.

"How have you been, Dimitri?" Lurbud asked, smiling for the first time since killing Suleiman.

"Bored in Minsk until I got a call to meet you here," replied Demanov, kissing Lurbud in the traditional Russian way. "It is good to see you again, Evad."

"And you too, old friend."

Lurbud and Demanov had fought side by side in Afghanistan. They had shared more freezing nights and narrow escapes than either could remember.

Demanov had stayed in the field after Lurbud's promotion and ended the war as the Soviet Union's third most decorated soldier. Since that time, he had gone on to be an instructor of the Spetnez, Russia's special forces, but had recently retired to a deteriorating existence. The stout, grizzled sergeant was a warrior in the truest sense of the word.

The safe room took up the entire top floor of the building and was designed to be used as a hideout for several weeks if necessary. There were beds for a dozen people. The kitchen shelves were crammed with canned food. Several huge drums were filled with water in case the building's supply was ever cut off. Light streamed through the multiple windows, but was diffused by the layers of caked dust that made it impossible to see into the room from the street.

"I trust everyone got past customs without incident?" Lurbud asked.

"There were no problems, we all arrived before the airport was shut down," Demanov responded.

Lurbud took a moment to scrutinize the troops Demanov had brought with him. They were all former Spetnez, men more loyal to Demanov than to their Motherland. Without exception, they were the finest trained commandos the Russian army had ever produced—their instruction went much further than Gregory Brezhnicov's KGB guards in New York, who had been murdered the day before by an unknown assailant. None of the men were especially large or hulking, but there was an air of competence about them which was chilling. Their minds and bodies had been sharpened to a rapier's edge by endless training and actual combat experience.

Though they never admitted it, both the United States and Russia "lent" some of their Special Forces troops to various war-ravaged nations so the men could gain practical understanding of battlefield operations. It wouldn't shock Lurbud to learn that these men had faced an American Ranger battalion on the hills above Sarajevo just a few years earlier.

"How did you assemble such a large force so quickly?"

"Army pay isn't what it used to be, Evad. As you know, the country's full of out of work soldiers. Finding commandos in Russia is easier than finding syphilis in a whorehouse."

"Did you have time to brief them in Minsk?"

"I told them that they would be fighting with you. That was all they needed to hear."

"Do you have any doubts about them, Dimitri?"

Demanov lit a cigarette and enjoyed the first few drags before answering. "In my career, I've trained Egyptians to fight Israelis, Angolans to fight South Africans, Nicaraguans to fight Salvadorans, and a dozen other groups to fight another dozen. I knew from the beginning that I was training a surrogate Russian army to fight a surrogate American one. Each time, I'd run across an American or two, 'advisors,' toting the most sophisticated weapons in their arsenal. But those contacts were fleeting. Just once I want to face the Americans in an open fight and prove once and for all who's been pumped full of propaganda and who is the best. Now that I'm finally getting my chance, I can't think of a better group of men to back me up—and that includes you, sir."

Lurbud was impressed with Demanov's speech and his old friend's conviction. "It seems that since the last time I saw you, you've become a philosopher."

"I haven't met a soldier who wasn't one," Demanov said seriously. "So why is it that the shadowy Kerikov has paid us so handsomely to be here?"

"What were you told by him?"

"That he needed a trained commando team ready to fight in the United States as the last part of a very old operation."

"Yes and no," Lurbud said, taking a seat on one of the cots. "You are needed, but your presence here is a deviation from a very old operation. The current unrest on the islands is a direct result of Department Seven's most ambitious plan, one which almost worked. Hawaii would have become a Soviet puppet if things had gone according to plan. We're here to mop up and cut our losses."

Demanov could not hide his astonishment. "I don't understand, Evad."

"Several months ago, Department Seven approached a very wealthy and eccentric local billionaire named Takahiro Ohnishi and asked him to assist us in an operation called Vulcan's Forge. In return for his help, Kerikov promised to use Russian resources to back a coup attempt that would split Hawaii away from the rest of the United States. Of course Kerikov never planned to aid Ohnishi in any way, but his involvement was necessary. Two different options had to be left open until certain scientific data was obtained concerning a volcanic island forming north of here. Now that we have this information the coup is no longer necessary and neither is Ohnishi. Unfortunately, Ohnishi has already started his rebellion. He must be stopped."

"That's where we come in," Demanov interrupted.

"Yes. We're here to eliminate Ohnishi. For now we wait until Kerikov gets in touch. There is another aspect of this mission I didn't tell you about, a submarine monitoring the volcano to the north. Kerikov is waiting for word from them before we put our plan into action." He lied to his friend. In fact, the *John Dory* was waiting for word from him. "I'm sorry to disappoint you, Dimitri, but you won't get the chance to take on the American army, only the guards around Ohnishi's mansion."

"They're still Americans, Evad. It'll be close enough."

ARLINGTON, VIRGINIA

As soon as Tish entered the rec room of Mercer's house, she threw herself onto the leather couch with an exhausted sigh.

"You didn't talk much on the way back from the White House," she said, not looking at Mercer. "You must be exhausted. I've been asleep for most of the day, but you haven't slept in thirty-six hours.

"Closer to forty," replied Mercer from behind the bar. He was making a pot of his barely potable coffee. "Want some coffee?"

"Are you crazy?" Tish sat up and looked at him. "Go to bed; you're dead on your feet."

Mercer let the coffeemaker drip directly into a mug before sliding the glass pot under the nozzle. He was about to take a sip, thought for a moment, then poured a dram of Scotch into the cup. The first taste was sublime.

"I'm afraid it'll be a while before I sleep. We have to talk."

The tone of Mercer's voice made Tish swing her long legs from the couch and stand up. She crossed to the bar and took one of the six dark cane stools. "Is something wrong?"

"Tell me about Valery Borodin," Mercer invited nonchalantly.

"I don't know any . . ." He saw that Tish was flustered by the question.

"Tish, right now I could have you detained by the FBI for your involvement in this plot. I haven't because you're Jack Talbot's daughter, but I'm not taking bets on how long I remain silent."

"Tell me first how you know about Valery?"

"I spoke with Dr. Baker at Woods Hole."

"I remember that old busybody from Mozambique. She wanted to be everyone's den mother. Figures she would talk." Tish settled down and turned her deep blue eyes to Mercer. "What do you want to know?"

"Let me make some assumptions first. You know he was a geologist, not a marine biologist, and that he was in Mozambique for a vacation, right?"

"Yes. He swore me to secrecy about that, though. He told me he would be starting a new project soon and that his superiors had allowed him some time off before his reassignment."

"Did he tell you who his father is?"

Tish was startled by Mercer's unsettling question. "Not at first."

"Did he mention that his father had faked his own death when Valery was a boy?"

"How do you know about that?"

Mercer wasn't about to admit that he'd been guessing about Valery's candor with Tish so he covered his relief with a gruff reply. "I can't tell you that, just answer my questions."

"Valery told me that his father had supposedly died in a lab explosion when he was still a baby. Then, about a month before we met, Valery's father reentered his life, acting as if all those years had never passed.

"His father was also a brilliant geologist, like Val, and needed his son's help on some secret government project. Valery both hated his father for vanishing and loved him for returning; he was hurting bad. He would cry some nights until I thought his heart would break. He was so alone and vulnerable."

"What else did he tell you about his father or his upcoming project?"

"Not much, really. He said they would be working together, he and his father, and that he was excited and frightened."

"Did he tell you he planned to leave Russia?"

Mercer's question made Tish blanch. "How did you . . ."

"Did he tell you?"

"Yes, but he couldn't do it until the project with his father was completed."

Mercer rubbed his knuckles into his eyes, trying to push away the sleep which threatened to overwhelm him. He poured another cup of strong coffee, this time omitting the Scotch.

"Tell me what really happened the night the *Ocean Seeker* exploded."

Tish said, acting confused, "I already told you about it."

Fury edged Mercer's voice. "Let me put some things into perspective here, Tish, so you know where I'm coming from, okay?"

She had never experienced such naked anger in her life. Mercer's voice, though not raised, drilled into her, forcing her back in her bar stool.

"Your boyfriend and his father are the architects of a plot that could tear apart the very fabric of this country. It started in May of 1954 when Pytor Borodin detonated a nuclear device, triggering a volcanic chain reaction that created a new metal whose value is incalculable. Since that time, he's ruthlessly murdered everyone who came close to discovering his secret.

"Do you remember the list of ships that Dave Saulman sent me from Miami?" Tish looked like she was going to be ill as she nodded. "That is actually a list of Pytor Borodin's victims. I hope you take note that the *Ocean Seeker*, the ship that blew up around you, headed that list. Borodin is also connected with a possible coup in Hawaii that could lead to race riots in every city in America.

"Valery Borodin and his father have masterminded a plot that could leave this country wallowing in economic and social chaos while the rest of the world prospers." Mercer's mouth was twisted into a disgusted rictus, but his eyes were slate hard. "I'm not some ultra-patriot who salutes every time I see a flag, but I don't want to see our government brought to its knees either. You have a choice. Tell me what I need to know, or I call the FBI and you spend the next century or two in a penitentiary with a cellmate named Leather."

Tish was sobbing now. Mercer wanted to take her into his arms, brush the tears away, and say he was sorry, but he couldn't. He had to be cruel.

"This is fucking useless," he said disgustedly, and reached for the portable phone lying on the bar.

"Wait," Tish said meekly. "Please wait."

Mercer poured a shot of brandy into a balloon snifter and placed it in front of Tish. She sniffed back her tears and sipped the amber liquor.

"What happened the night the *Ocean Seeker* was destroyed?" he repeated harshly.

"Around midnight a man came to my cabin. I'd never seen him before. He wasn't part of the scientific team or a member of the crew."

"A stowaway?"

"He must have been. He told me that Valery had sent him."

Mercer interrupted again. "What was he—white, Oriental, black?"

"He was Oriental. Maybe thirty-five or forty years old, about your size but amazingly strong. He told me that I was in danger and had to go with him. I tried to question him, but he said there was no time, just tossed me over his shoulder and carried me up to the deck. There was an inflatable raft tied to the stern of the *Seeker*. He threw me in and jumped after me.

"About five minutes after he started rowing us away, the *Seeker* exploded. I swear I don't remember anything after that. I think he knocked me out."

"Then you never heard Russian or saw the design on the stack of the ship that rescued you?"

"That part I do remember. I must have come to as we were pulled aboard that freighter."

"Why didn't you tell me about this before?"

"I didn't want anything to spoil Valery's chances of escape, so I stayed quiet. You see, the group he was going to work for, the one headed by his father, was incredibly ruthless. He told me that everyone involved with the project was sworn to lifelong secrecy and anyone who tried to leave the group before Val's father said they could would be hunted down and killed. He told me he knew his father would never let him leave. He was bound to the old man forever, he said. But he was still determined to get away. He said his father was completely insane and what they were working on could upset the balance of power all over the world. Valery told me before he left Mozambique that he would contact me just before he escaped. I assumed that this rescue was that contact."

"That may be, but he's made contact since then too."

"When, how?" Tish asked, a trace of excitement creeping into her trembling voice.

"The telegram I received, the one I thought was from your father, must have been sent from him. Christ knows how he made the connection between us." Mercer spoke slowly at first, but as ideas correlated in his brain, he talked faster. "I was suspicious about your rescue from the *Ocean Seeker*, it seemed too pat, but now it makes sense. Valery must have ordered an agent to board the ship and save your life when he learned that the *Seeker* was headed toward the volcano with you as a member of the research staff."

Mercer stood silently behind the bar, both hands cupped around his coffee mug. His eyes had lost their focus as he stared beyond Tish at a Ken Marschall lithograph of the Hindenburg, just before she exploded over Lakehurst, New Jersey. It was one of the only pictures that Mercer had gotten around to hanging apart from those in his study.

"He plans to steal his father's work when he leaves, doesn't he? That's why he just didn't run away with you in Mozambique."

"How did you figure that out?"

"It fits with his actions so far and with the brief description you gave of his psychological state. He would want to bring something of value with him so that he could provide for the two of you. At the same time, stealing his father's work would fulfill his need for revenge against his father for abandoning him."

"You can't know that." Tish was uncomfortable by Mercer's accuracy and covered it with an accusation.

"The first reason is obvious. He's going to want to be a provider for you and a possible family, unlike his father had been to him, and that data could make the two of you quite comfortable for the rest of your lives. I'm even more familiar with the second reason.

"Remember I said that I used to live in Africa when I was younger, that I was actually born in the Congo? Well, I left there as an orphan. My parents moved to Rwanda so my father could work on opening a copper mine. They were killed during an insurrection in 1964, ambushed going to a party on the first night of the fighting. Both of them were burned alive. My nanny, a Tutsi woman, took me back to her village the next day. I lived there for a couple of months until the fighting died down, then she turned me over to a World Health Organization team, who eventually contacted my father's parents in Vermont.

"Even though my grandparents were kind and loving people, I hated being with them and I hated my real parents even more for abandoning me. I felt utterly betrayed. I remember winter nights when I'd go cross-country skiing. I'd stop in some meadow, miles away from the nearest house, and scream at them, cursing them, accusing them of leaving me on purpose. It was the loneliest time in my life.

"If I could foster that much hate against my parents who actually died, I can only imagine the hate Valery must feel toward his father for leaving him for some government project and then just as casually returning."

"How did you ever get over your parents' death?" Tish asked quietly. Mercer's story had touched her deeply.

"An old farmer overheard me one night when I was about sixteen and we talked. He was the only person I ever opened up to. When I'd finished my story, he told me I was acting stupid and if I kept it up he'd slap me around because I was upsetting his dairy cows. I guess I'd received so much sympathy before that, I saw myself as a perpetual victim. By callously saying I was stupid, he made me realize that, in fact, I was. My parents' deaths were beyond their control—it was never their choice to abandon me. Finally I could accept that." Mercer poured a shot of Scotch into his coffee, then drained the cup in three deep swallows.

Tish didn't say anything, but the tension had eased from her neck and shoulders and her blue eyes were misted and soft.

"I owe you an apology," Mercer said softly. "I thought you were part of this operation. I thought you knew all about it."

"No," Tish said quietly, "I didn't."

"Do you still love him?"

"I don't know," Tish replied haltingly. "The time Valery and I had together was the most precious in my life, but it was so long ago. Is that shallow of me?"

"That's not for me to decide," he dodged the question adroitly. He took the bar stool next to her and held her slim hands in his.

"I was in love once." Mercer spoke slowly, deliberately. "I was twenty-five years old, taking summer classes at a mining school in England. She was four years older than me, a police psychologist just getting her start in the London constabulary. We spent every moment together that we could. I would commute a hundred miles to see her in the city, and she took the maximum number of sick days she could without being kicked off the force.

"One weekend toward the end of the summer, she was seeing me off at Paddington Station. We had just talked about marriage for the first time." Mercer's voice was barely a whisper, but the force of his words carried to the far corners of the room. "My train was just pulling out from the station. Suddenly there was gunfire. A man had burst into the station and opened up with a machine pistol. I watched from the window of the accelerating train as he emptied the clip, then dropped the weapon and pulled a revolver. By then the police had begun to swarm into the station. The gunman grabbed a woman and used her a shield, the revolver screwed into her ear. It was a standoff.

"Then the woman, my possible fiancée, started talking to the gunman, trying to calm him down, get him to surrender. It was her job. Later they found that the man, an IRA terrorist, had taken so much heroin that he probably never heard a word she said. She spoke for a only a few seconds before the gunman simply pulled the trigger and then turned the gun on himself.

"I saw their bodies fall across each other just as my

car pulled out of the station. I was too numb to try to get off the train. I just sat there as we sped north. I never returned to London. I didn't even go to her funeral. . . ." Mercer's voice trailed off.

"What was her name?"

"Tory Wilks," Mercer replied evenly. "You're the first person who's ever heard that story. I finished my classes in England and came home as if nothing ever happened."

"I'm sorry."

Mercer looked at her squarely. "We never had a chance to start a life together. I told you about Tory and what I lost because you at least deserve a chance. You once loved Valery Borodin and lost him because of circumstances out of your control." Mercer's voice firmed. "I'm going to make sure you have a fair shot at making it work."

"I don't understand."

"It's simple." Mercer smiled warmly, the wrenching emotions of a few moments earlier safely tucked back where they belonged. Again he was his normal sardonic self. "I'm going to help him escape."

"How? You don't know where he is."

"Don't I, though?" Mercer raised a mocking eyebrow. "I happen to know down to the inch where he is at this very moment."

"Where?" Excitement raised Tish's voice an octave.

"All in good time," Mercer replied vaguely. "I've got some things to figure out first. Why don't you take that nap you wanted?"

Tish saw that she could get nothing further out of him, so she went to the couch. She looked over at Mercer and saw he was already scratching away at a note pad with a fountain pen. She tucked the *Normandie* lap robe up around her chin, and for the first time in a long time, started considering a real life with Valery.

Ten minutes later, Tish sat up suddenly. "Mercer?"

He looked up from the pad. His normally dark complexion was drained and his wide set eyes were narrowed by exhaustion.

"I was thinking—Valery took a risk to have me rescued from the *Ocean Seeker* and put you in contact with me, right? Well, who tried to kill me in the hospital?"

Mercer stared at her for a moment, his weary mind grinding away at her question. He tore the top sheet of paper from the pad, crumpled it up, and tossed it into the plastic trash can behind the bar. "Back to the drawing board."

Several hours later, as the sun ambered the room with its dying rays, Mercer finally put down his pen, drank the last sip of his second pot of coffee and stood for a stretch. He had written twelve pages of notes and made eighteen phone calls. Tish was still asleep on the couch.

Mercer knuckled the kinks out of his lower back and squeezed his eyes tight, trying to clear his sleep-deprived brain. The caffeine he had drunk left him feeling weak and with a pounding headache. He pulled Dick Henna's card from his wallet and dialed his office number. Henna himself answered the phone.

"Mr. Henna, it's Philip Mercer."

"Do you have anything new?" Mercer liked the squat director for his bluntness.

"I need to get to Hawaii," Mercer stated flatly.

"I'm afraid that's impossible. Two hours ago all communications from the islands stopped, no telephones, radio, or television. All aircraft that could be routed to other destinations were turned back. Our reports from Pearl Harbor say the mob has started taking potshots at soldiers. I've gotten unconfirmed reports from ham radio operators that Honolulu is under martial law by authority of Mayor Takamora and that National Guard troops are shooting any white face they see."

"Oh, Jesus," Mercer breathed. "The fucking lunatic has started it."

"It appears so. There's no way to get you out there even if I wanted to."

"Listen, I have some theories that, if true, can clear this up in twenty-four hours, but I have to get to Hawaii." Mercer wouldn't allow his horror at Henna's news to dissuade him.

"Dr. Mercer—"

"I prefer Mister, or just plain Mercer."

"Really, most Ph.Ds I know flaunt their titles."

"I only use mine when I'm trying to get dinner reservations."

Henna chuckled. "I can respect that. Anyway, the President has authorized a covert action against Ohnishi in light of his involvement with this coup."

"Jesus." Mercer was shocked. "That's a stupid mistake. Ohnishi's just a pawn in this whole thing. Taking him out won't accomplish anything."

"You know something we don't?" Henna asked tiredly.

"Yes, I do, but it's going to cost you at least a ticket to that amphibious assault ship stationed near Hawaii."

"That's extortion."

"Extortion is such a genteel word, Mr. Henna. I prefer blackmail. What if I said I can hand over the mastermind of the entire operation?"

"I'm listening."

"I won't talk until you guarantee transport to that ship."

"Christ." Mercer could almost see Henna throw his hands up in exasperation. "All right, I'll get you out there. Now, what have you got?"

For the next twenty minutes Mercer spoke without pause and Henna listened. Hard.

"You got proof for any of this?" Henna asked when Mercer finished.

"Not one single shred. But it all fits together."

"I said it before, Mercer, if you ever want another job, the bureau would love to have you."

"Do you think the American Civil Liberties Union would stand to have an FBI agent making accusations like I just made? Shit, they'd skin us both alive.''

Henna chuckled again. ''You're right. I've got a meeting with the President in an hour. I'll take your proposal to him. The only way I can get you out there is as an observer, nothing more.''

''That'll be fine,'' lied Mercer smoothly. ''I really can't ask for more. Call me back when you're finished with the President.''

A minute after hanging up the phone, Mercer was between the sheets of his bed. Despite his battered body's need for sleep, he tossed and turned for twenty minutes before drifting into unconsciousness.

THE PACIFIC

Unlike most conventional helicopters, the Kamov Ka-26 lacked a stabilizing rotor in the stern; rather, it had two main rotors stacked on top of each other. Their counter-rotating blades kept the tiny copter from gyrating through the skies. The craft was much noisier than normal helicopters because of this arrangement, though the rotor noise couldn't drown out her two radial engines mounted in pods outside the cramped cabin.

The Ka-26, code-named "Hoodlum" by NATO, pounded through the clear skies at one hundred knots, near her maximum cruising speed. The sea below was an azure plane which rolled into infinity. The *August Rose*, mother ship to the small chopper, was nearly two hundred miles astern and steaming hard for Taipei, a gift to the Taiwanese ambassador. Dr. Borodin had ascertained the precise location of his island's birth, so the sophisticated gear on board the freighter was no longer needed.

The Hoodlum had been stored inside a huge packing crate on the deck of the refrigerator ship, her double set of rotor blades folded back along the twin booms of her tail. The chopper had remained hidden long after the freighter had started her long journey westward, away from the volcano, which was now no more than a few days from broaching the surface. Already dense, sulfur-laden steam clouds clung to the surface of the sea, marking the eruption.

With an operational range of 380 miles in her unitarian configuration, the Hoodlum remained on the *August Rose* until she was nearly two-thirds that distance away from the rising volcano. Only then had the pilot lifted from the deck with his two passengers.

Now, three hours after takeoff, the pilot was beginning to sweat, not from the humid air that whipped through the tiny cabin, but from fear. The antiquated radar on the twenty-five-year-old craft could no longer detect the *August Rose*, not that they had fuel to reach her in any case. They were alone, five thousand feet above an empty sea. The pilot looked back at his two passengers. The older one apparently slept while the younger one watched the ocean far below. The earphones over his head kept his fine hair from blowing about, but the wind worried at his olive drab flight suit. The pilot turned back to his instruments, scanning fuel, altitude, speed, and course in a quick glance before he gazed again at the endless horizon.

Valery Borodin turned away from the open door. He touched his father on the shoulder and Pytor's eyes cleared instantly. "We should be only about ten kilometers away."

The pilot overheard the comment through the intercom and replied, "Ten kilos away from what? We're at least three hundred kilometers away from Hawaii and running out of fuel. Do you mind telling me what this is all about?"

"Of course. Take us down to about two hundred meters first."

The pilot shrugged and complied. He doubted these two men were planning their suicides, so they must have a plan. Relieved, the pilot put the Ka-26 in a gut-wrenching dive. The rotors clawed at the air as they drove the chopper toward the surface of the sea. In an expert maneuver, the pilot pulled back on the collective pitch and leveled the craft at exactly two hundred meters. He looked back and was disappointed to see that his passengers appeared bored at his antics and expertise.

"Two hundred meters, sir."

The elder Borodin pulled a cylinder from the pocket of his flight suit. The yellow plastic case was no more than three inches in diameter and about a foot long. He pressed a red button at the top of the cylinder and casually threw it out the open door of the helicopter.

"What was that?" the pilot asked.

"A high-frequency transponder," Valery answered for his father. "Fly a one-kilometer box pattern and in a moment you'll see what we're up to."

The chopper banked sharply to starboard as the pilot began running his boxes. He had completed two kilometer-long legs when he saw a disturbance in the sea. The limpid blue water was frothing as if Leviathan itself was surfacing. The pilot brought the chopper to a hover near the boiling water.

The maddened sea grew more turgid until the bow of a ship burst from the waves, water streaming off her black hull. She rose swiftly, revealing her forward deck, studded with cranes; a boxy superstructure crowned with a single funnel; her aft deck; and finally her jack staff, sporting a limp Panamanian flag. It was like watching the death throes of a sinking ship, only in reverse. Water poured through her scuppers with the force of fire hoses as the ship wallowed in the frenzied swells of her own creation. After a minute the ship settled to an even keel, the waves dispersing quickly.

"Jesus," the pilot muttered.

"That," Borodin said with triumph, "is the watch dog of Ocean Freight and Cargo and our destination, the steamer *John Dory*."

If the pilot had had time to notice the decoration on the ship's funnel as he brought the Hoodlum toward the landing pad aft deck of this extraordinary vessel, he would have seen a black circle surrounding a yellow dot.

The Hoodlum settled on the rolling deck with deceptive ease. The pilot was truly a professional. The deckhands tossed chains around the four wheels of the copter and signaled him to cut power. An instant later the blades slowed to a stop, sagging like palm fronds.

Valery Borodin jumped from the craft, followed a moment later by his wheezing father. The elder scientist's skin had gone a chalky gray and his breath was short. Both men paused, waiting for the pilot to join them.

"What in the hell is this?" the pilot nearly shouted, his ears still ringing from the long flight.

"One moment and I'll let the captain explain." Borodin turned to the crew chief and made a cutting motion across his throat.

The chief waved his acknowledgment and signaled his crew. They quickly unshackled the the landing gear and unceremoniously pushed the Hoodlum into the sea. The chopper bobbed in the water for a few minutes, her rotor blades scratching at the paintwork of the *John Dory* before she filled with water and vanished. The pilot gave the tired little craft an ironic salute as he watched her go under. If he was bothered by the intentional destruction of his helicopter, it didn't show.

"You won't be leaving me that way, Valery," Borodin remarked casually as he turned away.

Valery stood as if he'd just witnessed a horrible accident, his eyes wide and his mouth hanging slackly. How had he guessed? Valery questioned himself. How could he know I wanted to escape using the helicopter?

Pytor answered his son's silent question. "Kerikov

contacted me after you tried to pressure him into rescuing that girl from the American research vessel.''

The plight of the beached whales weeks before and the effort to find out the cause of their deaths had been given a great deal of media attention that was picked up aboard the *August Rose* as she was monitoring the volcano. The radio reports about the NOAA mission had been very thorough, including interviews with some of the key scientific personnel. Valery recalled with pride that Tish had been brilliant during hers. Only he and his father knew that the *Ocean Seeker* was sailing toward her destruction as she embarked on her survey. In a gamble born of desperation, Valery had told Kerikov that if Tish Talbot wasn't rescued, he would destroy the volcano with the seismic charges stored aboard the *August Rose.*

''Kerikov wasn't impressed with your threat, Valery, and quite frankly neither was I. But I knew if she wasn't saved you would try to sabotage our mission, so he had her rescued at my request. You looked so smug when we heard on the radio that she was rescued.'' Borodin laughed shortly and looked over the still-wet rail of the *John Dory* at the small patch of bubbles that marked the grave of the chopper. ''You won't be leaving anytime soon. I still need you. Russia still needs you.''

That was the longest speech Pytor had addressed to Valery in the year since their reunion. It left Valery with such a cold, blinding hatred that his mouth felt the searing acids of the bile roiling in his knotted stomach. His fingers had gone white and bloodless as they curled into fists so tight that his bones seemed ready to tear through his skin.

Pytor Borodin saw none of his son's reaction; he had turned to greet the captain of the *John Dory*. Valery ambled toward them, his shoulders hunched and his trembling hands thrust deeply into the pockets of his flight suit.

''Welcome aboard, Dr. Borodin,'' Captain Nikolai

Zwenkov said, extending a hand. "I'm sorry I couldn't meet you on the landing pad, but I had to see that the ship was trimmed properly."

Borodin shook the proffered hand and introduced his son and the chopper pilot. Zwenkov was an ethnic Georgian and spoke Russian with an oafish accent, but he had the look of a stern, uncompromising professional.

"We must hurry and submerge once again. I don't want to give the American spy satellites a chance to spot us."

The captain led the three men into the ship's superstructure. There were no bulkheads or companionways, no cabins or bridge. The boxy structure was only a facade bolted to struts protruding from the rounded conning tower of a submarine. The sides and main deck of the *John Dory* were also just plates of steel welded to the hull of the sub, the cargo cranes, winches, and booms merely props. On the surface, from any range over two hundred yards, the freighter looked legitimate, giving no indication of her deadly secret within.

"It's like a K-boat," the helicopter pilot remarked, his eyes roaming the dank interior of the *John Dory*'s superstructure, referring to vessels used by Germany during World War I. They resembled freighters, but, in fact, were disguised gunboats. They would lure their victims within range with bogus distress calls, then reveal their large cannons hidden behind secret plates in their hulls. Thousands of Allied tonnage paid the ultimate price for falling into their traps.

"I like to think that this ship is a little more sophisticated," Borodin replied, rubbing the insides of his arms, "but the principle is the same."

"Come, Pytor, you look tired from your journey." The captain led them through a hatch and into the working part of the vessel, an old 285-foot Victor Class nuclear attack submarine.

Zwenkov moved through the maze of pipes, narrow hatches, and equipment with the agility of a child.

Twenty years in the Soviet Submarine Service had taught him how to avoid banging himself aboard these cramped vessels. He led Borodin and his son straight to his cabin after dropping the chopper pilot off with a subordinate.

Valery sat silently while the captain and his father chatted. Zwenkov would have killed his beloved Tish Talbot had Kerikov not been able to sneak an agent on-board the *Ocean Seeker* to save her. He wanted to beat Zwenkov for his anonymous barbarity. Yet Valery couldn't fully blame Zwenkov, for he was just a soldier doing his duty, following orders. The man behind those orders was his father.

A cramp seized Valery's gut as he thought how close he had been to escaping. The Hoodlum would have been the perfect way out of the demented world he found himself in. Valery was a man of science, dedicated to reason and thought. Yet his father had corrupted that pure world into a perverse dimension of murder and betrayal and unfathomable cruelty. Hatred boiled within him, hatred for his father's almost murdering the woman he loved, hatred for the untold murders in the past, hatred for abandoning a frightened little boy all those years before.

Only a few more days and it would all be over. If he didn't manage to escape, to rejoin the woman who'd been the source of his strength since his father had reentered his life, then his only other option was suicide. Valery promised himself that he would not die alone.

That decided, he found that his head had cleared. His mind was sharp and focused as he leaned forward to listen to the captain and his father.

"All I know is Kerikov radioed and said to suspend all activity until further orders. We are to remain on station, submerged, but with the antennae array extended, until we are contacted."

"But why? It makes no sense. We should make preparations to claim our prize." Dr. Borodin was speaking more to himself than the others. He rubbed his neck and throat absently. "I radioed Kerikov from the *August Rose*. He knows that the volcano falls outside America's two-hundred-mile limit. It belongs to the first nation that discovers it. By rights it belongs to us!"

"There is one more thing." Zwenkov's rumbling voice sounded almost apologetic. "Kerikov told me not to reveal this to you, but I've known you too long for secrets. He ordered me to load a thirty-kiloton nuclear warhead onto an SS–N–9 Siren missile and make it ready to launch."

Borodin took this news without emotion. It was as if his mind had turned in on itself, probing within to find answers. The hum of the sub's air-conditioning was the only sound in the spartan cabin for many long seconds. Finally Borodin looked first at Zwenkov and then at his son.

"He must mean to destroy the volcano—but why?" Borodin appeared more concerned with Kerikov's motives than with the fact that his life's work might be destroyed in a nuclear fireball. "There must be a leak somewhere in our security. He would have to destroy the entire project to maintain secrecy."

"Don't you understand that Kerikov has double-crossed you?" Anger made Valery's voice sound like a hiss. "He never had any intention of turning over the volcano to the government. He's used you since taking over Department Seven, hoping one day to sell your work right out from under you.

"The old regime is gone for good. The Russia you threw your life away for no longer exists. The world has changed since the 1950s, but you never took the time to notice. Vulcan's Forge would have only worked under a Stalinist regime, and that has been gone for decades. This whole operation was doomed the moment Gorbachev started glasnost and perestroika. Give up your old man's dreams and start living in reality.

"The Russian government would never attempt to occupy an island so close to American soil with one hand while the other was begging for economic aid. Kerikov knows this and he's made some sort of contingency plan.''

"How can you be so sure, Valery? You are only my assistant; you've not been told everything.'' Borodin dismissed the truth so easily because he really didn't understand it.

"Give it up, Father, there is nothing more and we both know it,'' Valery said sadly.

He saw, for the first time, how frail and weak his father looked. His eyes were rheumy behind his glasses and his once stocky frame had withered to a skeletal apparition. Borodin's skin had the pallor and texture of modeling clay.

"It will work out,'' Borodin said so softly that his lips barely moved.

Suddenly his body went rigid; his eyes snapped open as if they were ready to burst from their sockets. His lips pulled back, revealing his chipped and stained teeth in a death's head smile. He convulsed once, gasping for a quick breath before once again being grasped by the immense pain that tore through his body. His fingers crawled up his torso as if grasping his chest to calm the faltering heart within.

Pytor convulsed again, his heels kicking up from the floor as he made one last struggle, and then he was gone.

Borodin's prostate muscle had relaxed in death. The smell of urine hung heavily in the cramped office.

Zwenkov had seen enough death in his career to know that Borodin was beyond resuscitation. He crossed himself and leaned forward to close the old man's staring eyes.

"I am sorry,'' he said quietly to Valery.

Valery looked at his father for a long time before reaching out to touch the wrinkled hand. "It's funny, so am I.''

Death had cut through all of his hatred at the end, leaving him clean inside, as if reborn. His bitterness had vanished with his father's dying gasp and he knew it could not have been any other way. Even if he'd escaped with the data from the *August Rose*, he would've been forever plagued with this inner demon. But not anymore. The demon was put to rest, forever.

ARLINGTON, VIRGINIA

The insistent ringing of the phone dragged Mercer from a deep, deathlike sleep. His hand groped across the nightstand, knocking the Tiffany clock to the floor, then found the phone and swung the receiver to his head.

"H'lo." His tongue was cemented to the roof of his mouth with congealed saliva.

"Mercer, Dick Henna."

Mercer came a little more awake, opening his eyes. He was startled to see that night had descended—the twin skylights above his bed were black rectangles in the ceiling. He glanced across his balconied bedroom and saw that his whole house was dark. Tish, too, must have gone to sleep.

"Yes, Mr. Henna, what's up?" Mercer ran his tongue around his mouth and grimaced at the taste.

"The President accepted your proposal and, believe it or not, Paul Barnes from the CIA backed you up."

"That's surprising. I got the impression I was at the bottom of his Christmas card list."

"Kind of surprised me, too, but when it comes to the job, Barnes puts his personal feelings second. The commando assault that the President ordered will be postponed for at least twelve hours."

"So what happens now?" Mercer realized that his body was bathed in sweat. His sheets were a damp tangle around his legs.

"A jet will be ready for you at Andrews Air Force Base in about an hour and a half. You should be aboard the aircraft carrier *Kitty Hawk* by five tomorrow morning."

Mercer glanced at his scarred and scratched Tag Heuer chronometer. 9:15.

"Okay, I'll be at Andrews in about an hour." Mercer swung his legs off the bed, the cool air evaporating the sweat, making the dark, coarse hair on his chest and legs tingle.

"I'll meet you at the main gate with the recon photos you requested."

"Thanks, Dick." Mercer used the director's given name for the first time.

He cut the connection and dialed Harry White's number. After twenty rings, he hung up and dialed Tiny's. Tiny told him to hold for a second while Harry came back from the restroom.

"Harry, are you up for a little more baby-sitting?"

"That you, Mercer?"

"Yeah, Harry, can you come over and watch Tish again?"

"Why, what's she doing?"

"Sleeping in the nude."

"Yea, I'd love to watch that," Harry said with mock lasciviousness. "I'll be there in about fifteen minutes."

Mercer hung up, plucked the clock from the floor, and straightened the silver framed photograph of his mother that was the only other item on the nightstand. He flipped a bedside switch and light from three round Japanese lanterns bathed the room in a milky glow.

He stood up and moaned. The punishment his body had taken in the past few days was taking its toll. His shoulders were bruised a rich purple from his scrape against the metro train, and his feet and lower legs still stung from his leap into the Potomac. The cuts on his face had scabbed over, but they pulled every time Mercer moved his jaw. There was a livid red weal on his calf where the bullet had grazed him in New York.

"Jesus Christ," he muttered as he headed for the bathroom.

He took a steaming shower, popped a handful of Tylenol, and dressed quickly in baggy black pants and a long-sleeved black T-shirt. His socks and desert boots were also black. Feeling slightly more refreshed but by no means normal, he spun down the old rectory spiral stairs to the ground floor, his feet gliding over the steps.

Because his cooking skills fell far short of gourmet, his kitchen cabinets were nearly barren. It took him a ten frustrating minutes to make a mangled, runny omelet using his last three eggs, a slice of American cheese, a couple of cocktail onions pilfered from the bar and half a can of tunafish.

He carried the plate of food into his office, letting his hand brush against the large bluish stone on the credenza near the door as he entered. Setting the plate on his desk, he turned on the green shaded lamp. With a huge chunk of the omelet stuffed in his mouth he took a key from under a reference volume of mineralogy in the shelf behind his desk.

The key slid into the oiled lock of the closet adjacent to the office's entrance and the oak doors opened smoothly. In the closet were a fire retardant safe, a twisted and blackened piece of duraluminum that had once been a support girder in the airship *Hindenburg*, and a multidrawer cabinet which housed over a hundred valuable geologic samples he had collected through the years. On the floor of the closet sat an antique steamer trunk filled with souvenirs from his mission into Iraq.

Mercer dragged the heavy trunk out of the closet and propped open the lid. A Heckler and Koch MP-5A3 sat on top of the pile of equipment. The West German–manufactured machine pistol was a vicious weapon, capable of firing 9mm ammunition at over six hundred rounds per minute. Mercer lifted the nasty little gun and cleared the breach to ensure the action was still smooth, then set it aside and retrieved a Beretta automatic pistol. Since replacing the venerable Colt .45 as the primary sidearm of the U.S. Army, the Beretta had more than proved its worth in combat conditions. The pistol was in pristine condition like the H&K.

The next item Mercer pulled from the trunk was the heaviest by far—a nylon combat harness, a thick belt supported by suspender straps. The holster for the Beretta was attached to the suspenders so it would rest under his left shoulder for a quick draw and several nylon pouches full of clips for the machine pistol hung from the belt. A six-inch-long Gerber knife hung inverted from the suspenders. The final touches were a basic first aid kit and field compass in a slim padded case.

Mercer slid the Beretta into its holster and stuffed the combat rig into a light nylon duffel along with the machine pistol, then added a few other pieces of equipment. He zipped the bag, shoved the nearly empty trunk back into the closet, and locked the doors. He stashed the key back under the thick book and took one last weapon from his desk, first making sure it was loaded. Taking another big bite of his eggs, Mercer promised himself he'd never make another tuna omelet again.

"Mercer?" Tish called from the kitchen.

"I'm back here."

Tish entered the study wearing one of Mercer's Penn State sweatshirts. It came down to the midpoint of her smooth thighs and thrust up proudly over her unrestrained breasts. With her tousled hair and sleepy eyes, she looked vulnerable and incredibly sexy.

"That sweatshirt looks a hell of a lot better on you than it does me," Mercer remarked with a grin.

"Don't even look at me; I'm a mess." Tish ran a hand through her hair to get it away from her face. She noticed the duffel bag. "I heard you get up; what's going on?"

"I'm leaving for a couple of days. I think I can finally put an end to everything and with a little luck bring back Valery Borodin for you."

Tish's eyes brightened. "I was thinking earlier and couldn't believe how badly I want to see him again."

"Give me a couple of days and he's yours." Mercer was genuinely happy for her. "Let's go up to the bar; I need some of my famous coffee."

"What's that?" Tish asked as she turned to leave the study. Her gaze had fallen on the large stone near the door.

"My good luck piece," Mercer remarked, caressing the rippled surface. "It's a piece of kimberlite given to me by a director of DeBeers as thanks for saving his life after a cave-in in South Africa. Kimberlite is the most common type of matrix stone found in diamond mines." He explained, "By itself it's worthless, but nearly every diamond mined in the past hundred years has been found within a volcanic kimberlite pipe."

Mercer didn't tell her that this piece of kimberlite was far from worthless. Embedded in the underside of the stone was an approximately eight-carat diamond of startling blue-white color. Uncut, it was worth about a quarter of a million dollars, and if he ever had the stone finished, who could tell its value?

The door bells chimed, announcing Harry's arrival, while Mercer was making coffee. Harry let himself in and entered the bar through the library. He needed the doorjamb for support.

"Where are you going, a costume party as a ninja?" Mercer looked down at his black attire and shrugged.

"Actually, the theme is your favorite environmental catastrophe. I'm an oil spill. What do you think?"

"I think you're full of shit," Harry replied, seating himself at the bar. The cigarette in his mouth jumped with each word.

"Hi, Harry." Tish greeted the old man with a kiss on his gray stubbled cheek.

"You lied to me, Mercer. You said she'd be naked." Tish didn't understand the comment, but already knew Harry and Mercer well enough to not be offended. "Give me a drink, will ya'."

Mercer deftly poured Jack Daniel's and ginger ale. "Actually, I'm going to put another pin in my map." He jerked his thumb at the pin-studded map behind the bar.

"What color?"

"Clear," Mercer replied.

Harry knew that the clear pin in Iraq had been some sort of covert government mission and that the one in Rwanda denoted a violent episode in his friend's life. His whiskey-dulled eyes became a little sharper. "Where you heading?"

"I'm not supposed to tell you Hawaii," Mercer smiled, "so I won't."

"So I guess the whole thing comes full circle," Harry said softly, looking at Tish.

Mercer glanced at his watch and hoisted the nylon bag over his shoulder. "I've got to go. Give me your truck keys."

Harry fished the keys to his battered Ford pickup from his pocket and tossed them to Mercer.

Mercer snatched them from the air. "I'll be back in a few days; keep an eye on things." He gave Tish a light kiss and told her, "You be good and don't excite old Harry here."

On his way out of the house, Mercer paused in the library and smiled wickedly at the stack of framed pictures on the floor. The top photo, an 8×10, showed Mercer and another man standing on the crawler track of a huge Caterpillar D–11N bulldozer. The handwritten caption read, "Mercer, you did it again; this time I really owe you one." It was signed *Daniel Tanaka*. The logo stenciled on the engine cowling of the 107-ton dozer was the stylized hard hat and dragline of Ohnishi Minerals.

"Debt paid, Danny boy."

IN the black night, the sentry post at Andrews Air Force Base in Morningside, Maryland, looked like a highway toll booth. Several small glass buildings supported a metal roof that stretched across the entire road and bathed it in fluorescent lights. Mercer brought Harry's pickup to a stop, the ancient brakes squealing like nails drawn across a blackboard. The guard, an African-American barely out of his teens, regarded the decrepit truck with suspicion until Dick Henna, standing behind him, placed a hand on his shoulder. Through the open window of the truck, Mercer heard Henna reassure the young corporal.

Henna exited the small armored-glass guardhouse, walked to the passenger side of the pickup, opened the door, and slid in without comment. Mercer started rolling forward.

"I know that until recently you drove a Jaguar convertible," Henna said at length, his voice nearly drowned by the blasting exhaust. "I expected your second car to be a little better than this."

Mercer coughed as the Ford backfired and an acrid cloud of exhaust was blown into the truck's cab. He grinned. "Something old, something new . . ."

"Something borrowed, something blue," Henna finished the rhyme. "Got ya."

"But I think, under all the rust, this truck is brown. I'm not sure." Mercer looked at the large manila envelope in Henna's hand. "Is that for me?"

"Yes." Henna set it on the seat between them. "Two of the infrared photos from the spy plane, and contractor's drawings of the homes of Takahiro Ohnishi and his assistant Kenji. What the hell do you want this stuff for? You know you're only going as an advisor and observer."

"Absolutely," Mercer agreed quickly. "But when the assault occurs, I need some material to advise with, right?"

"Turn left here," Henna directed as they drove further into the sprawling complex. "You're one of the most ingenious men I've ever met, Mercer, but I've yet to figure out how you're going to get off the *Inchon* and onto Hawaii."

Mercer looked at him with mock astonishment, his face the picture of cherubic innocence. "Perish the thought, a cruise on an assault ship has always been a dream of mine. I have no intention of leaving the watchful eye of the navy. Seriously, Dick, you need someone out there who knows the whole situation and also understands something about bikinium. I don't think Abe Jacobs is up to it. Besides, I found out about this whole mess and I just want to see it finished."

Henna did not respond.

"Are you buying any of this?"

"No, I'm not." Henna grunted

"Good, because that's about the worst line of bull I've ever thrown." Mercer looked at Henna, the streetlights casting his face in either blinding light or impenetrable shadow. "If you know I'm planning to get off the *Inchon* as soon as I can and get to the islands, why are you letting me go?"

"Simple, I know you've withheld information from me." There was no anger in Henna's voice. "And that information is the key to ending this whole affair. You're the only person who knows what the hell is going on and suicidal enough to try and stop it."

"I appreciate your honesty and confidence," replied Mercer sardonically. "But dying isn't on my agenda of things to do and see on my Hawaiian vacation."

"Turn left."

Mercer swung the pickup and drove parallel to one of the base's steel-reinforced concrete runways. The blue lights which bordered the tarmac flashed by in a solid blur. In the distance, a jet roared off into the night.

They approached several massive hangars, the powerful lights around the buildings reflecting against their corrugated metal sides. Men in blue overalls walked purposely in and around the hangars, carrying tools, binders, and other paraphernalia.

"Swing into the first hangar," Henna directed.

Mercer slowed, passing several mobile generators used to jump-start the jet fighters. He pulled the truck into the hangar and stopped in a spot indicated by a grizzled chief master sergeant. The hash marks on his uniform sleeve, denoting years in the service, ran from his wrist to his shoulder.

Henna shook the chief's hand. "Everything all set?"

"Yes, sir." The chief said "sir" the way most men say "impotent"—either not at all or never above a bare whisper. "There's an extra flight suit in the office and a KC–135 stratotanker's ready to take off in Omaha. Another is standing by near San Francisco. Why the air force is paying for the transfer of a civilian to a navy aircraft I'll never know."

Mercer had seen the jet when he first drove into the hangar, but now took a moment to study his ride to the Pacific. The McDonnell Douglas F/A–18 Hornet rested lightly on her landing gear as if ready to pounce. She was like a leopard seated on its haunches, immeasurable power coiled up like a spring. The hard points under her razor-edged wings were bare of weapons, though two drop tanks clung there like fat leeches. Mercer took in her clean lines, the sharp needle nose, the twin outward-canted tails, the six stubby barrels of her General Electric gatling gun tucked under the canopy. She had two seats, which meant she was a training version.

VULCAN'S FORGE   267

"Ever been in a fighter before?" the chief asked with a patronizing smile.

"No," replied Mercer.

"Oh, Bubba's going to love you."

Mercer looked down at the chief. He was a good foot taller than the air force man, but the chief's wide shoulders and hard, thick gut made them appear physically equal. "Bubba?"

"Howdy," said a voice that came straight from a dirt farm in southern Georgia.

Mercer whirled around. The speaker stood near an office tucked against one wall of the cavernous hangar. The man's high-tech flight suit bulged where pads and air bladders would squeeze his body to keep him from passing out in the High-g world of the modern dog fighter. The pilot had a baby face and thin, mangled hair, and when he smiled, Mercer could see that a front tooth was missing. The helmet in his hand had "Bubba" stenciled between stripes of red, white, and blue.

The man looked nothing like Mercer's mental picture of the pilot.

"Billy Ray Young." The pilot extended a bony hand. "Jist call me Bubba." He grinned around the plug of tobacco firmly held in one cheek.

"Mercer." They shook hands. Henna couldn't help but chuckle at the pallor that had crept into Mercer's face.

"Kinda glad to have me some company on the flight," Bubba said. "I been to the stockade fer a spell and didn't talk to many folks there."

Mercer looked over at Henna. The FBI director said nothing, but his eyes sparkled with amusement.

"Come with me—ay'll git ya geared up."

Mercer followed the pilot to the office. Billy Ray kept up a solid monologue about his term in the stockade for flying his Hornet under the Golden Gate Bridge. His accent was so thick that Mercer understood maybe a third of the pilot's speech. Billy Ray showed Mercer how to fit into the constricting flight suit and, cinch up the various harnesses. Mercer felt like the Michelin Man strapping on a girdle.

Back out in the hangar, Dick Henna hefted Mercer's nylon duffel bag. "Bit heavy for a change of underwear."

"My toilet case is lead lined." Mercer grabbed the bag from him.

A mechanic took the duffel from Mercer and stored it in the area meant for the 1,350 rounds of 30mm gatling gun ammunition. He closed the hatch to the ammo bay and secured it with a special screwdriver, patting the fuselage affectionately before walking away.

"Giddyup there, Mr. Mercer, we's got a schedule to keep." Billy Ray Young was already in the Hornet's front seat.

"Mercer, don't worry about him," Henna said. "He's one of the best pilots in the navy. His record during the Gulf War was unparalleled."

"Is that supposed to make me feel better?" Mercer asked.

"No, not really." Henna smiled and extended his right hand. "Once you get to the carrier, a helicopter will transfer you to the *Inchon*. I'll get in touch with you there. Good luck."

"Thanks, Dick." Mercer walked over to the aircraft and mounted the metal steps to the cockpit.

The chief personally strapped Mercer into the ejector seat, briefly outlining the fifty things Mercer shouldn't do or touch while in the aircraft.

"Any parting thoughts, Chief?"

"Yeah, you puke in here and I'll have the deck officer on the *Kitty Hawk* make you clean it up." The chief slapped Mercer on the top of the helmet and scrambled down the mobile ladder.

"Y'awl set?" Billy Ray asked over the intercom.

"Let's do it, Bubba," Mercer said tiredly. Suddenly the five hours of sleep he had gotten earlier didn't seem like enough, but he doubted he would sleep much on this flight.

Billy Ray closed the canopy and fired up the two GE F404 turbofans. The sixteen-thousand-pound thrust engines sounded like banshees as he brought them to full power for an instant and then throttled them back again.

A tow tractor came out of the night's gloom and a lineman attached the tow bar to the front landing gear. With a slight jerk, the tractor edged the Hornet out onto the base's apron. Over the helmet intercom, Mercer listened to the chatter between the tower and several aircraft in the area. When Billy Ray finally spoke to ground traffic control, his accent nearly vanished. His voice was crisp and professional and Mercer began to feel a little better about the flight and the pilot.

"You barf easy on carnival rides, Mr. Mercer?" But not much better.

"Don't worry about me, Bubba."

The tractor stopped just short of the runway and the driver leapt from the vehicle and unhooked the tow bar. Billy Ray eased open the throttles and the twenty-five-ton aircraft began to judder under the massive power of her own engines. They taxied to the end of the runway and paused, waiting for clearance from the tower. The runway was a two-mile-long ribbon racing off into the night, edged by blue lights which seemed to converge at the distant horizon.

When they got clearance, Billy Ray let out an ear-splitting rebel yell and jammed the twin throttles to their stops, simultaneously engaging the afterburners.

Thirty-foot cones of blue-white flame knifed from the two turbofans as raw fuel was dumped into their exhaust. The Hornet reared back on her pneumatic landing gear as she started to rocket down the runway. Mercer was forced back into his seat as the aircraft accelerated.

At two hundred knots, Billy Ray yanked back on the stick and the plane arrowed into the black sky. Mercer's pressure suit automatically squeezed his chest, ensuring that blood didn't drain from his head and cause a blackout. He held onto the seat arms as he watched the altimeter needle wind around like a hyperactive clock.

Billy Ray didn't level out until they reached thirty-two thousand feet, and it took several minutes for Mercer's stomach to catch up to the hurtling Hornet. Sixty seconds later there was a jarring explosion and the thunderous roar of the engines died abruptly. Mercer thought for sure that Billy Ray had torn the guts out of her but then realized they had just broken the sound barrier.

"What ya think of her?" Billy Ray asked in the eerie silence.

"I can't wait until United uses these for their shuttle service," Mercer retorted. "Does she have a name?"

"Sure does," Billy Ray said with pride. "Mabel."

"Your mother?"

"No, my pappy's prize heifer," the pilot replied matter-of-factly.

Mercer slumped into his seat as much as he could and rested his head against the canopy. He closed his eyes for a moment and realized that sleeping would be a lot easier than he had first imagined. The only irritation was Billy Ray's off-key humming of "Dixie."

He was jolted awake once during the trip between Washington and the West Coast. That waking was the worst moment of sheer terror he had ever experienced. It was still dark outside and he could clearly make out the running lights of another aircraft that was so close he couldn't see the tips of its wings. Billy Ray seemed bent on ramming it. They were at subsonic speed, but the other plane was rapidly filling the Hornet's canopy. Mercer braced himself for the impending collision, but Billy Ray tucked his F-18 under the other lumbering plane with maybe twenty-five feet to spare.

Rapt, Mercer watched in fascination as a spectral boom came out of the murky night and into the halo of light around the fighter. Only when the boom attached itself to the tube just foreward and right of the Hornet's cockpit did he realize that the fighter was being refueled in flight. It took several minutes for the KC-135 tanker to fill the F-18's tanks. As the hose retracted toward the tanker, residual drops of fuel froze in the rarefied atmosphere and flashed past the cockpit like tracer fire.

"Thanks for the nipple; this baby was hungry," Billy Ray said to the crew of the stratotanker.

He waggled the wings of the nimble fighter, dipped below the slow-moving KC-135, and eased the throttles forward. An instant later, the tanker was miles behind them and the Hornet was approaching the speed of sound. Once the F-18 began flying faster than the roar of her engines and again the cockpit was silent, Mercer rested his head against the Plexiglas canopy. It took another few minutes for his heart to slow enough for him to fall asleep.

MV *JOHN DORY*

The radio operator tossed his earphones onto his gray steel desk under the massed banks of communications equipment. He nodded to his assistant, and hurried from the cramped room, a hastily scrawled page in his hand. The *John Dory* was running under the ruddy glow of battle lights as she had for most of this patrol but his little world was bright because of the lights on the sophisticated electronic radio gear. It took a few moments for his eyes to adjust to the gloom in the rest of the transformed submarine.

He passed through the small aperture of a watertight door and into the sub's control center. The two planesmen sat to the left in airline-style seats; the yokes controlling the rudders, and dive planes completed the aircraft cockpit facsimile. Behind them, the three men who monitored the ballast controls stood in front of a panel studded with two dozen valves and pressure gauges. The system was archaic, dating back to the earliest type of subs from the First World War, but still effective. Only the very latest Soviet subs utilized the modern ballast control computers that the Americans had been using since the 1960s.

The fire control station was to the left. It was the most modern piece of equipment on the boat, a twelve-year-old computer copied from the American UYK-7 command and control computer. The UYK-7 was the first type of C&C computer utilized on the American *Los Angeles* class attack subs. The Russian copy had been installed during the refitting of the *John Dory* in Vladivostok.

At the back of the control center, four engineers monitored the ancient reactor at the stern of the boat, their eyes and fingers never leaving the confusing mass of lights, dials, and switches. An identical panel was located in the reactor room and the two stations were electronically linked. This way there were actually eight pairs of eyes watching for any danger from the radioactive furnace burning away under its decaying shield of lead and concrete. The boat's periscope hung from the low ceiling like a steel stalactite. It acted as the only visible means to ensure the outside still existed once the sub dove beneath the waves, the passive and active sonars only reported the echoes of the real world.

"Captain, message from Matruskha." The code name for Ivan Kerikov referred to the intricate nesting dolls so popular with generations of Russian children. It was a fitting code for such a secretive and multitiered man.

Captain Zwenkov was hunched over the weapons officer's console, reviewing firing solutions for the sub's Siren missile in case it was needed against the volcano not more than twenty miles distant.

"This is good, Boris," the captain praised his weapon's officer and slapped him on the shoulder before turning to the lanky radio man. "What have you got?"

"Message from Matruskha, Comrade Captain," the radio operator repeated, handing over the sheet of paper. He stood at attention, waiting for the captain's response.

Zwenkov held the flimsy paper to one of the steel-caged battle lights and squinted to make out the writing. He grunted several times as he read it through. He then folded the paper carefully and slid it into a pocket of his stiff-necked tunic.

"Bowman, take us to periscope depth." Zwenkov's orders were quiet but clear. "But do not use the ballast. Take us up with engines alone, turning for two knots. We're not in any hurry. Sonar, secure the active systems. I don't want an accidental ping."

Zwenkov looked around the dim bridge as the men went about their jobs. Satisfied with their performance, he picked up a hand mike and dialed in the ship's intercom.

"This is the captain speaking." His voice was barely above a whisper. Crewmen not directly near a speaker had to strain to hear him. "I know we've been rigged for silent running for a long time, but the need for this precaution is almost over. We will be leaving station within twenty-four hours and heading for home. We cannot afford to be lax during these crucial hours; now is the time to redouble our efforts. There is an American carrier in the area as well as an amphibious assault ship. I don't need to remind you that there will be a fast-attack sub protecting the carrier and their sonar can hear a hammer drop two hundred miles away. They do not know we're here, and I don't want to give them a chance to find us. All conversations are to be in whispers. There will be no music in the mess rooms and any necessary repairs must first be cleared by me personally. All scheduled maintenance is suspended until further orders. That is all."

He hung the mike back in its cradle. The men on the bridge looked at him with a mixture of anticipation and excitement. Apart from sinking the NOAA ship a week ago, the cruise had been long and monotonous. The tension of remaining as quiet as possible for weeks at a time could destroy the nerves of even the best submariner, and they'd been at it for seven long months.

Now the captain was promising the men that they would be going home soon, and the anticipation creased their faces into smiles. The threat of an American hunter/killer sub in the area only served to spice that anticipation. After all, they were sailors in the Russian Navy and their job was fighting, not waiting.

Captain Zwenkov turned to the young radio operator. "Preset your system to alternate channel B. Every two hours starting at midnight you will receive a flash message. The message will be the word 'green' repeated for five seconds. Sometime tomorrow night the code word will be 'red.' It may not come during the two-hour cycle, so be prepared at all times. Every time you receive the message, tell me. Understood?"

"Yes, Comrade Captain." The radio operator saluted smartly and turned away.

"Captain, periscope depth," the dive officer reported quietly.

"All stop."

"All stop, aye."

"Extend the ultra-low-frequency antenna but don't let it broach the surface."

"ULF extending . . . ULF antenna depth one meter."

"Engineer, disengage reactor, bring her down to five percent power."

"Five percent, aye."

Although a nuclear reactor operates much more quietly than diesel electric propulsion, the powerful pumps used to keep the containment vessel cooled emitted a distinct whirling sound that a trained sonarman could distinguish over the noisy clutter of the open sea. By reducing power to the barest minimum, Zwenkov lowered his chances of detection by the lurking American sub and its very-well-trained sonarmen.

"Anton," Zwenkov said as he ran a hand through his short gray hair. In response, his executive officer stepped away from his station near the glass-topped plotting table just aft of the periscope. "Find young Dr. Borodin and send him to my cabin."

"Yes, Captain." The exec left the bridge, heading aft to the ward room, where he felt sure he would to find the scientist.

Zwenkov went to his cabin, just forward of the bridge. From the locked drawer of his plastic-veneered desk, he removed a half-full bottle of vodka and a cheap glass tumbler emblazoned with a picture of the immense television tower in East Berlin. The glass reminded him of his one vacation outside the Soviet Republics, to a city as bleak and depressing as his native Tbilisi in Georgia. He poured a half inch of the liquor into the glass, shot it down in one fiery swallow, and returned glass and bottle to the drawer.

Of course, alcohol was strictly forbidden on all Russian vessels, especially on submarines, but he figured a captain should have some privileges. A single shot, once a week, was all he usually allowed himself, though this week he'd taken three. The second drink he had taken soon after two seamen carried the corpse of Pytor Borodin to the sub's nearly empty freezer.

"Come," he barked after a knock on his door.

Valery entered, wearing a borrowed officer's utility uniform. He looked like a recruitment poster, dark handsome features, trim athletic body held erect with just a trace of tragedy around him that lent an air of mystery. Understandably, Zwenkov had not seen much of him since his father's death.

"Sit down, please," Zwenkov invited. "Would you care for some tea?"

Valery demurred with a hand gesture as he swung himself into a chair next to where his father had died. He eyed the other chair for a moment before turning to the captain. "You wanted to see me?"

Zwenkov knew that the direct approach was always best. "I just received word from Kerikov. He's ordered the destruction of the volcano."

Valery took the news without changing expression, he didn't even blink. He had expected something like this, but now that it came he felt nothing. Part of him was vindicated—the father who had abandoned him so young had wasted his entire life on a dream that would never be fulfilled—and part of him felt pain for the old man's failure. The conflicting emotions turned his face into a stony mask.

Zwenkov continued. "I'm waiting to hear from a commando team in Hawaii. Once I receive word, I'll fire the missile and obliterate the volcano. We then head toward Hawaii to extract the commando team."

"Did he give a reason?" Valery asked softly

"I'm sorry, Dr. Borodin, what was that?"

Valery cleared his throat, but his voice was still a whisper. "I asked if Kerikov gave you a reason."

"I'm a member of the Russian armed forces attached to the KGB, Dr. Borodin. When I receive orders I don't ask for explanations."

"You know it's a mistake, don't you?"

"That is not my concern," Zwenkov replied caustically.

"I heard what you said to the crew about the American submarines in the area. When you launch that missile they'll find us instantly."

"You may know geology, Borodin, but I know American tactics. When that warhead goes off, they'll rush to the area to investigate and we'll slip quietly away. The acoustics of the explosion will hide our underwater signature even at flank speed."

He had told Valery about the missile strike out of courtesy, since the young scientist and his father had put so much effort into the volcano's creation, but that didn't mean he liked Borodin nor wanted to have his orders questioned.

Since his father's death, Valery had abandoned any thoughts of suicide, admitting that he had been tempted in a moment of weakness. Now he realized that he would never be able to dissuade Zwenkov from destroying the volcano—but he still had a chance of escaping with his father's briefcase.

When the *John Dory* rendezvoused with the commando team, Valery would find a way to get off the boat, even if it meant swimming to Hawaii. He would escape. The volcano would be gone by then, but Pytor's notes would certainly be worth something to the Americans.

"Because our boat is about to enter a potential combat situation," Zwenkov said, interrupting Valery's thoughts, "you will be confined to your quarters. You are not under arrest, but a guard will be posted to ensure that you do not interfere with the operation of this vessel."

Zwenkov pressed the intercom button on his desk. The XO answered instantly from the bridge. "Yes, Captain."

"Send the security officer here to escort Dr. Borodin back to his cabin and have a guard posted there. There is no need for a sidearm."

A moment later, the security man entered the cabin and escorted a silent Valery Borodin away. A beefy guard already stood outside Valery's cabin when they reached it.

Valery threw himself onto his bunk after the guard closed the door with exaggerated courtesy. Waves of frustration pounded against the top of his head like a crashing winter surf.

He had been so close. The *John Dory* would have picked up the commando team near the Hawaiian coast under the cover of darkness and he could have easily slipped into the sea unnoticed.

Gone. His chances were gone. He would never be able to overpower the guard outside his door and make his way off the submarine.

He had lost.

He pounded his fists into his thin mattress, trying not to imagine how close he'd been to being with Tish again. The ache was strong enough to make him moan and toss about on the narrow bunk. Those beautiful weeks when they'd been together in Mozambique played through his mind like a romance film. Himself and Tish swimming and laughing and loving, carefree and gay. He could almost feel her thinking about him at this very moment, feel the connection they shared, the bond that wouldn't ever let them be truly apart. Valery closed his eyes tightly in a vain attempt to block out his loss.

"Goddamn it," he seethed, teeth clenched so tightly they were almost in danger of shattering, "Goddamn it."

NEAR HAWAII

The roar of the turbo jets woke Mercer and he knew the F/A-18 Hornet had just slowed to sub-sonic speeds. He blinked his eyes hard and rotated his stiff neck. The constricting flight suit dug painfully into his groin and had bunched up under his arms, but there was no way he could stretch out in the cockpit. Night still held the earth in its grip. The moon was big and fat overhead. Mercer was sure he could read by its pale glow.

"Where are we?" he asked Billy Ray.

"About fifty miles out from the *Kitty Hawk*; they're trackin' us now."

Ask any commercial or private pilot to name the most dangerous thing they could do with an aircraft and they will invariably say landing without power on rough terrain. Ask any naval aviator and the response would be landing on a carrier at night in rough seas. Knowing this, Mercer thought it prudent to keep quiet and let Billy Ray do his job.

Billy Ray "Bubba" Young had other ideas. He kept up a running dialogue of inane observations about farming, flying, and anything else that came into his head. Mercer could see his hands gesturing wildly as he talked. Only when they were ten miles out did the pilot regain his calm professionalism and get down to business.

"Control, this is Ferryman One-One-Three." Bubba gave the flight designation. "I have you in sight."

Mercer peered into the gloom ahead of the hurtling aircraft but it took him nearly twenty seconds to find the dim lights of the aircraft carrier which were just faint pinpricks of light like a constellation on the black surface of the sea. There was no doubt that Billy Ray possessed exceptional eyesight.

The Hornet was descending steadily, her powerful engines throttled back, her airspeed no more than two hundred knots. As they drew closer to the huge carrier, Mercer could see the lights on her stern; running lights, VASSI system lights to show the pilot his glide path, and the "ball" light that indicated the ship's roll. They meant nothing to him, but he trusted Billy Ray to know what he was doing.

"One mile out," the voice of the flight controller called.

"Confirmed," Billy Ray replied casually. There was a mechanical whine as the landing gear sank from the fuselage.

The few lights on the carrier made the sea look even darker and more ominous. By watching the ship's bow, Mercer saw she was pitching wildly. It looked impossible to land the Hornet on her deck.

"Call the ball," the radio buzzed.

Billy Ray slewed his aircraft through the sky to match the great ship's ponderous roll. When he felt they were aligned, he keyed the mike and said, "Bubba has the ball."

The flight was in his hands now, the carrier closing by the second, the Hornet still flying over one hundred and fifty knots, the controlled sway of the aircraft matching the flight deck's movement.

Three hundred yards out, the stall warning wailed—the wings were losing lift at the slow speed. Two hundred yards out, Billy Ray pitched the needle nose up at an even steeper angle, the aircraft was barely hanging in the sky. At one hundred yards the aircraft began to shudder, but Billy Ray held her up with a deft touch on the throttle. The deck was just a murky shadow ahead.

The entire situation seemed out of control. It was definitely unlike anything Mercer had ever experienced before—the wailing alarms, the mad movements of the fighter, and Billy Ray's rebel yell.

The wheels touched with a squeal of burned rubber; Billy Ray slammed the throttles to their forward stops and activated the afterburners, but the massive power of the engines could not pull the Hornet from the arrester cable that stretched across the *Kitty Hawk*'s deck. He shut down the engines as the plane's nose dropped to the deck. The instant deceleration from 150 knots to zero slammed Mercer into his harness, bruising both shoulders painfully.

As the turbofans whined into silence, Mercer exhaled the breath he was sure he'd held for the past two minutes.

"Ay should'a warned you about hittin' max power when we touch down. Gotta do that in case we missed the cable and need'd to take off again."

"No problem," Mercer said, too relieved to complain.

"Control," Billy Ray spoke into the radio, "give me the wire."

"You snagged two, Ferryman One-One-Three," the controller replied.

Billy Ray shouted triumphantly. "Ah haven't landed on a carrier in two months and Ah can still lay her down on the center wire."

To maintain flight status, naval pilots must consistently hook into the middle of the three arrester cables

that stretch across a carrier's deck. Hitting on number
one or three meant they came in too high or too low,
and if they do either too often, they're taken off active
status and sent to the mainland for additional training.
Billy Ray had executed a perfect nighttime landing.

As the F-18 was towed to one of the aircraft lifts by
a small utility tractor, the canopy opened and Mercer
breathed in the rich Pacific air. The smell of aviation
fuel and the smoke from the carrier's eight Forest-
Wheeler boilers could not dampen the tanginess of the
ocean. Mercer was amazed at the activity on the flight
deck; men scurried from task to task, aircraft jockeyed
around. An F-14 Tomcat streaked into the darkened sky,
a huge helicopter warmed up nearby.

Deck crews swarmed up to the Hornet. One pushed a
mobile ladder to the cockpit. Two men scrambled up the
ladder and helped Mercer and Billy Ray extricate themselves from the cramped seats.

"Good to have you back, Bubba," one of the men
said. "Your squadron leader wants to see you in the
briefing room right away."

"Fine," Billy Ray drawled. "Well, Mr. Mercer, been
a pleasure."

Mercer shook his hand and grinned. "If you say so.
I'm sorry I wasn't much company on the flight. I guess
I needed the sleep."

"Shoot, you were asleep the whole time? No wonder
you didn't answer none of my questions." Billy Ray
laughed.

Someone handed Mercer his nylon bag recovered
from the ammo well. The asphalt deck felt good under
his feet as he stretched his tired muscles. He realized
that the ship was barely pitching, it had just seemed violent as the Hornet had screamed in on its approach.

"Dr. Mercer, Commander Quintana wants to see
you," said a crewman. "I'll lead the way. Please stay
behind me, sir, the flight deck is a pretty dangerous
place."

No sooner had they stepped away from the aircraft than the huge square of the deck elevator vanished, carrying the Hornet to the hangar below. Mercer followed the crewman to the seven-story island, the only part of the carrier to rise above the flight deck. He could make out the bridge windows and the mass of antennae that shot up into the sky. Since the *Kitty Hawk* wasn't nuclear powered, she had a single funnel that cantilevered out over the starboard rail.

The wind that swept the deck pushed Mercer and his escort aft, toward the island. As they approached, Mercer saw a figure silhouetted in a doorway. When they were close enough, the Hispanic features and dark hair allowed him to correctly identify Commander Quintana. He was dressed in starched khakis, and though he seemed relaxed he held himself erect. Typical ramrod navy man, Mercer thought.

"Welcome to the CV63 *Kitty Hawk*. I'm Commander Juan Quintana. Why don't we step inside out of the wind?" Quintana made no offer to shake hands and spoke as if every word was capitalized and punctuated with a period.

Mercer followed him into the ship. The unitarian gray walls and stark lighting reminded Mercer of the basement of his grandparents' house in Vermont. The steel corridors were spotlessly clean but smelled of fuel oil and saltwater. Quintana led him up three decks and through a maze of corridors, to his office. Had Mercer not been used to the three-dimensional labyrinths of underground mines, he would have been thoroughly lost.

Quintana's office was small, but on a ship which housed more than 5000 men, space was at a premium. The walls were covered in cheap paneling and the carpet on the floor was thin but a definite upgrade from the steel passageways. Quintana's desk was wooden, standard government issue. In fact, it reminded Mercer of his own desk at the USGS. Since he believed that a clean desk was the sign of a sick mind, he assumed Quintana was indeed touched. The only items on the desk were a lamp, bolted to its surface, and a black, three-line telephone.

"The head is through that curtain," Quintana pointed. "You can leave your flight suit in there."

"Thanks." Mercer smiled his gratitude and headed for the bathroom.

A few minutes later he was seated in front of the commander sipping the coffee that Quintana had thoughtfully poured.

"The captain would have met you himself, Dr. Mercer, but he really doesn't like you boys in the CIA. Quite frankly, I don't like you, either." The distaste in Quintana's voice was hard edged.

"I'm glad we have that cleared up," Mercer replied with a grin, "I don't like spies either."

"I don't understand. I thought you're with . . ."

"The CIA," Mercer finished his thought. "No, I'm with the USGS."

"I've never heard of it," Quintana said cautiously.

"The United States Geological Survey, Commander Quintana," Mercer said with a smile. "I'm a mining engineer."

"It's bad enough using a navy jet to transport civilians, but this is ridiculous," Quintana said acidly. "You're just an engineer. What the hell is this all about, Dr. Mercer?"

The commander's arrogant attitude triggered Mercer's temper. "Don't act as if you had to pay for that flight yourself, Quintana, all right? I'm on a mission so far over your head, the people involved read like a who's who, and I don't recall any of them giving you permission to act like some simpering prima donna. As far as I'm concerned, your ship is just an airport where I'm changing planes, so stuff your holier-than-thou attitude, I'm really not in the mood." Mercer wouldn't normally have been that short with Quintana, but the tension was building within him and he needed an outlet. Besides, the commander was acting like a prick. "Your job is to get me to the assault ship *Inchon*, nothing more."

Quintana's eyes narrowed in rancor as Mercer spoke. "Fine, Dr. Mercer. It's 0430 now, first light in another two hours or so. A helicopter will transfer you over to *Inchon* then."

"That'll be fine. In the meantime where can I get something to eat?"

Quintana stood, his anger locked behind clenched teeth. "I'll take you to the officer's mess."

"By the way, tell the captain that Admiral Morrison sends his regards," Mercer said lightly as they left the office. The casual remark about the chairman of the Joint Chiefs was puerile, he knew, but the bulging veins on Quintana's forehead gave him a fiendish pleasure.

HONOLULU

Evad Lurbud always woke angry, even after a short nap. Anger was an integral part of him as much as his dark eyes or his powerful arms. It was an unfocused emotion, wild, yet so very important to him. It was the only thing that gave his life any meaning. If he could somehow vent just a little of that anger every day, then he knew he was alive.

As he swung his legs off the cot, he wondered what he would be like if he ever woke and found all the anger had finally left him. It had been his constant companion since the days of brutal beatings by his father and the intimate touches of his mother and aunt. He guessed if he ever woke without it he would put a bullet into his forehead.

The other bunks in the dim safehouse were occupied by his team. The bed above Lurbud sagged under the weight of Sergeant Demanov. Their snores were almost deafening.

Because the team had arrived only a day before Lurbud, he knew it was prudent to give the men a chance to acclimate to the Hawaiian time zone. The men had to be fresh this evening when it was time to move out. He glanced at his watch—6:30 P.M. He had been in Hawaii a little over twenty-four hours and now, as he stretched his muscles, he knew he was ready.

In one corner of the safehouse, two members of the team were playing endless hands of gin, trying in vain to alleviate the boredom between their scheduled two-hour reports to the *John Dory*. When they saw Lurbud looking at them, they came to immediate attention. Lurbud smiled and waved them back to their seats. He turned back to the bunks of sleeping soldiers.

"Gentlemen," he said softly.

With fluid grace, the men woke and slid out of their beds, coming to attention automatically. Their response was so instantaneous that even Lurbud was impressed. Sergeant Demanov broke rank and strode across the room to Evad. He was naked, yet showed no self-consciousness. His chunky body was covered in a thick pelt of hair.

"Not bad, eh?" Demanov asked, grabbing a cigarette and lighter from a table.

"Are you talking about your troops or your shriveled manhood?"

Demanov let out a deep belly laugh, smoke shooting from his nostrils in twin jets. "Best fucking troops in the world, they are."

Lurbud smiled, "I think this time even you are not exaggerating, Dimitri. I want them ready to move out by 1930 hours. It will take us at least an hour after that to get into position around Ohnishi's house."

"Have you given any thought to my plan?"

"Yes, this afternoon when the rest of you were sleeping. I don't think it would be a good idea to split our forces. We don't have the communications gear to co-ordinate a simultaneous attack against Ohnishi and Kenji. We will hit them in turn. With luck, Kenji will be with his master and the second operation won't be necessary. It is critical that we maintain our scheduled contact with the *John Dory*. If she's not waiting for us when we reach the coast, well, you know the consequences.''

While Sergeant Demanov and his team checked the equipment and weapons that had been smuggled into the safehouse months earlier through the Russian embassy's diplomatic pouch, Lurbud scanned the reports given to him in Cairo.

Ohnishi's mansion was protected by twenty guards, all of whom had military or police training and had attended numerous professional defense schools. These guards were better trained than most nation's elite defense forces. Lurbud had no doubt that his troops could handle them, but there he would certainly lose men. Ohnishi was old, wheelchair bound, and frail. He would pose no difficulty once the guards had been eliminated.

Kenji, on the other hand, was different. Lurbud had no plan of his house, no details of his security arrangements; even his personal details were sketchy. He was fifty-four years old, but the attached blurry photograph, though taken only a year earlier, showed a man who appeared twenty years younger. Kenji was a master of kendo, tae kwan do, and several martial arts that Lurbud had never even heard of.

A note from the KGB compiler who had put the dossier together stated that Kenji had mastered the art of nonweapons. He could use simple household items to kill or maim. The note explained that a similarly trained assassin had once slit the throat of a Hungarian dissident with a sheet of paper torn from a London phone book.

Lurbud sincerely hoped that they would catch Kenji at Ohnishi's. Heading into an assassin's lair without any tactical intelligence was tantamount to suicide.

At 7:30, Lurbud and his men left the safe house after checking that they had left no incriminating items behind. Despite the curfew, they left the city unmolested in a van that had been stored in a garage nearby. If Honolulu survived the crisis, the only evidence that they had ever been there was an empty barracks-like room and an abandoned van, both rented by Ocean Freight and Cargo months earlier. And since the break-in at the New York offices, OF&C had ceased to exist.

FORTY-FIVE miles away, the cooling breeze of evening was washing across Takahiro Ohnishi's glass-and-steel mansion. Ohnishi, seated in his wheelchair on the open balcony high above the rolling lawns, nodded solemnly as Kenji explained the current situation throughout Hawaii.

"Though it has been four days since he was killed, many of the National Guard units still believe that their orders are still coming from David Takamora; they don't know that Honolulu's mayor is now dead. MacArthur Drive leading to Pearl Harbor is blockaded by students armed with hunting rifles and fully equipped guardsmen. The airport is now closed to all traffic and the buildings have been evacuated except for mercenary guards I hired. The runways are blocked with airport maintenance vehicles that won't be moved without orders from either you or me.

"The microwave relay stations are also closed and guarded and the main phone cables have been seized. Hawaii is essentially isolated."

"Has there been any resistance from the media?"

"Yes," Kenji replied glancing at his watch. "The local heads of the networks are demanding some sort of interview with Takamora, preferably live, to calm the fears of the general population. One has threatened to start broadcasting reports about the violence to the mainland if Takamora doesn't appear soon."

"How do you plan to deal with him?" Ohnishi did not sound too concerned.

"As soon as he leaves his studio, I have an agent ready to take him out."

"Good. How violent are the streets right now?"

"From my men stationed in the hospitals, it seems maybe two hundred dead, around five hundred injured so far. Most of these are random acts like the ones seen in Los Angeles in 1992. Gangs of youths beating innocent people, vendetta retributions between gang members, that sort of thing. Some of the victims are those we've specifically targeted. Of our list of three hundred possible threats, eighty-six are confirmed dead, but many more have probably been eliminated. I don't have confirmation from our agents yet."

"It disturbs me that we have not heard from Suleiman about our arms shipment," Ohnishi said suddenly.

Kenji did not reply, but his gaze darted furtively to the face of his Rolex.

"Those arms are supposed to be here in a few hours, and we don't know what type of planes will be flying them in or the recognition codes the pilots will transmit. If we don't get those codes, we can't clear the runways.

"We are approaching a critical point. Soon people will begin to lose their fervor and want the violence to end. We must get those weapons and the rest of our mercenaries. The President of the United States will respond soon, I'm sure. The forces at Pearl may be bottled up for now, but they can be unleashed very quickly indeed."

"The President wouldn't dare order those troops to open fire. He'd be risking a sympathetic revolt on the mainland. Every ethnic minority in America would be behind us. Anarchy would reign in every town and street."

"He has other options, Kenji, an attack against me, for example. He knows of my involvement in this coup. He could target me alone and wait for the violence to die with me. Mobs like this only stay active with someone to control them. If we don't stay in contact with our lieutenants around the islands, they will quickly lose their fire."

"True," Kenji agreed, "and we must also think of Kerikov's response."

"I don't worry about him. His powers are severely limited."

"But the coup was his idea and was only supposed to happen on his orders. Surely he has a plan to stop it. We are jeopardizing his control of the volcano. He must have a way of protecting it in such a contingency."

Ohnishi smiled paternally. "You have always only thought of my protection, Kenji, and that is most admirable, but I believe that we are quite secure. There is no way Kerikov can stop us."

Kenji seemed relieved to hear his master's confident tone. "What will we do when we can't produce Takamora to lead the people?"

"Senator Namura is currently hiding outside Washington, D.C. He was my choice to lead the coup if Takamora had refused, so he will become the new leader. He has already accepted the honor. One of my private jets will fly him here as soon as it's safe for him to move."

"And Takamora's death?"

"We'll blame the U.S. military. Don't worry so, Kenji, all is working out well. Suleiman's weapons will arrive along with mercenaries to augment your forces. Namura will probably be here within twenty-four hours to place a stamp of legitimacy on what we've started. Neither the President nor Kerikov will have the time or fortitude to launch any major opposition."

From the corner of one eye, Kenji noticed a dark figure dart across the lawn toward the main house. The first man was quickly followed by two more racing from the shadowed protection of the jungle. Kenji crossed his legs casually, belying the instinctive tightening of his muscles. His hand rested naturally against his ankle.

"Maybe all contingencies have been thought of," he remarked. "I never thought we would actually get this far. Just a few months ago, a coup in Hawaii seemed like such a far-fetched idea.''

"It really wasn't so outrageous even then. The state was ripe for it, racism and tension was building. We only heightened it with our acts and now orchestrate its crescendo.''

The explosion wasn't strong enough to shatter the thick glass skin of the mansion, but it did rattle the balcony and startle a flock of dark pelicans into flight across the vast lawn. Ohnishi whirled around in his wheelchair, scanning his surroundings for a frightened moment. When he turned to his faithful assistant, Kenji had already sprung to his feet. The snub-nosed revolver from his ankle holster was held firmly in his hand.

The barrel was pointed directly between Ohnishi's wide staring eyes. "Don't move, old man," Kenji sneered.

Takahiro Ohnishi's age-weakened bladder released into his trademark black Armani suit.

THE WHITE HOUSE

Staff Sergeant Harold Tompkins was as about as nervous as a human being could get. He was on duty in the Situation Room when the video images from Pearl Harbor faded from the high-definition screen. He fiddled with the satellite feeds under the combined stares of the President, the chairman of the Joint Chiefs, the secretaries of State and Defense, and the directors of the CIA, NSA, and FBI.

One moment the image of Pearl Harbor was crisp and vivid and the next, the screen had gone blank. Had this been a commercial transmission, a ''Please stand by'' sign would have flashed and those assembled gone off for snacks or to use the bathroom. But this was not a commercial transmission; Pearl Harbor had just come under attack when the image had faded and these men expected Tompkins to get the video feed back on line.

''Anything?'' Admiral C. Thomas Morrison asked.

''No, sir, not yet,'' Tompkins managed to squeak.

''Jesus Christ.''

The air was thick in the twenty-by-twenty-foot vault buried four floors below the White House. A blue pall of smoke swirled from the cigarettes that these men would never admit to in public. Even the President, where he sat hunched at the head of the large refractory table, had a Marlboro hanging from the corner of his pensive mouth.

"If my wife sees me like this, she's going to kill me," he said to lighten the mood. The answering laughter had a nervous edge.

Despite the cigarettes, the hands made twitchy by endless cups of coffee and the grizzled stubble that covered their faces, these men were still as sharp as they'd been when called to the situation room twelve hours earlier. An aide entered from the single elevator and walked straight to Sam Becker, the head of the National Security Agency.

"Sir, here's the latest from the KH-11 flyby." He handed over a sheaf of infrared photographs taken by an orbiting spy satellite. "Just like the photos taken from the SR-1 Wraith, I'm afraid the analysts couldn't make much out of them. The heat signature from the volcano makes it impossible to locate any other thermal images."

"Damn," Becker said, leafing through the photos. "If my men didn't see a Russian nuclear sub, I don't see how Mercer could have. The NSA has the best photo interp people in the world. I hope you're right about him, Dick."

Henna looked up from the fan of papers spread before him. "I've got no guarantees, but so far the man hasn't disappointed. He told me over the phone that he had the *John Dory* pinpointed at the volcano site."

"If that's true, why didn't we just order him to tell us where that was?" asked Paul Barnes.

"Christ, Paul, you met him. Do you think he would have told us anything?"

"I agree with Dick on this one," the President remarked, rubbing his bloodshot eyes. "The deft touch is what's needed here, not a heavy hand."

"I think I have it, sirs," Tompkins interrupted. The men turned to the screen.

An image came into focus, a handsome Oriental man dressed in jungle camouflage. Behind him, marines were firing at an unseen enemy from the protection of sandbag bunkers. Two Abrams tanks sat squarely on a wide expanse of asphalt, their turrets pointed toward the main gates of Pearl Harbor. Their 120mm cannons were silent, but machine-gun fire spat from their coaxially mounted Brownings. It was a macabre scene because there was no audio.

Tompkins pressed a few more buttons on his console and the clamor of battle assaulted the room. The ferocity was stunning.

"Repeat your message, Colonel, we lost your transmission for a few minutes," Morrison said.

Over the sound of the battle, words matched the officer's moving lips. ". . . about ten minutes ago, sir."

"Colonel Shinzo, this is Admiral Morrison, please repeat," the admiral asked a second time.

"Sir, about ten minutes ago all hell broke loose. Without warning, the guardsmen and locals outside the gate opened fire. Small arms mostly, but the guardsmen do have rocket launchers and TOW antitank missiles. They are not making any move for an assault yet, but it's only a matter of time, sir."

Colonel Shinzo shouted something incomprehensible and ducked behind a sandbag wall. The camera must have been mounted on a tripod because it remained steady as a grenade detonated no more than twenty yards away. The image faded for a moment, then returned. Shinzo was again standing in view.

"What are you doing to hold them, Shinzo?"

"As ordered, we're firing over their heads, but my boys are taking too many casualties to remain passive much longer, sir."

"Colonel Shinzo, do you recognize my voice?" the President asked clearly, hiding his exhaustion.

"I believe so, Mr. President." The statement was more of a question.

"Colonel, you're doing a fine job there, but I want civilian and National Guard casualties at a minimum. Do you understand?"

"Yes, Mr. President," Shinzo said resignedly, knowing this meant losing a lot of his men.

The noise of the battle increased dramatically. Shinzo turned away quickly as the transmission broke off again.

The assembled men all turned to Tompkins, who was frustratingly twisting dials and knobs. "I'm sorry, but the transmission was broken at the other end. There's nothing I can do."

"That's fine," Admiral Morrison said dryly. "You're dismissed."

Tompkins gratefully hurried from the room.

"Can we trust him?" Paul Barnes asked. "I mean, he's a Jap after all."

"Shut your fucking mouth, you racist son of a bitch." Morrison was on his feet the instant Barnes finished speaking. "Shinzo wears the uniform of the United States Marine Corps. You question the integrity of one of my boys again, and so help me Christ I'm going to tear you a new asshole."

"Let's calm down here, gentlemen," Dick Henna said soothingly. "But Admiral Morrison has a point. We start second-guessing the motivations of our own people and we might as well go home and wait for Armageddon."

"I guess it's started," the President said slowly. Every man knew he meant a civil war. "The great melting pot has been simmering for two hundred–plus years and it's about to boil over. Unless this situation ends within a few hours, the news from Hawaii will light a powder keg in every big city in America. It'll make the Los Angeles riots of 1992 look like Mardi Gras."

The President was silent for five long minutes. His

most trusted advisors knew he was making a decision that might very well condemn the United States to the bloodiest war ever fought in the Western Hemisphere. The compassion they felt for him could not make the decision any easier.

His shaggy head was bowed over the table and his lips moved silently. Was he praying, or asking advice of the ghost of Abraham Lincoln, who was said to wander the White House? He raised his head, his shoulders squaring.

"Tom." Admiral Morrison looked the President square in the eye, awaiting his orders. "I want a Tomahawk cruise missile armed with a nuclear warhead launched at the volcano. If there is a Russian sub out there guarding it, it'll be destroyed by the blast."

So it was war. The United States was going to fight and perhaps lose everything democracy had created. Once again race would plunge America into a civil war, but this time there would be no North and South, no Mason-Dixon Line. The boundaries had blurred in the decades since then. Now the battles would be fought in every state and every town.

"Then order the *Kitty Hawk* and the *Inchon* to stand off, suspend all flights, and steam out of the area. I don't want them anywhere near Hawaii, is that clear? Tell the commander at Pearl to throw down their weapons and surrender the base."

A sigh ran through the room.

"I would rather sacrifice Hawaii than risk a war. Maybe their seccession will start a chain reaction and this country will disintegrate, but I'm willing to take that risk. I can't order our troops to kill Americans no matter what the consequences."

Tears ran unashamedly down his cheeks.

"Sir." Dick Henna was the first person to speak. "What about Mercer? We haven't even given him a chance."

"Dick, he's only one man. We're talking about a massive revolution supported by God knows how many people."

"Mr. President," Henna persisted, "What if he's right that this revolution is being masterminded by an outside influence? If he can cut that off, there will be no revolt."

"I spoke to the Russian President no more than two hours ago, Dick. He had no idea what I was talking about. Mercer was wrong about the Russians being involved. This whole thing was strictly Takahiro Ohnishi's."

"And what if this is something the Russian government didn't sanction?"

"That's a bit too far-fetched for me to believe. This is a massive operation. There's no way the head of the country wouldn't know about it."

"Ask your predecessors about Iran-Contra sometime," Henna retorted sarcastically.

The President ignored the remark.

"About the Russian government not sanctioning this operation, it may not be that far-fetched," Paul Barnes said, polishing his glasses.

"What do you mean?"

"This afternoon, the body of Gennady Perchenko was fished from a river in Bangkok. If you recall, Perchenko was the Russian ambassador to the Bangkok Accords, the one who outfoxed us into signing away any legal rights to that new volcano."

"Was there any indication of foul play?"

"In my business, there's never any indication, but I'd stake my career that he was murdered. Also, an informer reported seeing Ivan Kerikov flying into Thailand a few days before Perchenko's death."

"Who's Ivan Kerikov?"

"A real cagey KGB operator, sir. My contacts in Moscow tell me that there is a massive manhunt on for him even as we speak. It seems he has a record of working outside the fold and right now he's under arrest for misappropriation of government funds, equipment, and personnel, and a dozen other charges, including murder.

"He's come to the attention of the CIA a few times over the years. He ran a team of assassins and torturers in Afghanistan during the early 1980s and he was somehow connected to the Korean Air jumbo jet shot down in September of 1983. Most recently he took over Department Seven of the KGB.

"Department Seven is one of those groups we know very little about. They don't seem to have any active agents or any real goals. They just act as a sort of think tank as far as we can figure. Now, if Perchenko's death can be linked to Kerikov then we have a definite connection between that volcano and this Department Seven."

Sam Becker had been reading the file handed to him earlier, with the photos, and now he looked up sharply. "We have that connection."

"What do you have, Sam?" The President caught the strength behind Becker's voice and drew from it.

"On Paul's request last evening, I had the archive sections at Fort Meade pull anything they had on Soviet geologists from the fifties and sixties. The records were sketchy, but we just got lucky."

Since its inception, the National Security Agency at Fort Meade was the repository for every scrap of intelligence gathered from around the world. There was more computer power in the sprawling complex than anywhere else on the planet, and it was used to decipher even the most oblique reference or cryptic message from enemy and ally alike. If something had ever been put in print, spoken about over a phone line, or bounced off a satellite, NSA had a record of it. From the personal advertisements in the *Johannesburg Star* to mundane conversations between two sisters in Madrid to the dying gasps of three cosmonauts who secretly suffocated aboard the Soyuz space station in 1974, it was all stored on the magnetic tapes in NSA's archives.

Becker held up his slim file. "This is from the archive

director, Oliver Lee. According to Lee, personnel records from a research laboratory near Odessa show that an Olga Borodin has been drawing a decent pension from the state since an accident claimed her husband on June 20, 1963. Given the parameters of the search, her name caught Lee's attention, and after a bit more research he found that the laboratory was part of an agency called Department Seven. It seems the CIA know more about Department Seven than we do but the connection is obvious. Olga Borodin is the widow of a geologist named Pytor Borodin.''

''You mean the Russian specialist on bikinium?'' Henna interrupted.

''So, Dr. Mercer was right, the Russians are involved, just not their government.'' The President was truly shocked. ''Kerikov must be the mastermind and Ohnishi merely a pawn. The man's got balls, I'll say that much, but knowing this doesn't help us any. We still have a coup taking place in Hawaii and a valuable resource about to fall to this Ivan Kerikov.'' The President swiveled to face Henna. ''What do you propose?''

''Give Mercer until dawn,'' Henna said. ''If he has a plan, at least give him that much time. You saw from that last transmission that it's almost dark in Hawaii. Tonight should be relatively calm. The guardsmen don't have the right equipment for night fighting. If we don't hear anything by sunrise, continue with your plan, blow up the volcano and surrender the islands to Ohnishi.''

The President leaned back in his chair for a moment, staring at the soundproofed ceiling tiles, fingers laced behind his head. He made his decision quickly. ''All right, I'll give Mercer until seven A.M. local time, then I want that fucking volcano obliterated.''

Henna stood to leave the room. Mercer had arrived on the *Inchon* ten hours earlier and Henna had promised to get in touch with any final news.

''Dick?''

''Yes, Mr. President.''

"Why do you trust Mercer so much?"

Henna paused by the elevator door, his arms full of papers and files. "I'm basically a cop, sir, and cops learn to trust their instincts."

DESPITE the sophistication of the equipment in the White House Communications Room, Henna spent twenty frustrating minutes waiting for a connection to the *Inchon* and another ten for Mercer to be tracked down aboard the 778-foot assault ship and brought to the radio.

"About time you called."

"You've got until seven tomorrow morning your time," Henna said without preamble. "So you better have one hell of a plan in that Machiavellian mind of yours."

"What happens at seven?" Mercer asked airily.

"A cruise missile blows up Borodin's volcano and the President surrenders the Hawaiian Islands without a fight."

"Talk about your serious deadlines." Mercer paused, absorbing this latest piece of information. "Well, I'd best be off, then. Any parting advice?"

"Yeah. Right now Pearl Harbor is a war zone and we can only assume the rest of the islands are equally inflamed."

"I'm surprised it's stayed calm as long as it has. What else?"

"We've found a definite link between the coup and a Russian KGB director named Ivan Kerikov. He's the mastermind. He was last seen in Thailand but may be on Hawaii by now. Oh, yeah. I've had a team monitoring ham radio operators from Hawaii for the past couple of days. A guy there named Ken Peters, who works for one of the television stations, got hold of one of my people in California. He suspects that one of their reporters, Jill Tzu, may have been kidnapped by Ohnishi. She was doing a real in-depth exposé on him when she vanished.''

"Dudley Doright to the rescue. What else?"

"Just that Ohnishi's mansion is heavily guarded by some real fanatics, so be careful."

"Don't worry, Dick. I have no interest in Ohnishi's house. He's just a willing accomplice, not the linchpin."

The signal from the *Inchon* faded. Henna knew that Mercer had cut him off.

He settled the phone back into its cradle. If Mercer wasn't going to Ohnishi's mansion, then where was he going? And if Ohnishi wasn't the principal in this affair, who was?

HAWAII

Evad Lurbud's senses were so highly tuned that the explosion which echoed across the lawns from the main house rocked him back against his heels as if he had been physically struck. Sergeant Demanov placed a steadying hand on his shoulder.

"What in the hell was that?" the burly sergeant asked in a whisper.

"Don't know," Lurbud replied curtly, straining his eyes through the night-vision binoculars at the front of Ohnishi's glass mansion. "I can't see anything out of the ordinary."

Demanov, Lurbud, and two commandos were crouched behind a small stand of flowering rhododendrons placed like an island on the wide front lawn of the estate. The rest of the squad was similarly hidden behind other natural cover.

They had reached Ohnishi's as the shadows of twilight began smearing the beautiful grounds. Lurbud's team had made use of the jungle which surrounded the estate to approach to within two hundred yards of the house, then had dashed across the lawn in a leapfrog technique, moving from small grove to small grove.

Lurbud and Demanov were no more than forty yards from the marble porte cochere when the explosion occurred. The sound was accompanied by a flash of brilliant light at the side of the darkened house.

"I don't see anyone within the building," Lurbud said.

The night-vision glasses allowed Lurbud to see into the glass-walled house, but the main foyer entrance, curving staircase, and the rooms immediately to its left and right were all empty. He was about to signal the men behind him to move forward when a tiny movement within the mansion made him pause.

Someone was moving across the foyer toward the staircase. The figure was walking cautiously, twisting his body and neck as he peered around. When the man reached the base of the stairs, Lurbud clearly saw the assault rifle tucked under his arm.

"We've got company," he said tensely

Lurbud watched closely as another figure swept into the entrance foyer and scurried up the stairs. "Two so far," he remarked. "But something's not right. They look as if they aren't familiar with the house. It seems strange for Ohnishi's security to act like that."

"Could be standard practice after that explosion," Demanov suggested.

"I don't think so. I think I know why we haven't seen any of Ohnishi's personal bodyguards anywhere on the estate."

"American commandos beat us here?"

"That's my guess."

"Good," Demanov grunted, and quietly cocked his machine pistol.

KENJI, what's going on?" Ohnishi wailed.

"There was one contingency you never anticipated."

The revolver in Kenji's hand was steady. "Just as Kerikov sold you out and you sold out Kerikov, I have done the same to both of you."

"I don't understand, Kenji," Ohnishi pleaded.

"It's really quite simple. Ivan Kerikov hired me eight months ago to act as his watchdog, to report your activities to him."

Ohnishi slouched deeper in his wheelchair, his frail neck vanishing into his shoulders as he bowed in defeat. He already knew the rest of what Kenji would say, and the weight of truth was heavy on his wasted body.

"Kerikov had to maintain absolute command of every aspect of his operation. You were the only player that he did not directly control. That is why he enlisted me, to make sure that he knew what you were plotting."

"But I have known you all your life; you are like my son. How? How could you do such a thing?" Ohnishi might have accepted the betrayal, but he still had to know the reason.

"You know nothing about me except that which I've told you. It is true that at the beginning I saw you as my father, as my master, but like any son, I outgrew you. I searched for my own path. Which I found."

"Through Kerikov?"

Kenji's laugh was without feeling, so mocking that it sounded more like the bark of a rabid dog. "Kerikov is as much a fool as you were, old man. Soon after he approached me with his lucrative offer, I was approached by a group of men that gave me even more." Kenji related the story of his mother's enslavement as a "Comfort Girl" to the occupying Japanese army in Korea, his subsequent birth and his sale to his natural father. "I am half Korean, Ohnishi, a heritage that my father tried to bury, but a fact I could never ignore.

"In the years since Kerikov first approached you, he had to change his plans due to the collapse of his government. Not long ago, but before you began actively pursuing this doomed dream of yours, he sold you out to a group of investors. This group bought the volcano that Kerikov promised would make Hawaii a viable nation. What he did not know, or couldn't know, is that this group of Korean investors then contacted me. I don't know how they found out about my heritage, but they gave me the opportunity to prove who I really am. From then on, not only was I a spy for Kerikov against you, but also a spy against the both of you for my new Korean benefactors.

"You had no chance at all. Every move you made was counteracted by one of my allies. You bought weapons from Suleiman el-aziz Suleiman—I betrayed the Egyptian to Kerikov. The weapons that you so hoped for will not arrive. Nor will there be any additional mercenaries. Kerikov asked me to rescue a certain woman from the NOAA ship—I told my allies to have her killed in Washington D.C. Kerikov forced you to write that letter to the President, intending to hold it over your head, I sent it to the White House, knowing that would lead to the anarchy that now holds these islands."

"You sent the letter?" Ohnishi did nothing to hide his astonishment.

"Oh, yes. Mayor Takamora made a convenient scapegoat, but I was responsible for sending the letter. The volcano was too close to the surface to risk any detection and it was agreed that your letter would act as the best possible deterrent against the American forces finding it. The *Ocean Seeker* almost foiled these plans, but Kerikov dealt with it with a typical Russian reaction. After he had the NOAA ship destroyed, I knew that the American focus would be on to you and perhaps the Russians if they got smart, but we, that is the Koreans, would never be suspect. The volcano would be ours without ever having created or defended it.

"It was the perfect triple-cross. While you and Kerikov and the United States quarreled over the Hawaiian islands and the volcano, Hydra Consolidated would take the prize and no one would be the wiser."

Kenji was chuckling at the frail old man before him when an armed figure burst onto the balcony, his assault rifle covering both Kenji and Ohnishi. Kenji spoke to him in Korean.

"It's all right. This is Ohnishi; he won't give us any difficulties. All went well?"

"Yes," the Korean commando replied crisply. "Ohnishi's guards were taken out smoothly. The diversionary explosion worked perfectly; none of my men were even wounded."

"Good. We'll leave here for my house in just a few minutes. Make sure the remainder of the explosives are in place." The Korean soldier began speaking into a walkie-talkie. "You see, Ohnishi, this is where my true loyalties lie. When I told the Koreans about your coup, they thought it was the perfect cover under which they could claim the volcano. The United States and Ivan Kerikov would be too busy trying to quell the violence and silence you to notice us."

The sound of an automatic weapon ripped through the mansion like the tearing of a piece of canvas. Kenji rolled to the floor, shifting his aim from Ohnishi to the doorway leading to the balcony. The Korean soldier swung around so that he too covered the entrance. Silence hung in the air for a long moment.

"It came from downstairs. You must have missed one of Ohnishi's guards. Go check it out." Kenji waited until the Korean left before jerking Ohnishi to his feet and half dragging him toward his bedroom.

LURBUD gave the trigger of his machine pistol another tap as a figure lunged from the front door for the bushes just to its left. He knew he'd missed, but it would keep his opponent pinned for a few crucial seconds.

Sergeant Demanov followed Lurbud and two other troopers in the last dash across the lawn to the house. As they approached the thick slabs of glass of one wing, Lurbud tossed a grenade. The grenade cracked the glass as it hit, but did not penetrate. A second later, it exploded, shattering three panels in a plume of crystal and fire. Lurbud led his men through the resulting six-foot-wide hole. Their boots crunched across the fine glass chips spread out over the woven reed mat within. One of Kenji's men lay smeared against the far wall of the Japanese-style room, his body shredded by the razor-sharp glass.

The remainder of Lurbud's team had used similar techniques, blowing four other holes in the structure. What followed was nothing short of an all-out war, with both sides falsely assuming their enemy was an American commando team.

Cordite smoke hung heavily in the entrance foyer as Lurbud cautiously edged himself into the lofty room near one wall. In the whirling air, it was difficult to tell who was part of his force and who was not. A figure leapt from behind a huge terra-cotta vase, leveling his weapon at Lurbud. Sergeant Demanov dispatched the attacker with a quick burst.

Lurbud acknowledged Demanov with a nod and continued his sweep of the house. Gunfire echoed throughout the cavernous home and streaks of tracer fire, like comet tails, could be seen through some of the transparent walls. Halfway up the stairs, Lurbud came under a scathing fire, bullets ripping up the thick marble banister only inches from his body.

Lurbud leapt up and over the railing, exposing himself for a moment to the hidden gunman before dropping back to the first floor. He hit the hard marble and rolled once as more bullets sliced the air around him. More than one gunman had targeted him. He continued to roll, directing fire from his machine pistol at the vague outline of a man far across the foyer. The rounds caught the man low in the gut, the kinetic energy of the impacts lifting him bodily and tossing him through a bullet-riddled glass wall.

A grenade rumbled somewhere within the mansion,

shaking the entire building. It was immediately followed by the sound of huge chunks of glass shattering against the hard floor.

. Up and running, Lurbud changed clips for his weapon with expert hands. Someone loomed out from the reeking smoke and Lurbud almost tore him apart, but stopped in time as he realized it was Demanov.

"What's your estimate?" Lurbud panted.

"Ten to fifteen, maybe as many as twenty. It's hard to tell because this place is so fucking big."

Bullets flew over their heads as they both dove behind a sofa in what must have been the formal living room. Demanov returned fire quickly. Another fusillade pinned them back to the white-carpeted floor.

As soon as the firing stopped, Lurbud sprang to his feet and ran across the room. Bullets tracked his progress, edging closer and closer to his racing form. A Waterford crystal sculpture nearly seven feet tall exploded just behind him. He dove for the floor between two leather ottomans, breath jamming into his throat with the impact.

The firing stopped for a moment and he lifted himself. The gunman was in plain view. Lurbud opened up, stitching rounds across a massive Roy Lichtenstein painting before finding his mark. The gunman went down with three slugs buried deep in his torso.

Lurbud slithered across the room to the fallen assailant. Expecting to see a caucasian or Japanese from Ohnishi's security detachment, he was shocked to find that the gunman was Chinese or possibly Korean.

"What the fuck is going on?" he wondered.

Lurbud heard the distinctive crack of a pistol shot just as a bullet slammed into the corpse's chest inches from his hand. He lifted his machine pistol and fired instinctively, but his bullets hit nothing but more glass. The attacker had nimbly ducked behind a glass-cased suit of Japanese armor guarding a curve in the hallway leading to some of the guest suites.

Lurbud lurched to his feet and started down the hall, back pressed tight to the wall, hands steady on his weapon. He fired a burst at the priceless armor, which disintegrated under the hail of 9mm rounds. There was no one behind it. He continued on, passing the body of one of his own men further down the hallway. The Russian soldier's head had been completely twisted around.

"Jesus," Lurbud muttered, remembering that Ohnishi's assistant Kenji was a black belt of the eight don, a master virtually without peer. The dead Russian had to be his handiwork.

Lurbud tightened the grip on his machine pistol now that he knew the power of his quarry. He searched each of the opulent guest suites quickly but calmly, mentally blocking out the firefight still raging within the building. The door at the far end of the hallway did not lead to a room, but rather opened onto a stark concrete and steel service staircase.

He ascended cautiously, the rancid sweat of fear snaking down his flanks. It was impossible to hear anything in the echoing stairway because of the cacophonous battle.

After a few minutes, Lurbud reached the top of the stairs but there was no sign of Kenji, just a dimly lit landing and a fire retardant door. Lurbud jerked open the door, keeping his body safely out of the way.

When the gunfire he expected didn't occur, he ducked his head around the corner quickly. The room beyond was small, maybe twelve feet square, but tastefully furnished with a low bed, an antique dresser, and damascene wall coverings. A huge built-in mirror dominated the far wall. Lurbud knew it was one-way glass from the plans provided to his team.

Rather than waste time looking for the secret exit that Kenji must have used, Lurbud pumped a few rounds into the mirror and watched it tumble to the floor in a glittering cascade. Beyond lay Ohnishi's private bedroom and on the beautiful four-poster bed lay Ohnishi himself, naked.

His head had been severed from his torso, as had his arms and legs. Each appendage lay neatly in its proper anatomical position, but about two inches separated each from the trunk of the billionaire's body.

Evad Lurbud had been witness to and had in fact carried out some of the most vicious torture yet devised by mankind, but what lay before him brought vomit shooting out of his mouth. Ohnishi's withered genitalia had been cut off and placed a few inches from his groin. Lurbud knew from the amount of blood in this region that this had been the first member carved off.

Trying to regain his composure, Lurbud thought for a moment and realized that such a death took more time than he'd given the fleeing Kenji. Either someone else had been here first, or Kenji had done this prior to Lurbud's assault on the mansion.

If the presence of Korean guards was baffling, then Ohnishi's death was truly confusing. Kenji was Ohnishi's assistant of many years, by all accounts incredibly loyal. Why had he suddenly turned? Why had he killed his employer? Lurbud let these questions sink into the back of his mind as he continued his search.

Beyond the bedroom lay a dayroom as large as most suburban homes. The decor was very modern, including geometric and freeform art pieces and a glossy white pine floor. The pyramidal top of the mansion soared over Lurbud's head, supporting a huge primary-colored mobile by Calder, a smaller version of the one hanging in the east wing of the National Gallery in Washington D.C.

Lurbud dashed from the dayroom through the nine-foot-tall French doors at the far end and onto an open balcony that overlooked the back of Ohnishi's estate. He took a few deep breaths of the humid air, glad to be out of the smoke-filled house. Amazingly, he could make out the sounds of night insects over the din of battle below.

Kenji stood on the back lawn, a lean shadowy form in the rich moonlight. The instant Lurbud saw him, he raised his machine pistol, but Kenji was too far out of range. A glance to his left showed Lurbud the rope ladder, hanging over the side of the balcony that Kenji must have used to escape.

Below, Kenji stretched his arms over his head, and Lurbud swore he heard laughter. When Kenji's hands met, though Lurbud could not see the gesture, his finger touched the detonation button on a small radio transmitter.

A deep rumbling shook the building, buckling the entire structure. Some of the few still intact glass plates popped from their supports and flew onto the lawn. The rumbling deepened and the house began to shiver as the chain of small explosives planted around the foundation by Kenji's soldiers went off in a predetermined sequence.

The timing of the blasts corresponded with the harmonic resonance of the entire structure so that the rumbling deepened even as the sound of the small explosions diminished. Lurbud clutched at the railing as the building shook faster and faster. Huge rents appeared in the main support columns, those that took most of the strain of the massive glass roof.

The columns collapsed all at once and the roof shattered in a glittering explosion. The slab-sided glass walls toppled as the entire building turned into an endless a shower of glass. Tons of it poured down, killing all those beneath, slicing through flesh and bone without check. One moment the Koreans and Russians had been fighting a desperate battle and the next they were torn apart by an unimaginable force.

Lurbud had felt the balcony sway as the support columns let go. The lighted, almost crystalline pyramid above him shattered as if a bomb had gone off directly beneath it. He ducked under Ohnishi's breakfast table an instant before the shards sliced through the air like hypervelocity bullets. His left hand was caught in the hail of glass and he quickly pulled it to his chest. Three fingers were missing and a seven-inch-long fragment of glass was thrust halfway through his hand.

He had just started to scream when the whole cantilevered balcony let go. His last sensation, even before the pain of his mutilated hand had time to fully course through his nervous system, was of falling indefinitely.

USS *INCHON*

Mercer thanked the radio operator politely after hanging up on Henna and left the cryptlike Communications Room. His expression was neutral, and only a trained observer would notice the slight tenseness in his stride. His gray eyes were hard, devoid of emotion.

A woman he had dated several years earlier had said, the day their relationship ended, that the only way to tell what he was thinking was to ask him. His expressions, she complained, would never give him away, and his eyes, which are supposed to be windows into the soul, were really one-way glass that only he could see through.

He had scoffed at the notion, but any navy personnel that he passed would have agreed with her.

Because he had been sent to the *Inchon* for an undetermined number of days, Mercer had been assigned a cabin. It had the luxurious appointments of a cheap highway motel, but it was his own. He locked the door and stripped. After a cold shower to help wake him up, he dressed again, secreting equipment brought from his home.

When he was dressed, he did some quick shadow-boxing to ensure that nothing would fly free and that his equipment was unconstricting. His moves were fast and efficient, his mind focused to a pinpoint. Satisfied, he took several deep, calming breaths. He tucked his Beretta pistol into the waistband of his pants, the tails of his black shirt over it. Grabbing the nylon duffel containing his combat harness and machine pistol, he left the small cabin.

He passed a few dozen of the nineteen hundred marines on board as he headed for the flight deck. He could tell by their grim faces that the men didn't relish the idea of invading their own country.

Neither do I, he thought.

The flight deck of the amphibious assault ship was nearly three hundred feet shorter than the *Kitty Hawk*'s, but equally as pandemonious. An AV-8B Harrier jump jet thundered into the sky just as he walked onto the deck. Thanks to her ducted fans, the attack aircraft utilized only a tiny portion of the deck to achieve flight. The wind kicked up by her Rolls Royce Pegasus engines whipped the air furiously, sending grit into Mercer's eyes.

Several Sea Stallion and Sea King helicopters sat on the deck, their huge rotors hanging limply. Mechanics and other personnel were buzzing around, dodging small vehicles and each other in preparation for a possible battle. It was obvious that the President hadn't ordered the standdown yet. Mercer guessed that the commander-in-chief would wait until the last moment.

He shielded his eyes against the thirty-knot wind and surveyed the twilit deck until he saw the helicopter that had brought him from the *Kitty Hawk* early that morning.

A Sikorsky Sea King. Lieutenant Edward Rice, USMC, pilot.

The huge chopper sat just forward of the ship's superstructure. Mercer could see movement in the cockpit.

Eddie Rice had told him on the flight from the carrier that he would be ferrying some equipment back to the *Kitty Hawk* just after sunset. Mercer was thankful that Henna had called before the chopper returned to its ship. The hijacking would be a little easier since he knew the pilot.

No sense ruining a stranger's day, thought Mercer as he walked to the big helicopter. He approached the chopper from the port side and noticed with satisfaction that the crew door was open. He pulled the Beretta 9mm from under his shirt and threw his duffel bag onto the small platform below the chopper's flight deck.

He kept the gun hidden when he poked his head into the cockpit.

"Come to see me off, Mercer?" Eddie Rice smiled.

Without a doubt, he had the worst teeth for a black man that Mercer had ever seen. So much for stereotypes, he thought.

"I loved your flying so much, the navy decided I should go back with you," Mercer replied.

"They sent you to the *Inchon* just to bring you back to the *Kitty Hawk*?" Rice shook his head. "I've heard of the government paper shuffle, but this is nuts. Come on up; I'm just about cleared for takeoff."

Mercer tucked the pistol away without ever displaying it and slipped into the empty copilot's seat. As he had earlier that day, he felt like he was in a cocoon of dials and switches. He sat anxiously as Rice continued his preflight check. Waiting for the takeoff was agonizing and he kept glancing at his watch. He had eleven and a half hours until the nuclear strike.

"You got a date or something?" Rice asked, noting Mercer's agitation.

"Something like that," Mercer said grimly.

"Two more minutes and we're out of here." Rice tugged the microphone to his lips and began talking to the flight controller. A moment later, the two turboshaft engines began to whine. Needles on the instrument panel quivered and then started to climb as the General Electric motors warmed. Rice watched the instruments intently, his gaze darting from one gauge to the next.

When he engaged the gearbox, the engines' whine dulled for a moment as they fought the inertia of the stationary rotors, then picked up as the five great blades began to turn. The noise in the cockpit increased dramatically, forcing Mercer to don a helmet. Eddie continued to add power and the blades beat the air fervently. He eased back on the collective pitch and the 20,000-pound helicopter lifted into the dim Pacific sky.

"Piece of cake." Rice grinned as the *Inchon* vanished behind them. He turned to Mercer expecting a return smile, but was greeted by the gaping barrel of the Beretta. The grin melted from his face.

"Sorry, Eddie," Mercer said, his voice sounding tinny through the chopper's intercom. "But we're not heading for the *Kitty Hawk*."

"I guess we're not."

Mercer reversed his grip on the pistol and smashed it into the Sea King's radio, cutting the chopper off from the outside, then turned the weapon back on Rice.

"Listen, I'm on a secret mission. Hijacking a helicopter at the last moment was the only way to maintain security."

"Right," Rice said suspiciously.

"You know why the navy moved these ships to Hawaii." It was a statement, not a question. "You may be forced to invade your own country and kill your own people. Well, there's a chance I can stop it. I have to get to Hawaii and you're my best shot. It doesn't matter if you believe me or not, but you are going to take me to Hawaii."

"There's no way you work for the CIA. The few agents I've known would've just pulled the gun and given the orders. They don't like to explain shit. So who in the hell are you?''

''I don't work for the CIA, Eddie. I didn't lie this morning when I told you I was a geologist, but I'm also the only guy who can pull this off.''

''You know there's nothing I can do to you; I've got to keep both hands on the sticks to keep this eggbeater in the sky. So don't you worry about me. But my passengers might not like a sight-seeing tour.''

''Passengers? I thought you were carrying cargo.''

''When you see them, you'll know why I call 'em cargo.''

Knowing Rice couldn't leave his seat or contact any other aircraft or ship, Mercer ducked down until he could look into the cargo hold of the Sea King. There were five men in the 160-square-foot hold.

They were Navy SEALs, the best trained commandos in the American military, perhaps in the world. They sat in stony silence, oblivious to the noise of the chopper or the wind buffeting them from the open hatch. Like a computer that only works in a binary system of ones and zeros, the commander of the SEALs regarded Mercer as threat or nonthreat. His fathomless eyes were the bright blue of glacial ice. They held Mercer's for the fraction of a second it took him to categorize Mercer as nonthreat and turned away indifferently.

Mercer had never felt such an aura of utter malignance in his life than that surrounding these men. Rice was right to call them cargo. To call them passengers would be admitting they retained a trace of humanity.

He went back up to the flight deck and took his seat, donning his headset.

''See what I mean?'' Eddie grinned. ''Me, I've got no problems with Hawaii, in fact I'd love a Mai Tai, just give me a target destination and I'll get us there. Oh, you didn't need to smash up our radio, you know.''

''Yeah, why's that?''

Rice smiled crookedly. ''The call I received about two

minutes before you boarded. Seems my commander was contacted by the director of the FBI. Said he thought you'd pull a stunt like this and the SEALs would be a compromise between your plan and the president's. Those SEALs back there are under orders to follow you. He told me they might come in handy tonight.''

Mercer laughed so hard his guts ached. ''That son of a bitch,'' he said admiringly. ''No wonder he's the director of the FBI. My first hijacking and the victims turn out to be willing accomplices. Sorry about pulling the gun on you.''

''Ain't nothing. I was born in South Central. Wasn't the first time it's ever happened. Probably not the last, either.''

An hour and a half later, the Sea King blasted along the northern coasts of the Hawaiian islands, her watertight hull no more than fifty feet above the crashing surf, her sixty-five-foot rotor blades less than one hundred yards from the towering cliffs. Mercer had spent much of the flight in the cargo hold with the SEALs, poring over the plans to Kenji's estate and forming a battle plan. By the time the Sea King cleared the coast, all of them were satisfied that the assault could be pulled off successfully.

Back in the cockpit, Mercer could see lights, the concentration on Rice's face, but he also saw a slight trace of enjoyment too.

Maui and Molokai and the Big Island were behind them and now they skirted the northern coast of Oahu. Mercer thought about the dead whales found there only a month ago—the start of this whole chain reaction. Amazing how such an inane event sparked one of the greatest crises America might ever face.

''Do you have the coordinates?'' Rice asked, his eyes never leaving the moon-bathed waves below.

Mercer read the coordinates of Kenji's estate from the map provided by Dick Henna. Eddie Rice punched them into the navigational computer, waited as the machine processed them, then glanced at the readout. Banking the helicopter, he lifted her over the cliffs and headed inland. The moonlit scenery below them was a gray blur, the Sea King beating through the sky at nearly 140 knots, at times below tree top level.

Mercer trusted Rice's flying implicitly. He had no choice.

They rocketed over mountains only to plunge down the other side, the helicopter never more than a hundred feet from the ground.

"Ever done flying like this before?" Mercer asked, trying to act casual though his knuckles were white as he gripped his seat.

"Sure," Rice replied. " 'Course that was in Iraq, where there weren't as many mountains or trees or buildings to smear against."

Mercer tightened his grip.

"You ever done anything like this before?" asked Rice.

"Sure," Mercer mimicked Rice's deep baritone. " 'Course that was in Iraq, where there weren't any wise-ass pilots."

Rice laughed, then yanked the helicopter skyward to avoid a tall stand of trees thrusting up from the jungle.

As the terrain flattened out, Rice began to whistle. Mercer recognized the song as Wagner's "Ride of the Valkyries." He knew exactly how Eddie felt.

"We're about ten miles from your coordinates," Rice announced a few minutes later.

"Okay, the target is a compound in the middle of an old pineapple plantation. There will be a clearing about two miles north. It used to be an equipment storage area when the plantation was operational. There's an abandoned shed on its southern edge. We'll land there."

Rice didn't reply. He was watching the ground below. The low jungle canopy retained a semblance of regimentation from when it had been planted fields. He slowed the chopper to thirty knots.

"There," he said, spotting the clearing as he crabbed the helicopter to starboard.

Mercer saw the open ground a moment later, an area of about an acre; the abandoned metal building stood at its far end, the corrugated roof sagging in the middle.

"Ugly country in thirty seconds," Mercer said into his microphone, informing the SEALs in the cargo hold.

Rice used the last scrap of jungle cover before bursting into the clearing. The rotors kicked up a cloud of fine dust, cutting visibility down to nothing. He landed the big chopper by feel alone, settling her as close to the building as possible. Had there been paint on the huge storage garage, the Teflon rotors would have scraped it off.

By the time Mercer jumped from the chopper, the SEALs had already secured the building and the surrounding area. There was no one else in the vicinity.

The air was hot and incredibly humid; Mercer's clothing stuck to his body like a clammy film and the chirping of insects sounded unnaturally loud after his hours in the chopper. He buckled his combat harness around his lean waist, cinching the shoulder straps so they were snug but not binding. After pulling his MP-5 from the duffel, he threw the empty bag back into the chopper and turned to Rice.

"You know what to do?"

"I'll wait here until you contact me." Rice held up a miniature walkie-talkie given to him by one of the SEALs. "If I don't hear anything by five A.M., I'm outta here."

"Right."

Mercer looked at his watch, 9:35. In nine and a half hours the President would unleash the nuclear warhead and destroy the volcano two hundred miles north. A few minutes after that, Hawaii would become an independent country.

MV *JOHN DORY*

Although she was forty feet under the surface, the *John Dory* still felt the turbulence above that rolled her about fifteen degrees port and starboard. The radio operator clutched at a ceiling mounted support as he waited to gain Captain Zwenkov's attention. Zwenkov was once again in muted conference with the weapons officer, going over the firing solutions for the vessel's bow-mounted Siren missile for the tenth time.

"Captain," the radio man interrupted, "flash message received from the mainland."

Zwenkov turned, cocking one bushy eyebrow in question.

"The message read 'green,' repeated for five seconds, sir."

"Very well." Zwenkov glanced at his watch. 2200 hours.

This was the eleventh such message he'd received. He'd expected the "red" code by now, authorizing him to launch his missile, but it had not come. If it didn't come until the next scheduled contact in two hours, he would barely make it to the Hawaiian coast before dawn to extract the commandos.

"All right, Weapons Officer, one more time if you please." And they ran another plot for the nuclear missile.

EVAD Lurbud collapsed the portable antenna and powered down his radio. Using his mangled left hand had caused a bright wave of blood to seep out from under his hastily applied bandage. He let the pain wash over him, gritting his teeth to keep from screaming.

That he had survived four hours since the attack on Ohnishi's house was due mainly to his extensive KGB training. That he had survived the destruction of the house itself was little short of a miracle.

Once the bombs had detonated and the glass house had begun to shatter, Lurbud's dive under the table on Ohnishi's breakfast balcony had saved his life. The table had protected him from the exploding glass. When the main structure of the house tumbled, the balcony had fallen outward, carrying Lurbud with it. He landed on the lawn forty feet below, astonished to find himself alive. But by no means had he escaped unscathed.

His right shoulder joint had dislocated and his legs, torso, and face were severely lacerated by shards of glass. His right eye had been punctured so that the clear fluid within leaked down his face and dripped into the collar of his battle jacket.

With such massive injuries, the body's main defense is to go into shock. But there are many forms of shock, depending on the strength of the person. As endorphins and adrenaline coursed through him, Lurbud struggled to remain conscious and focused. After nearly twenty minutes, Lurbud began to move. Slowly at first, he raised himself onto his hands and knees, then to his feet. All that remained of Takahiro Ohnishi's palatial home were heaped piles of shattered glass and an empty skeleton of tubular struts. Lurbud staggered into the debris to search for the radio that would link him to the *John Dory*.

Where the scything weight of the falling building had sliced through a victim, the mound of glass was stained crimson by gallons of blood. In the dim moonlight, the blood looked black, but Lurbud could tell that dozens of such bloody piles dotted the charnel ruin.

Systematically he checked each body, scraping off the accumulated glass with the butt of his weapon to expose a recognizable portion. Korean and Russian alike had been diced so finely by the shards that easy identification was impossible.

With only fifteen minutes to spare before his next scheduled contact with the submarine, he found the bloody mass that had once been his radio carrier. Of the man, there was little more than strips of flesh, but the radio, in its armored plastic pack, had survived the cascade undamaged.

Propped against the sanguine heap, Lurbud made his first broadcast, repeating the word "green" for five seconds. Finished, he fell back against the pile, shards and chips digging into his flesh unnoticed.

Fighting the exhaustion brought on by the battle and loss of blood, Lurbud tended his wounds, winding a bandage around his mangled hand and gently mopping his sightless eye socket. To dull the ache growing in his skull, he shot a full syringe of morphine into his arm from the medical kit the radio man had also carried.

He recognized immediately how one could become addicted to the drug. Despite the pain clawing at his tortured body, his spirits had never been better. He felt buoyed and knew that he would survive to have his revenge against Kenji. All else faded in importance to him; the submarine, the volcano, even his own condition, as long as he could have his revenge. The van that the Russians had used to get to Ohnishi's estate was only a mile or so away. He could drive to Kenji's house and make him pay dearly for the suffering he'd caused.

Lurbud was lucid enough to know that he had to continue to make regular calls to the *John Dory*. Their action, if he failed to report, would surely jeopardize his chance at revenge on Ohnishi's former assistant.

It had taken him nearly two hours to stagger and crawl to where the van was hidden, his mangled body leaving a vivid trail of blood across Ohnishi's estate. The fifteen-mile drive north had taken another hour and a half; he had to stop about every ten minutes to allow his graying vision to return to normal.

Now he lay in a shallow ditch no more than one hundred yards from Kenji's home, peering at it through night-vision binoculars. The view dimmed and blurred from pain and effects of the morphine as he strained to focus his one functioning eye.

The sprawling two-story house was not nearly as grand as Ohnishi's, but it was very impressive. Constructed of dressed stones coated in beige stucco, the two main wings of the house spread from the central entrance like the blades of a boomerang. Each second floor window was a pair of French doors that opened onto narrow wrought-iron balconies. The fire-baked barrel tile roof and the expansive lawns betrayed the home as a former plantation from a bygone era.

A separate guest house sat on the other side of an olympic-sized pool from the main structure. After making his latest report, Lurbud knew that he had two hours to concentrate on Kenji. He was professional enough to realize that in his condition, he was no match for the Japanese killer. He had to plan carefully. Kenji's martial arts skill would render anything less than a long-range rifle shot useless. Therefore a diversion was needed to bring the Oriental out of his home and within range.

Lurbud slithered further into the ditch to get a better view into the rooms and hoped that something would present itself.

HAWAII

Way Hue Dong was the head of Hydra Consolidated, the Korean consortium that had bought the volcano from Ivan Kerikov. His grandson, Chin-Huy, sat at Kenji's desk smoking a fragrant Romeo y Julietta cigar. He was young, not much past twenty, but he possessed the eyes of an old man, eyes that had seen many things in the service of his family. When his grandfather had ordered him to lead the fifty-man contingent of troops to Hawaii, Chin-Huy had not questioned, merely obeyed.

His family had sent him or his older brothers to some of the most dangerous places on earth in search of profit. Whether it was poached ivory from war-torn Angola or stolen artifacts from the ravaged jungles of Central America, the younger members of the family had responded with vigor and initiative.

This mission, though potentially dangerous, had proved quite easy for young Chin. His local contact, Kenji, had done much of the work necessary to ensure that the family would not be bothered when they seized the volcano. Chin's men held the airport under the auspices of Hawaii's more fervent national guardsmen and few had had to be used at Pearl Harbor to incite the assembled students to open fire at the military compound. The only difficulties had been at Ohnishi's house, where more than twenty of his men had been cut down by a failed commando strike, presumably American.

All in all, Chin's role had been minor. All that remained now was confirmation from the mining ship en route to the volcano that its target was in sight. That would not take place for another ten hours or so. Once his family had possession of the volcano, Chin would recall his troops, making sure that their withdrawal would bring a swift end to the state's unrest. The violence now gripping Hawaii served only a limited purpose. Once the volcano was secure, it was best that the islands quieted.

"Your rewards will be great, Kenji. What do you plan to do with them?"

Kenji did not like the young man sitting languidly in his chair. Chin was brash, uncouth, and obnoxious.

"Do not speak too quickly; everything is yet to be settled."

"That commando team fell for your ruse perfectly—they attacked the wrong house, just as you planned." Chin waved his cigar in a dismissive gesture. "The volcano is within our grasp, surely you no longer worry."

"Ivan Kerikov believed that the volcano was within his grasp and Takahiro Ohnishi believed that Hawaii was within his, too. Both men were wrong. I will not believe that we are successful until the mining vessel anchors at the volcano site."

"Ach," Chin said, then launched into another story of his own bravery in the face of adversity.

He had told Kenji nearly a dozen such stories earlier in the afternoon, before Kenji had set out to murder Ohnishi. Chin's tales of bravado had a whining tone to them, as if daring Kenji to doubt them. Since Chin had not volunteered to lead his troops in the assault of Ohnishi's mansion, Kenji needed no proof of the boy's true character. Kenji had grown weary of the stories and the boy, yet listened as if rapt. It was expected of him.

Chin summed up, "If I could survive that and still keep the diamonds with me the whole time, surely I will get us out of this."

Kenji tightened his fists at his sides. He could disembowel Chin with his bare hands without raising a sweat and the idea was a pleasurable one, but he had to maintain his composure. His grandfather held Kenji's fate after he escaped Hawaii and he wouldn't jeopardize that for the mere pleasure of killing the boy.

"All operations are different, surely you know this. Because you survived many in the past does not mean you are protected in the present."

Though not chastened by Kenji's comment, Chin remained silent.

Kenji was content to lean against the paneled wall of his study, arms now crossed over his chest, watching Chin smoke his cigar. His years of training had taught Kenji to remain impassive no matter what the situation around him. The tension within him would make a weaker man pace, but Kenji simply stood, quiet and dangerous.

"What of the woman," Chin said, breaking the minutes long silence, "the reporter you have in the gardener's shed?"

"What about her?"

"She has refused to help us; surely it is time for her to die."

"Yes, maybe it is," Kenji said sadly.

"I will do it," Chin volunteered. "I want her first."

"Take her," Kenji replied casually, masking a sense of hurt.

At first, Kenji had entertained thoughts of taking Jill Tzu with him. There was something in the defiant beauty of the woman that made Kenji want to dominate her. Maybe it was because she knew of his Korean birth? He knew that she would never willingly be with him. Of course she could be drugged, like that American woman he'd rescued a week ago.

But Kenji knew that that was not a solution. Jill had to be eliminated, yet he had not been able to bring himself to do it. Chin's lurid request was the perfect opportunity. Jill would die, but her blood would not be on his hands.

Chin pulled his small feet from the desk and slammed them against the carpeted floor. Kenji expected him to skip from the room like a spoiled child granted his favorite wish. Instead, Chin swaggered out, eyeing Kenji in an adolescent attempt at domination.

JILL wasn't sure, but it felt as if night had descended once again, making this the fifth she'd spent locked up inside the maintenance shed. She could hear the incessant buzz of insects if she pressed her ear against the tiny crack under the door. The slit was too narrow for her to look through, not that it really mattered to her anymore. What was another night after all?

She'd entertained the thought of marking the floor by scratching the concrete with a sharp pebble to track the passage of time, but decided that it wouldn't do her any good. She knew she'd be dead before there were even a few gouges. She'd asked herself over and over why she was willing to be killed rather than report the propaganda Kenji had presented her with. Was her journalistic integrity worth more than her life? Were her priorities that messed up?

No, she decided. She could have done it, spouted off whatever he told her. She could have guaranteed her survival, but afterward, her life wouldn't really be worth living. Not because she would have helped that monster Kenji and not because she would have deceived the public. She would have disappointed herself and that was something she just couldn't do.

All her life she had faced the world according to her personal set of standards and not once had she ever broken her own rules. If she had, she would have been lying to herself. Jill remembered doing a report once on heroin use among teens in Honolulu. One junkie, a sixteen-year-old girl who supported her habit by hooking, refused to admit she was addicted to drugs. She accused Jill of faking a photograph of her shooting up behind a sleazy hotel. The girl had lied to herself so much that she couldn't even acknowledge the physical evidence of her problem. She'd told Jill that the needle tracks on her arms were tattoos.

Jill was afraid that if she broke her personal code, she would end up as self-delusioned as that junkie. Helping Kenji, even in an oblique way, would be a violation of that code. She couldn't do it, wouldn't do it, and would die for it.

Her mind had sharpened during the solitude of the past few days, driven by the same instincts which had kept man's ancient ancestors alive on the plains of prehistoric Africa. Like any animal, the human being can sense danger long before the threat is seen or heard. Jill knew that there was a new danger around her; she could feel a malignancy in the air as surely as if it were a physical sensation.

She had first noticed it about an hour earlier, primarily as a tightening of the atmosphere, an almost electric sensation. Soon she noted more tangible evidence of a change.

There was an audible increase in the numbers of guards pacing around Kenji's estate, more pairs of footfalls on the raked gravel walk next to the shed that was her prison. These new guards walked with a tighter cadence, more vigilant than Kenji's usual security. But in the past half hour or so, she had heard fewer and fewer people walking around, as if the new guards were vanishing into the night. She heard them walk past the building as if headed for the jungle's edge, but they never returned.

Now she heard new footsteps; there was an urgency in the strides. Jill knew instinctively where this man was headed.

The footsteps stopped outside the door and she heard keys jingling as merrily as a Christmas chime. The man thrust a key into the lock, turned it violently, and threw open the door. Jill had gotten to her feet and backed as far away from the door as possible.

The intruder was young, no more than a boy, but he carried himself with the negligent attitude of a world weary soldier, cocky eyes and a leering slit of a mouth. There was a pistol in a holster hanging from one bony hip.

He will rape me and then kill me, she thought as if reporting an incident that happened to someone else. I will be dead soon.

Chin-Huy approached, his small hands flexing in nervous anticipation. His eyes were dark spots on his face, like those drawn by a cartoonist. In them, she saw no depth. He drew closer, massaging his crotch languidly, his leer deepening by the moment.

Jill's attacker was small, no more than fifteen or twenty pounds heavier than she. She might have a chance fighting him off, if only he left his pistol in its holster. Incredulous, she watched as he undid the web belt and let it fall to the floor, the pistol landing heavily against the concrete.

The door was open behind him, beckoning her into the warm embrace of the night. Maybe she could duck past him before he could retrieve his weapon. Jill's eyes shifted past his shoulder to look at the rectangle of open country beyond her prison, and in that split second, Chin-Huy covered the last few feet between them. He struck her with a vicious roundhouse punch that drove her to the floor as if she'd been hit by a baseball bat.

Her connection to consciousness was just a thin strand. A quick hand darted out and kneaded one of her breasts painfully.

This is not happening to me, Jill thought. This is not me that's being touched.

Chin-Huy twisted her nipple viciously and she gasped, the pain bringing her back from the dark realm that draped her mind. She looked up into his face. His teeth were crooked and stained, his breath on her skin was hot and fast. His eyes had narrowed to pinpoints and lust had suffused his face with dark blood.

In the millisecond it took her to blink away some of the tears flooding her eyes, an arm had whipped around his neck and yanked him up, off his feet.

By the time Chin sensed something was wrong, his windpipe had nearly been crushed. He tried to whirl around and break the grip, but the arm clung as tenaciously as a remora. His body began to jerk and twitch as if controlled by a manic puppeteer. He slammed back with one elbow, but the blow lacked power and the man killing him didn't so much as grunt. The arm tightened even more, completely cutting off his air. Chin-Huy's tongue snaked from between his lips, tearing against his teeth so that his saliva was stained pink. With one final tug, Chin's neck snapped with a nauseating crackle.

Jill watched the man fall. Then her eyes scanned upward along the legs that stood behind the body of her would-be rapist. When she reached the face of the man who saved her life, she was greeted by a lazy smile and a pair of the most charming gray eyes she had ever seen.

"If he's my only competition for your affection, I bet you're free for dinner tomorrow night." Mercer grinned, then bent down and checked the livid bruise spreading across Jill's cheek. It was ugly and would last for a couple of weeks, but wasn't serious. Her eyes were brightening, so he wasn't too concerned about a concussion.

They were stunning, deep and black with such a trusting expression that Mercer looked into them much longer than absolutely neccesary. The emotions she'd bottled up for five days poured out as Jill ducked her head against his shoulder and cried. He murmured to her reassuringly, stroking her thick black hair.

"You're safe now, Jill."

"How do you know my name?" she asked meekly, her cheeks slick with tears.

"You're an unwitting victim in something much larger that I'm here to stop."

"You know about Takahiro Ohnishi and his coup?" she said urgently. Her resiliency marveled him.

"I know all about it." Mercer untangled her long arms from around his neck. "Jill, I have to leave you here for a while, but I'm sure that nobody will bother you again." He pointed to the dead soldier. "He was probably going to kill you, so now everybody thinks you're dead. When Kenji's eliminated, I'll come back for you and we'll all get out of here together. I have a helicopter waiting about two miles away."

"I understand," she said calmly. "What's your name?"

"Most damsels call me Lance A. Lot but you can call me Mercer." He smiled and was rewarded with one of Jill's. Christ, even in her condition, she was beautiful.

The corpse of the soldier was dragged out of the maintenance shed by one of the SEALs. Mercer closed the door but didn't relock it, then regarded the body.

"He's Korean," Mercer exclaimed, studying the mottled face. "I wonder who the fuck he was."

The SEALs simply stared flatly, not commenting.

On their approach to the shed, Mercer and his team had taken out eight Asian guards, some wearing fatigues like the figure at his feet and some wearing street clothing. In the jungle they had not taken the time to closely examine their victims, assuming that they were Kenji's personal guards. The discovery that the dead men were Korean put a new twist on the situation.

"I don't know who these guys belong to, but we'll assume they're not allies. That means we still have Kenji's guards plus these Koreans." Mercer spoke more for his benefit than the SEALs. "I doubt they know we're coming, so we have the element of surprise, but how effective is that against an unknown force?"

Mercer led them closer to Kenji's compound using whatever natural cover they could find until they were tucked safely behind the guest house. Near them, the azure pool shimmered with muted underwater lights. Kenji's house waited quietly twenty yards beyond the pool. Mercer surveyed the back of the two-story sprawling home through the night-vision goggles lent to him by one of the SEALs. Only a few rooms were illuminated, but the glasses easily probed the darkened rooms as well. Through the greenish hue, he saw at least fifteen armed men in the house, slowly pacing through the rooms, scanning the extensive grounds.

After about five minutes of studying the mansion, he gave the commandos their orders. They obeyed without question and left, blending into the night.

Waiting while the SEALs got into position was agonizing. Thoughts of fear and failure tried to weaken Mercer's resolve, but he crushed them down mercilessly. He had come too far to be afraid now, he told himself. Yet even as he mentally prepared himself for the assault, his mind drifted to a vision of Jill Tzu. He chuckled at himself. Of all the times to be thinking about sex. When the first crackling report of automatic fire rippled the silent sky, he shook his head quickly and moved.

As ordered, the SEAL team had crept around to the front of the house and opened fire, raking the edifice with a scathing barrage. Mercer ran across the open back lawn, praying that human nature would cause the men inside to turn toward the sounds, leaving him undetected. As his booted feet pounded across the grass, he crouched in anticipation of a killing shot from the second-story guards.

He covered the twenty yards to the house in record time.

Mercer leapt onto an immature palm and shimmied up like a monkey, feet and hands working in perfect harmony. Near its top, his weight bowed the tree inward and he dropped easily onto an unguarded second-floor balcony. The sound of gunfire intensified at the front of the house as the SEALs and the guards traded ammunition at a staggering pace.

Mercer kicked in one of the French doors and rolled across the room's carpet in case there was an unseen guard stationed inside. He came up onto his knees, the MP-5 tucked hard against his shoulder, and scanned the room quickly. Empty.

He stripped off his goggles and took a few calming breaths. The sounds of the fight below were barely muted by the thick walls of the plantation house. He had just turned to reach for the door when he noticed a shadow bisect the sliver of light at the floor. Mercer rested his hand lightly on the polished brass knob and felt it twist beneath his fingers. As the latch fully retracted, he yanked on the handle and brought up his machine pistol. The guard was caught unaware; Mercer pulled him into the room and jammed the barrel of the MP-5 into his belly. Just as Mercer felt himself being pushed backward by the man's weight, he pulled the trigger. The 9mm rounds tunneled through the guard, boring a cone-shaped wedge of flesh from his body that smeared against the wall behind him.

Mercer yanked his bloodied weapon from the falling corpse and turned down the wide hall. A fatigue-dressed Korean ducked out of one of the other rooms and Mercer managed to snap off a burst that caught the man high in the back. A quick check showed that one of the rounds had been fatal, while the rest had just mangled the ornate millwork of the door frame.

He did a sweep of the rest of the upstairs. The remainder of the elegant guest rooms in both wings of the mansion were deserted. One floor below, machine guns and grenades pummeled the masonry and shook the walls of the old plantation house. Mercer paused at the head of the stairs, the acrid tang of cordite smoke searing his nostrils.

A stab of fear lanced through his body. The battle below was like nothing he'd ever heard before, the ugly sounds of death echoing up the stairs. His experiences in Iraq and Washington were nothing like this. Those times, he'd been ambushed and hadn't had time to think. In the OF&C offices in New York, he had felt more in control. But this—this hell—was something different. He was about to voluntarily walk into carnage, and that terrified him. Grimly, he descended the ornate mahogany stairs, one finger squeezed firmly around the trigger of his MP-5. Just an ounce more pressure would unleash a hail of bullets.

In the mezzanine, two bodies lay sprawled in the rubble of the blown-out windows, one dressed in fatigues, the other, one of Kenji's men, in a dark suit. Cloying smoke layered the air, burning Mercer's eyes as he crouched just above the bottom of the staircase; bullets and shrapnel whizzed by like angered wasps. Obviously the SEALs' assault had lost none of its fervor. In an adjoining room, someone screamed in pain. Mercer knew, thanks to the plans provided by Dick Henna, that the wailing originated in a formal reception area.

Mercer didn't realize someone had spotted him until a stream of bullets tore into the railing and banister near him, shredding the wood like a chain saw. He tumbled down the remaining steps, ducking his head and hunching his shoulders. As he landed on the marble floor, he glimpsed the assassin, silhouetted in the doorway to the dining room. Mercer fired, but only one round went off before his clip emptied. The shot caught the Korean in the shoulder and spun him nearly completely around, but left him very much alive.

He started to turn back toward Mercer, Uzi clutched in his hands. Mercer launched himself from the floor, diving across a rich Turkish carpet while reaching for his holstered Beretta as he flew. The move threw off the guard's aim, giving Mercer time to torque himself as he landed and pump four or five rounds into him.

Mercer reholstered the Beretta and jammed a fresh clip into his machine pistol. He ducked around the doorway leading to the reception area, taking out three guards who were crouched under the shattered windows.

From the plans, he knew Kenji's study was on the other side of the entrance foyer, several rooms past the dining room.

Another guard spotted him as he raced back across the foyer and bullets tore up the marble at his heels. Mercer jinked once, then dove into the dining room, landing on a table large enough to seat twenty. The table had been beautifully set—Mercer's momentum shattered the ornate Royal Doulton china, turning it into a very expensive pile of trash on the polished wood floor. He tumbled over the far side of the table, knocking three chairs onto their backs.

He knelt up, steadying his H&K on the table. Shards of china dug deeply into the toughened skin of his knees through his black pants.

An explosion ripped through the foyer as the SEALs blew out the solid front door. A pall of smoke roiled into the dining room, and the Korean who had just fired at Mercer staggered into the room. Obviously he'd been standing near the door when it shattered and the wood splinters had torn through his body. Mercer's dispatching shot was a relief to the pitiable figure.

Mercer smashed through the door to the kitchen. There was more blood on the floor than in an abattoir; crimson smears streaked the walls and pooled under the two bodies crumpled below a blown-out window. The

SEALs certainly knew their business. Mercer returned to the dining room and cautiously nudged open the other exit door. The room beyond reeked of smoke. Flames licked at the ceiling from a destroyed television set a few yards beyond a large leather sectional couch.

One of Kenji's guards feebly tried to lift his weapon from where he lay, but he was missing a massive chunk of his left shoulder. Blood streamed from the wound.

Dispassionately, Mercer fired a short burst between the man's hate-filled eyes. The other guard in the informal living room, a uniformed Korean, was already dead.

Mercer took a few deep breaths as he changed clips. Glancing at his watch, he noted with surprise that only six minutes had elapsed since he had started running for the palm tree in the backyard. The adrenaline fizzing in his veins had made it seem more like six hours, yet each moment was etched into his brain like frames of film. Outside, the battle was dying down. Either the ranks of SEALs or guards had dwindled to nothing. He had no way of knowing.

Beyond the living room, a wide, window-lined gallery stretched the length of the northern wing of the house. The SEALs had shot out the tall transomed windows to his right, so the air was free of smoke. Opposite the windows, French doors opened into other rooms—a book-lined library, a silk-draped billiards room, a small cinema that had probably been the music room when the house was built at the turn of the century. The last door of the gallery led to Kenji's study.

Mercer stealthily made his way along the promenade, quickly checking each room he passed. The door just before the study was open, and as Mercer approached, a foot kicked out with incredible strength. The MP-5 flew from his grip, tearing some meat off his right index finger where it had caught on the trigger guard. Before he had time to react, a fist pounded into him, catching him just below the heart. Mercer's breath exploded in a wheezing gasp.

He staggered back a few paces, massaging his ribs. Kenji stepped into the corridor, wearing a black gi and no shoes. His dark eyes blazed with pure hatred as he gazed at the Occidental interloper.

"I do not know who you are, but I will take great pleasure in killing you for what you've done." His voice echoed from someplace deep within, an empty chasm which contains normal men's souls. Kenji had none.

Mercer struggled to draw his pistol, but Kenji paced forward cutting the distance between them in the blink of an eye. His foot flicked out with the speed of a viper's tongue and the Beretta spun away as Mercer's right hand went numb. Though Kenji was nearly twenty years his senior, Mercer had no hope of defeating him. Even if Mercer hadn't been battered so much in the past week, Kenji would still be able to take him apart at a leisurely pace.

"Are you another of Kerikov's errand boys?" Kenji asked mildly, cracking a hardened foot against Mercer's ribs.

Mercer fell against the wall, clutching at the rough stucco to keep himself on his feet. His chest felt as if it had been worked over with a baseball bat.

"What are you talking about?" he gasped.

A fist slammed into Mercer's stomach, doubling him over into Kenji's knee, which shot upward into his face. Kenji spun away as Mercer went sprawling onto the flagstone floor. "Did Kerikov send you with those assassins at Ohnishi's house?"

Mercer retched painfully, a trace of blood in the rancid bile that shot from his mouth and nose. Kenji's questions had thrown him off as much as the brutal hits he'd taken. Dazed by the punches and kicks, he wasn't sure he had heard correctly. "I'm not with your Russian allies."

Kenji kicked again, but Mercer managed to block the shot with his arm. Kenji was thrown off balance by the move, giving Mercer precious seconds to regain his feet.

"Where are your Russian sponsors, anyway?" Mercer

asked through gritted teeth as Kenji stalked around him.

Kenji gave a derisive laugh. "As dead as Ohnishi."

He threw a combination punch at Mercer, the first blow knocking against Mercer's skull and the other cracking two more ribs. Despite the pain, Mercer managed a counterpunch, but his fist felt like it merely bounced off the muscled cords of Kenji's throat.

"Like Ohnishi, the Russians were pawns to be used and discarded by myself and my true allies."

"The Koreans?" Mercer wheezed, understanding a bit.

"They have backed me for months in a double-cross against both Ivan Kerikov and Ohnishi." Kenji wasn't even breathing hard while Mercer was sucking in great draughts of air. "We triggered Ohnishi and Kerikov's pathetic coup and shifted American interest away from the volcano and its mineral wealth. To Kerikov, the coup was a means to an end; for Ohnishi, it represents a lifelong dream. To us, it was simply a diversion."

"You piggybacked onto Kerikov's plan, took his idea and his agents for yourselves. Then it was you who rescued Tish Talbot from the *Ocean Seeker*?" Mercer had to keep Kenji talking in a vain hope that a SEAL was still alive to save him.

"As ordered by Kerikov for the benefit of Valery Borodin, I believe. But she has no use in my plan, so my allies hired some assassins to execute her in Washington."

"Not quite." Mercer managed a wry smile. "She is very much alive and well."

"You?"

"Yes."

"No matter, I'll have her killed later on."

"The fuck you will," Mercer said, hatred giving him a reckless courage.

He dove at Kenji, slamming a shoulder into his chest. Both men flew backward, pounding into the wall hard enough to break away some of the plaster. Mercer recovered an instant before Kenji and fired three heavy punches into the older man's muscled torso. Kenji grunted with each blow, but still had the strength to pick Mercer off his feet and toss him away. Mercer scrambled up as quickly as he could, his cracked ribs keeping him slightly doubled over.

"I thought killing Ohnishi would give me the greatest pleasure, but now I realize your death will be even better," Kenji said menacingly as he came for Mercer.

Kenji's kick contained every ounce of strength in his body. It was a killing blow. Mercer bent backward the instant Kenji's foot rose, ignoring the pain that exploded in his chest with the movement. As he straightened back up, his hand reached for the Gerber knife suspended from his harness.

The steel pommel of the knife cracked against Kenji's foot with all the strength Mercer had left. The blow shattered the delicate bones as though they were glass, checking Kenji's attack. Mercer whipped the knife upward in a last desperate lunge. The tempered steel parted Kenji's abdominal muscles, sliced through the tough membrane of his diaphragm, and punctured his left lung.

Kenji reeled back, yanking the knife from Mercer's fingers. He stared down at the blade sticking from his chest with crazed and panicked eyes.

"You," he sputtered, blood spraying with his word.

Mercer had fallen to the floor after his attack. He was too weak to rise, so when Kenji pulled the knife from his body and turned the bloody blade at him, he had no defense. The savagery was draining from Kenji as fast as his life's blood, but he still had enough time to kill his last victim. Mercer lay sprawled like a temple sacrifice, arms at his sides, legs slightly parted. He could not avoid the blade plunging toward his chest.

The kinetic energy of the first bullet arrested Kenji's downward thrust and nearly stood him upright. The second shot tore another hole through his chest, shredding his' heart and damaged lung. The final shot blew out the back of his skull.

Mercer twisted around in time to see one of the SEALs, bloody and battered, fall to the floor. A full sixty seconds passed before Mercer recovered enough to get up and check on the wounded SEAL. When he turned him onto his back, Mercer was staggered. The man who had saved his life wasn't a SEAL at all.

Through a mask of dried and caked blood the unknown man opened his one undamaged eye. "*Spesivo*."

The use of Russian shocked Mercer for a second, then he understood.

"Kerikov."

"No." The man coughed up a bloody ball of phlegm and spat it on the floor. "I am Evad Lurbud, major in the KGB, Department Seven, and Ivan Kerikov's assistant. Thank you for allowing me to kill that pig."

"Where is Kerikov?" Mercer demanded sharply.

"Last I knew, he was headed toward Europe. Now, who knows? You are a member of the American Special Forces, yes?"

"I'm the guy who blew your entire operation."

Lurbud chuckled painfully, "I doubt that. No man could stop every contingency we laid down."

"I bet your men in New York wouldn't agree with you."

"That was you?"

Mercer smiled modestly. "It was nothing really. But it did lead to all sorts of interesting things, little things like disguised submarines named *John Dory*, man-made volcanoes, and long-dead scientists who do great Lazarus impressions."

Mercer could tell that Lurbud was truly shocked to see how much he knew.

"You guys made just enough small errors for me to figure out your little caper." Mercer ticked off each item on a finger. "When Tish Talbot was pulled aboard the *John Dory*, she saw the design on her stack and heard her crew speaking Russian. Then you used an OF&C ship for her official rescue, which made it easy to find the connection to the *Grandam Phoenix*, the ship you bastards started the whole operation with. And you didn't watch Valery Borodin closely enough, since he managed to send off the telegram that got me involved. I guess you can ultimately blame him for your failure. Without that telegram, no one would have ever suspected a thing.

"Too bad that your agents here in Hawaii turned on you. It's wise, when picking allies, to be certain of their true motivations. Ohnishi wanted an independent country more than he wanted the volcano, and Kenji, he must have had his reasons for bringing in those Koreans." Mercer had retrieved his weapons and now had the MP-5 pointed at Lurbud's chest.

"You can't kill me."

"Why in the hell not?" Mercer replied casually.

"If I don't radio the *John Dory* in an hour and a half, she will launch a nuclear missile at the volcano."

Mercer noticed the black radio pack wedged under Lurbud's body. He jerked it out by its nylon strap and held it at arm's length. Letting the Hechler & Koch dangle by its sling, he drew the Beretta, then calmly fired two rounds through the armored plastic shell. The radio sparked and smoked for a moment as it shorted completely.

He dropped the radio next to Lurbud's head. "Any other bargaining chips?"

"I am a major in the KGB. I am worth much to the CIA."

"Assuming I work for the CIA must be an infectious disease. You're the third or fourth person to think that. Too bad." Mercer aimed his pistol. "I'm a geologist," he said as he fired the last round from the Beretta. "Not a spy."

Mercer wearily started back down the gallery toward the main entrance of the house. He believed Lurbud about the nuclear threat from the *John Dory*. If Kenji and his Korean allies had somehow double-crossed Kerikov, he had no doubt that the Russian spymaster would reap some form of revenge. Destroying the volcano and the bikinium made the best sense. The hour and a half time limit would make things extremely tight.

He was just passing the last transomed window before the living room when a figure crashed through the remaining glass and fragile mullions. Mercer dove to the side, twisting in the air to bring the MP-5 up to bear. The attacker hit the floor, rolled, and came to his knees in an instant, his gun aimed at Mercer's head. Mercer was a fraction of a second too slow—the man had him pinned.

"I'm sorry if I scared you, Dr. Mercer, I wasn't sure who you were from outside," the leader of the SEALs apologized and lowered his weapon.

"Jesus," Mercer breathed, his heart slamming against his rib cage. "I was too petrified to be scared."

The SEAL's uniform was so tattered it was nearly unrecognizable. A wound in his shoulder bled freely. His face was streaked with dirt and dried blood. Despite the pain he must have felt, his eyes were impassive.

"What's the situation?" Mercer asked.

"All the guards are dead, the building is secure, but I lost my entire squad."

"I'm sorry about that," Mercer said, getting to his feet.

"It's our duty, sir."

"Radio the chopper and have the pilot land in the backyard. I've got some more work tonight."

While the SEAL made the call, Mercer wandered through the dining room and into the kitchen. Ignoring the two bodies on the floor, he searched through the three large refrigerators until he found something decent to drink. Though Kirin beer was far from his favorite, he gulped two bottles in record time. A minute later he was in the backyard, skirting the edge of the pool.

Jill Tzu had left the shed when the firing had stopped and was hiding near the guest house when she saw Mercer striding across the back lawn. Behind him, the main house burned in several places, the fiery light making his features appear sharp and uncompromising.

The Sea King thundered in over the grounds, its blinding searchlight playing across the estate as Eddie Rice searched for a clear place to set her down.

Reaching Jill, Mercer took her into his arms. She clung to him tightly, unaware that Mercer's ribs grated against each other as she squeezed. "Everything is all right now. You're safe. Kenji's dead." She nuzzled her head into his shoulder as if she were a small creature burrowing into the earth for protection. "Jill, I have to leave you here with one of my men for a while."

Jill looked up into his face with beautiful but frightened eyes. "Can't you take me with you?"

"I can't. There's still a lot for me to finish," Mercer said, then kissed her tenderly. "That's to let you know I would if I could—and that I'm coming back."

Mercer untangled her arms from around his body and nodded to the SEAL. "Try to contact the *Inchon* somehow, maybe through Pearl Harbor, and have another team sent here. Don't trust any local authorities. Also, guard her with your life."

He jogged to the waiting chopper and vaulted into its hold. Eddie lifted off immediately, sweeping the chopper over the dark jungle.

In the cockpit, Mercer threw on a helmet, keying the mike immediately. "Head north as fast as this bitch can move."

Eddie banked the chopper, then turned to Mercer, grinning, "I don't think you're gay, so that must have been a woman you were kissing just then. Where the hell did you find a woman in the middle of that fight?"

"You just gotta know where to look." Mercer chuckled in the murky light of the cockpit. He opened the last two beers he'd taken from the kitchen and handed one to Eddie.

"Not when I'm flying," the pilot demurred.

"I'm not with the FAA or the navy; don't worry about it."

"Good point," Eddie replied, and took a long swallow.

"Did those SEALs have any dive equipment on board?"

"Yeah. Like you asked, I went through their stuff while I was waiting. There's air tanks, regulators, masks, the works."

"Good." Mercer pulled a slip of paper from his pants pocket and handed it to Rice.

"What's this?"

"The Loran numbers of a Russian submarine about to start a nuclear war." Mercer had mentally calculated the position of the *John Dory* from the infrared pictures provided by the National Security Agency. "Punch them in and follow them."

"Problem," Eddie said after keying the Loran numbers into the Sea King's navigational computer. "We have enough fuel to get out there, but not enough for the return flight."

"There's a good chance there won't be a return flight."

"Why'd I know you'd say that?" Eddie muttered.

AN hour later the chopper was thundering over the ocean swells, a driving rain pelting the windscreen of the Sea King like grenade fragments. The wipers were all but useless. Occasionally, a bolt of lightning arced through sky, casting a brilliant incandescence into the cockpit.

Mercer sat quietly in a borrowed navy wet suit, content to let Eddie Rice do his job. It had been torture getting himself into the constricting neoprene, but now the tightness around his chest eased the pain from his cracked ribs. Unconsciously, his hand polished the barrel of his machine pistol as if he were at home working on a piece of railroad track. Hundreds of questions roiled in his mind, questions about Kenji, the Koreans, Kerikov, and Lurbud, but he could not allow himself to become distracted by them. He had to remain completely focused on the present and let the past sort itself out later.

He and Eddie were racing against an imminent nuclear launch. Failing meant not only their deaths but also the loss of one of man's greatest discoveries. The benefits of the bikinium were too great to let slip away now and on a personal level, Mercer wouldn't allow himself to fail, he'd suffered too much in the past week to not see this completed successfully.

"What's our ETA?"

"About another ten minutes."

Mercer glanced at the luminous dial of his Tag Heuer. "According to Lurbud's threat, the *John Dory* launches in thirty."

"I'm already ten knots over the safety limits of this bird in these conditions."

"Make it twenty knots over and that Mai Tai you wanted will be on me."

"Christ, I could use it now," Eddie replied miserably as he torqued more power out of the turbofans.

The chopper rocked and jerked in the storm as Rice fought to keep her below the *John Dory*'s radar. Her rounded nose nearly skimmed the white spume atop the waves.

"Bingo," Eddie nearly shouted a minute later, "target dead ahead."

"What's the range?"

"One mile," Eddie said, glancing again at the neon blue radar screen.

"That's got to be her. Take us down. I'll swim the rest of the way. When I jump out, take off again, but be ready to pick me up when that ship blows. Approach from the stern and make sure no one else gets aboard except me and the man I'll have with me."

"I told you, we don't have enough fuel to get back to Hawaii."

"That doesn't matter. Someone will figure out we're here eventually." Mercer didn't want to tell Eddie that if the SEAL failed to get through to Pearl Harbor, the President would launch his own nuclear strike against the volcano in just three hours.

"You're crazy, you know that?"

"It's the main reason I can't get life insurance."

The Sea King's engines wound down and the rotors whipped the sea into a salty mist as Rice brought her in for a water landing. Mercer waited at the open doorway of the chopper, sweating in the wet suit, the two large air tanks bowing his back. Around his waist he wore a leaded belt and a waterproof bag containing some other items borrowed from the SEALs. A razor-sharp dive knife was strapped to his right calf. The whole time Mercer had struggled into the gear, he had wracked his brain trying to recall everything that Spook had taught him about diving all those years ago in that flooded New York mine.

As soon as the rounded underhull of the Sea King touched the churned-up water, Mercer bit down on his mouthpiece, sucked in a breath of cool air, and launched himself out of the chopper.

The water was warmer than he expected. At first Mercer sank below the surface, then he adjusted his buoyancy by detaching one of the lead weights. He took a bearing from the compass on his wrist and, still underwater, started swimming toward the *John Dory*.

Mercer had made two potentially fatal assumptions when he launched himself from the Sea King. One was the that the ship they had picked up on radar was, in fact, the *John Dory*. There was a definite possibility that the craft ahead of him was an entirely different ship, one innocently steaming through the area. The second assumption concerned the hull of the Soviet submarine/

freighter. If there was no gap between the submarine's hull and the fake sides of the freighter, he would have no way of gaining access to the vessel. If he was wrong about either guess, he would be dead long before the Russian missile detonated.

After a few minutes of swimming, Mercer felt a vibration through the water—the pounding engines of a large ship.

Adding a little air to the compensator, he surfaced on the crest of a swell. Through the rain-lashed night, he made out the running lights of a large freighter about two hundred yards ahead of him. His breath hissed through the regulator, rain and spume splattered against his mask.

He ducked back under the surface and continued to doggedly swim toward the *John Dory*. The backs of his legs were beginning to ache and his breathing was labored.

The sound of the ship's props filled the silence of the sea, but the vessel itself was still hidden in the gloom. Mercer was hesitant to turn on his dive light for fear of being detected by a lookout on deck, but at last he took the chance.

The knife edge bow of the *John Dory* was no more than ten feet away and bearing down on him at eight knots. Mercer dove hard, but his reaction came an instant too late. The steel plates of the ship's bow scraped along his body, shredding the thick rubber of his wet suit. The thick crust of barnacles grated against Mercer's skin like a thousand tiny paring knives.

Mercer screamed into his mouthpiece as pain shot through his system, racing through his body to explode against the top of his skull. He felt the gray blanket of unconsciousness falling over his mind, but managed to push it aside by sheer force of will. He wouldn't allow pain to stop him now. He had only a few seconds in which to find a handhold of some sort before the vessel passed him. And if that happened, he had no chance of ever catching her.

Training the dive light upward, Mercer recognized the smooth curve of a submarine's hull. At least he had the right ship. He flashed the light to starboard and saw a space between the freighter silhouette and the sub's hull. He swam into the gap.

When his head broached the surface, he spat out his mouthpiece and gulped down the warm humid air trapped between the steel plating and the sub. The water in the four-foot-wide gap was churned in a vortex that carried Mercer along with the ship.

Since he did not have the luxury of time, he didn't bother glancing at his watch. He was certain that the sub was getting into position to fire the missile. He immediately set to work. The magnetic limpet mines he'd pilfered from the SEALs' stores stuck to the hull with a quiet snap; the timers had all been set, and as each one made contact with the sub's hull, it went active.

As soon as the explosive charges were planted, Mercer began climbing the spiderweb of steel girders that locked the bogus freighter hull to the submarine. Because of his injured ribs and the scuba gear hanging from his back the climb was exhausting. He wished he could dump the dive equipment, but if he hoped to escape with Valery Borodin, he needed it. At the top of the girders, he paused to look at his watch. Four minutes until launch.

Shit.

The sharp steel struts had ripped into his hands; blood poured from the wounds and dripped onto the deck where Mercer stood, just forward of the submarine's conning tower. The empty superstructure of the freighter soared thirty feet above his head. The cavernous space echoed with the hiss of water sliding across her hull and the beat of her props. The nearly total darkness smelled of diesel oil and saltwater. As quietly as possible, Mercer stashed his scuba gear and dive fins in a corner.

Two minutes.

He crept up the ladder of the rounded conning tower. As he neared the top, he made out muted voices. The language was unmistakably Russian.

He popped his head over the top of the conning tower and gave a friendly smile to the two shocked officers standing at the open hatch.

"Take me to your leader," Mercer grinned. Exhaustion and the adrenaline he was using as a substitute for real courage had made him giddy.

The two officers produced pistols in record time, leveling them at Mercer's head. One of them shouted down into the sub. Though Mercer did not speak Russian, he assumed that the captain had just been informed that they had a prisoner. Prompted by curt gestures from a pistol barrel, Mercer went down the hatchway and into the Soviet submarine.

At the base of the ladder, Mercer casually glanced around the vessel's control room. By the slack-jawed looks and the lack of movement, he rightly guessed that the launch had been suspended for the moment.

"Hi, my name's Barney Cull." Mercer stuck out his hand but no one made a move to shake it. "I'm offering a sale on hull scraping and wondered if you needed my services."

Captain Zwenkov stepped forward, his face set in a deep scowl. "Who are you?" His English was thick but understandable.

"Actually I'm Sam O. Var, your local Coffee Wagon Company representative. How are you guys fixed for blinis?"

Zwenkov said something that in any language would have sounded like, "Get him out of here and lock him up."

Mercer was hustled from the control room by two armed sailors. He called over his shoulder, "Don't think strong-arm tactics will get me to lower my prices."

He would have continued with the jokes but the pistol

stabbing into his kidney jammed the air in his throat. He was led through the sub toward the stern, thankfully away from where he had planted the charges.

He was stripped of his wet suit and after a rather extensive body search, one of his guards undogged a hatch and thrust Mercer into a small cabin. The hatch was closed behind him but not locked.

In the spartan room, a man a few years younger than Mercer sat on one of the bunks. He was handsome in that Connecticut shore, hair blowing in the wind, sweater knotted around the throat kind of way. Mercer assumed, correctly, that this was Valery Borodin. Borodin said something to Mercer in Russian.

"Sorry, I don't speak it."

Mercer's use of English drained the color from Valery's face. "I said, you're not a member of the boat's crew. Who are you?"

"I'm Philip Mercer, the guy you sent the telegram to."

"Who?" Valery's eyes narrowed in confusion.

"Philip Mercer. You sent a telegram to me in Washington, warning me about the danger to Tish Talbot."

"Tish sent you?" Valery stood, his voice brightening.

"No, you sent me." Mercer was getting confused himself.

"I don't know who you are, but you know Tish?"

"You didn't send a telegram to me in Tish's father's name?"

"No."

"Just after you had her rescued from the *Ocean Seeker*?"

"No."

"If you didn't, then who the hell did?" Mercer muttered. "Well, anyway, I'm here to help you get off this tin can."

"Did Tish ask you to come?"

"Not exactly, but she's safe and waiting for you right now in Washington, D.C."

"There's no way to escape. We're hundreds of miles from Hawaii."

"Listen, in thirty seconds this sub is going to have more holes in it than the golf course at Pebble Beach. I've got a helicopter waiting for us, so don't worry about it. Where's your father?"

"He died two days ago. Heart attack."

"For the pain he's caused, don't expect my condolences."

Mercer glanced at his watch and held up his right hand with fingers splayed. As each second ticked by, he curled one finger downward. With two fingers to go, several explosions rocked the *John Dory*. Immediately klaxons sounded throughout the sub. The dim battle lights blinked once, then shut off completely; a single white bulb lit as the emergency system took over. Above the wail of the sirens and the shouts of men, Mercer could hear the sound of water pouring into the vessel, signaling her impending death. Mercer thrust his hand down the front of his pants, ignoring Valery's startled look.

Few body searches ever explore the area between the scrotum and anus. As Mercer's fingers grasped the four-barrel pepperbox Derringer pistol held there by his jock strap, he was thankful that homophobia struck Russians, too. The gun, a favorite of nineteenth-century riverboat gamblers because of its small size, had been a gift from his grandfather years before and had remained in Mercer's desk at home since then.

He yanked the tiny pistol from his pants, mindful of the stray hairs caught in the gun's hammer. Although the Derringer was only twenty-two caliber, it was loaded with bored-out hollow-points filled with mercury. At a range more than ten feet the gun was useless. Closer, a hit would be fatal.

"Are you coming?" The sub was already listing.

Valery grabbed a cheap briefcase from the bunk. "Yes, I'm with you."

They stepped into the boat's central passageway, Valery clutching the briefcase to his chest like a mother protecting her baby. Panicked sailors and officers ran down the narrow corridor, ignoring everything except their own safety. Mercer and Valery blended into the stream of men rushing to the nearest hatch.

Bursting into the control room, Mercer saw Captain Zwenkov leaning over the weapon's officer. They were still going to launch the nuclear missile. Instinct made Zwenkov turn around and face his executioner.

The report from the Derringer was lost in the sounds of the dying vessel and her crew, but the bullet tore through the captain's head cleanly. His cap flew through the air, carried by the top section of his skull. The blood-splattered weapons officer whirled in his seat, but before he could move, a round caught him in the throat, ripping out his carotid artery and jugular vein, sending a fountain of blood across the ballistic control computer.

A crewman grabbed Mercer from behind. Mercer whipped around, smashing his elbow into the man's jaw. Blood and broken teeth sprayed from the Russian's lips. Another man, this one wearing the coveralls of an engineer, charged forward, and Mercer shot him point blank in the heart.

The little four-barreled pistol had only one round left, and Mercer didn't have any spare ammunition. "Valery, come on." With Valery close behind, Mercer shouldered his way to the hatch, shoving, kicking, and punching his way to the bottom of the ladder.

On deck, the list of the submarine was much more noticeable, at least twenty degrees. Mercer guessed that the vessel would flip onto her back in moments. The confused mass of men on the deck were too busy trying to launch an inadequate number of life rafts to notice Mercer as he led Valery to the cache of scuba equipment. The din of the klaxons echoed across the storm chopped sea.

"There's only one set of tanks," Valery pointed out.

"We'll buddy dive," Mercer said, slipping the heavy tanks over his shoulders.

"But I've never dived before."

"That's okay, this is only my second time, so we're almost even." Mercer shoved Valery into the gap between the sub and the outer plating and leapt after him, losing his mask in the plunge.

In the water, Mercer slipped Valery's hand through the straps of the scuba tank so they would not get separated in the confusion. Explosions rumbled within the sub's hull and burning oil filled the narrow gap with reeking smoke. Mercer worried fleetingly about the very real danger that the nuclear power plant would meltdown from the shock of cool seawater washing over its five-hundred-degree shielding.

"There will be a helicopter a few hundred yards directly astern. If we stay underwater, we won't be spotted."

A bullet plowed into the sea a few inches from Mercer's head, throwing up a tiny fountain of water. Mercer fired the last round from the Derringer into the gloom above them, grasped Valery's free arm, and ducked beneath the waves. He kicked downward, breathing as slowly as possible. About fifteen feet below the surface, he felt Valery tug the regulator from his mouth. The Russian took a few breaths, then thrust the rubber piece back between his lips. The *John Dory* was mortally wounded but her engines still pounded out eight knots. Mercer and Valery hung below the surface as the 285-foot hull glided over their heads. The concussion from the blasts that were wrenching her apart assaulted their ears painfully, but they had no time to worry about its effects. They began swimming away from the stricken vessel. Their progress was impeded by the turbid swells and their need to trade the life-giving mouthpiece.

After five minutes, Mercer brought them to the surface. The *John Dory* was a few hundred yards away and it was easy to see she was sinking. Her bow rode deep

and her props thrashed the water into a white froth as
they were pulled from the ocean. Only two of the lifeboats had been launched and the crew seemed too occupied, picking up survivors and corpses, to care about
the huge helicopter that swooped in overhead.

Eddie Rice settled the Sea King into the water and let
the rotors idle. Mercer could see the pilot scramble to
the cargo door of the Sikorsky machine. Rice popped
open a large drum of oil and spilled it onto the water.
The churned-up sea settled immediately under the
weight of the fluid.

Mercer and Valery swam toward the helicopter, their
heads repeatedly swamped by the storm. Both men
retched seawater regularly. They were only twenty yards
from the machine when one of the lifeboats began mo-
toring their way.

"Eddie," Mercer screamed into the night, "get ready
to take off."

The pilot must have heard Mercer because he vanished from the hatch. The last fifteen yards of the swim
were the most agonizing moments in Mercer's life. The
pain in his body was unbearable. His lungs burned, his
arms felt like lead, and saltwater had closed his eyes to
slits. He dug deep within himself, searching for any last
reserves of stamina to keep him going. There wasn't
much left but still he swam on with Valery right beside
him.

The outboard motor of the life raft was getting louder
as the small craft drew near. Neither man dared look
back.

Suddenly they burst into the calmed pool of oil that
Eddie Rice had laid down. The chopper's rotors were
beginning to beat harder. Mercer and Valery swam the
last few yards on will alone. Valery tossed his father's
briefcase into the open door and clung desperately to the
side of the chopper, his lungs pumping for air.

Mercer shoved him into the craft and stole a glance
over his shoulder. The *John Dory*'s life raft was only

about twenty yards behind and closing fast. Mercer knew he'd never clamber into the chopper before the Soviets were upon them.

"Tell the pilot to take off," he shouted, and let go of the Sea King.

Valery was nowhere to be seen. Mercer assumed that the Russian had passed out as soon as he was inside. He was wrong.

Valery reappeared in the doorway, a machine pistol held firmly to his flank. He fired a long, devastating burst at·the life raft, bullets and screams piercing the night. When the clip was empty, he held the weapon out to Mercer.

Mercer grasped the proffered gun barrel and hauled himself to the chopper. He hooked an arm through Valery's and the younger man hoisted him aboard. Mercer didn't even take time to catch his breath, he grabbed a headset and wheezed into the microphone, "Go, Eddie, goddamn it, go."

Only after the Sea King lifted from the water toward Hawaii did Mercer collapse to the deck, his eyes glazed over, his lungs nearly in convulsions. Valery sat down next to him, drained by exhaustion and an adrenaline overdose.

"My father told me that years ago he had stood by and watched as a lifeboat full of men was machine-gunned like that. He said that the men died for Russia's greater glory even though they weren't Russian. Now I have done the same. For what?"

"For the best reason of all," Mercer gasped. "To save your own ass."

He got to his feet and staggered to the open cargo door, wind and rain whipping around his body. He closed the door and returned to Valery's side. "Tell me, are you sure you didn't send that telegram?"

"Positive."

"I wonder?" Mercer mused, and then passed out.

ARLINGTON, VIRGINIA

Mercer sat at the back corner booth of Tiny's and slowly swirled his vodka gimlet so the cubes of ice clicked discreetly. He took a swallow and placed the glass back on the scarred tabletop. His movements were slow, deliberate. It had been three weeks since Eddie Rice had ditched his Sea King into the Pacific nearly a hundred miles from Hawaii and his body was still stiff and battered. Mercer fractured a leg during the impact and Eddie had given himself a severe concussion and turned his face into a vermilion patchwork of bruises and lacerations. The chopper pilot was still bedridden at the Pearl Harbor Naval Hospital. Valery Borodin wasn't so much as scratched during the crash.

He swiveled his head and surveyed the room. Tiny was out of sight behind the bar, searching for something or other. There were four or five other patrons, workers from the local trucking firm. Looking at them, Mercer felt vaguely conspicuous not sporting a baseball cap or at least a cigarette. Umber light slashed through the windows as the sun dropped beneath the smoggy horizon.

Mercer had been back in Washington just long enough to jam a clear pin into Hawaii on the map at home, call Dick Henna to set up this meeting at Tiny's, and give himself a decent buzz.

He drained the last of his drink and called to Tiny for another. The three gimlets already wending their way through his body were dulling the pain in his bruised joints.

Richard Henna came through the front door just as Tiny set the new drink in front of Mercer. Henna wore a dark suit and tie, his eyes hidden by the dark glasses seen on all FBI agents in the movies. Mercer stood slowly, supporting himself with one hand on the table, as Henna crossed the room to his booth.

"I see you're alive if not well." Henna shook his hand and the two men sat.

Henna removed his glasses and glanced around the dingy room. His expression matched one Mercer had made once in a public toilet in Istanbul.

"Lovely place you have here," Henna said sarcastically.

"It has its charms." Mercer grinned. "They water down the beer with bourbon."

"I'll stick to Scotch."

"Tiny, Scotch and . . ." He looked at Henna, cocking an eyebrow.

"Neat."

"Scotch and Scotch."

"So where have you been since the navy fished you out?"

The explosions that sunk the *John Dory* had been heard by the sonar aboard the USS *Jacksonville*, the *Los Angeles*–class attack submarine attached to the *Kitty Hawk* battle group. She was the vessel poised to launch a nuclear-tipped Tomahawk cruise missile at the rising volcano. The sub raced to investigate the blasts and in the process found the sinking Sea King and three passengers. After an hour of argument with the captain, radio communication with the commander of the Pacific fleet, and finally intervention by Admiral Morrison, the *Jacksonville* abandoned her mission and headed for Hawaii.

"I stayed in Hawaii until just this afternoon."

"A little rest and relaxation?"

"More like recovery and research."

Henna thought better than to press for Mercer's meaning. "How are you feeling?"

"Not bad. The cast on my leg came off yesterday and my ribs are okay as long as I don't try to sing opera."

Henna smiled, then thanked Tiny as his drink came. "I see how this place gets its name."

"He used to be a jockey," Mercer pointed out. "So what's been happening in Hawaii?"

"You were there, you should know better than me."

"No, I was up north on Kauai near a town called Hanalei, cut off from just about everybody and everything. The only news I heard was on the flight from L.A. to Washington, and even then I wasn't really paying attention."

"Well, let me fill you in a little bit." Henna shrugged out of his jacket and laid it next to him on the booth. "The state, hell the whole nation, was stunned when we told them exactly what had happened. The President decided to come clean on the whole affair from Ohnishi to Kerikov to the bikinium. Valery Borodin was at the press conference at Pearl Harbor to back him up. The CIA found some old photographs of Evad Lurbud to match his corpse found at Kenji's estate. Of course we needed two undertakers to make his body look human again after what he'd been through.

"The Russians deny all knowledge of the operation code named Vulcan's Forge, but admitted that Ivan Kerikov was known for operating outside government sanction."

"You said 'was known.' Is he dead?"

"No, he's vanished. He was in Thailand, then went to Switzerland, but from there, no one knows. He simply disappeared. The Russians are looking for him now, as well as the CIA and INTERPOL. He'll turn up."

"Don't count on it. If he's cagey enough to nearly succeed with an operation like this, he can easily stay lost too."

"Maybe you're right, I don't know." Henna nodded slowly. "Remember, though, there's also a group of very pissed-off Koreans after him."

"Have you been able to find out who was behind the Korean angle?"

"We got nothing from the bodies at Ohnishi's house, but the guy found near the gardener's shed at Kenji's was the grandson of Way Hue Dong, one of the seven richest men in the world. To further link him to what happened, the day after you were rescued, a small flotilla of ships, one of them specially designed for high-temperature dredging and all owned by one of Way's companies, arrived at the volcano site. You better believe they were surprised to see the U.S. Navy already there with a carrier and a half-dozen support ships. Way's already lodged a formal complaint with the World Court at The Hague, but he doesn't stand a chance of taking the bikinium from us.

"As for Hawaii itself—there was one more night of rioting after your raid, but that was it. Without the Koreans or Ohnishi to act as agitators, the mobs lost their will to fight and pretty much just went home. Hawaii's senators have both resigned, claiming health problems, but it was either that or face prosecution for treason. The President has pardoned all others involved, and a special task force has been set up to deal with any legitimate claims by the Hawaiians. He felt it best to sweep the violence under the rug rather than make the nation relive it for months in the courts. In all, about three hundred people died during the riots.

"The President's going to ramrod some funding

through Congress to try to end a lot of the racial tension in this country—education programs, urban aid, that sort of thing. The Los Angeles riots and now this recent crisis have finally brought people to their senses. The old adage, 'United we stand, divided we fall,' almost came true, and it's scared enough people who want to really do something about it. With the current conciliatory mood in Congress, he'll get all the funding he needs.''

Mercer interrupted. ''You can't change people's opinions with new laws and federal spending.''

''Thirty years ago doctors were advertising the health benefits of cigarettes,'' Henna countered.

''Touché.''

''It will take some time but at least we are finally on the right track. No one wants the type of ethnic strife that's tearing apart central Europe and the old Soviet republics. We've maintained racial diversity for two hundred years and we're not going to let it slip away now. America is famous for pulling through a crisis just as things reach bottom, and we'll do it again.''

''I hope you're right.''

Henna took a swig of his drink. ''Valery Borodin is with our own people at the volcano, assaying the parts of it now above the surface to see where to begin mining the bikinium. I believe Dr. Talbot is with him.''

''She is. As a favor to me, the president had her flown out there two weeks ago. I spoke to her on the phone yesterday, just before my flight back to Washington. She and Valery have rekindled the passion they once felt. Already they're talking marriage.''

Henna smirked. ''Kind of funny, you were the hero in all of this. I thought it was customary for the hero to get the girl at the end.''

''When they make the television mini-series, I'll make sure they change the ending,'' Mercer replied offhandedly.

''Well, don't think you're going to come out of this completely empty-handed.'' Henna fished a set of keys from his pocket and tossed them to Mercer.

"What are these?"

"The keys to a new, black SJX Jaguar convertible with tan interior, cellular phone, CD player, and an aftermarket turbo charger. It was the least we could do."

Mercer looked at the keys and gave Henna a sardonic smile. "After getting me shot at a few dozen times, nearly smeared against a train, almost drowned, beaten up more than once, crashed into the ocean, and within a few minutes of being nuked, you're right, buying me a new car *is* the very least you could do."

Henna knew by Mercer's tone that he wasn't really angry and gave a low chuckle. "The car's parked in front of your house. There are two things I want to know: how did you know to go to Kenji's house rather than Ohnishi's? And how in the hell did you pinpoint the *John Dory* when the experts at NSA couldn't find a damn thing?"

Mercer smiled slyly. "Finding the *John Dory* was easy. Those infrared photos showed a classic shield volcano, a number of small vents surrounding a central magma outlet. Normally those smaller vents are located on the side of the volcano and therefore under deeper water. Well, on all of the photos, there was a white hot signature nearly a mile from the central vent. At that distance, the thermal image would be yellow or orange, cooler because of the water depth. That white dot couldn't have been a natural vent; it had to be something man-made, like the nuclear reactor aboard the *John Dory* as she rode near the surface."

Henna was impressed. "And what about Kenji?"

"That was a hunch really, but I felt confident. I worked for Ohnishi as a consultant a few years ago in Tennessee. Ohnishi Minerals was interested in buying the second mining rights to some disused property owned by the Tennessee Valley Authority. Second mining is when the coal pillars that support the mine tunnels are ripped down to their very weakest tolerances. It's dangerous work and cave-ins occur frequently, but the profit margin is astronomical if the mines can be bought cheap enough.

"The TVA didn't want the old mines stripped the usual way, citing all sorts of possible insurance liabilities. I was brought in at the TVA's request because there had never been a cave-in on any of the second mining operations I'd worked on. TVA was still reluctant to sell after they read my geomechanic report, but Ohnishi Minerals managed to end run them. Ohnishi bought off officials, paid hundreds of thousands of dollars to some high-power lawyers, and in the end opened his own bogus insurance company to underwrite TVA's liability.

"What he did was illegal to a degree, but American mining laws are gray enough that he got away with it. At the time the vice president in charge of Ohnishi Minerals was a guy I'd gone through the doctoral program at Penn State with, Daniel Tanaka. When his crew was reopening the mine, I met with him and explained that I had faked some of the figures, underestimating the strength of the coal pillars. I had rightly guessed that Ohnishi would order him to pull out more coal than I said could be safely removed. We both knew that I'd saved the lives of his men, so he owed me a favor. I called him just before I went to Hawaii and he told me confidentially that Ohnishi himself had no knowledge of the details of the transaction when they had acquired the mining rights. Anything that could be construed as illegal or corrupt was handled by his aide, Kenji.

"I assumed that when Ohnishi was approached by Ivan Kerikov concerning the bikinium, he'd ordered Kenji to handle any of the details. Therefore Kenji was the real linchpin, not his boss. It wasn't until I reached Kenji's estate that I found out the Koreans had gotten to Kenji too. He was the perfect agent-provocateur, working all sides. Koreans and Ohnishi against the middle, Ivan Kerikov.

"As near as I can figure the cycle of double-cross,

Kenji screwed Ohnishi with the help of the Koreans while Ohnishi screwed Kerikov, who'd already sold him out to the same Koreans. Meanwhile those Koreans are screwing Kerikov right back by forming a partnership with Kenji. I think I have that right, but I'm not sure. The only thing that matters is that Ohnishi and Kenji are dead, Kerikov's in hiding, and the wily Koreans have nothing to show for their effort.''

"That sounds about the same way we figured it, too,'' Henna agreed.

Harry White staggered into the bar, a nearly spent cigarette clinging to his lower lip. He sat at the bar, hunching over in what he and Mercer referred to as "the bar slouch,'' and took a swig of the Jack and Ginger Tiny had already poured for him.

"It's hard to believe this all started over forty years ago with something as insignificant as the sinking of an ore carrier.''

"Not so insignificant if you were on that ship,'' Mercer replied, still staring at Harry.

"You know what I mean. The crew of the *Grandam Phoenix* died without ever knowing that they were the beginning of a conspiracy that nearly tore this nation apart.''

"Don't be so sure,'' Mercer said quietly, then called to Harry, "What, I come back from a trip and no sarcasm from you?''

Harry heaved himself from his stool and started toward the booth. "I see you talking to a guy in a suit, I figure the IRS has finally nailed you for tax fraud. I thought it best to stay away.''

Mercer laughed as Harry slid into the booth next to Henna.

"Richard Henna, director of the Federal Bureau of Investigations,'' Mercer said, drawing out each syllable, "I would like you to meet Ralph Michael Linc, former captain of the ore carrier *Grandam Pheonix*.''

For the rest of his life, Mercer would never again see

such a look of incredulity as those on the faces of Henna and Harry. Their jaws had both dropped noticably and they regarded Mercer with blank, expressionless eyes. Had he said he was the second coming of Jesus Christ, the reaction would have been more mundane.

Before either man could speak, Mercer explained. "After I got out of the hospital at Pearl Harbor, I went to Kauai because it's the closest big island to the new volcano. I went there hoping to find out if there had been any survivors from that night in 1954. I found a spry old lady, Mae Turner, who remembered a sea captain named Ralph Linc who washed up on shore four days after the *Phoenix* went down. He had lost a leg to a shark." Unconsciously Harry rubbed his good foot against the prosthesis strapped below his knee. "She nursed him back to health, but never heard from him again."

"How did you guess it was me?" Harry asked calmly.

"It was the telegram that started this whole mess for me, the telegram from Tish's dead father. At first I had no idea who sent it, but when I learned that Valery Borodin had been involved with Tish, I figured it must have been him, but he denied having sent it. I wondered who else would want me involved and knew that Jack Talbot was a friend of mine.

"Then I remembered talking to you the night before the telegram arrived from Jakarta. I remembered telling you that I thought he was working in Indonesia and wondered if he knew his daughter had been hurt. You were the only person who could have known I thought he was there. I started thinking about motive, about why you would want to get me involved and I came up with revenge so I figured you had to be a member of the *Grandam Phoenix*'s crew. Mae Turner confirmed my suspicion. I never did figure out how you got the telegram sent from Jakarta."

"Easy, really. I haven't been to sea since '54, but I still know mariners all over the globe. I just phoned a

friend who knew someone in Indonesia and had him
send the wire.''

''Why?'' Henna asked softly.

''We had a deal with those fuckers to scuttle the *Phoenix* for the insurance money. They were supposed to pick
us up. Instead, they gunned us down in the lifeboats.
They killed my entire crew. I caught two slugs myself.

''I blacked out after I got hit, and when I came to I
was holding onto an overturned lifeboat, with a Great
White using me as an after-dinner mint.

''I pulled myself up onto the boat, hatred keeping me
alive, and eventually landed on Hawaii. After Mae
nursed me, I went looking for those bastards. That's
when I changed my name to Harry White, so they
wouldn't ever know that one man managed to slip away.
I searched for twenty fucking years and didn't get anywhere.

''Every time a ship vanished near Hawaii, I checked
it out. Some were legitimate, sailboats found capsized,
storms, that sort of thing, but I knew some were caused
by the same people who killed my boys. But I never
could find a connection between those ships and mine.

''After twenty years, I finally gave up hope and
moved here to Washington. I felt like a failure. Then
they hit that NOAA ship, and I thought maybe after all
these years I'd have a chance at revenge. Surely the government would investigate and find some pattern to the
disappearances. I even thought I might be able to help
in some way, but, Christ, I'm crowding eighty now; who
the fuck would listen to me anymore?''

He turned to Mercer. ''When you told me that your
friend's daughter had been rescued from that ship, I understood how fate really works. I called my friend and
had his buddy in Indonesia send that telegram to your
office, hoping that I could avenge my crew through you.
Listen, Mercer, I was wrong to involve you, but I just
couldn't stop myself. I am sorry.''

Mercer looked at his old friend for a long moment,

his face a mask, his eyes neutral. "Do I call you Harry or Ralph?"

"I've been Harry White longer than I was Ralph Linc," he replied sullenly.

"Well, Harry, from now on if you want Jack Daniel's at my house, you bring it yourself, because I never drink the stuff." Mercer grinned and reached across the table to slap Harry on the shoulder.

Harry was nearly in tears. "Thanks, Mercer. Thanks for finally avenging the boys who died that night and thanks for understanding."

"Next time I fight one of your battles," Mercer admonished mockingly, "make sure it's not the goddamn KGB I'm up against, all right?" Mercer slid out of the booth and stood. "Now, if you gentlemen will excuse me, I have to pick up my private nurse from the airport. She couldn't get a seat on the same flight as me."

"Private nurse?" Harry and Dick said in unison.

"Well, not nurse, really, more like physical therapist. Her producer gave her one more week off, and I plan to spend it at a little bed and breakfast I know near Annapolis. It seems you're wrong, Dick, the hero does get the girl at the end."

Mercer left the bar before either man could speak. He only had thirty minutes to get to the airport and pick up Jill Tzu. It would be another hour's drive to the hotel, and a certain part of his anatomy was telling him he would need her type of therapy by then.

KHANIA, CRETE

Once an outpost of the mighty Venetian trading empire, the seaside town of Khania retains much of the influence of its renaissance benefactor. Though lacking the trademark canals of Venice, Khania can still fool even the most seasoned traveler into thinking he or she is on the Italian peninsula rather than the largest of the Greek islands. The calm Aegean spices the air of the resort town as breezes blow into the protected bay, past the stone lighthouse and domed mosque left over from the Turkish occupation. The cramped architecture of the port itself gives a person seated in one of the many quayside restaurants a feeling of contentment and belonging even as multitudes of tourists promenade by in arm-linked droves.

Khania sits nearly forty miles west of Crete's capital, connected to it by a stretch of new highway dotted with beautiful beaches and luxury condominium developments catering to Germans and Scandinavians wishing to hide from winter's fury. Because of the transitory nature of the population, no one paid heed to Khania's newest arrival as he sipped a Scotch at an outdoor cafe, watching the tourists load themselves up like pack animals with souvenirs and mementos of their stay on Crete.

He was dressed in creamy linen pants and a silk polo shirt, his feet shod in soft leather moccasins. If tourists had taken the time to notice him, they would have assumed that he was just another rich German "getting away from it all." They would have been dead wrong.

Ivan Kerikov had selected Khania with much care and deliberation. He knew that he was being hunted by the KGB, the CIA, and more importantly, Way Dong's security forces, so any hiding place must have several avenues of escape. Khania's transitory population almost guaranteed anonymity, while the island's rugged interior offered thousands of hiding places. If things became desperate, Libya was only a ten-hour boat ride away.

Kerikov signaled his waiter for another drink and sat back contentedly in the cloth and steel tubing chair. He could think of no better place to sit and wait without fear of detection while still enjoying the amenities of civilization.

Before leaving Zurich, he'd manage to empty several KGB accounts held there for agents operating in the West. He had enough money to live on for at least a year.

The waiter brought his drink and Kerikov thanked him with a grunt.

A year would be all the time he needed to utilize the information locked away in a bank's safe deposit box near Sygtagma Square in Athens. That information, stolen from the archives of Department 7, would be worth millions to the right buyer, one eager for the power to bring America to her economic knees.

Forge Books is pleased to present a taste of the
second Philip Mercer adventure,

Charon's Landing,

available in hardcover in the summer of 1999.

Howard Small leaned over the gunwale
of the charter boat and retched so violently that he nearly
lost his glasses. He spat several times in a vain attempt
to clear the foul taste from his mouth before straightening up. He laid his head back against the fiberglass
hull and moaned.

"Christ, Howard, we're still tied to the dock. Don't
tell me you're already sea sick," teased Jerry Small, captain of the fishing boat.

"Don't blame me, Jerry. It was that sadist there that
did this to me," Howard said, waving his arm weakly
at the other passenger on the thirty-foot craft. "We were
up until about four hours ago drinking tequila shots at
the Salty Dog Saloon."

In the opposite corner of the boat, the other passenger
smiled like the Cheshire Cat. He leaned negligently
against the transom, one long leg stretched out along a
bench, the other tucked against his chest, battered hands
cupping his bent knee. He wore faded jeans, a plain
black sweatshirt and a leather bomber jacket.

Despite the few hours of sleep the man had gotten the

night before and the massive amount of alcohol he must have consumed, the passenger's eyes were sharp and focused. They were an unusual shade of gray, hard, yet at the same time friendly and laughing.

"I know just what you need." The passenger glanced at his scarred TAG Heuer watch and noted the still distant dawn. "Just as I suspected, it's Happy Hour in Oslo, Norway."

He fished two bottles of Alaska Pale Ale from the plastic cooler on the deck next to him and tossed one toward Howard.

"Nothing like a little hair of the dog." The man grinned.

"At four thirty in the morning, this is the whole dog again," Howard complained as he opened the beer and took a long swallow.

"The fore lines are off, Dad, let's get going," said John, Jerry Small's teenage son.

"Get ready to cast off stern," Small said as the big, stern mounted Chevy engine rumbled to life.

John cast off the final line and jumped aboard their charter boat, *Wave Dancer*. The two passengers joined the captain and his son in the relative protection of the open-sided cabin.

They were the first vessel of Homer's charter fleet to head out in search of halibut, huge bottom feeding fish strongly resembling flounder. To starboard, the boat motored past one of the largest natural spits in the world, a mile long thrust of land, narrow enough that someone could throw a baseball from one side to the other.

The *Wave Dancer* rounded the tip of the spit. To port, the Kenai Mountains were a murky shadow in the dim light of the false dawn. The sun was just a stroke of blush against the horizon. The temperature was a raw thirty degrees, forcing the men to hold themselves close to the tiny heating vents in the cabin. Fortunately, the wind was mild and the seas were no more than three feet; a gentle ride for a boat designed to battle ten-foot swells.

"You don't strike me as one of the eggheads that Howard usually brings fishing," Jerry Small said to his other passenger.

The man smiled. "No, I'm an independent consultant, hired to check the viability of Howard's work for commercial application."

"Does my cousin's gizmo work?"

"If my recommendation holds any weight with Pacific Machine and Die, this time next year, Dr. Howard Small is going to be a very wealthy man."

Howard grinned around his hangover. This was the first he'd heard of the endorsement. "Thanks, Mercer."

"Don't thank me," Philip Mercer shook Howard's hand. "You did all the work. In a couple of years, the mining industry is going to be turned on its ear by what you've developed."

Professor Howard Small and his UCLA staff had developed a mini-mole, a type of tunnel boring machine that utilized the latest in laser guidance, hydraulic technology and micro-miniaturization. Their creation, dubbed Minnie, had just proven herself in her first true test. Unlike other tunnel-borers, Minnie was small and economical. A crew of twenty could keep the sixteen-foot-long machine running twenty-four hours a day as she chewed out a four-foot diameter tunnel. The borers used to dig the Channel Tunnel between England and France were six hundred feet long and required hundreds of men to maintain.

Mercer had been hired by Pacific Machine and Die, a huge mining equipment manufacturer, to evaluate Minnie's utility in hard rock mining. Mercer knew that his recommendation ensured that Pac Mac & Die, as the company was known, would be buying the rights to Minnie within months. Howard's long years of work were about to pay off.

This fishing trip was a way for both men to unwind after the long weeks of testing. An hour out of Homer, in a small protected cove, Jerry slowed the *Wave Dancer*, cutting her engines down to a slow trawl, then after a few adjustments, he shut down the engines and allowed the silence of the Alaska coast to wash over them.

"Best fishing hole in these waters," he announced, heaving himself from his seat to prepare the heavy rods.

Within a few minutes of getting the baited hooks in the water, Mercer heaved a ninety-pound halibut to the surface. Jerry and John used heavy gaffs to haul the fish over the gunwale. Its flat white body was smooth except for the two blisters on the top of the fish that protected its eyes.

"Great fish."

"Beautiful fish."

Five minutes later, Mercer and Jerry helped John land a forty pounder and then it was Howard's turn to haul in one of the monsters from two hundred feet down. There was no real sport to this type of fishing, it was just a test of strength to bring the sluggish creatures to the surface.

Howard had recovered from his hangover enough to begin enjoying the beers Mercer kept passing to him. Jerry Small, too, was drinking steadily. Only John, too young to drink legally, seemed to have any interest in remaining sober.

By ten in the morning, it seemed that they were catching the same fish over and over again, so they hauled in their lines and Jerry started out for another hole further from Homer.

About twenty minutes into the run, John pointed starboard and shouted, "Dad, what's that?"

Jerry throttled back immediately. Another boat bobbed eerily in the low swells about five hundred yards away. She was larger than the *Wave Dancer* by twenty feet, a commercial fishing vessel with a small cabin hunched over heavy bows, her afterdeck supporting what looked like a purse net derrick.

She was unnaturally low in the water and her upper works were darkened and scored by fire. There the unnatural silence of the crypt hung over her. No one moved on the deck or answered Jerry's call of, "Hello".

"What boat is that?" Jerry asked.

"Her name's burned off the transom," his son answered as he tied fenders to the side of the *Wave Dancer*. "But I think it's the *Jenny IV* out of Seward."

"I think you're right," Jerry said as the *Wave Dancer* brushed against the derelict.

Mercer jumped across with a line and secured the boats together quickly. He moved with a calm professionalism, as if finding burned-out wrecks was his normal occupation.

Six inches of sea water washed across the scarred plank decking of the *Jenny IV*, slopping from gunwale to gunwale as she rolled sluggishly. The waterproofing on Mercer's boots failed immediately. He looked around the deck, then quickly turned to Jerry.

"Radio the Coast Guard and report what we've found. Tell them to take their time, no one survived." Mercer's voice possessed an edge of command that hadn't been there before. He had seen the body in his first moment on board.

"John, make that call to the Coast Guard," Jerry Small said, then leapt onto the *Jenny IV*, steadying himself against a scorched deck winch when he saw the corpse on the deck.

If the condition of the boat was bad, the body on the deck was much, much worse. Whoever it was had survived much of the fire because the corpse's position indicated that he'd dragged himself from the cabin before dying. He lay stretched out on the deck as if crawling away from the flames. He still wore a safety orange coat over a checked flannel shirt, but from his pelvis down, there was nothing left but the blackened stumps of femur bones sticking obscenely from his hips. His hands were twisted claws.

Obviously there had been an accident on board and a raging fire, one that had caught the victim unaware, but there was no explanation as to why the fire went out before sinking the craft.

"Get back aboard your boat," he said to Jerry. "I need a flashlight and possibly an ax."

Jerry reboarded the *Wave Dancer* and handed the items over to Mercer. "Don't you think we should wait for the Coast Guard?"

A good point, thought Mercer, but something about this fire bothered him and he wasn't going to wait for the authorities to find out what.

Foreward, a door led to the below decks area. Mercer tried to wrench it open. The wood had been so warped by the fire that it jammed almost immediately. Mercer swung the ax a few times and the wood splintered. The door fell to the deck with a splash.

He flicked on the heavy flashlight and cast its beam around the cramped room below the pilot house. A small galley was to his left next to a couple of bench seats and a table that were all secured to the deck. Everything was burned horribly. To the right were three bunks; one contained another skeleton, this one burned so much that there wasn't any flesh left on the bones. Empty eye sockets watched Mercer almost accusingly, sending a superstitious chill up his spine. Placing his hand against a steel bulkhead he noted the metal was cold. The fire must have taken place at least twelve hours ago. Next to the door that Mercer had used another door led down a short hallway to the cargo holds. Of that door, nothing remained, and the casing and bulkhead near it had been blown outward by an explosion in the holds. That explained why the fire hadn't totally destroyed the boat. The explosion must have robbed the flames of oxygen.

Mercer wondered what a fishing boat could be carrying that would cause such an explosion. The vessel's engines were in the stern and logically the fuel tanks would be close to them, but there would be evidence of that sort of explosion above decks.

Murky green water reflected Mercer's flashlight beam as he trained it into the holds. The smell of burned wood and plastic couldn't mask the overpowering stench of years of fishing. Mercer took a cautious step into the flooded hold, feeling for a step as he made his way down.

He knew, as he stood thigh deep, that he couldn't accomplish anything here without diving equipment. He was just turning to leave when the beam of the flashlight reflected off something in the water.

He groaned aloud as he reached under the surface to retrieve it, soaking his arm in freezing water. It was a piece of bright stainless steel about ten inches long and six wide. Whatever had exploded on board had torn the steel as if it were paper. Mercer turned it in the beam of his flashlight and saw the name ''roger'' on one side, the last letter being the point where the steel was shredded.

He slipped the fragment into a cargo pocket of his leather jacket and made for the upper deck.

''Find anything?'' Jerry called.

''No,'' replied Mercer, noticing the damage to the net derricks for the first time.

The top of the A-frame fishing gantry was gone, the breaks clean and sharp. Whatever had destroyed the derrick had sheared it off.

''Did you contact the Coast Guard?''

''Yeah, they're sending a cutter from Homer, it should be here in about an hour.''

''Fine,'' Mercer jumped back to the *Wave Dancer*. ''There's no sense in us remaining tied up. Her lower decks are flooded and she could sink at any time.''

Jerry fired up the engine while his son cast off. Once they were fifty yards from the *Jenny IV*, Jerry idled his boat and kept her at a constant distance from the derelict. The men were silent for many long unsettled minutes, watching the deathly quiet *Jenny IV* as she swayed with the rolling waves.

''Well, I guess that takes care of fishing for the day.'' Jerry's voice was unnaturally loud.

Mercer turned to him and smiled back his own misgivings. ''Hell, fishing's just a reason to drink and I've never really needed an excuse for that.''